HORSE THIEF 1898

DEBRA KORNFIELD

BOOK ONE OF THE CALLY AND CHARLIE SERIES

Author: Debra Kornfield
Horse Thief 1898 by Debra Kornfield
ISBN: 978-1-953114-92-1
1. Fiction/Historical/General
2. Fiction/World Literature/Ireland/19th Century

Published by EA Books Publishing, a division of Living Parables of Central Florida, Inc. a 501c3
EABooksPublishing.com

Cover image by Joel Griswell
Cover design by Robin Black

ISBN: 978-1-953114-92-1

For my cousin Barb
who brainstormed this book with me
on a drive through a rainstorm in Kansas

And for the real horse thief
whoever he or she was
(with my apologies)

CONTENTS

WITH APPRECIATION

On an early morning walk while visiting relatives in Kansas City on a promotional tour for *Karis, All I See Is Grace*, I stumbled across historic New Santa Fe Cemetery. Wandering through the old gravestones, I noticed one engraved simply, "Horse Thief 1898." For a storyteller, such a thing kindles the imagination.

I mentioned the horse thief grave to my cousin Barb Jones later that day as we drove through a thunderstorm across Kansas. We brainstormed the origin and demise of the horse thief, and Barb said, "You could write a book about this!"

It could have ended there. But to my great surprise, a year later, God spoke to me. I sat in a leadership conference in Singapore, looking around the circle of gifted, effective pastors and leaders, asking the Lord whether I should be doing more with my life. Out loud (I thought), I heard a voice say, "I gave you the Cally story. Why haven't you written it?"

Startled, I looked around to see who else had heard the voice. Everyone seemed focused on the speaker. I wrote in my conference notes, "I think God just told me to write fiction. What sense does that make?"

But I went home to Pittsburgh and started writing. *Horse Thief 1898* became, for me, an amazing experience of my characters telling me about themselves and what happened to them. I had no idea Charlie was a piano prodigy until the moment I wrote it down. I didn't know Reeny and her baby would die, or that Cally would consult Miss Hilda. I kept telling my husband, "I'm so surprised by what happened today in Horse Thief! I never could have imagined it."

I owe Cally and Charlie my thanks for entrusting their stories to me.

I hope I have done them justice.

This book has been enriched by the encouragement and suggestions of my Word Weavers "Page 29" critique group, friends, family, and early readers, including David and Bonnie Liefer, Cathy Lawson, Timmy Podnar, Rhonda Herman, Meredith Dobson, Barbara Zimmerly, Elisabet Hogstrom, Joanne Spence, Meg Sateia, Marsha Wegner, Elaine Elliott, Janice Griswell, Shari Hobby, Karen Johnson, Rita Friesen, and my patient husband, David Kornfield. My love and thanks to each of you, and to anyone I have unwittingly forgotten.

Kirby Dilworth and others at the Carnegie Library of Pittsburgh, and Christopher Moriarty of the Friends Historical Library in Dublin aided my research. Drs. Andrew and Jeanne Kohn, both professional musicians, gave me valuable advice on the musical references. I am indebted to the Erie Canal Discovery Center in Lockport, NY, the Little House on the Prairie Museum near Independence, KS, Glenbower.com, and the National Susan B. Anthony Museum in Rochester, NY for valuable information and perspective.

After I launched www.HorseThief1898.blog, I received an email from William Malcomson VI! Will told me the research he found on the blog had helped him connect the dots of his family story! I plan to dedicate Book Two of the Cally and Charlie series, *Treasure Hunt 1904*, to Will and his living relatives. When you read the book, you'll see why.

Finally, if anyone out there has information about the historic horse thief, I would love to know it!

The Donnelly Family and Friends
Historical/*Invented for this story*/***Significant characters***
More information about both historical and fictional characters is available on www.HorseThief1898.blog

In Ireland:

Frank *and* ***Maureen (Reeny)*** *Donnelly, farmers in southern Ireland*
  Their children ***Cally*** *and* ***Teddy***, *five and three as the story begins*
  Their infant daughter who died in childbirth
Dugan *McCarthy, Reeny's younger brother, who marries* ***Aisling***
  Their children Caoimhe and Cathal
Colin Sweeney, Aisling's father, owner of the Old Thatch Pub *in Killeagh*
Micky *Donnelly, Frank's cousin, fisherman in Youghal, marries* ***Louise***
Miss Hilda, *midwife, healer, and contact with the faeries*
Father Michaelson, pastor of the Catholic church in Killeagh
Mrs. O'Shanahan, passenger on the Lion III *who befriends Cally and Charlie*

In America:

Roisin, *Reeny's cousin, who emigrated to the U.S. with her husband*
Malachy *Quinn*
*Patrick (****Paddy****), leader of a gang of boys in Albany;* ***Jeb***, *member of his gang*
Father Callahan, *pastor of a Catholic church in Albany*
*Captain Flannery (****Cap****), owner of the barge Mabel Lee*
Susan B. Anthony, pioneer for women's rights and suffrage, and her sister **Mary Anthony** in Rochester, NY. See Historical Figures.
River Rider, *Oneida tradesman; his family and community*
Mr. and Mrs. Woolsey, *Quaker farmers near Hershey, Pennsylvania*
Dr. George Tann, first African American doctor in Kansas; his wife Eliza. See Historical Figures.
Richard and Athena Williams, *their son Ben, Dr. Tann's friends in Olathe, Kansas*

Malcomson Family and Friends
Historical/*Invented for this story*/**Significant characters**

In Ireland:
David and Mary Ffennel Malcomson 1772-1844; Quaker shipper and industrialist.

> Their seven sons included **Joseph**, Joshua, John, Robert, **William**, and Thomas.

Joseph and Charlotte Pim Malcomson 1798-1858, head of Malcomson Brothers Shipping and Trading, built **Mayfield House**, Portlaw.

> Their children included David, George Pim, and Frederick.
>
> *For this story, I invented **Peter** as Joseph's fourth son and Jemima as Peter's younger sister.*

Peter, *captain of the* Lion III *and Cathleen O'Connell Malcomson, granddaughter of Daniel O'Connell, Irish hero. They inherited Mayfield House and live there.*

> ***Daniel*** *and* ***Meghan*** *Byrne; shipbuilder at family yards in Belfast*
> > *Martin and Molly*
>
> ***Margaret*** *(Gritty) marries* ***Percy*** *Grattan*
> > *Sarah (Sally) and Catherine (Cate)*
>
> ***Thomas*** *Malcomson marries* ***Cora*** *Sumner*
> > *Shane and Shauna (twins), Josephine (Josie)*
>
> ***Charles (Charlie)*** *Malcomson, age 10 as story begins*

Jemima O'Brien, poet, Peter's sister; widow of Aaron, lives with mother Charlotte in Dublin

***Silas**, Peter's cousin, and **Priscilla** O'Brien Malcomson, shipyard manager in Dublin*

> *Abigail and Martha*

William Malcomson, Peter's uncle, fifth son of David Malcomson, chairman of Limerick Steamship Co., bankrupter of Malcomson Brothers upon Joseph's early death

Mr. Hobbs, Charlie's tutor

Mr. Pearse, Charlie's piano teacher

Mrs. Grover, director of the Mayfield School for Girls
Zeke, gardener and handyman at Mayfield School for Girls
Lillian, maid at Mayfield House
Hesbeth, cook at Mayfield House (usually called Cook)
Evan, gardener and handyman at Mayfield House; also cares for the horses
Paudeen, *sailor who cares for Charlie on his voyages as a child*
Liam, *Charlie's friend; student at Foxwell Academy in Waterford*
Conor and Mary Sumner, Cora's parents; Mary works as a cook at Mayfield School for Girls
Mr. Barrow, *Charlie's teacher and mentor at Foxwell Academy*

In America and other countries:
Nathanael Malcomson, Peter's cousin; Silas's brother, printer, and **Sarah** O'Hanlon Malcomson, Quakers in New York City.

Their five children: Matilda, Tobias (Toby), Florry, Ben, and Jimmy.

James Douglass, runaway slave, member of Nathanael and Sarah's household.

Johnny O'Connell, Cathleen's cousin, living with his family in Albany, New York.

Jan Ignacy Paderewski 1860-1941, Polish pianist and statesman; *Charlie's mentor and teacher.*
See Historical Figures.

Olga Wisinger-Florian 1844-1926, Viennese artist and activist for women's rights; *Cora's mentor.*
See Historical Figures.

Scott Joplin 1868-1917, ragtime musician; *Charlie's inspiration at a critical time of his life.*
See Historical Figures.

Michele Esposito 1855-1929, an Italian composer, conductor and pianist, professor of piano at the Royal Irish Academy of Music; *Charlie's teacher in Dublin.*
See Historical Figures.

Glossary and Pronunciation Guide

Aisling: *ashling*

babby: baby

barmbrack: an Irish quick sweet bread with raisins

Bean Sidhe: *ban-shee,* a female spirit whose moaning foretells death

blether: longwinded nonsense

boxty, drisheen, Gubbeen cheese and farl: traditional Bealtaine foods.
    Boxty: a traditional Irish potato pancake. Drisheen: a gelatinous
    black pudding. Gubbeen cheese: semi-soft with a pink and white
    rind. Farl: flat, quadrant-shaped soda bread.

bumping: an Irish custom in which the birthday child is held upside
    down and his head bumped on the floor the number of times equal
    to his age.

clew: the bottom outside point of the main sail of a ship

eejit: idiot

Caoimhe: *kee-va,* means gentle, beautiful, precious

Ciaran: *keer-on*

Dubh Sidhe: *dov shee,* the dark faeries

dudeen: short clay tobacco pipe

duncher: a flat cap

garsún: *gaar-sahn,* boy

hat trick: A hat trick in football (called soccer in North America) refers to
    a single player scoring three goals in one game. Charlie is saying in
    chapter 36 Father wants all three of his sons to graduate from
    Oxford. Oxford was not yet coed, so his sister Margaret couldn't
    attend there.

Hold your wheest: Shut up

"Jesus the Very Thought of Thee" hymn: *Jesu dulcis memoria dans vera
    cordis gaudia . . .* A poem attributed to a French monk, St. Bernard
    of Clairvaux, in the 12th c., translated into English by Edward Caswall
    in 1849. It has been sung to a variety of different tunes.

kerfuffle: commotion, ruckus, fuss

Killeagh: *cilla*

knackered: exhausted, worn out

Lá Bealtaine: *bee-el-ten,* Irish May Day festival celebrating the beginning of summer

Laoise: *leesha;* means "radiant girl"

Let the hare sit: leave it alone

mo pháiste daor: my dear child

O God Our Help in Ages Past hymn: Isaac Watts and William Croft, 1708. After decades of oppression, singing was not common in Irish Catholic masses, but in the 19th century, those who did sing often borrowed from Protestant hymnody.

orphan trains or mercy trains: From 1854-1929, some 250,000 abandoned, orphaned, homeless children were taken from the eastern seaboard cities on "Orphan Trains" (Protestant) or "Mercy Trains" (Catholic) to families in the west to work on farms or in homes or factories. Some were treated well by the families who took them, some not. For many years there was almost no follow-up on the part of the organizers. An interesting novel based on significant historical research is *Orphan Train* by Christina Baker Kline.

oxter-cog: pull someone by the armpits

Paderewski: *paderevski*

páisti: affectionate name for a child

praties: potatoes

purler: fall, tumble

raparee: bandit, robber, scoundrel

Roisin: *ro-sheen*

Sláinte: to your health!

sticking out a mile: the best!

wean: child

wheekers: Wow! Hurrah!

wheen: a lot

Youghal: *yew-gull*

Debra Kornfield

PROLOGUE

Waterford, County Waterford, Ireland, 1855

"AAARRRGHHH!"

Joseph Malcomson's roar rang in the rafters of the Quaker Meeting House. He looked from one to the other of the implacable faces of the elders arrayed before him. Then he turned to stare at the congregation, first the men, then the women. Each man's hat was on his head. All but his son Peter, who looked at him hat in hand, his eyes shining. Each bonneted face gazed back at him with no apparent emotion besides the pity he saw in aunts, sisters, cousins.

"Come, wife. Children. We're done here." Joseph turned on his heel and marched out, head high. His wife Charlotte rose with dignity, followed by fourteen-year-old Jemima, her face flushed with embarrassment. Peter, on the men's side, glanced at the stern faces of his married older brothers and uncles, grinned, shrugged, and followed his father out the door.

No words were spoken until the family settled into their carriage. Charlotte turned toward her angry husband. "What did thee expect, Joseph? Did thee truly believe thee could flaunt the direct order of our Meeting and suffer no reprisal, even after their warnings?"

"I'll have no more 'thees' and 'thys' in my hearing!" shouted Joseph. "They have cast us out. We've no further obligation to follow their antiquated customs."

7

"They have cast thee out, husband, not me," Charlotte responded calmly. "I fully intend to continue my membership in the Society of Friends. Thy disregard of Quaker peace principles is none of my doing, as our Society knoweth full well. I say 'our' Society for I have no doubt Peter and Jemima will continue with me in good standing."

Joseph turned to his children. "Is it so, Peter? Jemima? You intend to flaunt your father's judgment in this matter?"

Jemima burst into tears. Peter put his arm around her and replied, "I don't know yet, Father. I'm quite fascinated by all this. I always thought our identity as Quakers was as much a part of us Malcomsons as—as the air we breathe. I need time to talk separately with thee—sorry, with you, Father—and Mummy, and perhaps my brothers and uncles as well. How is it Mummy can make a decision for herself, different from yours?"

Joseph and Charlotte looked at each other, her face as resolute as his.

"Thy father and I made a contract when we married, Peter. In some areas of life he cannot overrule me. Else I'd not have married him."

"I didn't know such a contract was possible, Mummy."

"Indeed, we were one of the first in Ireland to take this enlightened path, son. God imbued both your father and me with strong opinions. Our marriage contract hath allowed us to live together in harmony, without the subjugation and resentment so many women experience."

"My entire world hath broken open today! How intriguing. I will let thee know what I decide about the Society, Mummy, since Father hath offered me this choice. Father, I want to understand your point of view. Why *did* you disobey our Meeting, transporting soldiers to the Crimea against the elders' express instructions?"

"Jemima, stop your sniffling! This is about me, not you!"

"I—I'll try, Father. I worry for thy—for your—for thy soul."

"Humph. My soul is very well, thank you. The Meeting will be sorry enough when I stop supporting its good works. They cost money, and making money is what I do. Whether I transport the soldiers or someone else does, the war will kill them just the same. But I guarantee my competitors would not use their earnings to support soup kitchens and schools and the families of dead soldiers."

"So what it's all about for you, Father, is making money? You already own the largest fleet of iron steamers in the world. You're the Merchant Prince, so I've heard."

"Exactly right, Peter, and I didn't get here by mindlessly following impractical edicts. You mark my words, son. Those pompous elders will be at my door soon enough, begging for my patronage."

"I've heard the Merchant Prince described as vindictive and ruthless," Charlotte observed. "Here we are at Mayfield. Shall we take our supper early?"

"I will take Cormac for a canter, Charlotte. Do not expect me back until dark."

"A good decision, husband. Perhaps thee might leave thy ill humor in the fields. Come, Jemima. Peter."

"Father, I was thrilled to see you stand up to the elders. Can you please explain to me—"

"Come ride with me, Peter. God knows I've given you little enough attention of late."

"Yes! I have so many questions, Father."

Charlotte turned on the porch to gaze for a moment after her husband and son. *Peter is so needy of his father's attention and affirmation. How will this day shape him, I wonder. Grant him grace, I ask thee, merciful God.*

Debra Kornfield

CHAPTER 1

CALLY

Killeagh, County Cork, Ireland, November 1888

"SURE, YE'LL BE THE DEATH OF ME YET, Callandra Mae Donnelly, so ye will!"

Cally stood shivering and dripping, her body stiff as she gazed at Mammy's red and angry face. *I can't let her see my treasure.*

She gripped her wee mirror more firmly behind her back. While Mammy ranted, Cally's mind darted around their farm, seeking a better hiding place from her wee *eejit* of a brother. *Didn't Teddy throw it in the creek in a fit of envy?*

Something warm ran down from Cally's forehead, stinging her right eye. *I mustn't wipe it away, lest Mammy notice my treasure.* Distracted by the sting, Mammy's words scarcely penetrated.

"And haven't ye been nothin' but trouble and worry every minute of yer five years?"

Mammy paused to draw breath. Uncle Dugan's voice eased in, mellow and smooth. "Sure, Reeny, and wontcha let me peek at the wee lassie's injury? She's bleedin' on yer clean floor, so she is, Maureen."

Mammy shifted her glare to Uncle Dugan. Cally edged closer to the peat fire. The movement made her dizzy. She crashed to the floor, and everything went black.

11

ᏚᏂᏩᎧ

Cally's left eye opened, but her right one stuck. She whimpered.

"Ah, there ye are, lassie. Ye had me worried, so ye did." Uncle Dugan sounded far away. His face came close to hers as he whispered, "Don't worry about yer mirror, Cally. It's safe in my pocket. We'll talk about it when yer . . ."

Cally couldn't keep her eye open. Fraught images tumbled through her sleep. *Teddy waving the wee mirror before her outstretched fingers and then running like a* liltie *toward the creek before she could leap from the milking stool and chase after him.*

The glint of the metal as it spun toward the water. The shock and strength of the current as she plunged in after it. Her fingers closing over her treasure's round smoothness just as she slipped and cracked her forehead on a rock.

Teddy's shriek. Uncle Dugan hauling her out of the water and into the cottage, where Mammy made her stand up to give an account of herself ...

Cally moaned, her head a mighty ache pinning her to the bed. A soothing voice reached through her distress, this time Da's. "There now, lassie, I know it hurts. Ye'll be more prudent in the future, I don't doubt. Rest now, sweet one." Softly he sang.

> Too-ra-loo-ra-loo-ral
> Too-ra-loo-ra-li
> Too-ra-loo-ra-loo-ral
> Hush now, don't ye cry ...

A different dream surfaced. *Market day in town, clutching Uncle Dugan's rough hand, Mammy's eggs in a basket. A carriage with a broken wheel. A fancy woman stepping down, a round shiny thing in her hand. Her words spoken oddly while her laddie stared at Cally. "Oh, do you like my wee mirror, lassie? May I show you how pretty you are?"*

Uncle Dugan's nod. The surprise of her own reflection, curly red hair

framing wide green eyes, a wee nose, freckles everywhere. Lifting her
gaze to the woman's gentle brown eyes.

"Yes, tis a dainty wee thing. I found it in a street stall in Bombay.
Would you like to have it, páistí?"

Mammy's brusque tones collided with the dream-memory. "Wake
up, now, Cally. Miss Hilda's come to tend ye."

Still, only her left eye would open. At the level of her eye, Cally saw
her mammy's tummy, round and big, pressed against the bed. She
stretched out a finger and touched it. *Another babby? No one told me.*

Mammy moved back as Miss Hilda sat on the bed, slowly easing
Cally to sit supported against her side. "Drink this, lassie. It tastes bitter,
but it will make ye feel better. Give her a few swallows whene'er she
stirs, Reeny, slowly so she won't throw it off. It'll comfort her some
while the swellin' goes down. Ye made a good fist of sewin' the wound
on her forehead."

Miss Hilda eased Cally back onto the pillow. "She'll be needin' yer
good broth, too, Reeny, as much as she'll take. She's had a desperate
wheen of bleedin'. Ye must keep her in bed. I'll come again in two days
unless Cissy McDougal starts her birthin'."

Mammy turned away, and Cally's mind returned to the mystery of
the kindness in the mirror-lady's eyes. *Life is more. Bigger than I*
thought. Scary but—but—happy. I didn't know.

Cally tucked the mystery away deep inside. As deep as the hole she
would ask Uncle Dugan to dig for her treasure at the back of the potato
patch, with a big rock over it like all the other big rocks piled there.

C320

"I won't never touch yer treasure, never again, Cally. I promise,
cross my heart."

Teddy's anxious whisper reconnected Cally to her pillow, and her
aching head, and the scent of burning peat. At Mammy's heavy footfall,
he scuttled away. *I must get better, to ease Teddy's worry.*

Cally sipped the broth Mammy brought, though her tummy heaved, and her head throbbed. Mammy held her steady and tucked another pillow behind her. Such a wonder, this unexpected kindliness. *I must think about it more, when I am not so, so knackered.*

CB&O

January 1889

Cally held her knees tight against her tummy. *I could use the bucket, but Mammy will make me empty it, and last time I spilled. The outhouse is better, so I spill where I'm meant to.*

Cally chuckled inside at her own humor. She lifted Teddy's hand from her arm, waited while his breathing settled, then grabbed her shawl and slipped through the back door. Sitting on the stoop, she pulled boots over her bare feet, then ran down the path, giggling as her steps squeaked in the new snow.

A bright moon emerged, and Cally stopped to admire it. "*Cuir do phíopa ar do ghualainn trí ardú na gealaí*" (Put your pipe upon your shoulder by the rising of the moon), she whispered, Da's bedtime song fresh in her mind. Then she dashed to her destination.

Returning, Cally slowed to make her steps noiseless. She pulled off her boots and eased open the door, pressing icy fingers over her mouth to muffle her breathing. From her parents' bedstead across the single room of their cottage, she heard voices.

"Sure, I hoped the accident might have tamed her, but she's still as wild as ever."

"Still and all, yer too hard on her, Reeny. She's but a wee lassie. Can't ye find some patience for her, as ye did when she was laid up?" Cally strained to hear Da's soft voice.

"I ne'er thought to raise a tomboy, Frank, in soul I didn't. Think of what she did yesterday, slidin' down the hill with her skirts over her head fer all the world to see her pantaloons. Sure, I do think sometimes she's no daughter of mine."

Mammy's voice softened. "This one, now. I'm prayin' to the Virgin to give me a real sweet babby. One who loves to help me in the kitchen and learns her stitches and speaks soft as a lassie should and—"

"Why, Reeny, ye're not thinkin' right! God gave us our precious daughter Cally! We're to love her, not try to make her over. And we're to be grateful fer whatever *wean* God sends us."

Cally's eyes flooded with tears. She couldn't breathe. She hurried to her bed and buried her head under her pillow to muffle her sobs. *Mammy's always nicer to Teddy than to me. But she just said out loud she doesn't want me. She hopes the new babby is nothin' like me.*

Cally wept for a long time, anger rising through her grief. She remembered Da's words of support. *But does he secretly wish I was a different kind of lassie, like Mammy does?*

Cally couldn't decide. His affection was the calm center of the whirlwind always swirling around her and Mammy. *But does he really love me? I must watch and listen . . .*

Mammy shook Cally awake. "Must I *oxter-cog* ye from yer bed, ye slough about? The house so cold and the fire not yet stirred and no peat to put on it. Why, yer da's been out this long time carin' fer the animals. And Daisy not yet milked . . ."

Cally stopped listening. She dressed and hurried to her chores. Inside, she made a secret promise to herself. *Unless she makes me, I won't speak to Mammy again. I'll do what she bids me, but I won't try to win her love. I'll be as cold as this air making my breath come out like smoke. And I'll watch Da and Uncle Dugan. Will they even notice I've changed?*

Cally finished her milking and settled her plan in her mind. "And I hope if it's a lassie this babby dies," she told Daisy.

Da yelled. Cally ran to the door of the barn. Uncle Dugan raced down the lane, his feet slipping on the snow. Pivoting toward the house, she saw a trail of scarlet staining the snow.

"Cally! Cally! I need ye to keep an eye to Teddy! Right now!"

Cally couldn't move. Da shouted again. She forced her legs toward the house.

All she remembered later, as she and Teddy huddled under their bed covers for what seemed like forever, was blood.

And Mammy screaming.

Then, silence, thick as a slice of Mammy's bread. Peeking from the covers, Cally saw Da cuddle a wee bloody body. Then he threw himself over Mammy and wailed, a keening that curdled Cally's blood. Teddy shook. Miss Hilda hurried in. Da shouted, "Too late! Ye're too late!"

And Uncle Dugan stood by the door twisting his duncher, crying, "I tried, Frank! I tried!"

Cally knew her world had shattered. *And I know it's my fault.*

CHAPTER 2

CHARLIE

Mayfield House, Portlaw, County Waterford, Ireland, April 20, 1889

STRAIGHT AND TALL AS HE COULD STRETCH, Charlie stood before Father, eyes shining. The captain spoke magical words from behind his big desk.

"So, you have reached ten years, Charles Henry. You are old enough to sail with me when your school term ends."

Charlie swallowed. His voice came out all trembly. "Ye-yes, sir. Thank you, sir."

"All right then. Cathleen, do you have Charles's birthday gift?"

"Yes, Peter."

Mummy extended a brightly wrapped package. Charlie pulled aside the tissues to reveal a sailor outfit, complete with a white hat and a scarf in blue and green, the colors of his father's shipping line. *Sticking out a mile! I never imagined turning ten would be so grand!*

"Let's try it on, shall we, Charlie?" Mummy said, holding the pants up to Charlie's legs. "The end of term is only eight weeks away, so I'm sure it will still fit you."

"Charles," Father said sternly, "You're to mind your schoolwork for these eight weeks. I expect a good report from Mr. Hobbs."

"Yes, sir." *But I'm to sail with Father on the* Lion III! *How can I possibly think about sums and history and French?*

૭૪৪৩

Charlie swallowed a big bite of toasted *barmbrack.* "Good morning, Mummy."

"My dear son. Good morning, Lillian."

Lillian curtsied. "Good morning, Mrs. Malcomson. Would ye like a cup of tea in your hand? I'll ask Cook to poach yer egg. Will ye have kippers and bacon like Master Charlie, so?"

"Thank you, Lillian. Tea and egg will be lovely, with a wee slice of barmbrack."

"Yes, ma'am."

Mummy sat across from Charlie. "I have a surprise. Your father's cousin Priscilla and the girls are coming on the train from Dublin this afternoon. Once Mr. Hobbs releases you from your studies, you may play with Martha and Abigail in the garden."

Charlie's face fell. *Last time, they left upset. I never knew why.*

"You look concerned, Charlie. Are you thinking of the *kerfuffle* the last time the girls were here?"

Tears filled Charlie's eyes as he remembered Abigail backing away and Martha gasping when he boasted the *Lion III* was in port. *The girls ran to their mother and they all left.*

"Why do they talk and dress funny? Why didn't they want to see Father's ship?"

"Have you finished your breakfast, Charlie? Let's go into the sitting room until Mister Hobbs arrives. I want to tell you a story."

On the settee, Mummy pulled Charlie close. He shifted to watch her face.

"Charlie, Cousin Priscilla and her family are Quakers. So was your father when he was young. We can talk about that another time, yes?"

"But I don't know what a Quaker is."

"Quakers are also called the Society of Friends. They love God. They

18

believe in peace. They try to help people solve their disagreements by talking instead of fighting."

"Those seem like good ideas."

"I agree. Your great-grandfather was a strong Quaker. His name was David Malcomson. He was a prominent industrial leader in Ireland and became wealthy. When David grew old, his eldest son, your grandfather Joseph, stepped in to manage what became Malcomson Brothers Shipping and Trading."

"Joseph was Father's father?"

"Yes. Sadly, Grandfather Joseph died before you were born. He built this house when your father was a baby."

"My grandfather built Mayfield? I didn't know that!"

Mummy laughed. "Yes, this house is special. Grandfather Joseph and his four brothers ran their businesses according to Quaker beliefs in honesty, fair trade, respect for each other, and treating their workers well. About thirty-five years ago, though, Grandfather Joseph made a decision his brothers didn't agree with. Have you learned in your history lessons about the Crimean War in Russia, Charlie?"

"Yes. Men from England went to Russia to ask Czar Nicholas to stop the war."

"Those men were Quakers, and one of them was your father's uncle. They tried to convince Czar Nicholas Jesus doesn't want people to fight each other. Nicholas listened, but he decided to declare war anyway. The men returned sad and disappointed. They declared no Quaker, in England or Ireland, could be involved in the war in any way."

"But what did Grandfather Joseph do, Mummy?"

"The British government asked Joseph to transport soldiers to Russia in his ships. The other brothers said, 'Absolutely not!' But Joseph did it anyway, using two ships, the *Kangaroo,* and the *Lion II.* So Grandfather Joseph could no longer be a Quaker, and he could not continue in business with his Quaker brothers."

19

"Mummy, Lion is the name of Father's ship! The *Lion III*."

"Yes. The Russian navy destroyed the *Lion II*. The Quakers believe this was God's judgment on Joseph."

"So … Abigail and Martha were upset because the *Lion III* has the same name as what they think is a bad ship?"

"Yes. Oh—I hear the doorbell. Mr. Hobbs is here, so we'll save the rest of the story for another time."

"Oh, Mummy. This can be my history lesson for today! Can't you ask Mr. Hobbs to let me have more time with you?"

"No, son. Run along. I must attend to business for the school, but I'll be back before Priscilla and the girls arrive."

⋐⋑

Look at me, Mummy! Charlie danced from one foot to the other, his eyes on Mummy's face while she told Cousin Priscilla about his brother Thomas at Oxford. "He has chosen to read philosophy. He always did have his head in the clouds, that one."

Charlie couldn't speak unless spoken to, and he must greet Cousin Priscilla before he was free to play. *I see Martha and Abigail under the beech tree at the end of the garden.* Heaving a sigh, he tuned in again to what Mummy was saying.

"Yes, I've hardly seen my sweet grandchildren since Daniel and Meghan moved to Belfast. They grow up so fast—Martin is six already and Molly is four. Margaret is with them now, shopping for her wedding trousseau. We are in a fluff over her wedding plans." Mummy laughed. "We count on you and Silas coming to the wedding, Priscilla, yes?"

Charlie took a step closer, and Mummy pulled him into a hug. "This young man will sail with his father this summer, coming home two weeks before the wedding."

Charlie took his chance. "Good afternoon, Cousin Priscilla."

Her laugh trilled. "Go on, Charlie. I know thee are anxious to enjoy this fine afternoon."

Charlie couldn't contain a loud whoop as he dashed through the French doors and across the lawn. "You're it!" he yelled as he touched Abigail's shoulder. In a flash she leaped to her feet and was after him, skirts and bonnet ribbons flying.

⚛

Hurrah, my favorite: beef wellington and champ. Charlie's mind filled with questions as he listened to the adults converse, but he must be seen and not heard. He made a funny face, rewarded by his cousins' suppressed giggles, then turned his attention back to Cousin Priscilla.

"Yes, Peter. Dear Silas hath spent more time in America this year. We miss him terribly. Since thy brother Frederick and my brother Ephraim are managing the Dublin shipyard so well, our Meeting hath asked Silas to give assistance to the Quakers' educational work in the Carolinas. Sadly, freeing the slaves did not change the Americans' attitudes toward them." Priscilla paused for a bite of champ.

"Silas hath written extensively about America's founding principle, all people created equal. He travels from city to city, encouraging American Friends in their labors of support for the emancipated. He borrows from the abolitionist speeches of thy grandfather Daniel, Cathleen!"

What does abolitionist mean? I must remember to ask Mummy.

"Intriguing," said Father. "Children, you may be excused. Will you play for us, Charles?"

Charlie's face grew warm. A thrill traveled all the way to his toes. *I haven't yet played for Father the second movement of Mozart's Piano Concerto No. 9.*

As he left the table, Mummy said to Cousin Priscilla, "I'm glad there is a piano aboard the *Lion III*, for Charlie has been invited to play with the Waterford Chamber Orchestra in October, and he mustn't get out of practice."

⚛

I'm too excited to sleep. What a grand day!

Mummy blew out the candle. Charlie counted on his fingers: *One, I learned Grandfather Joseph was a rebel! Two, Mr. Hobbs let me go early to play with Abigail and Martha.* He sighed. *I wish I could play with children more often. I hardly ever see the girls at Mummy's school, even though it's right in our house.*

He turned over and snuggled into his pillow. *Three, Cook made beef wellington and champ! Four, Father is home. Five, I know he liked what I played.* He smiled.

The themes of the 9th Concerto echoed through Charlie's mind and into his dreams.

CHAPTER 3

CALLY

Killeagh, May 1889

CALLY STROKED SIMON THE HORSE until Uncle Dugan emerged from the house wearing his duncher. "Ready, Cally? Up ye go, Teddy."

Cally and Teddy still fit on the wagon seat with Uncle Dugan. Teddy began chattering, giving Cally freedom to daydream as Simon trotted into Glenbower Wood. Soft spring loveliness soothed her into feeling almost happy. Pheasants and red squirrels scurried out of their way and the song of linnets and warblers quieted as they passed. The lake's surface ruffled under a light breeze.

"Uncle Dugan, stop!" Cally's outburst surprised even her. "Look! Look at the kingfisher!" They watched, breathless, as the bright blue bird floated over the surface of the water, then suddenly dived, emerging with a small silver fish flailing in its beak. The bird flew toward them, disappearing in the shadows under the bridge.

Uncle Dugan's eyes crinkled as he smiled at Cally, then took up the reins. They rounded a bend, trundled over the noisy River Dissour, passed the Old Thatch Pub where two men waved, and rumbled on into town. But Uncle Dugan didn't take their normal route to the shops. He drove past them and slowed Simon to a stop near the church.

Teddy asked, "Why are we here, Uncle Dugan? I 'member we used to come here, before—"

"It's four months today since yer mammy died. Yer da let me bring youse to see her grave. The cemetery is back behind."

Cally's pleasure in the outing drained away. She clutched Simon's bridle. "Take Teddy, Uncle Dugan. I'll—I'll just wait here with Simon."

"I won't make ye go, lassie. But I wish ye would, so I do. Ye never had a proper chance to say goodbye to yer mammy. Or to yer wee sister."

Cally froze, remembering. *Miss Riona took us away to her house. We stayed there many days. When Uncle Dugan finally fetched us, our cottage didn't seem like home anymore. Da hardly noticed we were there.*

Her uncle's light touch brought Cally's thoughts back to the present. She wiped her suddenly sweaty palms on her dress and grasped Simon's bridle more tightly, shaking her head no. Uncle Dugan looked sad, but he gave her a hug before walking away with Teddy.

Cally fidgeted, secured the bridle, jumped down from her seat and walked all the way around Simon and the wagon. She stopped to stroke Simon's nose, then walked around the other way. *How could I say goodbye? If Mammy and the baby are angels now like Miss Riona told us, they must know what a bad girl I am, even worse than Mammy always thought.*

"But I am a little bit curious," Cally whispered to the horse. "I don't know what a cemetery is. Maybe Mammy and the *babby* are in a new angel window in the church. I'm going to peek at Uncle Dugan and Teddy. Stay here, Simon."

Cally ran to the church and along the wall, then peeped around the corner. She saw a low fence and a bunch of strangely shaped stones in a grassy place. *I came to church so many times and never saw this place!*

She couldn't see Uncle Dugan and Teddy. *I'll have to go closer.* Cally tiptoed to a gate in the fence and slipped through. Hiding behind a large stone, she looked around. Nothing. She chose another hiding place and ran toward it. Uncle Dugan stood up and saw her.

"Cally, I'm glad ye decided to come. Yer mammy's grave is right over here."

Cally walked slowly toward Uncle Dugan. He came to meet her and grasped her hand. As they walked around the last large rock, Cally saw Teddy sitting on the grass beside a small stone with markings on it. She sank down beside him.

"What does it say?" she whispered.

Uncle Dugan traced the letters as he read them.

MAUREEN EILIS McCARTHY DONNELLY

MAY 9, 1864-JANUARY 23, 1889

AND HER INFANT DAUGHTER

"Why do they have a stone?" Cally asked. "Miss Riona said they are angels now, like in the church windows."

"The stone is for us, not for them," Uncle Dugan said. "It gives us a place to come to when we're missing them."

"Does Da come here?" Teddy asked.

"I don't know. He doesn't want to talk about it."

"He doesn't talk to us at all," Cally blurted, tears springing to her eyes, just as Teddy said, "Da doesn't love us anymore."

"I know, lassie. I know that's how it feels, Teddy." Uncle Dugan squatted and gathered Cally and Teddy into his arms. "I know it's hard, I know. But it's not yer fault."

Uncle Dugan kept talking, but Cally's tears stopped and her body grew rigid. *It is my fault. I know Da can never love me again. But why is he angry at Teddy? Should I try to tell Da it wasn't Teddy's fault, only mine?*

Cally made her body soft again so she could hug Teddy and wipe his tears. She hummed one of the lullabies Da had sung to them back when he had loved them both. Teddy grew still. He slumped against her, and she stroked his dark hair. After a while she realized he was asleep. She looked up at Uncle Dugan.

"Lassie, will ye stay here with him while I go into the church for a few minutes? I must speak to Father Michaelson."

I don't want to be alone by Mammy's stone. But she nodded and shifted Teddy's weight so his head was in her lap. It seemed a long time until Uncle Dugan came back. He lifted Teddy into one arm and took Cally's hand to walk back to Simon and the wagon.

Cally expected to drive straight home, but Uncle Dugan pulled up to the Old Thatch Pub. Inside was dark and quiet. "Mr. Sweeney?" Uncle Dugan called. A plump, cheerful young woman appeared, and suddenly Uncle Dugan didn't seem to know what to say.

"Why, Dugan!" the woman said. "These must be yer niece and nephew. Aren't they sweet! What is yer name, lassie?" Cally pulled back behind Uncle Dugan's legs, and he found his voice. "This here is Callandra, Aisling, but we call her Cally, and this one is Teddy."

"I'm right happy to meet youse both, so I am," Aisling smiled. "Can I get ye anything, Dugan?"

"Do ye have a taste of treacle pudding fer the *weans*, Aisling? That would be grand."

"Yer a sound man, Dugan, so ye are. And a half 'un fer yerself, then?"

"Could ye sit with us a spell, Aisling?"

Cally looked from Uncle Dugan to Aisling staring at him. "I'll fetch the pudding," she said. "Sit yerselves wherever ye like."

"Wheekers!" Teddy exclaimed. "Treacle pudding! Thanks, Uncle Dugan!" Aisling laughed, Uncle Dugan took a deep breath, and the strange moment passed.

Aisling was wonderful company. Cally found herself telling about the kingfisher. Aisling said he probably had a little cave in the bank under the bridge. She seemed to know all about the creatures of the forest. Cally was sad when Uncle Dugan told them it was time to go home.

Besides Mammy's grave, she had something else to think about in bed that night: *What happened between Uncle Dugan and Aisling today?*

Debra Kornfield

CHAPTER 4

CHARLIE

Mayfield House, Saturday, June 1, 1889

"CHUCKLES!"

"Gritty!"

Charlie jumped up from the piano to give his sister a hug. "You've been gone forever!"

Eyes sparkling, Margaret said "Martin and Molly sent you presents! But I have no idea where Elaine packed them . . ."

"They are in the purple valise, Miss Margaret. I knew ye would want them right away." Elaine curtsied and grinned at Charlie.

Margaret grabbed Charlie's hands and pulled him into an improvised jig. "I'm to be a bride, Chuckles!" she sang. "Your Gritty is marrying the sweetest man in all the world! Oh—I almost forgot! Meghan helped me choose your wedding suit. Now don't you dare grow while you're on that ship. Elaine! Help me find Charlie's suit so he can try it on!"

Everything for Gritty is exciting. But soon she'll be married and won't live with us anymore.

"Chuckles, why the sad face? Percy and I will be here so often you'll hardly know I don't live here. And you can visit us! Waterford isn't far from Mayfield, you know."

29

It won't be the same. But Charlie pretended to be happy about the fancy suit. Elaine combed his blond hair with a sweet-smelling oil and took him to stand before the tall hallway mirror. *I do look nice. Will Father notice how grown-up I am?*

Margaret walked into Charlie's mirror-reverie. "See—didn't I tell you? You look wonderful, Chuckles. You even have a bit of room to grow." She threw her arms around him. "I'm so proud of you, little brother. Thank you for agreeing to play for our reception! Let Elaine help you get out of this suit, so you don't mess it up. Then back to your practicing—for the wedding, I hope."

"Nope. The third movement of Mozart's 9th piano concerto, for the concert in October. It's tricky. I have to get the fingering right before Mr. Pearse comes tomorrow."

∞

Father himself woke Charlie. "It's our day to sail, son!"

Charlie pressed his nose to the window of the carriage taking them to Waterford. *The Lion III will glide down the Suir to the River Barrow, through the East Passage, past the Hook Lighthouse and out to sea. With me aboard!*

"I've assigned sailor Paudeen to show you the ropes," Father explained. "We'll dine together every evening, and you can report to me what you've learned that day."

"Yes, Father." Charlie couldn't contain his smile.

"This isn't a vacation, son," Father admonished. "Mornings, you'll have sailor duties. Afternoons, you'll practice the piano, just as at home. I know you'll make me proud, Charles."

"Yes, sir." Charlie looked down at his bright sailor whites, fingered the scarf around his neck, and shivered with anticipation. *I'll be part of Father's world, the one he lives in when he's not at home.*

The Waterford harbor came into view. Father said, "Son, you will share a cabin with Paudeen next to mine. You must stay out of the way while the ship is loaded. Paudeen will show you where you can watch. Follow his instructions exactly. You're to practice the piano for at least one hour this afternoon. I will see you at tea."

"Yes, Father." *I WILL make Father proud.*

෪

Charlie gazed out to sea, dreamily watching a multi-hued sunset paint the huge expanse of sky and reflect bright colors onto the ocean.

"Tis a balmy evening, isn't it, Charles." Father's voice startled Charlie.

"Father! Di—did I do something wrong? I didn't expect to see you again tonight."

"No, nothing's wrong, Charles. My officers have everything under control. Your mother suggested I tell you more about our family story, and I have some time before you go to bed."

"Oh, thank you, Father. Can you tell me about the *Lion I?* I know the *Lion II* was destroyed in the Crimean War, but I don't know about the first *Lion.*"

"Have you heard about the hunger years in Ireland, when the potato crops rotted, and many people starved? I was seven when that famine began in 1845, so I remember the terrible struggles of those years. Your mother was but three and has few memories of her own."

"Did you live at Mayfield then, Father?"

"I did, yes. I never wanted to live anywhere else. I'm happy knowing Mayfield is always waiting for me, no matter how much I travel."

"Did Mummy grow up at Mayfield too?"

Father laughed. "Oh no, Charles. She only came to Mayfield after we were married. She grew up on a farm in County Kerry. You can ask her about that."

"Yes, Father."

"To save their families, thousands of people left Ireland during the famine and in the lean years following. They traveled to England, to

Canada, and even to Australia. But mostly they sailed to America."

"Like us!"

"Yes. Irish Quakers worked hard to help people in Ireland who couldn't afford to emigrate. They ran soup kitchens and opened schools, so poor children could learn to read and learn skills other than farming."

"Like the school Mummy runs at Mayfield House?"

"Exactly, though the children studying at your mother's school pay a fee to attend."

"But what about the *Lion I*?"

"The *Lion I* was my father's first ship. It was made of wood. *Lion II* was made of iron."

"And *Lion III* is made of steel."

"Yes. For five years of the Great Hunger, my father used the *Lion I* to transport Irish families to America. Other ships packed people into their holds by the hundreds, giving them inadequate food and hygiene. Many got sick and some did not survive. My father booked only the number of people for whom the *Lion I* had berths, fed them well, kept the ship clean, and never lost a single passenger. I am proud to hold the same record on *Lion III*."

"Did he make the passengers pay more?"

"No. Tickets cost the same as what other companies charged, so the *Lion I* did not profit from those voyages. In fact, the *Lion I* brought food back from America for Quaker soup kitchens and schools. There were only eight thousand Quakers in Ireland, but their efforts helped more people than any other group in Ireland at that time."

"You seem proud of them, Father." Charlie took a deep breath. "So why aren't we Quakers?"

"Ah, bright lad. That's a question for another day. It's getting late."

"But Father, what happened to the *Lion I*?"

"She was stolen by pirates."

Charlie gasped. "Really?"

"Really true. I'll walk you to your cabin, Charles. Tell me how you like sailing so far. I'm told the passengers enjoy your practicing."

"Can't we talk about the pirates?"

"No. We'll talk about that another time."

I don't like Father's voice getting hard like that. He swallowed, then lifted his head. "I like seeing how everything works, and the songs the sailors sing. The whale we saw yesterday was grand! But—but Father, is it always so calm and peaceful on the ocean? I thought—I guess I expected more excitement and adventure."

Father laughed. "Calm and peaceful is exactly how we like it, lad. Don't tell me you're craving trouble! The Atlantic is a fickle mistress. Off to bed now, son."

෮๏

Charlie dreamed he was riding his horse Midnight, smooth and easy. Then she started jerking against the reins and refused to obey him. She bucked, trying to throw him.

Something clipped Charlie on his ear before hitting the bulkhead beside his shoulder. Paudeen's voice startled him fully awake. "Charlie, we've run into a storm. Yer to go to yer father's office to wait it out safely. Get dressed, put on yer coat, collect everything that's loose in this cabin and lock it into the drawers. I'll be back fer ye in five minutes."

Finally, an adventure! Charlie laughed. A dim light came through the porthole. He quickly followed instructions, then Paudeen practically carried him against the force of the wind the short distance to Father's office. Dumped, breathless and dripping, in a chair fastened to a bulkhead, Charlie barely heard him yell, "Tie yerself to the chair with this rope." Paudeen threw him a towel and was gone.

Charlie grabbed the chair as the ship rocked. A sailor hastily locked away everything from Father's desk—a photo of Mummy, papers and books, and Father's collection of curios from ports around the world.

33

With but a glance at Charlie, he left, taking the lantern with him.

Charlie slipped and slid on the chair while he struggled to secure the rope around his body in the darkness. *It's a good thing I've been practicing my knots.* A sliver of fear pierced him. *I'm in the center of the ship, with no portholes. Couldn't they have left me a lantern?*

He tied his last knot and took a deep breath. *Father thinks I'll be safest here. But I want to see the storm! Maybe I can even help the sailors!* Charlie scrubbed himself with the towel. *Father's treating me like a* wean! *I want to see what's happening!*

Nausea flooded Charlie as the floor tipped one way and then another. Something crashed, and he flinched. *That will be me, sliding and falling like a* lummox *if I take off this rope. But maybe Father and Paudeen have forgotten all about me! I can't stay here in the dark by myself!*

Charlie retched. *What did Mummy tell me to do when I'm afraid? Sing.* In a wavery voice he sang a hymn he remembered from church, "O God, our help in ages past . . ." He had just started on, "our shelter from the stormy blast," when the ship's horn blasted. Only the rope securing him kept Charlie from bolting out of his chair.

"And our eternal home," he quavered. *I don't want an eternal home! I want Father! I want light! I want the ship to stop bucking!* Charlie threw up again. *I must obey Paudeen. But I feel awful.* Panic filled Charlie's throat and he heaved once more. Without thinking, he started untying knots. Once free, he felt for something to hang on to so he could reach the door. His hand bumped a metal rung. And then another not far away. And another.

I never noticed these rungs before. Charlie held on with all his strength. When the floor tipped, he slid forward and grabbed the next rung.

Finally, he felt the door handle. *Oh no! I'm locked in!* But by turning the handle as hard as he could, he managed to open the heavy door.

Thunder assaulted his ears. Icy water drenched his legs. *How did water get in here?* Shaking with cold, he slid through the door. The ship tilted and the door slammed shut just as he found a rung to cling to.

Shivering and wet to his knees, Charlie peered down the passageway. *Which way shall I go? Hmm, I'll go aft and take the starboard ladder.*

He struggled down the passageway, feeling for one rung at a time, fighting the pitch of the ship. Cold water splashed up to his waist as thunder roared again. *I see a bit of light!*

Charlie turned left at the end of the passageway. A gust of wind and water poured through an open hatchway above the starboard ladder, throwing him hard against the bulkhead. Water sloshed over his head. Breathless, he struggled to his feet, searching for a handhold. Another gust of wind and water knocked him down, bashing his head against the floor.

CR&O

"Charlie, wake up!" Paudeen's voice came from far away. *I don't want to wake up. My body hurts. Oh, my head.* Charlie's stomach heaved. Hands, cool against his cheek, turned his head to the side. A damp cloth soothed his hot forehead, and Charlie sank back into sleep.

When he woke again, all was quiet. He lay with his eyes closed, savoring the stillness. *The ship is no longer bucking. I'm warm.* Gingerly, eyes still closed, Charlie reached toward the pain in his head and felt a sticking plaster. He turned carefully to his other side and fell back to sleep.

"Charles, wake up." *Father. I must obey.* Charlie forced his eyes open and squinted in the light. Father's face was stern. Tears coursed suddenly down Charlie's face. *I wanted to make him proud.* Father put a finger to his lips. "Hush, son. You're safe. You've no need to cry. Paudeen will bring soup. Drink it. I'll return later. I must understand why you disobeyed me."

ርሄ

"We've lost a day because of the storm, but fortunately we haven't lost much else. We're on course to dock in New York on Wednesday. Now, Charles, tell me. Why didn't you obey me and stay in my office as Paudeen told you?"

Now I'm for it. "It was dark. I was sick, and scared. I knew I should stay, but I was all alone and—and I just couldn't. I'm sorry, Father." Sorrow and shame erupted in a sob.

"We are fortunate a sailor noticed the open hatch and found you. Had the passageway continued to fill with water, your disobedience might have had a different outcome. But here you are, with nothing worse than a headache. By the time we dock you should be back at yourself."

"I'm sorry, Father."

"You must learn the importance of obedience, Charles."

"Yes, Father." Charlie turned his head. *I mustn't cry. Father will be even more angry.*

"You've missed two full days of piano practice. You must make that up; I promised your mother. You can return to your sailor work on our return trip."

He is so disappointed in me. "Yes, Father."

"We'll be in port for several days while the ship is repaired. You will stay with our Quaker relatives in New York City."

"Yes, Father." *We have relatives in New York City?*

"Paudeen will help you bathe and change your bedclothes while you go on deck for a while."

"Yes, Father." *What will it be like to stay with Quakers?*

CHAPTER 5

CALLY

Killeagh, August 1889

Washing her face, Cally touched the scar on her forehead. *I haven't seen my treasure for a long time, not since Teddy threw it in the stream and Uncle Dugan buried it. I want to see my scar. I could ask Uncle Dugan to help me.*

As she milked Daisy, Cally kept thinking about her treasure. *I wonder if I'll look different now. I want to look like Aisling, so I do. I love watching her. She's so pretty and cheerful and kind and smart. I wonder—what does Aisling see when she looks at me?*

Cally poured goat milk into the churn. Taking a deep breath, she decided. *I must find out. I'll ask Uncle Dugan to dig up my treasure.*

The minute Teddy ran with Shep to play behind the cottage, Cally ran as fast as she could up the hill to the potato patch where Uncle Dugan bent over the weeds.

"U—Uncle Dugan!"

"Cally, what's wrong? Tell me quick!"

"Noth—nothing's wrong. I just want to ask ye something. Is this a bad time?"

37

"It's a fine time fer a break. Have a drink of water and tell me what's on yer mind." Uncle Dugan wiped his forehead with his sleeve, settled his duncher back on his head, and held out a dipper.

"I—I want my treasure." Cally was still out of breath. "Please, Uncle Dugan."

Shep and Teddy raced around the cottage and up the hill. Uncle Dugan leaned to put the dipper back in the pail and whispered, "When ye come ter fetch the praties fer dinner, I'll have it fer ye." He winked at Cally and said in a normal voice, "Ye'll have to come back, Cally. I don't have the bucket ready fer ye yet. Maybe after ye put Teddy in the bath."

Bath! Then today is Saturday. And we'll go to church tomorrow with Aisling! All but Da.

Cally chased Teddy back down the hill. "Feed Shep, Teddy. I'll pick herbs for champ while the water heats for yer bath."

Cally glowed inside, thinking of Aisling's bright smile as she said, "That is durn good goat cheese, Cally, so it is! Isn't that so, Dugan? Next time I'll teach ye to make champ." Cally remembered the special look on Uncle Dugan's face as he nodded to Aisling. *She acted like showing me how to make yummy champ from potatoes, milk, goat cheese, and herbs was the most fun in all the world.*

"I want to be like Aisling when I grow up." Cally said out loud as she washed her herbs. The thought surprised her. *But it's true.*

CB&O

"Here ye are, lassie. It stayed clean fer ye. I wrapped it in a cloth and put it in a box—like true buried treasure!" Uncle Dugan's eyes twinkled in the way Cally loved. She took the wee mirror and turned it over and over, examining every detail of the metal's ornate pattern. Finally, she took a deep breath and looked at her reflection.

"Cally, what's wrong? Why the tears, lassie?"

"Oh, Uncle Dugan, I still look like a wee *wean*!"

Uncle Dugan's arms were around her in an instant. "But, my darlin', ye are but a wee *wean*. Though yes, ye have had to carry a load too heavy fer yer wee shoulders, so ye have. Is that what's troublin' ye? If so, does it help ye to know it troubles me too, that yer childhood is bein' swallowed up in tryin' to take care of yer whole family?"

Cally looked up from the mirror to study Uncle Dugan's face through her tears. *He doesn't usually talk that much. I must understand what he is saying.*

"Uncle Dugan, I don't rightly know what ye mean. I just thought God might have let me grow up more, to be able to cook and clean and care for Teddy and Da." Fresh sobs shook Cally's slender body. "Oh, Uncle Dugan, I hoped I would look like Aisling! But I don't!"

"There now, lassie, cry it all out. It does a body good to let the feelings come." Uncle Dugan's hug was warm, strong, comforting. Cally felt herself relax and her sobs eased.

"Cally, Aisling is a grown woman. She's fourteen years older than ye are. Ye aren't meant to look like her for fourteen more years! The problem isn't with ye, lassie. It's not yer fault ye are having to grow up too fast . . ."

Not my fault . . . That's not true. Mammy told me I would be the death of her, and I wished fer the babby to die. Cally didn't hear anything else Uncle Dugan said. A chill settled over her, stealing away the comfort of his arms. She stiffened, dried her eyes, and handed her treasure to Uncle Dugan. "Put it back—I don't want it anymore."

Cally hurried down the hill with her bucket of praties. *I must see to Teddy's bath, and make the champ, and set the house to rights before Sunday.*

When her work was done and she lay finally in her bed beside Teddy, Cally made a promise inside her heart. *I won't cry any more. Never again. It does no good and changes nothing.*

03℞

"What's wrong with Cally?" Aisling whispered to Dugan on the way to church. She turned to look. Cally hunched in the wagon bed staring out at the landscape, apparently oblivious to Teddy's chatter and Shep's head on her lap, his brown eyes fixed on her face. "Even Shep knows somethin's not right."

"I don't know. She looked in her wee mirror yesterday and got upset that she wasn't grown up yet. She looks like my early memories of Reeny, but I wasn't sure she would like to hear that."

"She looks like ye, too."

"Sure, and that's why ye are so fond of her, is it, Aisling?"

Aisling laughed and glanced back at the children. Cally pretended to be asleep, watching Aisling through mostly closed eyes. "Well, I'm fond of Teddy too, and he looks like his da. But tell me more about what happened yesterday."

"She cried, wishin' she looked like ye. I tried to comfort her, but she pulled away from me. She's been like this ever since. I'm right worried, so I am. She's gone into her own world and I can't reach her."

"We must both of us watch and seek a clue, Dugan. It stabs my heart, seein' her like this."

Dugan nodded. Aisling was quiet for a moment and then said, "Do ye know, Dugan, I have never once heard Cally mention her mammy or her baby sister. Not once.

"Ye are right, Aisling. Nor have I. I don't think she has grieved them properly."

I can't tell them Mammy and the babby's dyin' is my fault. They would never forgive me. I couldn't bear it. Cally sighed and squirmed and pushed Shep off her lap, so they would know she was awake and give over this kind of talk.

Cally let her hand lie in Aisling's like a lifeless thing as they walked into the mass. Aisling cast a worried glance at Dugan, and then back to Cally. As the familiar Latin rhythms began, she whispered to the children the words of the mass from Father Michaelson's catechism. *I shall go in to the altar of God, to God who giveth joy to my youth. . . Our help is in the name of the Lord. . . Thou wilt turn, O God, and bring us to life . . .* "Oh Lord, may this be so," Aisling whispered in her heart, "for me, for Dugan, for Cally and Teddy, and for their da."

CHAPTER 6

CHARLIE

New York City, June 25, 1889

CHARLIE STOOD AT THE PROW of *Lion III*, his gaze darting from the vast assortment of ships to the wharf teeming with people to the immense buildings thrusting toward the sky. *I always thought Waterford's port huge and busy. But this . . . !*

New York City heaved and swarmed and towered before him. *I feel dizzy.*

"Your first time, is it, lad?" A hand landed on his shoulder. Charlie looked up, squinting against the sun's glare.

"I feel so—small, Paudeen. And scared. I never felt like this on the open sea. Even in the storm, I knew it was just wind and water and thunder. But this—I have no idea what this is."

Paudeen laughed. "Sure, it's frightenin', so it is. Give me a clear horizon, endless space, sunrises and sunsets stretchin' across open sky any day. But ye won't be alone to face it, Charlie. Ye are to stand right here, both legs the same length until yer Cousin Silas comes for ye. Ye know him? Good, then. Yer father will see ye at tea at yer relatives' house two days from now. Yer to mind yer elders, practice yer piano every day, and rest when ye are tired. The Captain wants ye full

43

recovered for the return voyage."

The long speech pulled Charlie's attention from the complex scene before him. He flung his arms around Paudeen's waist, embarrassed as a sudden rush of tears dampened the sailor's whites. "Take a grip, lad. Ye are a brave sailor. Look now—that's Trinity Church! The tallest building in New York City. I'll see ye in about ten days, Charlie." And he was gone.

Charlie looked up, up, up to find the top of the spire on the church Paudeen had pointed out. The building grew larger by the minute as the *Lion III* approached the quay. He gripped the railing and searched the crowds for Cousin Silas. *Why did Mummy never tell me I have cousins in America? What will Cousin Nathanael and Cousin Sarah be like, and their five children?*

Charlie's head ached by the time Cousin Silas walked up the gangway. "Thee looks pale, laddie" he said. "Come, thee can rest while we drive to Nathanael's house. Hold on tight to my coat while we walk. I don't want to lose thee in the crowd. James is holding the brougham as close as he can to the end of the ramp. Thy gear is already stowed."

Charlie held on, put his head down, and focused on keeping his balance as Cousin Silas pushed through the throng to the carriage. The press of people, the heat, the noise, and the assault of too many smells overcame him. His stomach heaved before Cousin Silas finally lifted him into the haven of the carriage. "There, *garsún*, thy father told me thee hath not been at yourself since thy *purler* in the storm. Stretch out on the bench and put thy head in my lap. Good man. Now rest. Thee will have plenty of time in these next days to see the city."

Charlie closed his eyes. He awoke to excited voices as James opened the carriage door. Charlie focused on one voice, the one saying "A bowl of soup and a good night of sleep will set him right, so it will. Come children, thee can meet thy cousin in the morning. Matilda, won't thee mind them so I can attend to Charlie?"

༺༻

While he waited for James to bring the carriage, Charlie labored over a long list he was writing, titled "Ten Days in New York City." *I want to remember to tell Mummy everything.*

Fourth of July in America!

The Statue of Liburty

The Harbor, Trinity Church

Watching construcsion of the World Building

Central Park

New York Times Building (new!)

The Sience and Invention fair

Cousins Matilda, Tobias, Florry, Ben, and wee Jimmy (named
    after James)

Quakers, different and same

James

The piano at the Presbiteeryan Church

Surprise concert with Mister Pader-something!

Cousins Nathanyel and Sara moving to bigger house (September)

Cousin Silas and James's lekch

Cousin Nathanael interrupted Charlie's puzzlement over how to spell "lecture." "It's time to go, lad." Charlie jumped up, shoving his list and pencil into his pocket as the family crowded around to say goodbye.

Cousin Sarah wiped a tear. "Thee packed my letter to my sister Priscilla, yes, Charlie? Give Margaret and her intended our best wishes. It hath been a right pleasure to have thee with us these days. Thy music was a balm to my soul. God hath wonderful plans for thy life; don't thee forget that, Charlie." She blew her nose.

Cousin Nathanael helped Charlie into the brougham. He waved to his cousins until they turned the corner at Water Street. *I want to see everything.* "Cousin Nathanael, could I ride up front with James?"

"I don't see why not." Nathanael stuck his head out the window and yelled to James to stop the carriage. Charlie let out a whoop in the early morning coolness as he clambered up to the bench. *I want to look and look and look.*

As the ships at anchor in the bay came into view, Charlie had a startling thought. *Waterford will never again be the center of my universe.*

挄掀

Mayfield House, August 6, 1889

Charlie ate breakfast in the kitchen. *Too many people in the dining room. After today, life can get back to normal in this house.* He speared a kipper. *Father hasn't talked to me since he got home. I think he's still angry. He won't thole disobedience.*

"God has graced us with perfect weather for the wedding!" Mummy entered, waving at the patch of rosy sky visible through the kitchen window. "Stay out of the way, Charlie, and don't muss your wedding suit!" Charlie smiled at her and rose. *Soon I'll get you back, Mummy.*

At the piano, Charlie watched through the open drawing room doors as men set up rows of chairs in the garden. Then he turned to a last run through the pile of music Gritty had asked him to learn and play for the reception. *All I've done since I got home is practice, practice, practice. Mr. Pearse only let me prepare for the wedding AFTER full workouts for the October concert. I hope Gritty and Percy will be happy.*

He pulled Clara Schumann's Scherzo No. 2 from the stack, but a nearby conversation distracted him. Peering around the piano, he saw two men he didn't recognize, their heads together. A creaky voice said, "Hide in the closet of your bedroom while everyone gathers in the garden, and you'll have the house to yourself. Everyone believes you are a cousin from Scotland, but they won't notice if you're not at the wedding. Now repeat what I told you."

Charlie pulled back when the old man's watery eyes swiveled his direction.

"The safe is in the master's dressing room behind an ocean painting," the man whispered. "I won't let ye down, sir. I'm a dab hand at safe cracking. Best I meet ye at the Clodagh Bar tomorrow after I bid farewell to the Malcomsons. No use risking capture by giving ye the haul here at the house."

What? Father's safe?

"It's time justice is served." The old man's voice quavered but his eyes were fierce. "Carry out your part and your reward will be generous."

What does this mean? What should I do? Charlie looked around, his body tingling with alarm. *Father's in his study talking with Percy's father, and Daniel is with them. They won't like being interrupted. Mummy's dressing for the wedding. Lillian's busy. I haven't seen Gritty at all this morning. Meghan took Martin and Molly for a walk. Oh—I know! Thomas! Mummy expected him to arrive after I went to bed last night.*

Charlie peeked around the piano. The men were gone. He strolled through the drawing room, inclining his head to the smiles of many guests. He walked normally down the hallway, then flew up the stairs to Thomas's room. Without knocking, he threw open the door and rushed in. Thomas's wedding clothes were laid out on his bed, but he was still in his bathrobe, finishing his breakfast. "Charlie, what . . .?"

Seeing no one in the hallway, Charlie closed the door. "Thomas, I need your help!" His brother's eyes widened as Charlie related what he had overheard.

"Some *raparee* means to rob us? While Margaret and Percy are saying their vows? What a lark! This is more fun than a dozen weddings!" Thomas set his plate on the tray and began pacing. "What did the old man mean about wanting justice? Never mind, we must concoct a plan. Let's think while I dress. Neither you nor I can miss the wedding." The last bit was muffled as Thomas pulled off his pajama top. "But we must alert the police!"

"Everyone is too busy. There's no one to send."

"I know! We'll ask Zeke at the girls' school to take a message! He's a sound man. Look in the desk for paper, pen and ink while I get this durned suit on. I'll write the message and you can run around the house to deliver it."

"But—but I've never in my life gone to the school without Mummy."

"This is an emergency, isn't it? Do you have a better idea? Here, I'm ready to write."

Thomas mumbled as he scribbled. "'Zeke, please take this message to the police station immediately. Thank you. Thomas Malcomson.'

"Now to the police. 'A hired thief with red hair, spectacles and a twangy voice intends to rob my father's safe while my sister Margaret gets married in our garden. Please send someone quickly to hide in my father's dressing room to catch him. The wedding is at 11:00. Thank you. Thomas Malcomson, Mayfield House.'

"There. Here are the messages. Put them both in your pocket. Don't run, Charlie. Walk as if you do this every day. At the wedding, we'll both have to act like nothing is happening except hitching our sister. Off you go."

Charlie carefully smoothed the messages in his pockets so they wouldn't be noticeable. He smiled at a guest in the hallway, walked down the stairs and out the front door past a dozen more guests arriving for the wedding. He wandered the length of the house and around the corner. Then he raced to the door of the school, rang the bell, and stood panting. A woman he recognized vaguely opened the door.

"Good morning, ma'am. I am Charles Malcomson. I have a message for Zeke, please."

"Today is Zeke's day off, Charles. He may be at his cottage. I am Mrs. Grover, director of the school. If you leave the message with me, I can deliver it to him tomorrow."

"No, Ma'am. That is, the message must be delivered right away. Can you tell me how to get to his cottage? How far is it?"

"Zeke lives in town. Your sister's wedding is at 11:00, is it not? The only way you could be back on time would be to take a carriage or ride a horse. Is it something I can help you with, Charles?"

Charlie shifted from one foot to another. *Should I trust this woman? Mummy must trust her since she works at the school.* "What I really need is to get an urgent message to the police. I hoped Zeke could take it."

"The police? Why?"

"A man is planning to rob my father's safe while we are all in the garden for the wedding. I overheard him talking to another man in our drawing room."

"Oh my. I understand the urgency. If you go, you will be late for the wedding and upset your family. Charles, may I send Cora, one of my older girls who rides well? She can go first to the police with your message, and then to Zeke's house. He will surely give assistance if he can."

Charlie handed Mrs. Grover the envelope for the police. *Am I doing the right thing?*

"I can see you are concerned Charles. Take some deep breaths. You have done what you can. Relax now and focus on this special event for your family. I'll add a note to explain to the police why Cora is delivering your message. They should wear plain clothes and enter through the servants' door, yes? Tell me exactly how to find your father's dressing room."

The day grew warm. Charlie smoothed his hair as he walked back to his own side of the mansion. Lillian met him at the door, her expression anxious. "Where have ye been, Master Charlie? Everyone has been looking for ye. It's time fer the family to enter. Yer Grandmother Charlotte and yer other relatives have already been seated."

Charlie joined his family, gathered outside the drawing room door. Late-arriving guests hurried past them as a string quartet played the lively traditional "Haste to the Wedding." *Only Thomas and I know there will be drama during the wedding inside too.* Margaret, radiant in her wedding dress, clung to Father's arm, her bridesmaids around her. Elaine held Martin's ring pillow, her hand on his shoulder.

Thomas looked at Charlie, his eyebrows raised. Charlie gave him a small shrug before saying, "You look beautiful, Mummy." She gave him a hug, straightening his collar.

The wedding guests quieted as the strings shifted to Bach's "Air on the G String." *Time to go.* Thomas walked first, escorting Mummy. Then Daniel with Meghan, followed by Charlie before Molly scattered her pink rose petals.

After the bridesmaids, Gritty will walk in with Father to Schubert's "Ave Maria." Elaine will send Martin with the rings at the right time. Will the police be able to enter the house quietly enough not to alarm Elaine or late guests? Thomas and I didn't think of that.

As he walked, Charlie tried to locate the creaky old man among the guests but found he couldn't do so and maintain decorum. *Mrs. Grover told me to relax and focus on the wedding.* Reaching his seat, Charlie mentally rehearsed the first piece he was to play for the reception.

CRUD

Squeezed with Thomas into a large easy chair across from Father behind his big desk, Charlie couldn't stop trembling. The long reception was over. Margaret and Percy had departed amid a flurry of rose petals, and most of the people too. Mummy invited the remaining house guests to rest in their rooms until supper. *I'm glad supper won't include me. I'm exhausted.*

The redheaded man pretending to be a Scottish cousin stood handcuffed between two plainclothes policemen, a grizzled man beside them. "Zeke," Thomas whispered. The chief of police, in full uniform, sat in another chair.

Father cleared his throat and demanded an accounting of what had transpired in his home that day. Thomas jabbed Charlie with his elbow until he stood. "Fa—father, the man you need is still a guest in our house." Charlie paused and swallowed, fighting a tremor in his voice. "I saw him during the reception. He's your uncle, I think. A scary old man named William. Before the wedding I heard him talk to this man about wanting justice."

Father turned to Zeke. "Find out from Lillian what room William occupies and invite him to speak with me."

Charlie sat down. *Will Father be angry about what I've done?* Thomas put his arm around Charlie's shoulder and grinned. "Father, if Uncle William is the true villain, Charlie is the hero of this story. Shall I tell Father what I know, Charlie?"

Charlie nodded and pushed back into the cushions as Thomas stood. Pacing before Father's desk and waving dramatically, he recounted the story Charlie had whispered to him during a break at the reception. *Thomas never sits still while thinking or talking.*

"But Father," Charlie felt heat in his face. "A girl at the school named Cora rode to town to give Thomas's messages to the police and Mr. Zeke. Can we tell her thank you in some way?"

"I will consider how we may thank Miss Cora, Charles. Do continue, Thomas."

A knock came at the door. William entered, smiling. Seeing Father's stern face and the others in the room, he stopped short, causing Zeke to bump into him. Zeke grabbed the old man to steady him and shut the door behind them. The language that poured from the old man's mouth Charlie had never heard before, not even among the sailors on Father's ship. It was punctuated by words like "justice" and "unfair" and "after all I did for Malcomson Brothers."

When the flow finally stopped, Father turned to the chief of police.

"Perhaps, sir, your men could take our 'Scottish cousin' to jail, while you stay to hear Uncle William's story? Thomas, Charles, Zeke, you may go. I am grateful to each of you for your part in today's events. Uncle William, please sit down and explain to me why you feel unfairly treated by the Malcomsons."

Thomas protested and Father allowed him to stay, but Charlie was glad to escape. He ran to the drawing room, the kitchen, and finally found Mummy in her bedroom. She was seated on her settee, drinking tea with Grandmother Charlotte, Aunt Jemima, and a woman he didn't know.

"Charlie! I've been wondering where you were. You played so beautifully! Margaret and Percy both asked me to tell you thank you, thank you, thank you. Everyone had kind words to say. I am so proud of you, son."

Grandmother and Aunt Jemima agreed. "Indeed, thy music was unforgettable, Charles."

"Charlie, this is my dear friend Maggie. She was my nanny when I was growing up. I am delighted she came to celebrate with us her namesake Margaret's marriage."

"I'm pleased to meet you, ma'am."

"And I you, Charles."

"You look tired, Charlie. Give me a hug and you can go rest."

Charlie snuggled close for a moment, basking in Mummy's praise, and comforted by her warm affection. *How good to feel normal and safe before I go to bed.*

CHAPTER 7

CALLY

Killeagh, April 1890

CALLY EASED HER HEAD AROUND the doorframe far enough to see Miss Hilda, who stood with her back to the open doorway, mixing herbs and oils on the worktable in the center of the room. Slipping through the door, Cally hid behind a set of shelves supporting a dozen pots. The scent of herbs made her eyes water. She pinched her nose and held her breath to keep from sneezing.

Humming as she worked, Miss Hilda stopped mixing and covered the clay bowl with a cloth, then reached for another bowl. Her practiced movements calmed Cally's anxious thoughts. She could hear through the door a lapwing singing its early-morning song, *pee-wit, pee-wit*.

"Ye might as well come out, lassie, I know ye are there." Miss Hilda's words startled Cally. *So, it's true: Miss Hilda does have eyes in the back of her head! I should run away now.* But as quickly as the thought crossed her mind, Miss Hilda turned around and held out her arms. "Come, Cally. Tell me what troubles ye."

Trembling, Cally emerged from her hiding place and walked step by step toward Miss Hilda. She couldn't remember why she had come, only that she needed to talk with someone, and it couldn't be Uncle Dugan or Aisling. As Miss Hilda's arms folded around her, despite herself Cally burst into tears. *I promised myself never to cry again! What's wrong with me?* Miss Hilda held her, taking up again the sweet melody she had been humming.

When Cally's sobs eased, Miss Hilda gave her a cloth to blow her nose, settled her into a chair, then said, "First things first. Have ye breakfasted, lassie? I was just about to eat some toasted barmbrack. Ye'll join me, won't ye? And take a cup of tea in yer hand?"

Cally crunched her barmbrack and savored the fragrant tea, almost forgetting the weight of her troubles in the comfort of a full tummy.

"Now, Cally," Miss Hilda said after she washed and put away their teacups. "Tell me why ye came to see me this beautiful morning. How are Teddy, and yer da, and yer Uncle Dugan?"

Jolted back to reality, Cally's eyes again filled with pesky tears. She pressed her fists into her eyes to make them stop. *What must Miss Hilda think of me? A six-year-old can't be a crybaby!*

"It's all right, Cally. Even I weep sometimes. This world can bring us much pain."

Miss Hilda cries sometimes? Cally could not imagine it. She peeked through shaky fingers to see whether Miss Hilda was funning her. But her gaze was quiet, and calm, and gentle. Slowly, Cally lowered her hands and tucked them under her thighs.

"Miss Hilda, I don't know what to do. Da is sad, and nothing I do or say ever makes him happy. He doesn't even see me, unless Teddy is crying, or I don't do the chores just right. He doesn't speak to us. He's mad at Uncle Dugan. And he got angry when Father Michaelson said God's will was best, after Mammy and the *babby* died." Cally stopped, frightened by the emotion that welled up when she remembered Da pushing the priest out of their house and slamming the door.

After a moment, she continued. "Da doesn't sing or play his uilleann pipes. He works or he sits by the fire, or he comes in late from sitting by

Mammy's and the *babby*'s grave. He doesn't even smoke his *dudeen*. Sometimes I see tears on his face. I don't know what to do. I—I'm afraid of what bad thing might happen next." So many words tumbling from Cally's mouth surprised even her.

Miss Hilda's warm eyes didn't leave Cally's face. "I see, lassie. And ye feel responsible for all of them, Teddy, yer da, and yer Uncle Dugan, isn't that so?"

"I *am* responsible. There's no one else to take Mammy's place." *To try to be the girl Mammy wanted.*

"This is a heavy burden, Cally. How do ye think I can help ye, then?"

Cally took a deep breath and clenched her hands. "I heard some women talking at market. They said ye can do spells, to keep the dark faeries from doing their bad things, so they said."

"I can, Cally. But it will cost ye. The Dubh Sidhe will want something from ye, to stop making trouble for yer family, so."

"Wh—what will they want from me?"

"I don't know. I'll have to ask a good faery to find out. Come back in a week, Cally, and I'll try to have an answer for ye. But don't ye think ye should talk with someone about this, yer da or yer Uncle Dugan, or even Father Michaelson? Ye are trying to save yer family by yerself, Cally, an' that's too much responsibility for a wee lassie. Would ye want me to come to yer house and help ye talk to them?"

"Oh no, Miss Hilda. They might be angry with me. I don't think Da believes anymore in the good faeries, not since Mammy died. He won't listen to me or to Uncle Dugan. And he gets angry if anyone even mentions Father Michaelson. Please, Miss Hilda, please don't tell anyone I came here. I must go. Da thinks I'm in the upper pasture with the sheep. I've left Teddy alone with them much too long! I'll come back in a week, if I can."

"I'll watch for ye, Cally. Come whene'er ye are able. And here, take these sweeties to share with yer brother. He's sure to be worried about ye bein' gone for so long. Fair play to ye."

Miss Hilda stood for a long time watching Cally scramble down the steep path, balance her way across the creek on slippery stones, and then begin the long climb past the peat bog to her family's upper pasture. *What will the Dubh Sidhe demand from the brave grieving lassie?*

Hilda sighed. She would have to start the ritual of contact with the little people. "What can't be cured must be endured," she muttered, as she began snipping herbs from her pots. "But it do be hard to know which is which for yon wee Cally. Should I or should I not have a talk with yer man Frank Donnelly?"

☙❧

Cally rounded the bend and clamored over the low stone wall into the upper pasture. Spotting her, Teddy ran as fast as his four-year-old legs could carry him across the uneven turf, dodging sheep as he ran, Shep careening after him.

"I thought ye weren't coming back," he wailed, throwing himself at her so they both tumbled to the ground. Shep barked frantically, running around and around the emotional children.

"Not coming back?" Cally giggled, tickling him until he laughed and tickled her back. "What do I have in my pocket, then, just for ye? No peeking, ye have to guess, so ye do!"

Teddy didn't care to guess. He soon had his hand in Cally's pocket, blue eyes still reddened from his tears, pulling out Miss Hilda's sweeties. "For me? I haven't seen sweeties since Boxing Day!" Shep barked louder, hoping to be included in the disbursement of treats. But a sudden crack of distant thunder startled the children.

"I'll open the gate to the sheep pen, and then help ye gather them in," yelled Cally, dashing for the enclosure at the far end of the pasture. Shep and Teddy herded the anxious sheep toward the gate as raindrops spattered around them. Cally ran to pick up a lamb and carry her inside, the ewe bleating after her. When all were secure, Shep and the children, completely soaked, scrambled down the hill toward home.

Shivering, Cally blew on the banked coals until flame licked up the side of a fresh chunk of peat, and then pulled the kettle over the fire. "Wrap yerself in the blanket from our bed until the room is warm," she instructed Teddy. "I'll put praties in the fire to roast."

Busy with dinner and chores and tucking Teddy in, Cally only had time to review what Miss Hilda had said when was in bed herself. *Was going to talk with Miss Hilda right or wrong? What have I started? What will the faeries say? What will they demand in payment to stop bringing trouble to my family?*

The questions frightened Cally so much she sat up in bed. She became aware of Da and Uncle Dugan speaking at the other end of the single room which was their home.

"Ye can't go on like this, Frank!" Cally leaned forward. *Uncle Dugan never speaks so strongly.* "It's not good for ye, it's not good for yer *weans*, it's not good for the farm, and it's not good for me. Somethin' must change! Ye need help, Frank! And I don't know how to help ye."

"Ye have been helping, Dugan, so ye have. Ye kept the farm functionin' when I simply could not do it. Ye have been there to help Cally care for Teddy. Take yer hurry in yer hand, can't ye, Dugan? Let the hare sit."

"Frank, it's been more than a year since Reeny, God bless her memory, took yer wee *babby* to Heaven with her. More than a year. Still ye're but a shadow of the man ye once were. If ye were alone, ye could slough about fer as long as ye had a need to do it. But ye have two *weans,* Frank, who need ye. This family cannot go on like this. Won't ye talk with Father Michaelson? I know ye were angry with him, but won't ye forgive him and let him try to help us?"

Cally held her breath. *Uncle Dugan, at least, might understand me goin' to see Miss Hilda, why I had to talk with someone.*

Da spoke more loudly. "I told ye, Dugan, I need more time! I know Reeny was yer sister, but she was my *wife,* the mother of my *weans*! I can't just let her go! The last conversation I had with Reeny was an argument, Dugan. An argument! How can I forgive myself fer that, I ask ye!"

Tears pooled in Cally's eyes and spilled down her cheeks. She knew what that last argument had been about. *It was Da speakin' up fer me! Is he sorry he did so?*

Uncle Dugan's voice hardened. "No. No, Frank. Ye are out of time. Haven't ye even noticed that Cally's cut to the onion? Don't ye care how desperately Teddy wants yer love? This stops now, Frank. Today. Tonight."

Da raised his hand, but Uncle Dugan wasn't finished. "And me, Frank. Do ye ever take yer thoughts away from yer own pain to think about someone else? Sure I am grateful ye and Reeny took me in when our mam and da died, ye know I am, and I've tried to repay ye. Now I want to marry Aisling, but where would we live? I can't invite her to share the barn with me."

Da said something Cally couldn't hear.

"No, hear me out, Frank. I'm not seeking to abandon ye. Aisling loves the *weans* too. She'll be happy if I can build us a cottage here on the farm. But to do that, I need yer help, Frank. I've been carryin' the work of the farm almost entirely by myself. No, stop, Frank. I've more to say. If ye won't take a grip, me and Aisling will find a room in town. Her da will let me work at the tavern. We have our own life to think about now, Frank. I'm not asking fer yer answer right now, tonight. But soon, ye must tell me."

Cally heard the door open and close, Uncle Dugan going to his bed in the barn. She held her breath to stifle a cry. *No, Uncle Dugan, please, please don't leave me! I can't bear it! Da—please—I'm afraid. And so knackered. Don't I matter to ye at all?*

Cally hunched her wee shoulders, trying to ease the tight ache they so often felt. *If Da stays the same, and Uncle Dugan leaves, how can I keep going? What if more terrible things come from the Dubh Sidhe?* Cally buried her face under her pillow and wept herself to sleep. Breaking her vow, the second time in one day.

Debra Kornfield

CHAPTER 8

CHARLIE

Mayfield House, Sunday, April 20, 1890

"HAPPY BIRTHDAY, CHARLES. You are eleven today, I believe.

"Thank you, Father." *What is this about, I wonder.*

"Sit down, son. I must talk with you about a decision we are facing. First, though, about this summer: I plan to take you sailing with me again. But I must know whether you will obey me without question."

"Yes, Father."

"See that you do. Now, your mother is concerned about your music. I need to understand, Charles, what the piano means to you, and what thoughts you have about your future. It seems you have a gift, and we must decide how to steward it properly."

"Thoughts about my future? I—I don't know what you mean, Father."

"Let's review this last year. The first musical event I recall since your last birthday was the impromptu concert in New York City, when the First Presbyterian Church organist heard you practicing and invited you to open a concert he had already organized for Mr. Paderewski. This was Mr. Paderewski's first New York concert, I believe. You received a standing ovation, and strong praise from Mr. Paderewski himself. He wanted to take you back to Vienna immediately to be his student."

Charlie flushed. *That was such a surprising evening. My cousins—*

But Father was still talking. "Charles, that concert was the first time I realized how unique your gift is, and why your mother insisted you not slight your practice time aboard ship."

"Thank you, Father. Hearing Mr. Paderewski play was amazing. I was so happy you could be there."

"The second event was Margaret and Percy's wedding reception, where despite your worry over the robbery, you played the most beautiful pieces ever to grace our drawing room. Your music attracted as much attention as the bride and groom."

Father has never talked to me this way. "Father, may I ask—have you been able to talk with Uncle William?"

"Yes, son. I believe we reached a reasonable settlement, which seems to have eased his bitterness. But we were discussing your music. The third event was with the Waterford Chamber Orchestra in October. I missed that concert because I was sailing, but on my return, Mr. Pearse was ecstatic. That is not too extravagant a word. He claimed it as a highlight of his career."

Father looked intently at Charlie. "I wasn't here, but I have wondered ... Be frank with me, Charles. Tell me how things have been with him since then."

Charlie rubbed his palms, suddenly sweaty, on his pants. "Must I, Father?"

"Yes. This is important, Charles."

Charlie took a deep breath and spoke quickly. "Father, ever since that concert, Mr. Pearse is never happy, no matter how hard I work. I dread my lessons." Charlie lifted his eyes to Father's face, afraid of what he might see there.

"Go on, son."

"I love the music, but I don't like him yelling at me all the time.

Forgive me, Father. I know you pay a lot for him to teach me. But every time I play in public, Mr. Pearse yells more."

"Thank you, Charles. That is exactly what I needed to know. Now let me tell you of an offer your mother and I have received. In the months since he met you in New York City, Mr. Paderewski has not forgotten you. He wants you to move to Vienna so he can teach you. His agent has written, saying there is a school in Vienna you could attend as a boarding student. One of his more accomplished students would teach you whenever the maestro is away on tour."

Charlie sat up straight. "But—I would have to leave home? Live far away from you and Mummy? Oh, Father!"

"This would begin in the fall, with the new school term. You could still sail with me this summer, for two crossings if you wish, since we have no wedding to worry about. Thomas might join us for one of them, as a break from his studies at Oxford. And you would come home from Vienna for your midterm break, and for Christmas."

"But Father. What if I miss you and Mummy too much? What if the other students at the school don't like me? How could I go to school there? I am only beginning to study German. And I've never been in a school before—I've always had Mr. Hobbs as my teacher. What if I miss the birth of Margaret's baby? What if Mr. Pearse is angry? What if—" Charlie was on his feet, his voice rising with each of his questions. "What if Mr. Paderewski doesn't like me?"

"Calm down, son. There is, indeed, much to consider. Your mother and I have discussed this extensively, but we have not decided yet. Sit down, Charles, and listen."

"Yes, sir." *Move to Vienna? By myself?*

"I propose that you and your mother travel to Vienna to speak directly with Mr. Paderewski about his vision and hopes for you. This will interrupt your studies with Mr. Hobbs, but your mother wants to visit the school while it is in session to get a feel for what the teaching and the students are like."

"Are we going soon, then, Father?"

"I have purchased passage for May 5, two weeks from tomorrow. You will sail south on a naval ship to Brest, then travel east by train to Paris, Munich and on to Vienna. Ah, here is your mother now, home for luncheon. My dear, I have just explained to Charles the decision we have before us and the journey you and he will undertake to explore it."

"Charlie, sweetheart, you look like the weight of the world has fallen onto your shoulders! Come here and give me a hug. Better?"

"I—I ... Maybe ..."

"I stopped by the school on my way home from mass. Look what I brought you from Cora, Charlie—she carved this little horse herself! Do you know she will be graduating from our school in a few weeks, then traveling to London for art school? We will miss her. She says she will miss you too, son. You may go around to say goodbye to her before we leave for Austria."

Charlie swallowed and took a deep breath. "It looks like Midnight!" He settled back in his chair, tracing the flowing lines of the beautiful little horse. *It's easier to think about Cora than about this conversation with Father. I'm glad she became my friend.*

"So, Charlie. What do you think of Mr. Paderewski's invitation?"

My music matters—to someone famous! But—

"What if he yells and throws things like Mr. Pearse does?" Charlie didn't realize he had spoken out loud until Mummy pulled him once again into a warm hug. To his chagrin, he found himself in tears as Father spoke.

"Charles, you are too old to be making this fuss. I assure you we want only what is best for you and will decide accordingly. Go wash your face and then play for me what you have been learning while I was gone."

ᘓᘔ

May 5, 1890

"Are ye ready fer yer grand adventure, then, Master Charlie? Yer mother has run to the school and will be back soon. Yer father had to leave for his ship a coupla hours ago." Lillian busily packed a luncheon for Charlie and his mother to eat on the way to the Waterford port, but Charlie noticed her wipe away a stray tear now and then.

Impulsively, as she turned from the table, he launched himself into her arms. "I'll miss ye that much, so I will, laddie. I've been with ye most every day yer whole entire life—except when ye went sailing with yer father. This house won't be the same without ye."

"I'll miss you too. Lillian. I promise, I'll bring home a present for you from Vienna!" Charlie flashed her a grin and was rewarded by a smile in return.

"Go then and put on yer jacket so ye are ready to jump into the carriage the minute yer mother returns."

Charlie picked up his jacket and wandered around his home, memorizing every detail. He was peeking into Father's study when he heard his mother call him. To his surprise, Mr. Hobbs stood on the front step, with Cora and Mrs. Grover a few steps away. Mummy was saying, "We'll be guests of Viscount Heinrich von Taffe. His father Eduard knew both my grandfather and Peter's father. Ah, there you are, Charlie. It's time for us to go."

Mr. Hobbs stepped forward to grasp Charlie's hand. "I've just come to say goodbye, lad. I've enjoyed my years teaching you. If you decide to stay here, it will be my joy to continue. But if you choose Vienna, I wish you well. This trip will be good for your fluency in German!"

"Thanks, Mr. Hobbs. I'll see you in a month!" Charlie turned to Mrs. Grover and Cora. *I already thanked her for my beautiful little horse and said goodbye, so why . . .?*

"With permission from your mother, we came with a question, Charlie. Would you be willing to play for our graduation ceremonies after your return? I know our girls would love that. You can choose for yourself what you wish to play."

Charlie looked at Mummy, who nodded. "Yes, Mrs. Grover. It will be an honor."

"Have a wonderful trip, and please come visit us on your return. We would like you both, Mrs. Malcomson, to share with our students what you see and learn as you cross the continent."

Mrs. Grover turned and nodded at Cora. Taking a deep breath, Cora said in a rush, "Mrs. Malcomson, I have been corresponding with a Viennese artist named Olga Wisinger-Florian. She has asked for a sample of my work and wants to send me a small painting of hers. If it's not an inconvenience, ma'am, could you deliver this to her? I've written her name and address on the packet. If it is not an imposition, ma'am." Cora blushed as she extended a small package.

"I'll tuck this in my satchel to keep it safe. Cora, you never cease to amaze me! I would not have guessed you were in contact with a famous Viennese painter! We will be happy to take this to Mrs. Wisinger and bring back her gift for you. Your art already makes us proud, my dear. One day you too will be famous."

Cora curtsied, blushing even more deeply, and stepped back to stand close to Mrs. Grover. But she turned again to Charlie. "Charlie, may I—that is, perhaps I should be asking you, Mrs. Malcomson. I want to care for Midnight while you're gone. It would be a pleasure."

Mummy nodded. She turned to speak to Lillian hovering in the doorway. "Lillian, please tell Evan Miss Cora will be caring for Midnight. He need only groom and ride Patrick, Rose, and Dancer while we are gone."

"Yes, ma'am." Lillian curtsied.

Charlie waved to them all and climbed into the carriage. *Today is full of surprises. I didn't know there are woman artists in Vienna, or that my grandfather knew a Viennese viscount. What else don't I know? Everything.*

CRSO

Charlie woke early, feeling hungry. He listened for a moment to the clack-clack of the train, then climbed down from his bunk and dressed quietly. Leaving Mummy asleep in her berth, he slipped through the sliding doors connecting their sleeper with the dining car.

"Bonjour, Monsieur Charles. Did you sleep well?" The waiter pulled out a chair and handed him a menu.

"Oui. Merci," Charlie replied. "May I have croissants and hot chocolate?"

As he munched, Charlie gazed at vineyards, a lovely river, and the small villages the train trundled past. France seemed as pretty and green as Ireland. Soon, though, the sky clouded over. By the time Charlie finished his breakfast and made his way to a seat in the lounge car, rain spattered the windows.

Charlie pulled out his German textbook, anxious to review basic conversation before their train stopped in Munich. "Ich trage, du trägst, er trägt . . ." he muttered, then "Oh, Mummy!"

Mummy laughed and slipped into a seat across from him. "Good morning, Charlie. You were so focused you didn't see me. Your German declension sounds good! Do you want to continue, or are you ready for a break?"

Charlie closed his book. "Mummy, how did your grandfather know Viscount von Taffe?"

"I beg your pardon? Oh. I never know what will pop out from your busy mind, young man. The von Taaffes are still members of the Irish nobility even though they have lived in Vienna for many generations. When Grandfather O'Connell found himself unwelcome in Ireland for a time, he traveled to the major cities of Europe seeking political support for his hope to gain Irish independence peacefully. He met many Irish living in Europe. I remember Viscount Eduard visiting my grandfather when I was a little girl in County Kerry."

"Mummy, if you grew up in County Kerry, and Father grew up at Mayfield, how did you meet him?"

Mummy's laugh trilled. "It's lovely traveling with you, Charlie. All right, I'll tell you our story. Your father and I met in Dublin. He was a student at Trinity College, and I was training as a teacher at a Model School. Girls didn't go to college back then. We met at a pacifist political rally. Grandfather O'Connell taught me his pacifist beliefs, which were no more popular among Catholics when I was growing up as they are now. Peter was raised as a pacifist Quaker. That was what first brought us together." Mummy gazed out at the rain, as if she had forgotten Charlie was there. Finally, she sighed and continued.

"Our Lady of Mercy Training College for women opened a few years ago. Maybe someday I'll go there and learn more properly the work I do at our school."

Charlie watched her, puzzled at the sadness in her face. "Mummy, what is the difference between Catholics and Quakers? And why doesn't Father go to church with us?"

"Oh, Charlie. That's a long story. When your father and I began to grow fond of each other, he told me he would never become Catholic, and I told him I would never give up my Church. He explained the Quaker criticisms of the Catholic Church, and said his relatives, including his mother, wouldn't like us to be married. So, we separated. But a few months later we bumped into each other at a Dublin social event. We admitted we didn't like being apart. He decided he could handle disappointing his Quaker relatives and agreed to have our children baptized in the Catholic Church."

"But Grandmother Charlotte loves you!"

"Yes. Once the decision was made, she chose to handle it graciously. After all, her own husband, your grandfather Joseph, had left the

Society of Friends long before. My father, however, disowned me for marrying a Quaker."

"What does 'disowned' mean?"

"It means I never had contact with my family again. But after my father died in 1877, we decided to give his name to you. I'm sad you never knew him, Charlie. He was a marvelous person. And so was my mother, Catherine. And my twin brothers."

"That's so sad, Mummy. Even your brothers don't want to see you?"

"I confess I haven't tried, Charlie." She gave a short laugh. "I'm afraid to be rejected all over again. We did invite them and their families to both Daniel's and Margaret's weddings, but they didn't come."

"Well, someday I'm going to make friends with your family, Mummy, and tell them you are wonderful and miss them."

"You are? That's sweet, Charlie. Perhaps your generation will be more open-minded."

"At least you still have your nanny, Maggie. She came to the wedding."

"Yes! That meant so much to me! I'm glad you got to meet her, Charlie."

"So, here's what I know, Mummy. Quakers are simple, and Catholics are fancy. Quakers are different, and Catholics are ordinary. They both have a lot of rules, but the rules aren't all the same. Catholic masses are in Latin. Quakers don't have masses. They just sit around not saying anything, and then someone speaks, and then there's more silence. At least that's how it was at Cousin Nathanael's house in New York."

"That is all true, Charlie, but think about the ways your father and I agree. We both believe God cares about everyone, not just rich people. Both of us oppose violence and political oppression. We believe all people should be treated with respect and honor, no matter their country or language or wealth or the color of their skin. We believe in doing whatever we can to bless the people we know, beginning with our own family and reaching out from there."

"Is that why you have the school at Mayfield, Mummy?"

"Partly, Charlie. But the main reason is that Mayfield House became too expensive for us to maintain and it's too large for just our family. Also, I love teaching. Since your father is gone so much, it helps me to focus on something else I love."

"I've never seen you teach, Mummy."

"Hmm, that may be true in the formal sense. But every mother teaches her children."

"So, what kind of girls go to your school? It's strange to live in the same house, but not know them."

"Our school serves two groups: those from wealthy homes, who can pay and who help us with the costs of maintaining Mayfield, and those from poor homes, who pay what they can. We believe poor girls have as much right to an excellent education as rich girls—or rich boys, for that matter. No one chooses their gender or what family they will be born into. It's not fair that boys are favored over girls in Ireland."

"Mummy, is Cora a rich girl or a poor girl?"

Mummy smiled. "Cora is rich in every respect except financially, Charlie. Her parents have always done their best to give her opportunities to learn and to use her gifts. She has studied at Mayfield School for Girls since she was tiny. Her mother works at the school as a cook to help pay her fees."

"Is Cora the only child in her family?"

"Sadly, yes. Her older brother, Shane, got sick and died when he was eleven—the same age as you. Maybe that's why Cora is so fond of you. Perhaps you remind her of her brother."

"Mummy, the rain has stopped! I see mountains. And look—we're coming into a big city!"

"This must be Munich! I believe we'll only be at the station for a couple of hours. We'll sleep one more night on the train and arrive in Vienna early tomorrow. Shall we get off and look around? I'm longing to stretch my legs. I've heard the new train station is twice the size of the one I knew. And we could walk to the Marienplatz. Let me check how much time we have."

Mummy rang a tinkly silver bell to catch the attention of the coach attendant. "Will we have time for a walk to the Marienplatz, monsieur?"

"I believe so, madame. You may wish to flag a carriage to return. We'll depart for Vienna at half past four. I'm told Bavarian pastries are marvelous, madame."

"Merci, monsieur. Charlie, let's grab our wraps and have an adventure!"

❀

As the train gathered speed leaving Munich, Charlie began a letter to Mr. Hobbs about their trip so far. The ancient port at Brest. The Champs-Élysées and Arc de Triomphe and the amazing new Eiffel Tower in Paris. The elaborate Great Hall of the Munich central train station, and the fun of buying Bavarian pastries for the people who served them on the train. "I will have to come back to Munich," wrote Charlie. "We hardly had time to see anything. But now we are on the last part of our trip. I wonder what Vienna will be like!"

Debra Kornfield

CHAPTER 9

CALLY

Killeagh, April-May 1890

"THEY WANT YER TREASURE. I don't ken what that is, lassie; they didn't tell me. But that's their price fer stoppin' the mischief against yer family."

Cally caught her breath. *How do the Dubh Sidhe know about my treasure? What else do they know?* She wrapped her arms around her chest, as if to hide herself and her secrets.

"I—I don't know, Miss Hilda. I didn't know their price would be so high. I have to think about it." Cally didn't wait for a response. She darted out of the house and down the hill as fast as she could go. She didn't stop running until she reached the edge of Glenbower Wood.

Why did I come here? Isn't this where the faeries live? I should be running away from them. But it seems like someone is taking me. Cally found herself walking straight into the forest, off the beaten path. At the edge of her awareness were tinkling sounds, as if the faeries were laughing at her.

Deeper and deeper into the woods she walked, pulled by an invisible cord. Down a gentle hill, across a brook, up the other side and now climbing steeply, until the hill leveled into an open place surrounded by oak trees. Cally half expected to see a ring of toadstools, but instead, she saw a cross made of stone, with a stone kneeling bench in front of it. *What is this place? Why am I here? Is this a dream?*

Cally no longer felt she was being pulled. She looked around carefully, turning in a slow circle. She could hear nothing at all. No birdsong, no rustling of small creatures, no murmur of leaves. Weary, she stretched out on the grass and fell into a deep, dreamless sleep. When she awoke, before she opened her eyes, she realized something covered her, and her head was cradled in someone's lap. The scent of honeysuckle wafted over her. A female voice sang softly, and a hand gently stroked her hair. *I feel like I'm full of sharp, rough edges, and the song and the hand are smoothing them away. I don't want it to end.* She lay still, savoring the unfamiliar sensation of being cared for.

When next she woke, Cally was alone. It seemed nature had been holding its breath, waiting for her to wake, for as she blinked her eyes open, the glen filled with birdsong and skittering and chattering. A breeze still carried the scent of honeysuckle.

Cally sat up, too gentled inside to immediately take back up her mantle of responsibility. She began walking down the steep hill, caught up in the sweetness of the song that still echoed around her. Wondering but not worrying, she touched her hair where the hand had stroked it.

Though she had not been to this place before, she knew the way home. *Somehow, I know I don't need to worry. Someone bigger than me knows what to do about the Dubh Sibhe and my treasure. I feel—relieved. Light. Happy.*

Just as Cally reached home, Uncle Dugan and Teddy trotted down the lane in the wagon. Cally ran to pet Simon. Teddy yelled, "Cally, look what Aisling gave us! New clothes for May Sunday! Come on, let's try them on to show Da!" Teddy scrambled down from the wagon, grabbed Cally's hands and danced her around in a circle.

Uncle Dugan grinned as he handed parcels down to them. *We're going to the* Bealtaine*? What will Da say?*

"Go on, Cally. Get changed while I care for Simon. I'll carry in the rest of our packages."

Cally caught her breath. *When have I last received a present, just for me?* Though Teddy ripped open his package, she carefully untied the string and eased aside the paper on hers. Aisling had made her a brightly colored dancing skirt and a frilly blouse with a bow at the throat! And there were new underthings, and sandals, and a purple bonnet.

"Let's wash first, Teddy. We're too dirty to put on these new things. We've some water in the bucket. Leave yer clothes on the bed and come outside with me. I'll help ye."

Teddy was too excited to fight her. Soon he was scrubbed and dressed in new breeches, buckled under his knees, and a blue shirt that matched his eyes. He had new socks and shoes, and his very first hat, with a perky blue ribbon. When he was ready, Cally pumped fresh water from the well for a shivery wash and dressed herself.

"Ye needn't worry about making supper tonight, Cally. Aisling sent us home with sausages and salad. She helped me pick out the sandals fer ye too. They came to Killeagh all the way from Cork City, so they did." Uncle Dugan beamed as Cally and Teddy twirled so fast her skirt flared out and they fell in a laughing heap on the grass.

Uncle Dugan ran to the barn for his harmonica and taught them dance steps they would need for May Sunday. They were practicing when Da came down the hill from the upper pasture. Cally saw him stop a short distance away, watching them with a mixture of joy and sorrow on his face. Teddy and Uncle Dugan saw her staring and turned to look. Da started to say something, but stopped, and walked past them into the cottage. Cally and Teddy looked to Uncle Dugan to find out what they should do.

Uncle Dugan knelt and gathered the children into his arms. "We must be patient with yer da a little longer, sweet *páistí*. By next year I think he'll be joinin' us with his pipes and his song. Some things take time to heal and cannot be rushed. We'll put the new clothes away and say no more about May Sunday today, yes Teddy? It's only two more days. I'll tell ye a secret: Aisling has been chosen for the May Queen's court! Won't it be fun to see her dressed up as a lady in waitin'?"

Drying the last dishes after Aisling's good supper, Cally heard a knock on the door. Three men she vaguely remembered seeing in town asked Da to sing and play his pipes for the festival. Da didn't say a word. He pushed past them, out the door and up the hill. The men turned to Uncle Dugan. He held his hands out and shrugged, and the men went away.

CB&ED

Cally smoothed her dancing skirt and straightened Teddy's hat. Dawn lightened the Sunday sky as Uncle Dugan drove into Glenbower Wood. Cally could faintly hear pipes and fiddles. Folks dressed as festively as she passed them on foot as Uncle Dugan pulled Simon up behind a long row of horses and carts and attached a feed bag for him. "Hurry, *weans*! I know the best place to watch the procession of the May Queen and her court."

Cally saw torches in the distance and heard flutes before she could tell which one of the dancing ladies was Aisling. The crowd clapped in time to the music. Before long Aisling dipped and turned before them, handing Cally a flower from her bouquet. Everyone fell in behind the procession as it passed, following the dancers down the road, over the bridge, and into the meadow where pipes and fiddles joined the flutes, and everyone began to dance.

Later, Cally and Teddy watched Uncle Dugan hurl a stone as far as he could. Though he didn't throw it the farthest of all the men, Cally saw his joy in the game, in his strength. It was something to tuck away, to think about later. From loaded tables they stuffed themselves full of boxty, drisheen, Gubbeen cheese and farl. They clapped, spun, or stomped through jigs, reels and hornpipes, and laughed or wept by turn through the singing competitions. Uncle Dugan whispered to Cally that her da had won the singing prize many times in the past, and next year might again. Before Cally could feel too deeply her yearning to hear Da sing once more, Aisling whirled her away into another merry jig.

Darkness fell as Simon trotted them all home. *This has been the best day ever,* Cally thought dreamily. Da was not in the cottage. Uncle Dugan carried Teddy, fast asleep, to his bed and told Cally he would be with Aisling at the Old Thatch Pub. Before Da came home, Cally too was asleep, cuddled around Teddy, their May Sunday clothes neatly folded at the end of the bed.

ᏣᎬᏃ

Cally blinked bleary eyes the next morning, waking from a dream of twirling so fast her skirt flew straight out in a circle around her. Suddenly she sat bolt upright, alarm ringing through all her senses. Da—why was Da sitting by her bed, holding Teddy on his lap, watching her? What new terrible thing had happened?

"Da, wha—what's wrong?" she stammered.

"Sure, nothing is wrong, Cally. That is, a lot of things have been wrong, and I've finally understood my part in that. Come here, lassie. There's room for both of ye."

Marveling, Cally pushed aside her blanket and stepped hesitantly toward her father. As he lifted her to his lap, and she felt his arms close around her and Teddy, she burst into tears, burying her face in her father's worn work shirt. Da held them and rocked them for a long time, humming a gentle melody the children had not heard for a long, long time.

Finally, Cally's sobs subsided into hiccups. Da laughed. Cally jerked up and stared at him in amazement. *Da is back? Da is back!* A surge of hope spread its warmth through her shivering body. Teddy laughed too, and finally Cally joined in. Bemused by a sound not heard in this house for many months, Uncle Dugan poked his head through the open door and soon chortled along with them.

Da stood up, spilling the children onto the floor. Grabbing their hands, he began dancing a jig, improvising the music with his voice.

A sweet lightness thrilled Cally as she threw on her clothes and ran to the outhouse, then to the shed to milk Daisy. *Da is back! DA IS BACK!!*

CRBD

Da played his uilleann pipes that evening, the first time since Mammy and the *babby* had died. After a while, he set them aside and looked soberly at each of his children. "*Weans*, we must talk. Yer da has been very sad. Sure, an' I have made life difficult for ye both. I am sorry, so I am. Can we have a new beginnin'?"

Cally and Teddy both shouted, "Oh, yes, Da!" and threw their arms around him. Uncle Dugan's grin was wide enough to split his face in two.

"In soul, I am thinkin' this family needs a holiday," Da continued. "What do ye all think of a trip to the beach?"

Cally pulled back, puzzled. *What does Da mean? A holiday? A beach? What is that?*

Da didn't notice. "My cousin Micky has long asked us to visit, but we always thought we were too busy with the farm. He has a cottage near the lough where he fishes salmon. I'll send him a letter, so I will, and as soon as we hear back from him about dates, we can plan our trip. I'm quite sure he would accept some of our wool in exchange for feedin' and housin' us for a week. Youghal isn't far. What do ye all think?"

Cally was even more confused. *Da has a Cousin Micky? What is a lough, and salmon, and Youghal? I've never heard those words before.* Teddy too stared at Da as if he were speaking a foreign language.

"Who will care for the animals, Frank?" Uncle Dugan asked. "Do ye want me to stay here while the rest of ye go to Youghal?"

"No, I've already thought of that, Dugan. Ye are part of this family too, and do ye think Aisling could join us? I'll ask yer man Eamon, from the next farm over, if his young Tiernan can stay here while we're gone and tend to the chores. Eamon owes me a favor from when he was laid up with the hatchet wound in his leg."

"Well, that would be grand, Frank. My mouth waters already thinkin' of Micky's salmon. Do ye know, I only met him the once, at yer and Reeny's weddin'? Sure, ye *weans* are in for a treat, Cally and Teddy, so ye are!"

Well, if Uncle Dugan thinks so . . .

"It's past time ye two were sleepin' with the angels," Da observed. "Go on now. I'll be there in a wee minute to sing ye to sleep."

Sing us to sleep? I have no idea what Da's strange talk means, but I'm starvin' hungry for his sweet lullabies. Cally and Teddy tucked into bed in record time. A worry flitted through her mind, as it did every bedtime, about what she should say to Miss Hilda, but it quickly faded into the happiness of Da's beautiful ballad.

Sure a little bit of Heaven fell from out the sky one day
and it nestled in the ocean in a place so far away
and when the angels found it sure it looked so sweet and fair
they said suppose we leave it for it looks so peaceful there

So they sprinkled it with stardust just to make the
shamrocks grow
it's the only place ye'll find them no matter where ye go
then they darted it with silver just to make the lakes
look grand
and when they had it finished sure they called it Ireland.

Debra Kornfield

CHAPTER 10

CHARLIE

Vienna, May 13, 1890

CHARLIE FIDGETED, arching his fingers against each other as he waited for Mr. Paderewski. *I don't remember ever going so long without playing the piano as I did while traveling from Waterford to Vienna. Yesterday afternoon's two hours helped, but I'm still out of kilter. What if after this whole long trip Mr. Paderewski changes his mind about wanting to teach me?*

Charlie looked up to see Mummy watching him, concern on her face. "Son, remember that your father and I are on your side—no matter what Mr. Paderewski says."

"Thank you, Mummy. It's just—I don't know what I want."

"It is a big decision, Charlie. But we don't need to make it today. Think of this as another adventure. Another part of your education, learning about the world. Isn't it incredible to be in the very city where Haydn, Mozart and Beethoven composed their gorgeous music?"

"I guess so."

""I have a surprise for you. I bought tickets to a recital Saturday night at the Schönbrunn Palace. The concert will feature young composers at the beginning of their careers, Richard Strauss, Luigi von

Kunits on the violin and our own Mr. Paderewski. Won't it be grand? I'll look forward to it all week."

A booming laugh interrupted Charlie's response. Mr. Paderewski bustled in with another man, scattering raindrops as he pulled off his coat and cap, red hair standing out in all directions. Charlie leaped to his feet, his heart pounding.

Mr. Paderewski ran his fingers through his hair, saying, "Gustav, this is the young man I've been telling you about, Charles Malcomson. Wait until you hear him play! Charles, Mrs. Malcomson, may I present my friend Gustav Mahler, visiting family in Vienna. He's out to change the way we understand and play music. You'll hear a great deal about him in years to come, I guarantee you. Well, come in, come in. Please sit down. Beastly weather today. Let's begin with a cup of tea to relax our young friend, eh, Gustav? He looks rather terrified, don't you think? We'll have to show him we're really not frightening—at least *I'm* not."

Mr. Paderewski poked his friend with his elbow and rang a bell. "Tea, please, Frau Schmit. Four of us. Please include some of those little cakes I love."

The avalanche of words eased as Frau Schmit passed steaming teacups and delicious Punschkrapfen. *I've never eaten anything like this before. I wonder what it is.*

Mr. Paderewski swallowed three before addressing Charlie once more. "So, young Charles, you have come all the way to Vienna just to taste Punschkrapfen, is that not so? Anything else that happens will be secondary to apricot, rum and pink fondant." Mr. Paderewski wiggled his red eyebrows at Charlie, who laughed despite himself.

"All right then, so we understand each other. Life is to be enjoyed, and friendship is to be enjoyed, and music is to be enjoyed, and none of the three is complete without the others. So, we must be friends if we are to create beautiful music together. Don't you agree, Frau Malcomson?"

Mummy looked startled but managed to smile and nod.

"More tea, Charles? No? Then I want you to sit back now and close your eyes. Yes, just like that. I will say some words. After each one, please say out loud the first thing that comes to your mind."

This is the strangest thing I've ever done.

"The first word is glory."

"Bach's Toccata and Fugue in D minor."

"Mystery."

"Grieg's Concerto in A minor."

"Transparency."

"Haydn's Violin Concertos."

"Collaboration."

"Mozart's Sonata for Two Pianos."

"Challenge."

"Beethoven's C minor piano sonata."

"Not Chopin?"

Charlie opened his eyes. "I don't yet know Chopin, sir. Except the piece you played in New York."

"All right. Close your eyes. Joy."

"William Vincent Wallace, Midnight Waltz."

"Peace."

"John Field's Nocturne Number 5."

"Sadness."

"O'Carolan's Farewell to Music."

"Ah, I see your own Irish composers touch your heart most deeply. Don't ever lose that connection, Charles. Now close your eyes again. Just two more. Freedom."

"Midnight."

Mummy interjected, "Midnight is Charlie's horse, named after Wallace's waltz." Charlie's eyes flew open. He saw Mummy gazing at him with an odd expression he didn't know how to interpret.

"Ah. Eyes closed, Charles. One more. Love."

"Mummy," Charlie said, and burst into tears. He felt Mummy's arms close around him and leaned into her, his eyes still closed as if to shut out the whole stressful experience.

"Gustav, let's give Charles a few minutes to compose himself. Relax, my boy. I know this has been hard, but I have learned so very much about you. We will be back in a quarter of an hour."

Charlie breathed in Mummy's smell and nestled into her warmth. *How can I possibly leave her? I can't.* He sat up and told her so.

"My sweet lad, I am praying for God's direction. Let's keep an open mind for the rest of this week. If you still feel the same then, your father and I will seriously consider your feelings."

"Mummy, why were you looking at me like that?"

"Like what, Charlie?"

"I don't know. I never saw you look like that before."

"Well, I can try to tell you. I was astonished at your responses, Charlie. You have such depth, young as you are. I felt sympathy for you, facing this big decision. I felt a desperate need for wisdom regarding how to steward the gifts God has given you. I felt affection and pride. Your life is a mystery that will unfold to us step by step. I have no idea how all of that found expression in my face!"

"I don't want to think about it anymore, Mummy. I'm tired. Will you sing to me?"

"With pleasure, my son. *Sure a little bit of Heaven fell from out the sky one day . . .*"

Mummy sang the last lines, "*then they darted it with silver just to make the lakes look grand and when they had it finished sure they called it Ireland,*" as Mr. Paderewski and Mr. Mahler walked back into the room, quietly this time. Charlie looked up and smiled at them, more confident now. *I'm not ready for this man. Not yet. So, it doesn't matter whether he likes me.*

"Charles, will you play for us? Anything at all. Whatever you wish." The men sat on a couch across from the piano. Charlie walked toward the gleaming instrument, flexing his fingers. *I get to play this beautiful instrument. I don't have to think about anything else.*

⊰⊱

"What a lovely estate Viscount von Taffe is sharing with us! That gallop was such fun! Charlie, I think your practicing has given you more energy, not less. You gave me a great run on that little mare. My big Murgese could hardly keep up! Oh Charlie, look at this! It's an invitation from Mrs. Wisinger-Florian to dine with her tomorrow evening. I am delighted!"

"Is she the artist Cora told us about?"

"Yes. I sent her my card and explained my errand for Cora, and this is her response. Whew, I need a bath. You do too before we meet with Mr. Paderewski again this afternoon. Today is Thursday, yes? It's hard to keep track in such a different rhythm from home."

"I've been confused too."

"So, today we will have luncheon with the von Taffes and this afternoon we see Mr. Paderewski. Tomorrow we will visit the Peterskirche Gymnasium, to consider it as a school for you, and we'll dine in the evening with Mrs. Wisinger-Florian. Saturday we'll tour the Schönbrunn Palace and Gardens before the special concert there that evening. Viscount von Taffe and his wife will accompany us."

Charlie felt his stomach clench at the mention of the school. *Oh, but it doesn't matter, since I've already decided I won't go there. It will just be an educational experience.* He chuckled at his own pun.

"What are you laughing at, Charlie?"

"Oh, nothing, Mummy. That all sounds fun. I can't wait for the concert."

Mummy gazed at him but said only, "All right then. You're on your own until luncheon."

 CRITICAL

Mr. Paderewski welcomed them cordially, and again rang for tea. When they were settled, he said, "Frau Malcomson, Charles, I have given careful thought to your situation and mine, and I have a proposal for you to consider." He stopped and looked at each of them.

"As you know, the concert your son graced in New York was my first time to play there. It opened the door for me to tour some of the great cities of America, beginning with a month in New York in July of next year. I would like very much for you to spend that month in New York with me, Charles." He sipped his tea.

"Might that be possible, Frau Malcomson? I could give Charles lessons between concerts. Before you answer, let me share with you the rest of my thoughts."

Charlie and Mummy looked at each other in surprise. Mr. Paderewski munched a pastry before he continued. "I believe, Frau Malcomson, I have been too hasty in inviting Charles to move to Vienna. I myself was twelve when I left home to study in Warsaw, a year older than Charles is now. I had the support of a kind and generous family. Yet the transition was difficult for me. I missed my father, and perhaps because of that, I got into some trouble. But that's a story for another day."

Mr. Paderewski took another swallow of tea.

"Frau Malcomson, I believe we must allow our fledgling Charles to grow happily and naturally. I do not believe he is ready for the stress he will endure if we pull him from your nest too soon. Charles has a very sensitive temperament. This is wonderful for the depth of his musical interpretation, but I fear if we continue with the plan I so rashly urged you to consider, we may crack something inside him."

Mr. Paderewski's gaze moved from Mummy to Charlie and back again. "Now, if the upcoming American tour is a success, I expect to travel to New York with some frequency thereafter. Your husband is often there, is he not? I propose we put that natural connection to use, so I may see Charles with some regularity and can therefore influence his development. But for now, Frau Malcomson, I believe his place is at home. His teacher—Herr Pearse, is it?—may be willing to take some suggestions from me, yes?"

Charlie jumped to his feet halfway through this long speech, doing an Irish jig Mr. Paderewski completely ignored, until suddenly he was on his feet too, jigging along in imitation of Charlie's steps. Mummy clapped the rhythm, and the dance went on until Charlie collapsed beside her, gasping for breath.

"I take it, Frau Malcomson, my conclusions have met with approval by your son?"

Charlie didn't wait for Mummy to respond. He said, "Thank you, thank you, Herr Paderewski! I know this is the right decision because I already made it for myself. Mummy, we don't have to visit the school! Could I—" Suddenly Charlie felt shy. "Could I instead have a lesson with you tomorrow, Herr Paderewski? I want so much to learn from you."

"Hmm, allow me to consult my schedule, Herr Charles. Surely, we can fit you in somewhere, since you have traveled so far. But it will cost you."

Charlie looked at Mummy in alarm.

"It will cost you practice time between now and Saturday. You mentioned on Tuesday Mozart's Sonata for Two Pianos. Have you played this piece before? Yes? Then, I would like to play it with you at the concert on Saturday night. We can work on it together tomorrow at—let me see—four o'clock. Will that fit your plans, Frau Malcomson? I have a copy of the second piano part here somewhere. Give me just a moment to find it."

"Yes, sir."

"And before we meet tomorrow, I will write out a list of the work I would like young Charles to accomplish before we next see each other in New York. I'll send with you a letter to Herr Pearse detailing my recommendations for his support of Charles's development. Is all of this acceptable to you both?"

Mummy squeezed Charlie's shoulders. "My son's happy face tells me you have judged him correctly, Herr Paderewski. My husband will be surprised, but I am sure he would want me to express our gratitude for your generosity to Charlie and to us. We are in your debt, sir. Should your travels ever take you to Ireland, please plan to visit us in Waterford."

"It is my great pleasure to know your remarkable son, Frau Malcomson. It will be an honor to contribute to his growth as a musician and, I hope, as a person."

Mr. Paderewski turned to Charlie with a stern expression. "I expect you to work hard between now and tomorrow afternoon, young man." He wiggled his eyebrows and Charlie giggled. "Allow me to escort you to the door."

CRBO

Charlie could hardly sit still while Mummy and Mrs. Wisinger-Florian talked. The fingering and phrasing Mr. Paderewski had taught him poured through his mind, and he found his fingers moving on the table where they sat after dinner. It took him a while to notice tears on both women's faces. They in turn did not see him looking from one to the other as Mrs. Wisinger-Florian said passionately, "I intend to do all I can so young women like Cora may receive the training and respect and opportunities you and I were denied, Frau Malcomson. Cora shows great promise. I hope one day I may have the privilege of meeting her."

She stopped and wiped her eyes on a dainty handkerchief. "Meanwhile, I wish to encourage her however I can from a distance. I will not keep you longer now. Charlie needs a good night of sleep in preparation for tomorrow's concert. I'm pleased I was able to obtain a ticket! If I am not able to greet you amid the press of people there, please know it has been a delight for me to meet you, and to learn more about Cora from you."

Mummy wiped her own eyes, smiled at Charlie, and rose from the table. All the way home, she chatted brightly about Mrs. Wisinger-Florian's art and her warm hospitality. Charlie went to bed still puzzled about what had caused the women's tears.

⊂ℨ⊅

A telegram addressed Mr. Peter Malcomson May 19, 1890: *Lovely time in Vienna. Good decisions made. Going home earlier than planned. Will advise. My love, Cathleen.*

⊂ℨ⊅

"Why, Herr Paderewski! We didn't expect to see you again!"

"I brought a farewell gift for young Charles. And I wanted to tell you myself what great pleasure playing with Charles brought me, Frau Malcomson." Mr. Paderewski bowed and extended to Charlie a bulky parcel tied up in brown paper. "Don't open it until you reach home, Charles. It can be your next German lesson with your Herr Hobbs."

Charlie returned the bow. "Danke, Herr Paderewski."

"Frau Malcomson, a letter to Herr Pearse is in the packet of lesson plans I gave you, but would you please remind him to write me each fortnight about Charles's progress? And remind him he must allow the boy to develop naturally, with pleasure, not pressure. Now I must run. I look forward to seeing you in New York next July. But—may I have just one word with you, Frau Malcomson?"

Mummy looked at Charlie. He frowned but carried his package into the next room. *What could Mr. Paderewski want to say to Mummy that I can't hear? Maybe she'll tell me on the train.*

⊂ℨ⊅

Mummy hugged Father tightly. "Peter, it's so good to have you home again. Welcome back! I'm glad we had a day at home ourselves to prepare for you!"

Father turned to Charlie. "I see you're off for a ride on Midnight. Go ahead, son. Enjoy the beautiful afternoon. We'll catch up with each other at supper."

☙

Walking into the dining room, rosy from his ride and his bath, Charlie paused as he heard Mummy say, "He's begun translation of the newspaper articles Mr. Paderewski gave him, as an assignment for German class. Mr. Hobbs showed me. It's quite remarkable, Peter. Our son's performance with Mr. Paderewski in Vienna is in all the papers." Charlie shrunk back into the doorway, embarrassed. *What will Father think?*

"They're calling him 'Charles *der Kleine, der Groβe*,' Charles the Small Great One. And Peter, Mr. Paderewski spoke with me privately when he came to say goodbye. He said—"

"Ah, there you are, Charles. Cathleen, will you please ask Cook to serve? I was just about to tell your mother about a letter from Thomas, Charles. He's coming home for the summer and will sail with us!"

Botheration! I thought I was going to discover Mummy's secret!

☙

"It's been a delight to have you with us this summer, Thomas. I believe it has been a good break for you too, has it not, son?"

"Great fun, yes, Mummy. Thanks for the sailing, Father. What a lark voyaging with you and Charlie. No storms this time, eh, little brother? Now, just one more year at Oxford! Mummy, Father, can we discuss what comes next after graduation? I'll tell you my plan fast all at once, and then you can react, and then we can have a good conversation about it once you're over the initial shock. Perhaps at Christmastime."

Mummy laughed, but Father gazed at Thomas intently. "Let's have it then, Thomas."

Thomas stood up from the table. "I want to work for the railroad in America. There, I've said it. Ready for our race, Charlie? I bet you a pound Dancer and I can beat you and Midnight to the river!"

⋙⋘

"Thomas, you remember Cora, don't you? The student who rode to the police to get help on the day of Margaret's wedding?"

"I know who you're talking about, Mummy, but I've not met her." Thomas, his arm around his mother's waist, looked down into her face.

"I want to ask a favor, Thomas. Cora has just graduated from our school, and has moved to London to study at Louise Jopling's new school of art. She's never been so far from home before. Could you run down from Oxford from time to time to see how she's making the adjustment? It would mean a great deal to me, as I'm fond of Cora and believe she has a wonderful future as an artist. I've written her a letter, with her address on the envelope. Could you deliver it for me?"

"Jeepers, Mummy. I don't know how soon I'll find time to go to London. I have much to make up from taking such a long break this summer. But I'll try, just because I love you."

Thomas planted a wet kiss on Mummy's cheek and squirmed out of reach of her tickle, calling from the carriage door, "I'll see you all at Christmas! Tell Margaret not to let my niece or nephew grow up too fast without me! Goodbye, Father. Don't fret. All will be well. Spend your pound wisely, Charlie." And he was gone.

Charlie heaved a sigh and turned toward the drawing room. *Having Thomas home was great fun, but I've sorely neglected my practicing.*

Debra Kornfield

CHAPTER 11

CALLY

Youghal, County Cork, Ireland, July 1890

DA SAID YOUGHAL WASN'T FAR, but it seems far to me. We're stuffed in here like praties in a bucket. Cally, Teddy, Aisling, and Shep sat on top of, between, or around goat cheese and butter, all the clothes any of them owned, Da's pipes, and the food Aisling packed for their picnic lunch along the way.

Cally glanced forward. *Uncle Dugan and Da must be talking about something important. I can tell by the way they wave their hands around.* She sighed and shifted a bag of cotton behind her back. *I still don't know where we're going or what it will be like.*

As Aisling and Teddy played a game of naming the types of trees they passed, Cally worried. *Will Tiernan take good care of Daisy and the sheep? Won't they miss us? What about my treasure? Might the faeries find it and steal it while no one is there to protect it?*

The wagon rounded a curve. Cally caught her breath and stared. *Oh. No wonder Da didn't explain this to me. It's too big for words.* She stared and stared at the ocean and still could not fathom what she was seeing. Without thinking, she gripped Aisling's hand. Shep leaped from the wagon, barking and racing toward the water. Uncle Dugan pulled to a stop and they all clambered out to pick their way over rocks and sand to the shore. Da squatted, drawing Cally and Teddy close.

Even Teddy was speechless. Then, with a whoop, he pulled away and dashed toward Shep, who barked and frolicked at the edge of the waves. Da freed Cally and they ran toward the water, yelling at the top of their lungs. *The water is salty! I never imagined such a thing!*

Too soon, Aisling called them for the picnic she had spread on a blanket. Everyone talked at once while stuffing themselves with cheese and bread and apples. After lunch, the adults stretched out on the sand for a rest, but Teddy, Shep, and Cally ran back to the water.

"It's time to go on!" Da yelled too soon. "We'll have many days to play in the ocean!"

A tangle of red roses blooming beside Cousin Micky's front door enchanted Cally. "Red rose, proud rose, sad rose of all my days" murmured Da.

"What did you say?"

"That's from a poem by William Butler Yeats," Da said. "It's about the suffering and the beauty of Ireland. Yeats likes to write poems about roses, so lovely despite their thorns."

"I love them. If I ever have a daughter, I'm going to name her Rose."

Da smiled at Cally as Micky welcomed them in. His house boasted a separate bedroom, something Cally had never seen before. The front porch and the whole wide beach stretched out for the children and Shep to play on. By the third day they had grown brave enough for Cousin Micky to begin teaching them to swim.

Sleeping required some adjustments, though. Cousin Micky gave his bed to Aisling, Cally, and Teddy. He slept on the sofa in the main room. Uncle Dugan, Da, and Shep chose the front porch, where the whole family gathered after dinner to talk, laugh, tell stories and gaze at the moon's reflection on the waves.

No! I don't want to go to bed! Not even if ye tuck us in, Aisling! It's not fair! I'm not a wee wean like Teddy is. Almost Cally said what she felt out loud. Then she noticed Da looking at her so lovingly, she didn't have the heart to upset him.

"I want to teach ye a bedtime prayer my mammy taught me when I was a little girl," Aisling told them as they snuggled under the covers. "It's very simple, but I still say it every night before I go to sleep. Would ye like to learn it?"

"Yes!"replied Teddy, sitting up again. Cally crossed her arms over her chest and didn't move. *It's not fair!*

"This prayer is from Psalm 4 in the Bible. I'll say the first part and then ye can repeat after me. *In peace I will lie down and sleep.*"

"In peace I will lie down and sleep," Teddy repeated. Cally glared at Aisling and remained silent. Aisling didn't seem to notice.

"For ye alone, O Lord, will keep me safe."

"For ye alone, O Lord, will keep me safe," mimicked Teddy.

"Now let's say the whole thing. *In peace I will lie down and sleep, for ye alone, O Lord, will keep me safe.* Well done, Teddy! Do ye think ye can say all of it by yerself?"

"In peace I will lie down and sleep, for ye alone, O Lord, will keep me safe."

Cally couldn't help echoing the prayer in her mind as Teddy recited. *But I'm not going to sleep. It's not fair! I'm not tired! I want to hear the adults'* craic. She fought to stay awake long after she heard Teddy's light whiffling snore. *I can hear their voices but not their words. It's not fair!*

On the third night, Cally sat up carefully to not wake Teddy. *They won't notice if I sit quiet as a mouse by the window in the main room.* She slid out of bed, carefully opened the door, and crept into the sitting room. The front door was open, so she could hear clearly. She made herself comfortable on the sofa.

"So, I've been talking to Dugan about the idea I've had of moving to America," Da was saying. "Did ye ever go there, Micky, during yer navy days? No? Well, Dugan and Reeny's cousins live there, in upstate New York."

Cally gasped, then covered her mouth with her hand. *What is Da saying?*

"Ye might move?" Aisling sounded upset. "But that means ye would take Cally and Teddy with ye? Ye would leave Dugan and me alone on the farm?"

"Nothing's been decided, Aisling." Uncle Dugan's voice comforted Cally as well. "It's just talk, so far. Frank feels restless, that's all. He can't get used to the farm and house without Reeny. He believes he needs a change, but it needn't be so dramatic as a move across the ocean."

Across the ocean? But the ocean goes on forever! It has no end!

"I would miss the *weans* terribly, Frank. I hope ye find a different solution, in soul I do."

I hope so too. Cally began to shiver. She crept back to the warmth of the bed and settled in beside Teddy, leaving as much space as possible for Aisling. *Now what will I do? If I ask any questions, Da will know I listened. But I don't understand. Now I have even more to worry about. I wish I hadn't snooped.*

○§○

Placing a star-shaped shell on the tiptop of their magnificent sandcastle, Da declared it perfect. Teddy ran down the beach with Shep while Cally sat back to admire their handiwork. "It is grand, Da. Just like every day here has been."

Da sat on the sand next to Cally. "I've been wondering . . . What is it that brings a look of worry to my wee lassie's face when she thinks no one is watching? Will ye not tell me what troubles ye even in this beautiful place, Cally?"

Startled, Cally looked anxiously at Da's face, then down at her fingers making whorls in the sand. "I—I don't know if I can, Da. It might make things worse. I don't want to spoil our holiday."

"Cally, *weans* aren't meant to keep worrisome secrets from their fathers. I know I'm the cause of that and I'm right sorry, so I am. I'm ready now to be the one who carries this family. Can't ye let me have some of that worry back?"

Cally erased her whorls with the flat of her hand and started finger-drawing again. *I wish I could ask Miss Hilda what to tell him. Oh! Miss Hilda offered to talk to Da! That's what I should do!* Relieved, she lifted her eyes to his face and was surprised to see tears pooled in his eyes.

"Da, I will tell ye. But not now. I'll ask someone to help me explain, after we get home. Will that be all right?"

"All right, Cally. Ye have held this family together for a long time, ye and Dugan and Aisling, so I must respect yer wishes. But don't ferget, will ye, Cally? Fer my sake."

"Yes, Da."

"It's time we head back to Micky's fer tea. He'll have fresh salmon fer us if he's had a good catch today. Won't that be grand?"

"Da, why isn't Cousin Micky married? It seems sad fer him to live all alone."

"I'll tell ye a bit of the tale while we go after Teddy and Shep. Micky was my best pal when we were comin' up, so he was. His parents' farm was right next to ours, until they lost it during the Great Hunger. His parents emigrated to Australia, but Micky refused to go. My family took him in. We were both *weans* then, Micky a year older than me. When he was old enough, Micky joined the Irish navy. That's when he learned to love the ocean."

Cally had one ear tuned to Da's story, and the other to Shep's bark, farther down the beach than she thought Teddy should have wandered. She sped up her pace. Da didn't seem to notice.

"At one of his ports, Micky fell in love with a beautiful girl. He visited her every chance he could, but she refused to leave her country, and Micky didn't want to live there. He bought his beach cottage here at

Youghal when he left the navy and as far as I ken, has never looked at another girl since. I've noticed him, though, watching Dugan and Aisling. Haven't ye seen that too, Cally? I wonder whether he might start changing his mind, so I do. Ye can watch him too and let me know what ye think."

Da laughed, but Cally was distracted, worried now about Shep and Teddy. Shep's barking, still distant, was his anxious-bark. She started running down the beach. After a moment, she heard Da running with her. Cally heard footsteps pounding behind her and soon Dugan and Aisling passed them. Cally could now see Shep racing toward them. Da, with a look at Cally, took off as fast as he could.

"Wha—what happened?" Cally panted, as she came close to the group huddled around a small figure lying on the sand.

"Teddy may have broken his leg," Aisling told her. "Dugan has run to fetch Micky and wood for a splint. We're afraid to move him until we can stabilize his leg. It looks pretty bad, Cally, but I'm sure Micky will send for help."

Without waiting for Aisling to finish her explanation, Cally pushed Shep aside and knelt beside her brother. Teddy groaned as tears rolled down his cheeks. Cally looked from his face down his body, and saw his left leg jutted at an odd angle.

"No, don't touch it, Cally. Let's do all the pain at one time, when Dugan gets here with the splints. Here, ye can help me warm his hands while we wait for a blanket."

Da began singing a song Teddy loved. Teddy shivered despite Da's shirt tucked around his bare chest. Cally and Da each chafed one cold hand. Shep lay down carefully beside Teddy, who nestled into his warmth. Aisling paced, looking anxiously down the beach toward Micky's cottage. "I see them!" she yelled and took off toward Uncle Dugan and Micky.

"The first aid will be here soon," Micky shouted as they drew closer.

"They told us to wait and not splint it ourselves. But we have a blanket, and hot tea, and laudanum for the pain."

Da tucked the blanket around Teddy's body as well as he could without moving his leg. After a dose of bitter laudanum, Teddy relaxed and fell asleep. "Does anyone know yet what happened?" Micky asked.

"Not really," Aisling replied. "But see those rocks there? My guess is he was jumpin' on them with Shep and fell, and Shep pulled him this far before Teddy screamed so much, he stopped. Dugan and I heard Teddy yellin'."

"I blame myself," said Da. "I should have known better than to let Teddy run off like that."

No! I know this is my fault! The Dubh Sidhe are angry because I haven't given them my treasure. Cally pinched her nose to keep herself from crying.

"The important thing is caring for Teddy," Micky said. "Ah, hear is the medicine wagon."

"Cally!" Teddy, woken by the wagon's bells, clung to her, his voice beseeching.

"She can't go with us, son. Only one of us can be with ye fer yer operation," Da explained as he gently pulled Teddy's arms away from Cally. He nodded to the medicine wagon men that they could splint Teddy's leg and lift him into the back of the wagon. Da climbed in with him, but Teddy still sobbed, holding his arms out to Cally as the wagon pulled away.

Uncle Dugan, Aisling and Cousin Micky turned to go back to the house, talking intently, with Shep bounding ahead of them. Cally shifted to watch them go, then ran after the medicine wagon as fast as she could until it disappeared around a curve. Cally slowed to a walk, her head down.

What should I do? They don't seem to know it's my fault. Mammy, the babby, Da's long sadness, now this. What if Teddy dies too? Cally threw herself down, pounded the sand with her fists and cried and cried and cried.

It was dark when Cally felt Shep's tongue on her face and opened her eyes. Blinking in confusion, she pushed Shep's head away to see Uncle Dugan and Aisling, lantern swinging, bending over her. The anxiety on their faces made Cally sit up, rub her face with the back of her sandy hands, and say, "What's wrong? Is it the operation? Is Teddy—"

"We don't know anythin' about Teddy yet, Cally, because we've been lookin' fer ye. If ye don't want us to worry about ye, then don't run off without tellin' someone where ye're goin'. Each of us thought ye were with someone else, until at dinner no one could find ye." Uncle Dugan's voice was stern, and Cally shrank back.

Aisling dropped to her knees and pulled Cally into a hug. "Let's go home and find out if Micky has news about Teddy. It's all right to be sad about what happened to him, Cally. But please be sad *with* us. We're all sad. We need to be together."

But ye don't realize Teddy's accident is my fault. Tears welled up again as Cally stood, brushed herself off and let Aisling take her hand. But she forced the tears down, and the three of them walked in silence back to Cousin Micky's house.

ೞ

"Here's what I think we should do, so," Da began, as the family gathered on the porch at sunset, three days after Teddy's accident. "The doctor says Teddy can come home tomorrow, but his leg must mend for at least a fortnight before he can travel. I know ye and Aisling need to go home, Dugan. I will drive ye, the day after tomorrow, check out everything at the farm, and come back two days later. Will ye be all right stayin' with Teddy, Cally, to care for him with Micky's help until I get back? Can ye go two days without fishin', Micky?"

"Aisling and I have been talkin'." Uncle Dugan's voice was gruff. "We hate to leave the wee lad, but if we don't go home now, the cottage won't be finished before our weddin' date. We could put off the weddin', but . . ."

"No, no. I already have that date on my calendar," Micky said. "I'll be glad to take charge of Teddy while ye are gone, Frank. With Cally's help, of course. And if ye need more time at home after being gone so long, Frank, don't ye worry none. We'll be fine."

Cally realized she had been holding her breath. She let it out with a whoosh, and everyone laughed. Teddy would be home tomorrow from the doctor's surgery. He was "stabilized." Whatever that meant exactly, it must be good. *I'm glad, glad, glad Da trusts me to stay with Teddy. Even though he doesn't know the accident was my fault. I hope, hope, hope the Dubh Sidh will stop now and not make more bad things happen.*

Cally glanced at Cousin Micky to see what he really thought about Da's plan. His smile warmed her all the way to her sandy toes.

೦೪ಞಿ

"Cally, Teddy, this here is my friend Louise." Cousin Micky walked in carrying groceries. Cally jumped to her feet and curtsied. From the couch, Teddy waved his hand, while Shep ran around in a circle. Cally gave him a kiss. "Good dog, not jumpin' on her."

"Louise brought supper for us. Wouldn't ye like somethin' besides salmon?" Micky laughed, and everyone joined in.

He has the best laugh. I wonder what kind of friend Louise might be.

Cally scrambled to set the table. As they ate mutton stew and soda bread, she learned the word "librarian." Miss Louise ran the Youghal library.

"I've brought ye wee ones some books," their visitor said brightly. "Wouldn't ye like to read to Teddy to help the hours pass, Cally?"

Cally shrank back, embarrassed. "I'm sorry, ma'am. I don't know how to read."

"Don't ye, dear? Well, I think we have another project on our hands, Micky. Ye are a bright lassie, I can tell that already. Would ye like me to teach ye, then?"

Cally's face must have told her the answer because Miss Louise fetched her satchel and looked at her calendar. "Hmm, I could ask Jill to run the chess club, and Lauren to handle the book club, and Jake to look after the bazaar . . . Yes, I think I could come every day next week, after the library closes. Unless that would be too much of my company, Micky?" Her eyes twinkled, and Cousin Micky's face flamed.

"Fer Cally's sake, surely, is it, Louise?" Micky laughed.

Cally looked from one to the other, her suspicions growing. *It's the same look Uncle Dugan gives Aisling. Learn to read! No one has ever, even once in my life, suggested such a thing!* A thrill started in Cally's toes and traveled all the way to her eyes. She couldn't stop smiling.

"Well then, Teddy, would ye like me to read a book to ye now? And soon, it will be yer big sister reading to ye. Won't that be grand, so?"

Will I really be able to do this? I've never even seen a book besides Mammy's big Bible. Cally and Teddy sat one on either side of Miss Louise, mesmerized by the wonderful tales she told them from the books she had brought. They stared in delight at the pictures.

Finally, Miss Louise exclaimed, "Oh, just look how late it is! I'm sure these children should be in their beds, Micky. I'll leave ye the books, Cally and Teddy, so ye can tell the stories again to yerselves, just by looking at the pictures." She turned again to Cousin Micky. "The books will be due in two weeks. But I can trade them for other books, if Cally wants to come to the library while ye stay with Teddy. Ye can tell her how to get there, yes, Micky?"

Miss Louise took us around the world with the stories she read. I never knew the world is so big, and so interestin', and so different from Ireland. Cally didn't know how to put all this into words, but her eyes shone as she followed Cousin Micky, carrying a drowsy Teddy to their bed. *I wonder if there are any books in the library about the Dubh Sidhe and the good faeries. Or about New York in America. Or about crossin' the ocean. Dare I ask Miss Louise?*

Debra Kornfield

CHAPTER 12

CHARLIE

Mayfield House, Christmas 1890

SIPPING EGGNOG, Charlie gazed happily around the drawing room, elegantly decorated with red velvet ribbons and holly. Martin and Molly, eager for action after early mass, poked and shook the packages under the tree. Everyone waited for Father to authorize lighting the candles, singing of their traditional Christmas songs, and opening the gifts. But Father, chatting with Daniel and Percy, seemed in no hurry.

Everyone is here: Daniel and Meghan, Gritty and Percy, Thomas and me. And for her first Christmas ever, Gritty's baby Sally. She's cute, but she'll be more fun once she's seven like Martin or five like Molly. What's taking Father so long to begin? And why isn't Thomas joining in the conversation with Father? He looks—hmm. Nervous, maybe.

"Ma'am, a guest has arrived." Lillian curtsied and returned to the kitchen to help Cook prepare their Christmas feast.

Mummy threw a look at Thomas, who blushed and grinned. Charlie sat up straight. *What's this?* He didn't have long to wait. Mummy walked in escorting a young woman Charlie at first didn't recognize. When he did, he leaped to his feet, throwing his arms around their visitor. "Cora! I didn't know you were coming! You look—different."

Charlie stood back to appraise Cora from top to toe. Despite her warm hug, Cora wasn't looking at him. *Thomas.* Just for a moment, Charlie saw something pass between them. *Aha.*

"My parents will be along shortly," Cora told Mummy. "They need to visit a shop, but since your house was on the way . . . Thank you for inviting us, ma'am. Sir."

"Do you know everyone, Cora? Charlie, of course. And I know you've met Thomas. These are my other two children, Margaret, married to Percy and mother to wee Sally—

"God bless the child," interposed Cora.

"And Daniel, married to Meghan. Their two rapscallions are Martin and Molly. Family, this is my dear friend Cora Sumner, famous artist-in-training, recently of London. Her parents will join us shortly."

Everyone bowed or curtsied, with a scattering of "pleased to meet you." Molly took Cora's hand and pulled her to the tree. Cora looked over her shoulder toward Thomas. He had regained his seat but gave her a warm smile. *I bet I'm the only one who noticed that. Christmas has just become more interesting! Now I understand Father. He's been waiting for Cora and her parents.*

"Charles, while we await the Sumners, how about some music. What have you to offer us this Christmastide?"

"Do you mean music for singing, Father?"

"No, we'll light the candles and do our singing once Cora's parents arrive. Have you a Christmas piece you can play for us?"

"I can play part of Handel's '*Messiah.*' You'll have to imagine a choir, orchestra, and soloists."

"That will be grand, Charles. Thank you."

"But this is just background music. Not a performance." Charlie grinned at Thomas, who had found an excuse to sit by Cora. As he played, Charlie heard "*Nollaig Shona Dhaoibh!*" at the front door. "Merry Christmas to you, too, Mary. Mr. Sumner. Lillian will take your coats."

Father rose. "Ah, now we can begin! Our family has no Mary to light the candles, so we counted on your coming, Mrs. Sumner. Mr. Sumner, welcome to our home. I have met your wife before, of course, at our school. Please, sit here. Will you have some eggnog?"

"God bless the child," Cora's parents said together, smiling at Sally.

What have we done other years, with no Mary to light our candles? Oh, now I remember! Last year Mummy and Daddy invited the Grovers. And the year before they invited the Murphys.

"So—now we can sing, Charles. What shall it be first?"

Charlie started into "That Time of Year Has Come Around Again." His eyebrows shot up when Thomas pulled out a harmonica to play along. "Just something I've been picking up," he murmured.

"Well then, would ye mind some harping?" Mr. Sumner pulled a handsome set of uillean harps from the bag he had set on the floor beside him. At the first notes, Martin and Molly jumped up to dance, and soon everyone jigged and laughed.

From the piano bench, Charlie saw Lillian and Cook swinging and turning in the hallway. "Mummy, can't they come in?" he whispered. Their voices joined the celebration.

"Oh, my roast!" Cook ran out of the room, with Lillian following. Everyone laughed, and Charlie switched to a St. Patrick's Day dance set, yelling *"Sláinte mhaith"* (Good health! Everyone responded, *"Sláinte mhòr"* (Even better health) and they were off. Charlie sat back and clapped as Mr. Sumner's pipes took over the rhythms.

"This isn't Christmas music," observed Mummy.

"I know, but how often do we have a piper in our house?" Charlie laughed.

"How about a hornpipe, then? Peter, will you play one for us?"

"Hardly a traditional Christmas, this, Cathleen. But to please you, my dear, yes, I will." Father went out and reappeared with his horn. "Can you do this, Charlie?"

"I don't know. You start, and I'll see whether I can catch on."

"We know how to hornpipe." Mr. Sumner lay aside his pipes and pulled his wife to her feet. "Anyone else?"

"Well, of course," Father said. "We're a sailor family, after all."

☙❧

Ha! They no longer consider me a wean. Charlie hugged a pillow on the sofa near the door after Daniel and Meghan took Martin and Molly to bed and the Sumners and Gritty's family went home. *Whew, but I am tired.* He fondled his favorite gift, a wee colt Cora had carved to accompany the mare she had given him before his trip to Vienna. *How long ago that seems now. Mr. Pearse and I weren't getting along. But Mr. Paderewski helped.*

Charlie yawned and tuned in to the adults' conversation. Thomas spoke. "Yes, I met her in London, and we've become friends." *Right.*

"She's a lovely girl, and I'm fond of her," Mummy said. "I'm glad we could meet Mr. Sumner today, after knowing Mary for all the years Cora spent at our school. I've always admired Mary's determination to do all she can for their daughter."

"So," said Father, glancing up as Daniel and Meghan rejoined them. "We've received Christmas letters from my mother, my sister Jemima, Silas and Priscilla, and from Nathanael and Sarah in New York. Who wants to read the first one to us?"

Charlie didn't remember the end of even the first letter. He opened his eyes to see the fire burning low in the grate, no lights except the candles, and no one in the drawing room except Mummy and Father. *I guess they decided I could sleep here,* he thought drowsily. Gradually he realized Mummy and Father were talking about him. He closed his eyes as though still asleep.

"What do you think, Peter? Has Charlie made progress in the areas Mr. Paderewski expressed concern about? I mean about letting Charlie be a child and finding playmates for him." Mummy laughed softly. "Did I tell you Mr. Paderewski didn't think an eleven-year-old should know the meaning of the word 'collaboration'? He just threw that in to see what he would do with it. Charlie knew exactly what the word meant."

"Yes, you told me all about that conversation, Cathleen. It made me realize Charlie has been surrounded almost exclusively by adults his whole life. He certainly enjoys Martin and Molly!"

"He does, though they are younger than he is. But I don't think the lads we've invited to play with Charlie have been a grand success, Peter. He seems to find their games silly and their conversation boring. Do you have any ideas? Should we put him in Foxwell Academy in Waterford? That seemed to work out well for Thomas."

Charlie sucked in his breath, almost giving himself away. To cover it up, he turned over on the sofa. He imagined Mummy looking over at him, with the bemused expression she sometimes wore when she didn't think he was watching.

"Hmm. Wouldn't consistent practice time be more difficult? Let's keep looking for a lad who shares Charles's interests. Do you know anyone with a passion for horses?"

"Oh, good idea, Peter! I'll ask Percy. He knows the Waterford families better than we do. And Peter, last week, Mr. Pearse informed me he wants Charlie to enter a piano competition in Dublin in June, after the school term ends. But we've planned for Charlie to sail with you in June. Can you schedule an early July sailing, to get Charlie to New York in time for Mr. Paderewski's first concert? He'll be one of the first to play in a new concert hall, built by Andrew Carnegie. If it's completed in time. I would love for Charlie to be there."

"With this much advance notice, I can adjust my sailing schedule, Cathleen. Now, I, for one, am tired. Shall we take our young prodigy to bed?"

෴

Charlie heard Thomas's voice in the kitchen. "Oh, how I miss your cooking when I'm at Oxford. Won't you go back with me? I know I'm your favorite Malcomson, Cook."

Charlie chuckled along with Cook. "Ah, go on with ye now, Master Thomas. Who would take my place here, so? Sure, I know what yer after—an extra pie to go in that basket for yer picnic with Miss Cora. But what I don't ken is, who has picnics in the wintertime? Has yer book-learnin' addled your mind? Are ye sure Miss Cora will take kindly to this notion, so?"

"Ah, Cook. Who else in this world talks to me like you do? I'll be sure to give you a full report on how well Miss Cora likes your picnic."

"Every jig and reel, so."

"Every jig and reel, yes, ma'am." Charlie pictured Thomas saluting to Cook and heard them both laugh.

"Off with ye, then. But don't say I didn't warn ye."

Thomas walked through the dining room toting a large basket. He almost didn't see Charlie. "Hey, baby brother. You woke up late. Got plans for today?"

"Yes. Mummy has asked a lad from town to ride horses with me. He should arrive soon."

"Well, have a good time. I'll see you at tea."

☙❧

"Yes. Send Charlie to bed. He's a pipsqueak and won't understand what I need to talk to you about. Oh, don't look at me with such a sad face, Charlie. I don't care. You can stay if you want. If Mummy and Father agree."

"Thomas, would you be interested in sailing to New York with Charles and me next July? It may be too soon to decide, but if I can convince your mother to go as well, and perhaps Daniel and Margaret and their families, we could make a grand outing of it. Yes, I know my dear, I've taken you by surprise. I've been thinking about this since we had our talk the other night."

"It's a lovely idea, Peter! I've been hearing how delightful it is to float down the Erie Canal, and the charms of the hotels near Niagara Falls. Wouldn't that be fun?"

"Yes, it would. We'll develop these ideas further, Cathleen. Now, what is on your mind, Thomas? Do you wish to talk about your brainless idea to work for the railroad in America?"

"Well, that's a good beginning, Father. No pussyfooting with you. Yes, I do want to talk about that, and it's not brainless at all. It's an opportunity for advancement. I'll tell you all about it, but first I have something else to discuss. It's about Cora."

Ha! I knew it!

"Cora has confided in me that she suffered from cholera this fall. That's what is different about her, Charlie. She's lost a great deal of weight. She was so sick she had to spend several weeks in hospital and was not able to complete her studies this semester. She is worried you may think she has been irresponsible with the financial help you are giving her."

"Oh, my dear Cora! Why did she not tell us herself? Do her parents know?"

"Well, she didn't tell them, Mummy, not wanting them to worry. But surely they've noticed the changes in her, just like you did, Charlie. So many people have died in this epidemic in London. You can't tell anyone, Charlie, else I'll thrash you and throw you in the river." Thomas turned on him with a threatening expression.

"I won't, I promise, Thomas. But is Cora all right?"

"She will be. She's still recovering."

"How can we help, Thomas? Has she had adequate medical attention?"

"She says so, Father, but I'm not convinced she has. When she wouldn't see me for a month this fall, I thought she was rejecting me as her friend. It never crossed my mind she might be in trouble. When she did agree to see me, she was so tired and weak we just sat in her house and read a book together, and then she showed me her latest artwork. She's really very talented."

"I know that, Thomas. I've not the least doubt she'll make a great success of a career in painting and sculpture."

"Your faith in her matters a great deal, Mummy. So, today we went on a picnic—"

"You what? You took a sick girl out into this cold air?"

"Well, not exactly, Mummy. Do you remember the Millers, the family of my chum Edward from Foxwell? They have a greenhouse filled with gorgeous plants and flowers. They set up a little table for us, and it was charming. Cora painted it—maybe she'll show you."

"You've always been creative, Thomas. What a lovely idea!"

"Well, I guess we're each creative in our own way, Mummy."

"Back to practical matters, Thomas. What do you propose we can do for this girl?"

"Well, the first thing, Father, is for you to understand there's not a lazy or irresponsible bone in Cora's body, and you should continue her financial support even though completing art school will take her a little longer than she thought."

"That is reasonable, Thomas, under the circumstances."

"Thank you, Father. Secondly, do you have any contacts in London who could recommend a good physician? I want to be sure she's getting the best care."

"This girl has become important to you, I see, Thomas. Please tell me more about that."

Thomas flushed. "Well, Father, I think I want to marry her. Are you shocked? I haven't said one word in that direction to Cora, but I believe she has an idea of how I feel. The thing is, Father, she's not from a wealthy family. Will that be a problem for you? I couldn't bear to ask for her hand only to discover you disapprove. I don't want to hurt her in any way. I'm happy you invited her family for Christmas, but how would you feel if the Sumners became related to us? And Charlie, add this to the topics you will not discuss with anyone outside of this room, or—"

"I know. You will thrash me and throw me in the river. Tempting as that is, I will not say anything, Thomas. Remember, Cora was my friend first. I'm sad she's been sick."

"Thomas, let's come back to practicalities. First, I have no objection to your marrying Miss Cora. I've heard her praises sung by your mother for years now. But what is your sense of timing with all this?"

"Well, Father, art school for Cora will take one more year. After my graduation, I want to get a job with the railroad. It's growing fast in the more western and rural parts of America right now, and they need people with good minds for administrating the complexities of all that growth. But I need experience. Are there any Malcomsons still involved with railroads, Father? Anyone in London who might take me on and teach me the rail business, from the ground up? That's what I want. Then when Cora finishes art school, we could marry, and at the right time emigrate to America. That's my grand plan so far."

"I'll write a letter for you, Thomas, to my uncle Thomas in London. And I will educate myself on the current state of railroads in America. But what about all this training in philosophy I'm paying for at Oxford? Will that go to waste, in your grand plan?"

"Not at all, Father. I've learned to think systematically. I've learned oratory, which will come in handy when I run for office someday. Your grandfather Daniel has become one of my heroes, Mummy! Sometimes for fun I practice giving one of his speeches, especially the ones about emancipation in America. Father, philosophy has expanded my mind far beyond Waterford, I can tell you that. And I've become a good writer, too. I intend to continue reading William James, Herbert Spencer, Friedrich Nietzsche and Alexander Bain and I may write some journal articles. I have definite opinions about some of what they're saying."

"Why does that not surprise me," Father responded drily. "Well. You've given us a lot to think about. Cathleen, will you please say a prayer for Miss Cora, for her health and peace, and for Thomas and this grand plan of his?"

"With the greatest pleasure, Peter. Our Father in heaven, Thou knowest the important matters weighing on our minds. Wilt Thou touch and heal dear Cora completely, and give her the strength to complete her studies? And wilt Thou bless our Thomas, with so much to consider in these next months? Give them Thy wisdom and protect their friendship. And now together we pray, Our Father, who art in heaven, hallowed be Thy name . . ."

CHAPTER 13

CALLY

Killeagh, November 1890

"KEEP PRACTICING. READ TO TEDDY every day," Miss Louise told me. "It will get easier. Just don't give up. And don't be shy about asking yer Da for help."

Cally sat on a rock by the stream, daydreaming in the sunshine of a rare warm day. *I missed reading some days when Uncle Dugan and Aisling got married. Even Teddy was too excited to mind. But Miss Louise was right. I can read most anything now.*

Cally stood, climbed on the rock, and reached for a stray apple still clinging to a bough. As she munched, she continued her mental review of the last months. *Since to read I needed books, and the only person we know with books is Father Michaelson, he and Da finally talked to each other. I don't think they're friends, exactly. But at least Da is going to church with us again.*

Cally wandered toward the barn to feed her apple core to Simon. *I never had time to myself like this before Aisling came to live on the farm with Uncle Dugan. She makes my life so much easier! She says now I'm seven, once winter comes, she will teach me to write.*

Stroking Simon's nose, Cally spoke her thoughts out loud to him.

"When I turned seven, Uncle Dugan asked me what I wanted for a birthday present. I asked him to dig up my treasure, so I could see what I looked like, since I've never been seven before. I was disappointed. I look the same as when I was six. Uncle Dugan buried my treasure again."

Finding a brush, Cally began untangling Simon's mane. "Da surprised me when Miss Hilda talked to him. I never saw Miss Hilda so—so strong. Is that the right word, Simon? Anyway, Da listened quietly, looking very sad. Then he asked Miss Hilda to go back to the Dubh Sidhe and tell her he's responsible for this family now, and the faeries are to leave us all alone." Cally sighed, remembering the anxiousness and then the relief of that day. Simon nuzzled her neck.

"If the faeries want somethin', they must tell Miss Hilda to come to him, not to me. Can it really be that simple, do ye think? I'm trying not to worry, because so far they haven't done anythin' else bad. I think they know Da is strong. But Teddy can't walk right. He drags his leg. I don't know whether he will ever get better." Cally leaned against Simon and let her sorrow overflow into tears. Simon stood quietly, letting her rub her wet cheeks against his mane.

"I still can't tell Da about me makin' Mammy and the *babby* die, Simon. I can't bear to think of losin' him again, now he's my Da once more. How can he not be angry, if I tell him?"

The barn door creaked open, wide enough for Teddy to pull himself through. "Cally, Aisling wants yer help to fold the sheets. It took me a long time to find ye, so ye better hurry."

Cally sighed, kissed Simon, smiled at Teddy, held out her hand, and walked with him through the sunshine and up the hill to Aisling and Uncle Dugan's wee bungalow.

છ৪৩

Killeagh, Christmas 1890

"She's beautiful. Thank ye, Aisling." Cally gazed at the lovely doll she held, complete with eyes that opened and shut.

"Came all the way from Cork," Aisling said, tilting her head. "So, I'll teach ye to sew, Cally. We can make doll clothes for her together. And when ye're ready, I'll help ye sew a new dress fer yerself. Ye have outgrown this one."

"But ye were going to teach me writin', Aisling."

"Oh, we'll have plenty of time for both, *páistí*, ye'll see. Winter is for learnin' and for makin' things, don't ye think?"

"And Uncle Dugan will teach me to play my new harmonica!" Teddy laughed out loud.

I don't hear him laugh much anymore, Cally realized suddenly. *His leg must hurt him more than he tells us.*

For a moment, the brightness faded from the day. But Da said, "How about some music?" And soon they swept from one Irish ballad to another, Da's rich voice filling their home with every emotion in turn.

☙❧

Youghal, April 1891

"Miss Louise! Cally can read everythin' now! And she can write, too! And I can play my harmonica!" Teddy was the first to hug Miss Louise and Cousin Micky, with Shep bouncing and barking in circles around them.

"Is that so, Teddy? I can't wait to see for myself. But ye must call me Cousin Louise, now. Startin' tomorrow." Cally, climbing the porch steps with her arms full of bundles, saw Miss Louise look at Cousin Micky. *I saw that look when we were here before,* Cally thought. *Maybe I knew this marriage would be happenin' even before they did.*

"So, ye'll have to tell me whether Cally and Teddy's weddin' clothes are what ye imagined, Louise." Aisling handed a bundle to her soon-to-be cousin-in-law. "I could use a drink of water, so I could, if ye don't mind."

"Or what about a cup of tea in yer hand, Aisling. I have it all ready, keepin' warm on the stove. And then we can look at the clothes."

Cally plopped her bundles and herself on the porch swing, gazing out to sea. *So much has happened since we were here before.* "Life seems too good to be true, don't ye think, Shep?"

Shep barked, and nudged her, and she ran with him down to the water.

CஇஜD

This is the golden moment of the day, soon to be replaced by silver, Cally thought as she settled on the porch with her back against the wall of the house. *This is the magic moment when faeries are about.* She sat up straight. *Oh! I thought about faeries and wasn't afraid! How glad I am to have Da back.*

No one seemed to notice she had come back out after tucking Teddy into bed. *Sometimes I feel invisible. Tonight, I'm glad of it. I must find out what the adults have been talking about. It will affect my life too, I think.*

Cally sat still, watching the sun set while she listened. Uncle Dugan sat like her, his back against the wall on the other side of the porch, with Aisling nestled beside him. Cousin Micky and Miss Louise sat together on the creaking swing, one of them giving it a gentle push now and then. Da, on the steps, absently scratched Shep's tummy.

"So, Frank. The last time ye were here ye talked about going to New York, America. Is that bee still in yer bonnet?"

As Cousin Micky threw this question into the quiet of the night, Cally noticed Uncle Dugan sit up, his gaze fixed on Da. *He doesn't know what Da will say. But he's afraid he won't like it.* These thoughts came to Cally without effort, as if she could see what lay beneath the surface as easily as what had been brought into full view already.

"There's no simple answer to that question, Micky. Ye are one of my oldest friends. Perhaps ye can explain to Dugan what I haven't found words to make him see. Ye too have suffered a great loss—no, at least three great losses—that have changed the way ye think and live yer life. Yer marriage to Louise gives me hope to move forward one day myself. But I'm not there yet. It's hard for Dugan to understand that."

Cousin Micky nodded, his hand in Louise's, his attention on Da.

"Dugan thinks I should be fully able to embrace the life I had before Reeny died. But part of me died with her, and it's not comin' back. It's a new life I need, not a fixin' of the old one. I've no vision fer findin' that new life on the farm where I've lived since I was born. I long for a new place, a new beginnin'. Is that so hard to understand? Everything there reminds me of Reeny. There's no place I go or anythin' I do that isn't tangled all around her. How can I find new life when the old is so much with me?"

Da shifted his body toward Dugan. "Dugan, ye too experienced great losses, the loss of yer own parents and brother and sisters to the black fever. Can ye not let yerself remember that pain, at least enough to feel empathy fer me? Ye know I love ye and Aisling—ye are and always will be a big part of my heart. Yer carin' fer the farm and for the *weans* when I couldn't is a debt I'll carry all my life. I know ye love Cally and Teddy like they were yers. They will miss ye dreadfully. But ye will have babbies of yer own to pour yer love into. It's time fer me to take mine and nourish the seed of new life in me that longs for different soil in which to grow."

A long silence followed this speech. Cally grew sleepy. She began easing to her feet, but Miss Louise spoke. Cally slumped back down.

"Frank, I'm a newcomer to this family, so perhaps I have naught of great value to offer ye. But I would like to tell ye a story, if I may." Miss Louise looked questioningly at Da, then at Cousin Micky, and then at Dugan and Aisling. Each nodded and settled back into their places.

"Once upon a time in a faraway place, a good faery buried a treasure."

Cally's sleepiness vanished. She sat up straight and waited.

"Many men heard about this treasure, and some set out to search for it. But the faery had set a spell. Only a man with a pure heart, a purity forged through suffering, could discover it. Men with hearts full of greed and selfishness would find no value in it.

"Legends grew up about this treasure hunt. Always there was a clue whose deciphering would lead to the next clue and then to the next, until the treasure could be discovered. Many thought they understood the first clue, but they were disappointed, and their search led to harm rather than riches.

"I thought of this story, Frank, when I heard ye say there is a stirrin', a restlessness in ye to find a place that can give ye new life. I see yer heart longs as well fer peace, and fer the freedom that comes from finding yer true place in the world. I see in ye a longing so strong fer that joy. In the legend, that longing is the mark of a man who could find the treasure, fer it is a pure one born from the bitter experience of death."

Miss Louise sat back and set the swing moving again with her foot, the cross around her neck gleaming in the moonlight.

"Yer discovery of the treasure ye seek, Frank, will be lifegivin' to those ye love, for we can't give away what we don't possess. Do ye ken what I am sayin', Frank? Yer restlessness is pushing ye toward a path of discovery. And though it may be a hard and perplexin' path, there will be about it a fragrance, a breath of love that is but a taste of what the treasure holds fer ye. A song just out of yer reach, but clear as glass on the edges of yer dreams.

"Ye will know ye have wandered from the path, when ye no longer detect the fragrance, the breath of love, the song ye hear just before ye awake and long to remember the whole day through. If that happens, ye must stop where ye are and be still. Do not try to go back. Walk forward in that stillness until ye receive those gifts back again. Then ye will know ye are on the right path."

Miss Louise's voice stopped. For a long time, no one stirred, as each one gazed into the silver on the waves. Cally never knew how she moved from the porch to her pillow. She dreamed of a treasure even greater than her mirror. And when she woke, she heard the echo of a song on the edge of her dream, whose ending she could no longer remember.

CRSO

Killeagh, May 1891

"I've done it, Dugan. I bought passage for me and the *weans* on a ship called the *Lion III*, leaving Waterford on Monday, July 6. Talk is the captain of this ship has never lost a passenger, in all his crossin's over the mighty Atlantic, even in the worst of storms. People tell of a clean ship, and fair treatment, and adequate food, all due to the captain's roots in Quaker piety. And the crossin' cost me no more than any other ship, and fer any other I would have to travel across Ireland to depart from a different port."

Cally's heart raced. *So, we are truly going to do this? Cross the endless ocean to a place we know nothin' about? And leave behind Uncle Dugan, Aisling, Cousin Micky, Cousin Louise, Shep, Simon, Daisy, Miss Hilda, Father Michaelson, Glenbower Wood and our farm and our home and everything we have ever known?* She put her hand protectively on Teddy's shoulder, nestled beside her.

"I know this is a shock, Dugan, though it's one ye've known was comin'. I know, a thing that may someday happen, and a thing happenin' right now, are totally different. Ye and Aisling must depend more on her family now. I'm leavin' ye a thrivin' farm in good order. I've no doubt ye'll accept this and wish us well. And allow us to make a happy partin'."

Uncle Dugan's eyes never left Da's face. He didn't say a word, just walked out the door and let it slam behind him. *Like the door that will be slammin' on us and Killeagh.* Cally watched Da stare at the door for a

121

long time. Then he opened it carefully and walked through, leaving it open behind him.

CHAPTER 14

THE CROSSING

Youghal, Sunday, July 5, 1891

"CALLY! TEDDY! It's time to go!"'

Cally and Teddy ran up the beach to Cousin Micky's cottage. Brushing sand from their feet, they put on their new shoes and turned toward Uncle Dugan and Aisling. *This is the moment I've been dreading. How can I possibly say goodbye? Soon we'll be on a ship crossing that endless ocean. What if we never reach the other side?* She threw herself into Aisling's arms, sobbing. "When will we see ye again? Will ye even remember us?"

"Sure, sweet lassie, and Teddy, I'll remember ye both forever and a day, and love ye always. Every time ye look up and see the moon, ye can know yer Uncle Dugan and I are lookin' at the very same moon and lovin' ye from afar. Tell them, Dugan, what we're thinkin'."

"Sure, Aisling and I are savin' our pennies so we can go visit ye in America next year, so we are. Won't that be grand? And we'll be watchin' fer yer letters, and promise we'll write back soon as we know yer new address. Tell us all about the voyage and New York and our cousins there—every wee detail. Cally can help ye write, Teddy, until ye learn to do it yerself."

Cousin Micky intervened. "Climb up in the wagon, now. We've a long drive ahead, near fifty miles to Waterford. I'm right grateful yer cousin in Kilmeaden will let us spend the night, Dugan. From there it'll be but a short drive tomorrow to the Waterford quay. Ready, Louise?"

"Cally! Come on now!"

"I'm just sayin' goodbye to Simon, Da." Cally gave his nose one last kiss and buried her face in his mane, letting him dry her tears one last time. Then she climbed into the wagon with Teddy and Da, who insisted Louise ride in front beside her husband. "I wish Shep could have come with us, Da. I miss him so much already."

"I know, lassie. I miss him too, but with his injured paw he wouldn't have been happy on this trip. Micky, I think we're ready. Thank ye again fer drivin' us to Waterford so Dugan and Aisling can return to the farm."

"It's always a treat fer us to spend time with ye and yer *weans*, Frank. Maybe we can join Dugan and Aisling in their plan to visit ye next year. Wouldn't that be grand?"

Cally looked carefully at each item in the wagon with them, counting on her fingers. *The bag with Teddy's clothes, my clothes, and our special things. Da's duffle. Food fer the journey today and tomorrow. The surprise we brought to thank Cousin Micky and Cousin Louise fer drivin' us so far.*

"I think everythin' is here, Da." She lay her head on Da's lap, closed her eyes, and thought about their special things. *My treasure. The doll Aisling made fer me, and the doll clothes we sewed together. The sewing basket Miss Hilda filled fer me.* The Fireside Stories of Ireland *Cousin Louise gave me for my birthday and the* Red Fairy Book *she gave us fer Christmas. The new dress Aisling helped me make, and Teddy's new shirt and pants. His wee train and his harmonica.*

She sat up. "Da, how will Teddy get new cars fer his train? Uncle Dugan promised to make more cars fer him, and more track."

"I bet he'll be workin' on that this winter, Cally. Won't it be grand to see them next year?"

Next year is as far away as the other side of the ocean.

Mayfield House, Monday, July 6, 1891

Lillian squinted in the dim light of the barn. "Ah, there ye are, Master Charlie. Don't ye look handsome in yer new whites! Yer carriage is here, and yer mother is looking fer ye, so she is. Yer brother Daniel and his family are already tucked into their own carriage."

"I was just saying goodbye to Midnight."

"All right then, run now. Have a wonderful time with yer family."

"Thank you, Lillian! I'll see you in a month!"

Mummy stood by the carriage. "Charlie, don't you look handsome in your new whites! I think you've grown six inches since your first set two years ago!"

"Thank you, Mummy. I was just saying goodbye to Midnight."

"Climb aboard, son. We'll pick up Margaret and Sally in Waterford on our way to the quay. Daniel's carriage will follow us. Percy will meet us there."

"Isn't this exciting?" Mummy continued as the carriage rolled onto the road to Waterford. "A whole month of vacation with our whole family!"

"Except Thomas. Tell me again why he can't go with us?"

"Well, since graduating from Oxford last month, he hasn't worked long enough to earn time off. It's right he be treated exactly like any new employee of the railroad, even though Uncle Thomas owns it."

The carriage hit a bump, and Mummy grabbed her hat.

"Our Thomas didn't seem upset about it. I suspect being near a young lady in London named Cora is more important to him right now."

"My friend Cora!"

"Yes, Thomas says she has grown well and strong since we saw her last, Charlie. I'm so grateful."

CℬℛО

The Lion III, *Wednesday, July 8, 1891*

"Who are those people I've seen you talking to, Chuckles?" Margaret walked with Charlie along the stern deck, watching the sunrise.

"They're a family from County Cork, hoping to make a new start in America. I noticed them when they boarded, because they were upset. No one had told them they couldn't stay together on the voyage. The lassie is seven, too old to stay with her father and brother but too young, really, to be by herself in a crowd of women and girls she doesn't know. They spend much of their time on deck so they can be together, often on the deck I'm responsible to clean."

"What about the children's mother?"

"She died giving birth to their wee sister, who also died. The father, Frank, told me. The children are sad about leaving their home in Killeagh, County Cork. I've been teaching them to tie knots! But I wish I could do more for them, Gritty."

Margaret sighed. "I'm sure they appreciate your kindness, Chuckles. Surely every one of these people in steerage has a story of hardship to tell."

"Are you enjoying the voyage? How is Sally?"

"Sleeping right now. Percy stayed with her so I could get some air. It's getting cold and windy, though."

"I'm worried we're in for a storm."

"Oh, there's Paudeen. Maybe he can tell us."

"Ma'am, I must ask ye to go to yer cabin until further notice. We believe severe weather is coming. Charlie, advise everyone on this deck to go below. Yer father says—"

"No! I won't do it! Don't make me!" shouted Charlie, his body shaking violently. Hands fisted, he glared at Paudeen. Then he crumpled, bursting into tears.

"Charlie, what—?" Paudeen and Margaret said at the same time, reaching for him.

"I can't. I can't go back into the dark, all alone. I can't do it." Charlie's words were barely intelligible through his sobs. His shoulders heaved, his trembling fingers covering his face.

"Charlie, that's not what I was going to tell ye. Yer father asked that ye assist with the sail on the foredeck. Can ye do that? I know ye understand what to do, and others will be with ye."

Supporting him, Margaret said, "Charlie I've never seen you like this. What's going on?"

"I—I don't—don't know." Charlie pulled his hands from his face and saw a man approach, hat in hand, trailed by two children. *Frank?*

The man addressed Paudeen. "My name is Frank, sir. I couldn't help overhearing. I can help, sir. I'm not a sailor, but I'm strong and I can follow directions. Will ye let me take Charlie's place? Sure, he's not in good shape for this, I'm thinkin'."

Frank turned to Cally and Teddy. "*Weans*, go below. Teddy, stay with Cally and do whatever she tells ye. I'm goin' to give the sailors a wee hand here. When the storm passes, I'll find ye. Cally, look fer the nice woman ye were tellin' me about—Mrs. O'Shanahan, is it? Ye and Teddy stay with her until I come for ye. Be strong and don't worry, lassie. See what fine sailors we have taking care of us? Go on now."

Frank watched his children stumble down the deck, holding the handrail and each other. Turning back to Paudeen, he said quietly, "Sure, Charlie has been a big help to us, so he has. I'm grateful for the chance to repay him in this small way. Won't ye let him stay out the storm with his family? He's still young—only twelve, so I believe."

Paudeen thought quickly. He had never disobeyed an order from his captain. But lightning flashed and a torrent of rain suddenly pounded the ship. "Charlie, go with yer sister, then. Right now! Frank, walk this deck to be sure all passengers are below. Then go to the foredeck. I'll advise the sailors there to expect ye in Charlie's place and tell ye what to do. Thank ye, sir."

☙❧

"Charlie! What's wrong, son? Margaret, run to Sally and Percy; I'll care for Charlie."

Charlie climbed into Mummy's berth and pulled the blanket over his head. He heard an object crash to the floor. He heard screaming. In an instant, he was back in the dark in Father's office, tied to a chair, all alone.

"Charlie, Charlie, you're safe, son. I'm here with you. Don't be alarmed. I'm getting in bed with you so I can hold you. There, *mo pháiste daor* (my dear child), can you feel me with you? You're not alone. I'm with you, I'm with you. . ."

Gradually, Charlie realized the screaming came from his own throat. Mummy held him, murmuring, until he quieted, his trembling body calming.

"That's right, Charlie. Relax, my son. I'm here with you and I'm not going to leave you."

Mummy began to sing, a familiar song from church. *Jesus, the very thought of Thee with sweetness fills my breast . . .* The bed pitched, but Charlie nestled into Mummy's embrace, focusing on her soothing voice until he fell asleep. He dreamed he was a baby, rocking in a cradle. The cradle became his horse. A boy now, he rode Midnight on a warm summer day, faster and faster, and then he found himself once more tied to a chair in the dark in Father's office. He woke screaming again as his body hit the floor with a thump.

"Oh, Charlie, are you hurt? I'm right here, son, but I'm tied to the chair so I can keep my balance. Hold on just for a minute. I'll find you and help you up."

Sobbing, Charlie rolled one way and then the other in the dark as the ship bucked. He tried to get up and fell again. Finally, he felt

Mummy's hands on his back. "Let me help you, Charlie. You're safe. I'm right here with you. There's another chair right beside mine. Take a deep breath and let's crawl together to the chairs. Do you feel it right here? That's right, son. Let me tie you in. This is a bad one, all right, but we're safe and we're together. We must wait it out and pray for Father and for our sailors fighting the storm. Charlie, you're shaking like a leaf. Take another deep breath. Hold it—and now let it out slowly. Now one more deep breath . . ."

"Mummy, I—I dreamed I was locked in Father's office, in the dark, all alone while the ship pitched like a wild thing. What's wrong with me?" Charlie sobbed. "Wh—why is my body shaking like this? Father must be a—angry with me that I didn't obey his orders." Charlie's voice ended in a shriek.

"Calm down, *mo mhac daor*. I'm right here with you. Take a deep breath. That's right. Now another. Better?"

"I—I think so."

"Charlie, perhaps this storm has reminded you of the other storm when you got hurt. Yes? That must have been a terrifying experience for you, more than I even realized."

"B—but that was two years ago!"

"I know, son. I can't explain it, but clearly some part of you remembers that experience."

"Thank you for staying with me, Mummy."

"Of course, *mo pháiste daor*."

"I know Father will be angry. Oh!" Charlie cried out as the ship contorted.

"Hold on to me, son. This storm can't last forever. We must be patient and trust God. I'm sure your father is entirely focused on handling the ship in this storm. I doubt he even knows you're with me."

"Mummy, a man named Frank took my place. Is—is he all right?"

"I'm sure he is, son. The best thing we can do is ask God to help him, your father, and all the sailors and passengers. Will you pray with me?"

CR80

I'm scared.

But Da said: Be strong, find Mrs. O'Shanahan, take care of Teddy, he'll find us after the storm.

Be strong, find Mrs. O'Shanahan, take care of Teddy, wait for Da to find us.

Be strong, find Mrs. O'Shanahan, take care of Teddy, wait for Da.

Be strong, find Mrs. O'Shanahan, take care of Teddy, wait.

Cally chanted this litany hundreds of times as the ship tossed in the wind and waves like a toy boat. Cooking was forbidden, so their only food was bread. In the dark and the crowd of women, she couldn't find either her berth or Mrs. O'Shanahan. She sat in a corner, wedged against the crack between two barrels of foodstuffs, with Teddy's head in her lap.

He had fallen asleep, she thought, but suddenly Teddy sat up and began to sing. *O God our help in ages past, our hope for years to come. Our shelter from the stormy blast and our eternal home.* There was a stir among the women, and then a quiet, a listening. A few others joined Teddy's clear treble: *Under the shadow of Thy throne, Thy saints have dwelt secure. Sufficient is Thine arm alone, and our defense is sure. . .*

Be strong, find Mrs. O'Shanahan, take care of Teddy.

Time like an ever-rolling stream bears all its sons away . . .

Be strong, find Mrs. O'Shanahan.

Be thou our guide while troubles last, and our eternal home.

Be strong.

CR80

"My dear, I only came for a moment to learn how you fared during the storm. We saved the ship and the passengers, but we lost two men. I don't yet know the details. Forgive me that I cannot stay with you. I must learn the names of our lost sailors. I must—"

130

Father stopped, and Charlie heard him move. "Cathleen, is that Charles in your berth? I ordered him to the foredeck. What is he doing here? I have not yet released the men from their stations."

"It's a long story, Peter. There will be time later. I know you must go now to care for your crew. We are fine. God be with you, my darling."

Charlie held himself rigid a few moments after his father went out, then turned toward the bulkhead. "I knew he would be angry."

"Oh, Charlie, I didn't know you were awake. Son, your father is exhausted and upset. Two sailors were lost in the storm. This is the first time he has lost anyone, in all his years as captain. I'm so glad you were safe here with me. If two strong sailors were swept away by the fury of this storm, imagine a twelve-year-old boy . . ."

ᏧᏊᏋ

Cally woke to the smell of breakfast. The ship had stopped rolling. *Da. Where is Da? Perhaps he couldn't come while we were sleeping.* In the dim light coming through the portholes, Cally looked around carefully and located Mrs. O'Shanahan applying a bandage to a woman's leg. *She must have knocked into something in the dark.*

Teddy slept soundly, his head pillowed on his hands. Cally eased away from him and joined the line of women waiting for relief. *I bet Da is sleeping too. Sure, he'll send for us soon, so he will. I want to be able to tell Da I followed his instructions.* After her turn in the head, Cally made her way to Mrs. O'Shanahan and settled into a spot where she could see Teddy.

A man called through the hatch, warning, "Man coming down." *It's Da! Finally! Oh, I'm SO glad!* Cally threaded her way toward the ladder. *But those aren't Da's legs and feet. And head.* She let out her breath with a whoosh of disappointment. *Oh, it's the sailor who talked to Da when that boy Charlie started cryin'. Why is he here? WHERE IS MY DA?*

"Attention, please. I need to speak with Mrs. Fiona O'Shanahan, a girl Callandra Mae Donnelly and a lad Theodore Francis Donnelly. Please

131

meet me on deck. Thank you."

CRITICAL: centered ornamental divider

"No, Paudeen, no! It can't be true! Paudeen, please tell me it's not true!"

"I'm sorry, I can't stay to talk more right now, Charlie. Mrs. Malcomson?"

"Come here, Charlie. Tell me what this means."

"Oh, Mummy, it's the man Frank who took my place! His death is all my fault! Oh Mummy, if I had obeyed Father, he would still be alive! How can I ever forgive myself? What will become of Cally and Teddy? Oh, Mummy, I can't bear this!"

CRITICAL: centered ornamental divider

"Cathleen, how shall I bear this? It's my fault that man Frank went overboard. He stepped into the breach caused by my wrong judgment, asking too much of Charles. And the brave sailor who tried to save him—what can I tell his widow and his wee son? And Frank's two children now orphans . . . Cathleen, I know I must go and give to my men what comfort I may, but please, for a moment, just hold me. Please. Just for a moment."

CRITICAL: centered ornamental divider

It's my fault. It's the Dubh Sidhe's vengeance on Da because he stood up to her. I should never have gone to the faeries for help. Everything I touch, everyone I love . . . Mammy, the babby, Teddy's leg, now Da . . . What if Teddy is next? Should I give him to Mrs. O'Shanahan and then throw myself overboard, so I don't kill him too? What shall I do, what shall I do . . .

Cally hunched in a corner of the deck, as small as she could make herself, rocking her body back and forth, back and forth. Teddy put his arms around her, but she did not respond at all. Mrs. O'Shanahan tried to take her below for lunch, but Cally's body seemed a dead weight.

"We best give her a wee bit of time, Teddy. Sure, it's a shock fer both of ye, so it is. A terrible, terrible waste of a good man's life, so. Come now, lad. We'll save some food for yer sister. In time, she'll come back to us. Ye'll see. Sure, she needs to grieve, so she does, and so do all of us for the loss of two strong Irish men in this cursed storm. It was no one's fault. It was the will of God, so it was, and didn't I hear the Bean Sidhe moanin'? We must learn to accept it."

೦೩೮೦

I can't remember what the man said who prayed over Da and the sailor. Cally sat holding Teddy's hand as his sobbing gradually eased. *I remember the name Colin along with Da's name, Frank. The captain said they were both brave. The sailors and passengers said* Our Father who art in heaven. *But I can't remember anything else, except Teddy squeezing my hand and the splash when the bodies hit the water.*

Mrs. O'Shanahan appeared and pried Teddy's hand away from hers. Cally stumbled back to the corner of the deck where she had sat, day and night, since Da left them. She rocked and took up her inner litany. *It's my fault. It's my fault. What shall I do? What shall I do?*

Debra Kornfield

CHAPTER 15

CHARLIE

The Lion III, *Friday, July 10, 1891*

Charlie turned from swabbing the deck to see his eldest brother approaching.

"Hey, little brother!"

"Hey, Daniel! I haven't seen you here before."

"I've come by each day, walking the decks for exercise, but didn't want to interrupt your work. I've watched you chatting with those Donnelly children. Since the storm, though, you're different, Charlie. Are you all right? You sit at supper and don't say a word."

Charlie hung his head. "I'm sad, that's all. And anxious about what will happen to Cally and Teddy. It's my fault they lost their father. I don't know how to help them."

"Well, you're not the only one concerned. Father has called a meeting of the whole family after supper this evening in his office. He asked Mrs. O'Shanahan to come as well, at least for the first part. She's a passenger who has been caring for the children. Father thinks she may be able to give us some insight into their situation."

"Have you met Cally and Teddy, Daniel?"

"Yes. I've tried to engage Martin and Molly in playing with them, since their ages are practically the same. But I can't say it's been a great success. The orphans don't understand much English, and my children, sadly, are rusty with Irish. Callandra and Theodore, of course, have suffered a great loss and are surely not their normal selves. My heart goes out to them. The lassie, especially, seems very withdrawn. A sailor named Paudeen will care for the four children during this family meeting. Father says you can vouch for him."

"Oh yes, Paudeen's the best! He took care of me on my first voyage with Father."

Daniel looked at Charlie quizzically. Charlie blushed. "He *did* take care of me. It wasn't Paudeen's fault a storm came, and he had to help secure the ship. I'm the one who didn't follow orders. Paudeen's tops! The children will have a lovely time."

"All right then. I'll expect a good report from Martin and Molly. Forgive my hesitance. It's not every day I leave them with a sailor, Charlie."

"Well, you won't be sorry. But about Cally—I agree, she is sad in a way I can't touch. She says she won't go back to her uncle and aunt in Ireland. I don't understand why. Before the storm, she told me she loves them." Charlie pulled his sailor cap tighter over his furrowed brow.

"Well, the *Lion III* won't return to Waterford for at least a month. Maybe by then she'll get past the initial shock and think more clearly. The boy seems quite dependent on her. I suppose that's natural, since he lost his mother so young." Daniel took a step closer. "Just between us, Charlie, I'm intrigued by Father taking such an interest in these steerage passengers. It must be your friendship with them."

My friendship with them is what left them orphans. But I can't say that. Daniel won't understand. "No. It's because Frank—their father— and the sailor Colin are the first people Father has ever lost on the *Lion III*. He took pride in his perfect safety record, the same record held by our grandfather."

"I know. But I think there's more to this, Charlie. I've never seen

Father so distressed. Well, I'll let you get back to your chores. I'm glad you like sailing, Charlie. Much to Father's disappointment, I'd rather build ships than sail them. This voyage hasn't made me love it more."

Charlie picked up his mop. "I'm not as keen on sailing as I was, Daniel, but please don't mention that to Father. See you at the meeting."

CRBO

"Everyone settled? I'm sorry we must squeeze into such a small space. There's a bottle of port on my desk for you, Daniel and Percy, and sherry for the ladies. Please help yourselves."

Charlie hunched in a corner away from Father's direct gaze. No one moved except nine-month-old Sally, playing with a toy on a rug. All eyes were on Father's face.

"I wish to discuss what we as a family can do for the Donnelly children, who were orphaned when their father was lost while helping our sailors during the storm."

No one spoke. Charlie tucked his hands under his thighs. *Father seems heavy and—and unsettled. I'm afraid. I know he's still angry with me for not following his orders. For good reason. So much suffering has come from what I did.*

"May I present Mrs. Fiona O'Shanahan, who has generously cared for the Donnelly children on this voyage. We will listen to her counsel, and then release her while we discuss how to proceed."

Mrs. O'Shanahan curtsied. "Yes, thank you, Captain, sir. The first day of the voyage, wee Cally was upset, bein' separated from her father and brother for sleepin' and eatin'. Her berth is beside mine, so her father asked me to watch her, though truly Cally doesn't require much lookin' after. We're both from County Cork, so we are. I'm from the city and they are farmers, but sure, it does give us a sense of kinship, so."

"What do you understand about the children's situation, Mrs. O'Shanahan? Have they talked about where the family was going in

America, whether they have relatives there and if so where, or any other practical information that could help us?"

"Sadly, I think those particulars drowned with Mr. Donnelly, sir. The lassie, Cally, poor wee lamb, has spoken almost nothing since the storm. The laddie, Teddy, says his mother's cousin is to meet them. He doesn't know whether this cousin is a man or a woman. He thinks he or she may have red hair like his mother and Cally."

"If we are unable to locate this relative, Mrs. O'Shanahan, might you wish to take the children with you to your new life in America?"

Mrs. O'Shanahan curtsied again. "Oh Captain, sir, forgive me, please, sir, but I'll be movin' on from New York to Boston, so I will, to stay with my daughter who is soon to be birthin' her fourth *wean*. My heart is sorrowin', sir, for Cally and Teddy, so it is."

She paused to swipe a tear and take a deep breath. "But I mustn't be expected to care for them beyond our dockin' in New York City, sir. My daughter's family is already stretched as far as they can manage with the birth of this new *babby*. I haven't the courage even to suggest they take in two orphans. I beg yer understandin', sir. I'm not a hardhearted person, sir, so I'm not."

Mummy spoke. "We fully appreciate your situation, ma'am. Please be at peace. As Captain Malcomson's wife, I thank you for your service to them during these initial days of their loss. We believe God will show us a way to care for them." Mummy's warm and gentle voice seemed to settle Mrs. O'Shanahan. She stopped twisting her apron, and Father looked at Mummy gratefully.

"Sir—ma'am—if I may but say one last thing. Cally, she'll need tenderness, I'm thinkin', sir. She's lost everythin' but her brother, sir. And if I may say this in confidence, sir—ma'am." Mrs. O'Shanahan lowered her voice, but Charlie could still hear her. "Cally cries out in her sleep, sir. I believe she is frightened of the faeries, especially of the Dubh Sidhe. This may be why she's afeared of returnin' to Ireland."

Mrs. O'Shanahan straightened and spoke normally. "She says nothin' when I ask, so I don't know fer certain, sir. But if she's had dealin's with the faeries . . ." Her voice trailed off and she gave herself a little shake. "Well, sir—ma'am—I believe that's all I know to tell ye."

"Thank you for speaking with us, Mrs. O'Shanahan. May God go with you to your new life in Boston, and may he bless your daughter and her family."

"Thank you, Captain, sir."

Father held the door while Mrs. O'Shanahan curtsied her way out, then turned to Charlie. "Charles, you know the Donnelly children better than any of us. What do you think we should consider regarding these children's future?"

That's the first time he's spoken to me since the storm. Charlie couldn't think past that. He opened his mouth, but nothing came out.

Margaret cut in. "Father, may I ask a question before we go on? Percy and I don't understand what these children's future has to do with us. Their father died by an act of nature. It was an accident. A tragic one, certainly, but why are you and Mummy so concerned about these orphans? Surely, in the *Lion III's* steerage as in much of Ireland, there are countless children in difficult situations. We can't care for all of them."

Father looked at Mummy, and a look passed between them Charlie didn't know how to interpret. Father seemed to gather himself together. "Thank you, Margaret, for voicing a question that may be in all of your minds. As captain of this ship, I feel responsible for Frank's death and its consequences. His death and the sailor Colin's are a blow to me personally, and I wish to do what I can to care for their children. Will you support me in this?"

"Support you? How?"

Another look passed between Father and Mummy. She spoke. "Margaret, we're thinking of keeping Cally and Teddy with us until the

Lion III sails again, then take them back to their relatives in County Cork. Charlie has heard the children mention both Killeagh and Youghal, so we're confident we can find their uncle and aunt. Keeping them with us may alter our vacation as a family, though, so we wished to discuss it with you before we decide."

Margaret's brow puckered, and her voice raised just a little. "Would they do everything with us? Our outings and concerts in New York City, visiting our relatives in Albany, floating on the Erie Canal to Niagara Falls?"

Is Gritty speaking for everyone? I wonder what the others are thinking.

"Well, that's what we want to discuss, Margaret. Perhaps Nathanael and Sarah would be willing to keep the children while we go to Albany and Niagara Falls. They are a generous and hospitable family. Right, Charlie and Peter?"

Charlie saw Gritty relax. "That sounds like an excellent solution, Mummy. Perhaps the children could stay with Nathanael and Sarah the entire time. That might be best for them—less upsetting than moving around. The Windsor Hotel isn't far from Nathanael's house, so we can check on the children and perhaps invite them on an outing or two, but enjoy just being our family the rest of the time."

Daniel stood. "I like that idea, Margaret. We've already planned for Martin and Molly to spend the night with Nathanael's family while we attend Mr. Paderewski's opening concert at Carnegie Hall. That will be a chance for all the children to be together." Daniel looked at Percy and then at Father. "I for one am ready for a taste of port. May I serve you, Father? Percy? What about you ladies? Sherry, anyone?"

After everyone settled, Father said, "I still need to hear from Meghan, Percy, and Charles. What has each of you to say to my proposal?"

"I think Nathanael and Sarah must be saints as well as Quakers, to add two more to their five, and our two as well Saturday night!" Meghan laughed. "I am anxious to see how my children adapt to their family before I leave them for a whole night. Yet I do want to attend the concert, since this Mr. Paderewski has all of you so entranced."

"I will support whatever you all decide," Percy stated. "Right now, Sally needs her bed. May Margaret and I be excused?"

Charlie looked from one to the other of the faces of his family. *Focus on how we can help the children, not on Father. . .*

Mummy caught Charlie's eye and gave him her warm smile. "Don't worry," she seemed to be saying. "We'll work this out." Charlie's brow puckered, but he took a deep breath and turned back to Father.

"So, Charles. I still need your perspective on the Donnelly children."

"Father, since Cally seems terrified of returning to Ireland, I don't think we should force her. Perhaps by the time we sail she'll be able to tell us why she's afraid. I've seen Cousin Sarah's special way with children. Maybe Cally will be more open with her."

"That seems a reasonable hope, Charles."

"I have a different question, Father, about Teddy. Have you noticed his limp? Could we take him to a doctor, to find out whether anything can be done for his leg?"

"That is a fine suggestion, Charles. I will send a telegram tomorrow inquiring about orthopedists of high reputation in Manhattan." Father looked around the room, his gaze softening as it fell on Sally, fast asleep now against her father's chest. "We will discuss the matter with Nathanael and Sarah when we arrive and proceed from there. Cathleen, will you bless us as we go to our rest?"

Charlie let out a breath he didn't realize he was holding.

"With pleasure, Peter. *Be present, O merciful God, and protect us through the hours of this night, so that we who are wearied by the changes and chances of this life may rest in your eternal changelessness; through Jesus Christ our Lord, Amen.*"

Father left immediately to check in with his officers. Charlie waited until his brother and sister left, then slipped out as well. Glancing back, he saw Mummy following him.

"Mummy, do you think the guests in the lounge would mind if I play the piano a little while?"

"That's always been your way to work out your feelings, hasn't it, Charlie. I think our passengers will love it. May I walk with you?"

"Of course, Mummy."

"These have been such difficult days. I admire you for returning to your work this morning, but I know it will take some time to work through in your mind and heart all that has happened."

"I don't know how I can ever get past this, Mummy. How can I get over knowing I was the cause of a good man's death? A death that left two children orphans!" Charlie burst into tears and stopped in the passageway, burying his head in his arms against the bulkhead. "Please go on, Mummy. I just need a few minutes to myself."

Mummy put her hand gently on Charlie's head for a moment, and then turned to join Daniel and Meghan, on their way to collect their children from Paudeen.

When he felt in control again, Charlie walked to the lounge. Without greeting anyone, he sat down at the grand piano.

◌⃝◌

Cathleen said good night to her grandchildren, then placed her hand on Teddy's shoulder and turned to Paudeen. "Where is Cally?"

"I took the children for a walk on the deck, ma'am, since it's such a beautiful evening. All four were with me, but when we entered the lounge, Cally was missing. I couldn't leave the other three. I'll take Teddy down to his berth now. Perhaps she's gone to bed."

"She went to the deck, Mrs. Malcomson," Teddy said. "She wanted to be alone."

"In her usual place on Charlie's deck, I imagine, Teddy? I'll check on her. Look for me there after you take Teddy, please, Paudeen."

"Yes, ma'am."

"Good night, Teddy."

Cathleen watched Teddy limp away. *What a good idea Charlie has, of seeing a doctor about that leg.* She glanced toward the piano. *As usual, Charlie's completely lost in his music.* Raising a hand, she prayed a silent blessing over him, then nodding and smiling at passengers who greeted her, made her way into the moonlit night to look for Cally.

Cathleen marveled at the calmness of the ocean, sparkling silver in the moonlight. *Who could ever guess we've just been through such a violent storm?* Stopping briefly, her hand on the railing, she looked out to sea and prayed for the souls of the two men they had lost. *Frank taking Charlie's place is a picture for me of what Jesus did for us. Oh, Father, both my husband and my son carry a heavy burden of guilt over what happened. Please show them the way forward.*

Rounding the bend onto what she considered Charlie's deck, Cathleen saw a bundle half-hidden behind a lifeboat bound to a ladder to the upper deck. As she drew closer, she saw Cally sound asleep, her face marked by crying. Cathleen sat on the deck with her back against the bulkhead. Gathering the wee lassie into her lap, she began to sing.

It seemed a holy space to Cathleen as she sang. Time seemed suspended between the moon and the trail of silver in the water. She sang all the lovely Irish lullabies she could remember. Beginning a hymn, Cally stretched and rearranged herself against Cathleen's chest, then with a soft sigh, breathed evenly once more.

So absorbed was she, Cathleen startled when Paudeen appeared before her. He bowed, then lifted the child from her lap. *So small for her age yet carrying such heavy responsibility.* Cathleen rose, feeling strangely bereft.

Cally sighed and nestled into Paudeen's embrace. Noting his raised eyebrows, Cathleen shrugged and lifted her hands. "I don't know,

Paudeen. There is something special about this lassie, beyond my understanding. Let me pray before you take her to her berth."

Cathleen placed a gentle hand on Cally's shoulder. "*O God, almighty and merciful, you heal the brokenhearted, and turn the sadness of the sorrowful to joy. Let your fatherly goodness be upon this child. Remember in pity both her and all those who occupy the steerage on this voyage. Lift up those who are cast down. Cheer with hope all who are discouraged and downcast, including this precious child. Though Cally be troubled on every side, save her from despair. Grant this, O Lord, for the love of him who for our sakes became poor, your Son our Savior Jesus Christ. Amen.*"

CHAPTER 16

CALLY

The Lion III, *July 10, 1891*

CALLY DREAMED SHE WAS IN GLENBOWER WOOD, *at the top of the hill with the stone cross and the scent of honeysuckle. She was in a woman's lap, with her head against the woman's shoulder. The woman sang and gently stroked her hair.*

Cally felt heavy, so weighed down she couldn't move, or speak, or even think. As the woman sang, though, she began to feel lighter. The pressure in her chest and in her head started to ease, so she could breathe more deeply. She could feel her body start to relax, as if her tummy was not coiled up quite so tightly.

The woman's song was sweet and clear. Cally didn't want it to stop. Some seemed familiar, but it took too much effort to figure out when she had heard them before. She stretched, and then relaxed into the singer's warmth.

In her dream, Cally felt herself drifting into sleep. But then someone else lifted her. Someone strong. Uncle Dugan! She sighed and nestled into Uncle Dugan's embrace, and he carried her to her bed, where she heard the little whiffling sounds Teddy made when he was deeply asleep.

CRITICAL

Saturday, July 11

A whiff of honeysuckle awakened Cally. She lay for a moment with her arm around Teddy, savoring the comfort the scent gave her. People moved quietly nearby. She opened her eyes and at first thought she was in a box, but when she turned over, she realized the box was open on one side. Dim light came through a round window, and she saw many other three-sided boxes stacked around her.

At first, it all seemed like part of her dream. But as women and girls stirred and then sat up and climbed out of their boxes, and then a woman she recognized walked toward her, Cally remembered where she was. *I'm on a big ship. Going to America. That woman's name is Mrs. O'Shanahan. Da—*

Cally gulped sudden tears. She turned and closed her eyes just as Mrs. O'Shanahan reached her berth, making little clucking noises. *Don't come. Stay away! Leave me alone.*

"There's my girl. I know ye are awake, lassie. It's no use pretendin' yer not. It's a new day. A day to practice facin' into yer troubles instead of away from them. Come now, let's go relieve ourselves, and then dress and see about breakfast. Oh, but ye are dressed already. Didn't ye ever change into yer night clothes last night, then? I remember now ye were out very late. What were those people thinkin' of, then, keepin' children from their necessary sleep?"

Cally closed her ears, and her heart, to Mrs. O'Shanahan's voice. She did allow herself to be pulled out of bed and to the line of women at the head. Reaching its brief privacy, she realized she felt different. *I feel— what word is right? Lighter. Looser. Like I can breathe again.*

The wondering feeling persisted, as Mrs. O'Shanahan pulled her back through the crowd of women to her berth and while she went through the motions of waking Teddy, helping him dress, and taking him to stand in line for his turn at the head.

The sense of wonder stayed with her the rest of the long day. She played with Teddy on the deck, saw the sailor boy Charlie smiling at her, and even noticed the pretty sky and the waves sparkling in the sun.

CRBO

Sunday, July 12

"Man coming down."

It's Da!

Cally leaped to her feet. She looked around for Teddy and saw him playing with a wee lassie in the open area beside the berths. She threaded her way toward him. *I must get Teddy ready to go up on deck.* But the legs descending the ladder were clothed in white. Cally crumpled and stuffed her fist in her mouth to stifle a wail. *Da is gone. Da is never coming back. Da is gone. Da is never coming back. We are alone. Be strong. Take care of Teddy. Be strong . . .*

"I need yer attention, please."

It's that Paudeen-sailor, the one I ran away from.

"Please heed these announcements. We know ye are runnin' low on provisions. The captain bid me tell ye that at noon, today, tomorrow, and Tuesday, the galley will send down food fer ye. We're runnin' low up top too, but we will share with ye what we have."

A great cheer arose from the women.

"Now, bein' the Lord's day, the captain will lead prayers on the decks at 11:00, usin' the loudspeaker from the bridge. Are any among ye gifted with singin', who could join him on the bridge to lead some hymns? I see two hands . . ."

Cally pressed her hands to her eyes to stop a flood of tears. *Da could have sung better than anyone.*

"We expect to dock in Manhattan, New York City, mid-mornin' on Wednesday. Yer breakfast on Wednesday will be yer last meal on board. Once ye are called to debark, ye will go directly to the Barge Office to pass through immigration. If ye don't have the proper papers . . ."

Cally's mind raced. *What will Teddy and I do on Wednesday? We don't have any papers. Will Mammy's cousins be there to find us? I don't remember their names, or where they live. I only know Da was laughin' with Uncle Dugan, sayin' all the McCarthy family looks alike, red hair and freckles like him and me. How will I find them?*

Cally's body jerked with shock when the sailor said, "Now, I need to speak with Miss Callandra Mae Donnelly. Please come with me."

For a moment Cally couldn't move, though she saw Teddy jump to his feet. Seeing Mrs. O'Shanahan coming toward her, though, she bolted for the ladder, where Paudeen's long legs were disappearing. *What could the sailor be wantin' with me? Have I done somethin' wrong?* Cally looked back at Teddy and tried to smile. "I'll be right back," she yelled, though whether that was true, she had no idea.

Paudeen stood at the top of the ladder, beside a woman in beautiful clothes. A memory flashed through Cally's mind, too quickly for her to grasp it. The woman bent down, and Cally found herself looking into kind brown eyes. *I think I've seen these eyes before . . . Have I?*

"My name is Mrs. Malcomson, Cally. I am sad about the loss of your father in that terrible storm. My husband is the captain of this ship, and we would like to help you if we can. I believe you know our son. He is a young sailor named Charlie."

Charlie is the son of the captain? I didn't know that!

"I see you do know him. Cally, will you go with me to my cabin, to talk with Charlie and me about what you will do when we arrive in America? We want to help you. We won't make you do anything you don't want to do. But we have some ideas. Would you like to hear them?"

"Ye promise I can decide fer myself? Cross yer heart?"

"Cross my heart, Cally. I know you feel a great responsibility for your brother Teddy, and I honor that. I have no desire to make your decisions for you."

"Could Teddy come with me to yer cabin?"

"Why yes. That's a fine suggestion. I'll wait here while you call him."

☙❧

Cally and Teddy sat on chairs opposite Mrs. Malcomson, swinging their legs and sucking peppermints. Charlie, sitting on the berth, sucked one too, to keep them company. *I'm glad Charlie is here. He was our friend before the storm, before Da—*

"So, Cally and Teddy, may I ask you some questions? You see, since your dear father is no longer with you, Captain Malcomson and I think the best plan is to take you back to your uncle and aunt in Ireland. Would you like that?"

"No, ma'am. Sure, we cannot go back."

"Can you tell me why, Cally?"

"No, ma'am, I can't tell ye. I can't tell anyone. It wouldn't be right."

Teddy jumped to his feet. "But Cally! Uncle Dugan and Aisling love us. They could be like our mammy and da." Teddy turned to Mrs. Malcomson. "I want to go back to our farm, please, to live with Uncle Dugan and Aisling and Shep and Simon and Daisy."

"Teddy, no! We must stay together! That's the last thing Da told me: Take care of Teddy. Ye have to stay in America with me!"

"Well, Uncle Dugan wasn't here, so Da couldn't tell him to take care of us. But if he *was* here, Da would have asked *him.* That's what *I* think." Teddy spoke loudly, then ducked his head and turned red.

"This is a big decision, Cally and Teddy. You have time to think about it. It will be almost a month before the *Lion III* sails back to Ireland. For now, let's talk about some other questions. Would that be all right?"

The children glared at each other, flushed and breathing hard. Cally took a deep breath and nodded.

"You have relatives who will meet you at the dock in New York, is that right? Can you tell me about them?"

"All I know is she is Mammy's cousin, and she looks like Uncle

Dugan and me. I don't know what he looks like. Did ye ever hear Da say their names, Teddy?"

Teddy shook his head. "I don't think so."

"There will be hundreds of people at the wharf, Cally. Do you know your father's plan for where to meet your cousins?"

Both children shook their heads.

"I have your father's bag here—can you get it, Charlie? Paudeen brought it from the men's steerage so it wouldn't get lost. I have not opened it. Would the two of you be willing to find out whether it contains the information we need?"

Cally looked at Teddy, and saw his eyes brimming with tears. *It's not right. Da wouldn't want us to touch his things.*

"I understand how difficult this is, Cally."

"C—could ye or Charlie open it, ma'am, instead of us?"

"If you are sure that's what you wish."

Cally looked at Teddy again, and he nodded, wiping his eyes and his nose on his sleeve.

"Charlie, could you help me, then?"

Charlie pulled the bag into the space in front of the children, then unfastened the clasps and opened the flap. A large object, wrapped in Da's clothes, took up most of the space. As Charlie unwrapped it, both children burst into tears. Cally threw her arms around Teddy, and they wept together. Mrs. Malcomson handed them her handkerchief. Charlie sat quietly on the floor, waiting for the storm of tears to ease.

"I see your father was a musician. This was his harp?"

"Y—yes, ma—ma'am. He useta win prizes." Teddy began crying again. Mrs. Malcomson got up and found another handkerchief.

"Charlie is a musician too. He hasn't learned the uilleann harp, but he does play the piano. Would you like to hear him play if there's time before prayers?"

"I'll be glad to play for you, if you would like that, Cally and Teddy."

The children looked at each other and sniffled. They said nothing.

"Shall we see what else is in your father's bag?"

Charlie lifted out a set of clothes, revealing papers at the bottom of the bag. He handed the top one to Cally.

"This is Da and our mammy. Da used to keep this picture by his bed."

"I see. She is lovely like you, Cally. And your father looks like you, Teddy."

"Ye—yes ma'am."

Cally swallowed hard, then handed the photograph to Teddy so she could examine the next paper Charlie handed to her. "This is torn out of Mammy's Bible. Why would Da do that? It says, 'Bir-ths and Bap-tisms.'"

"I'm impressed, Cally! I didn't know you are such a good reader."

"Y—yes, ma'am. Cousin Louise taught me. Why would Da tear a page out of the Bible? Cousin Louise taught us never, ever to tear books."

"Was your Bible big and heavy?"

"Yes, ma'am."

"Perhaps he thought the whole Bible was too big and heavy to carry with him."

"Then he should have left it with Uncle Dugan, not torn it out. Look, Teddy. It has Da's name on it, Francis Cashel Donnelly, and his parents, and Mammy's name, Maureen Eilis McCarthy, and her parents, and their marriage day, December 23, 1882. That's the same as Da's birthday, 'cept he was born in 1861. And Mammy's death January 23, 1889."

Cally glanced at Teddy and spoke more quickly. "And my name Callandra Mae Donnelly and my birthday, October 17, 1883. And yer name and birthday too, Theodore Francis Donnelly, March 13, 1885. And Infant Girl died January 23, 1889. And more spaces after that."

Cally handed the Bible page to Teddy, sat still with her head in her hands for a moment, then accepted the next paper from Charlie. "This says, 'To the pr—priest in New York, America. Francis (Frank) Cashel Donnelly is a member in good standing of the Roman Catholic Church in Killeagh, County Cork, Ireland. Father Joseph Michaelson.'"

"That sounds like a useful introduction to a new parish. I am Catholic too."

"Yes, ma'am. I guess we don't need it now." Cally wiped her eyes. Charlie waited until she was ready to look at the next paper.

"This is a funny drawing of a man on a ship and a lady with a crown on her head and something in her hand. It says, 'Wishing ye well, mate.' It has a lot of hard to read names." Cally handed the paper to Mrs. Malcomson.

"These are all men's names. Toby, Henry, Eamon, Liam, Aiden, Connor, Brody, and one I can't read either."

"Oh, those are our neighbors and Da's friends from town. I don't know what this one is." Cally extended the last paper to Mrs. Malcomson.

"It seems to be a business contract. Let me see. Dugan Branigan McCarthy promises to pay Francis Cashel Donnelly ten pounds sterling per month to purchase your father's house and farm. He's to keep this amount stored in a locked box, added to monthly, and take it to your father when he visits America next year, at which time the purchase will be considered paid in full. Dugan is in possession of an identical contract. It's signed by both men and a witness."

"Oh."

"Is that all of the papers in the bag, Charlie? There are no identity papers, or information about the children's cousins?"

Teddy said, "Da kept a letter in his pocket. In case someone stole his bag, he said."

"I see. Perhaps that letter contained instructions for meeting your relatives in New York. And maybe your father tucked your Irish identity papers in with it."

Teddy looked at Mrs. Malcomson and shrugged.

"This makes it harder for us to find your cousins. We'll arrive two days late, because of the storm. Can either of you think of anything that might help us find them?"

Both children shook their heads.

Charlie paused from returning Da's things to the bag. "Mummy, could we post an announcement in the New York papers? Perhaps Cally and Teddy's relatives will see it. We could ask them to go to Cousin Nathanael's house."

"What a good idea, Charlie! Cally and Teddy, Cousin Nathanael and his wife Sarah are relatives of ours in New York City. We will stay near them, in a hotel, while the *Lion III* is repaired and re-provisioned."

"Maybe Cally and Teddy could stay at Cousin Nathanael's until their relatives come."

"What do you think, Cally and Teddy? Of course, we will try, first, to find them at the port. But if we don't, I like Charlie's idea: to post your location in the newspaper."

"Will ye tell in the newspaper that Da fell in the ocean?"

"No, Teddy. We will only tell them about that in person."

"So, we will look fer Mammy's cousins when we get to New York," Cally said. "And if we don't find them, we will stay at yer cousins' house until they find us through the newspaper."

"How does that sound to you?"

"What if yer cousins don't want us to stay at their house?"

"Then we will talk about what to do. But they are kind people, Cally. Did I tell you Nathanael and Sarah have five children? Their oldest is a year older than Charlie, and the youngest is just a baby. They probably have one or two children close to your ages."

Teddy stood up. "Are they rich, like Martin and Molly? Do they know how to talk right?"

Mrs. Malcomson laughed. "I don't know, Teddy. I've never been to their house in New York. But you have, Charlie."

"They speak Irish at home, and American English when they go out. They are not rich, but they do have a big house," said Charlie.

"Cally, how does this plan sound to you?"

"Can we think on it a wee while, Mrs. Malcomson, before we decide?"

"Certainly, dear. We have two more days on the ship. You know the deck where Charlie works. When you decide, you can tell him, then he can tell me. All right?"

"Yes, ma'am. Thank you, ma'am."

"Would you like to take your father's bag with you now, or leave it here with me?"

"It would be safer here, ma'am. There are so many people where we sleep."

"That will be fine, Cally. Perhaps my husband can assign a sailor to help you look for your relatives once we dock in New York City."

"The only sailor we know is Paudeen, ma'am. And Charlie."

"I'll ask whether it can be Paudeen. Would you two like to take a peppermint with you?"

"Oh, yes, ma'am! And—and can we hear Charlie play the piano?"

"You certainly may. You need to practice anyway, don't you, son? But it's only half an hour until prayers, so listen for the announcement."

CRRO

I've never heard music like this before. Charlie's fingers move so fast. Cally gripped Teddy's hand. *Oh! I just remembered! Mammy told Da one time, "What, is my cousin Roisin daft? Who in their right mind would want to leave Ireland and go to America?"*

Cally whispered to Teddy, "Roisin, that's Mammy's cousin's name. I'll tell Charlie tomorrow."

CHAPTER 17

CHARLIE

The Lion III, *Tuesday evening, July 14, 1891*

"OH! I DIDN'T SEE YOU THERE! I thought I was alone."

"We listened to yer music yesterday too, but ye didn't see us 'cause that rich lady Martin and Molly's mammy called us to play with them. An' she gave us sweeties, too, and taught us a game with cards."

"That sounds nice, Teddy."

"Yes, and we decided to go to yer cousins' house in New York to wait fer Mammy's cousin. And Cally remembered Mammy's cousin's name: Roisin McCarthy. Cally was supposed to tell ye yesterday but Mrs. O'Shanahan said we needed a bath and Cally was mad and then when we went to yer deck ye weren't there, so."

"Cally was mad at Mrs. O'Shanahan?"

"Yes. Cally said she doesn't ever want to see Mrs. O'Shanahan again, and I said that wasn't nice, and then we both got mad. Sure, it *wasn't* nice, Cally, so."

Charlie laughed. "Well, Mrs. O'Shanahan is going to Boston, so you'll get your wish soon, Cally. Want to go watch the sunset with me before you go to bed?"

◌৪০

"You sent for me, Father?" *I've been dreading this. But now that it's happening, I feel nothing.*

"Yes, Charles, come in. I've asked your mother to join us."

"Oh, hello, Mummy."

"How was your day, Charlie? Here, son, sit by me."

Charlie stayed leaning against the door. "I watched the sunset with Cally and Teddy."

"They seem very fond of you."

"Well, I'm fond of them too."

Father cleared his throat. "Charles, this conversation may not be easy for either of us. Your mother told me you feel responsible for Frank Donnelly's death. I don't believe—"

Charlie's body jerked forward. "I am, Father! If I had carried out my duties, Mr. Donnelly would still be alive. It's simple logic, Father!" *What is wrong with me? How embarrassing to cry in front of Father!*

Mummy jumped up, but Father gestured her back and rose himself. "Come here, son."

What—?

Father walked around his desk and embraced Charlie's stiff body. After a moment, Charlie realized Father wept too. He drew back, gulped, and stared. *Father never hugs me. And he never cries.*

Father pulled out a handkerchief and snorted. "I told you this wouldn't be easy for either of us. Sit down, Charles, and listen. I'll try to explain why Mr. Donnelly's death was not your fault." He took a drink of water and poured a glass for Charlie.

"Charles, I have been unwise in my expectations of you. No, let me finish. I forgot what it's like to be ten, and eleven, and twelve. Your mother has been helping me think about myself as a boy. It took some effort, I confess, but as memories began coming back to me, I realized how inappropriately I have treated you."

His mouth open, Charlie stared at Father.

"Had I been wise, my son, I'd have realized how terrifying this storm would be for you, after your frightening experience two years ago. And it was foolish of me to expect you to fight the storm as if you were a fully grown, experienced sailor."

Charlie shook his head vehemently.

"No, just listen. I have caused you to suffer unnecessarily, and that pains me deeply. I was not wise. I was wrong."

"Oh, no, Father."

"Son, I know you want to please me. I am honored that you want me to be proud of you. I am proud of you, Charles. I am proud of you because you are my son."

"But—"

"Charles, it is possible for me to make wrong judgments. I am not perfect. I make mistakes. Sometimes my mistakes hurt other people. I asked too much of you, more than you were capable of doing, and I am deeply sorry."

"But, Father—"

The captain threw up his hands and looked at Mummy. She nodded at him. "You're a bright boy, Charles. You spoke of logic. Use your reasoning skills rather than your loyal, respectful, obedient son skills, and see where you come out."

"I—I'll try, Father."

"Thank you. I don't seem able to adequately express myself. The point is, Frank's death was not your fault, Charlie. It wasn't. It was mine. Can you accept that?"

Charlie said again, "I'll try, Father. But—"

"Please, no more buts, son. Perhaps your mother can help you understand better than I can." The captain took a deep breath, drank some water, and wiped his face with his handkerchief.

"I do have another question for you, Charles. Paudeen tells me you've been thrashing and crying out in your sleep. Can you tell me about that?"

Charlie shrank back in his chair, trembling.

The darkness.

The terrible rocking of the ship.

Left alone, tied up in the dark.

The water—

He heard moaning. He only realized it came from his own throat when he felt Mummy's arms around him. "It could have been me who drowned! I hate sailing! I hate this ship! I—"

Charlie gasped and covered his face with his hands.

"I didn't mean that. Truly. What's wrong with me?"

Charlie buried his face in his arms. He didn't dare look at Father. There was a long silence. *He must be so disappointed and angry. Even angrier than I am at myself.*

But Father's voice when he finally spoke was gentle and sad. "Son, I am so sorry for your suffering, and for my part in causing it. I wish I could take it from you."

⟡

Charlie gave a huge yawn as he leaned against the port deck rail, watching the land come steadily closer, his bag at his feet. *Huh. I didn't have any nightmares last night. The first time since the storm. I thought I would spend the night thinking about that conversation with Father, but instead I just went to sleep. Good thing, since I have my lesson today with Mr. Paderewski.*

Charlie turned to admire a graceful sailboat and saw Cally and Teddy walking toward him. Each gripped one side of a cloth bag.

"Oh my! At first I didn't recognize you two!"

"We're wearin' Martin and Molly's clothes! See, even though Molly is younger than Cally, Cally is small, so Molly's dress fits her."

"And even though Martin is older, you're big, so his clothes fit you! How convenient, Teddy! But why aren't you wearing your own clothes?"

"Mrs. Malcomson wants us to look like part of yer family, and get off the ship with ye, Charlie. Oh, there she is. She'll tell you. Oh, and there's Paudeen!"

"Good morning, Charlie. What do you think of your new brother and sister?"

"Good morning, Mummy. Is that what Teddy and Cally are now? I'm sorry I missed breakfast. I don't think I've ever slept so late."

Mummy smiled. "Clearly you needed the sleep. Now, I want you three to pretend you are brothers and sister, so Cally and Teddy won't have to go through immigration at the Barge Office. It's a small bit of subterfuge in a good cause, Charlie, since we have no papers for them."

"What is sub ter —"

"Subterfuge means being a little bit sneaky. I bet you never imagined my mother could be sneaky, did you, Teddy."

Mummy poked Charlie and laughed. "We're arriving later than we expected. So, here is my plan. Paudeen, hire a carriage to take Charlie directly to the Fifth Avenue Presbyterian Church. Don't leave him until you are sure Mr. Paderewski is there."

"Yes, ma'am."

"While Charlie is having his lesson, take Cally and Teddy, with this letter, to Cousin Nathanael's. The address is on the envelope. Once Nathanael and Sarah have read the letter and Cally and Teddy are settled at their house, return to the church. Oh, and please tell Sarah we plan to be there for supper at six o'clock and are looking forward to seeing them."

"Yes, ma'am."

Mummy took a breath. "When Charlie's lesson ends, take him to the Windsor Hotel. By then, the rest of the family should have arrived, and you will be free, Paudeen." Mummy tucked a bill into his hand. "Keep the change, dear Paudeen. You have been such a help to us. We'll see you back on the *Lion III* three weeks from now for our return voyage."

"Thank ye, ma'am. I'll go now to fetch Mr. Donnelly's bag from your cabin."

"Charlie, enjoy your piano lesson." Cathleen bent down. "Cally and Teddy, I'll see you in a few hours, at Cousin Nathanael's house for supper. Don't worry. Paudeen will take good care of you. Nathanael and Sarah are lovely, kind people. Charlie says their children are lovely and kind too." She gave each child a hug. "I must go get our own things ready."

Charlie saw Cally and Teddy's eyes follow Mummy to the end of the deck. They brightened when Paudeen reappeared.

Setting Frank's bag on the deck beside the children, Paudeen touched Teddy's shoulder. "*Weans*, look! We're sailing through a passage called The Narrows between two large bays. We're leaving the Lower Bay and entering the Upper Bay. Manhattan, where we will dock, is in the Upper Bay. We'll be there soon!"

Charlie smiled at the children's wide eyes, turning their heads to take everything in, and at Teddy's hand sliding into Paudeen's. *I bet you feel overwhelmed, just like me my first time here. But Cally—you haven't said one word. I wonder what's going on in your pretty head. You let your chatterbox brother speak for you. Your whole world has turned upside down, and you have no idea what will happen to you and your brother next.*

The Upper Bay was getting noisy. Warning beeps from barges competed with toots from tugboats and a deeper, single blast from their own ship's horn. *That means we're altering our course to starboard.* He chuckled as Paudeen explained this to the children just after Charlie thought it. With Paudeen there to point things out to Cally and Teddy, Charlie returned to his own thoughts.

What will it be like to see Mr. Paderewski again? I haven't practiced much on this voyage. I wonder whether he'll notice. It's a good thing we decided I should not move to Vienna, since Mr. Paderewski spent this last year in Paris. I wonder what it's like to be him? All of Europe seems to be in love with him, yet his son is sick. I can't imagine how hard that is.

Teddy yelled, "Look at that! That's the lady in Da's drawing! With the crown on her head! Look, Cally! Did ye ever see anything like that in yer whole life?"

Just wait until you see Manhattan!

ഗ≈ാ

"Whew! I'm not late after all—there's Mr. Paderewski getting out of that carriage. Thank you, Paudeen. I'll see you at supper, Cally and Teddy. You'll love Cousin Nathanael and Cousin Sarah and their children." *What good memories I have of my time with them! But now I must focus on music, nothing else.*

"Hello, Herr Paderewski!"

"My dear boy, it is so good to see you! You've grown! Let me see your hands. Yes, you will have an easier time now with some of the chording. How was your voyage? How is your family?" They walked together into the church. "I am afraid I have some upsetting news, both for you and for me. I will tell you about it after we greet your friend, the organist. It was kind of him to allow us to meet here."

Settled at the piano, Charlie turned toward Mr. Paderewski. "You have bad news, sir?"

"I do indeed. After playing thirty-six concerts in England, I arrived in New York on Monday. As I disembarked, Mr. Tretbar, who arranged this American tour for me on behalf of Steinway pianos, informed me I would play my first concert the very next day—last night! And he has scheduled eighty concerts for me to play in just three months! Eighty! It is impossible! Mr. Tretbar seems blithely unaware of what he is demanding of me. And in cities like New York, Boston, and Chicago

161

where I'm to play multiple concerts and recitals, it is to be a different program every time. He has advertised music I have never played in concert before, not once!"

Mr. Paderewski paced back and forth, his voice rising as he talked.

"I should have time to recuperate from the voyage, and several days between concerts, to rest and to practice for the next one. Mr. Tretbar apparently thinks I am a machine. If I have a day without a concert or travel, I am to consider myself fortunate."

Mr. Paderewski wheeled, sat down, and spoke more quietly. "I was so distressed I inquired immediately when the next ship would depart for Europe. But Mr. Tretbar says most of the tickets for the eighty concerts have already been sold, and if I disappoint him, I may never be invited to America again. You see, Charles, I am in a difficult situation. I may only be able to give you one more lesson while we are both in New York. It crushes me to say this, but I need every bit of time either to rest or to practice. Do you understand? Can you forgive me?"

How disappointing! "Yes, of course, sir. This sounds quite dreadful."

On his feet again, Mr. Paderewski leaned over Charlie's chair.

"You must learn from this experience of mine never to agree to something unless you understand clearly what you are agreeing to. Eh, Charles?"

He paced again. "I cannot imagine how I will survive these next weeks. I played two concertos and Chopin last night at Carnegie Hall, then, because the rehearsal with the orchestra took place this morning, I spent the entire night practicing for the concert this evening, a completely new program. It is insane! A schedule I am utterly unprepared to face."

The master gave a huge sigh, followed by a huger yawn.

"Charles, do you remember playing Mozart's Sonata for Two Pianos with me in Vienna?"

How could I forget? "Yes, sir."

162

"Could you play it with me again? We could use this as an encore Saturday evening. What do you think, Charles? Would your mother allow you to practice with me tomorrow night? To practice on two pianos, we'll have to go to the Steinway warehouse. I have the score here with me. You will have a day to review it."

"We can try, sir, if it would be a help to you. I haven't played it since Vienna."

"That's the world I live in now. But let us turn to your music. I promise, I will look carefully at my New York City schedule to find a time for your second lesson. I too am staying at the Windsor Hotel, so I will leave a message for you there. Now, show me your finger exercises. Have you been practicing your Czerny?"

ભ્જ

Nathanael opened the door. His arms, stretching out to give hugs, stopped mid-air. Instead of cousins, he saw a tall, swarthy sailor and two *weans*.

"I see from thy blue and green scarf thee is from the *Lion III*, so come in and tell us the reason for this surprise visit. Sarah! Have we refreshments for our guests? No, children, these aren't thy cousins. I'll introduce them when I know who they are. Now, sailor . . ."

"Paudeen, sir. I expect ye are Mr. Nathanael and Mrs. Sarah. And yer children. I'm pleased to make yer acquaintance."

"As are we, Paudeen. Please enjoy this fresh-pressed peach nectar and Sarah's famous biscuits. Do thee like sweet biscuits, lassie? Laddie? Now then."

"Sir, Mrs. Malcomson has sent ye a letter explaining everything. If ye still have questions after ye read it, I'll try to answer them."

"Sarah, sit here with me and we'll read Cathleen's missive together. . . Oh. Oh my. Lord have mercy. We are so very sorry for thy terrible loss, Cally and Teddy." Nathanael and Sarah's eyes filled with tears.

Nathanael lowered the paper, looked long at his wife, then at Cally and Teddy, and finally addressed Paudeen. "We will be delighted to have Cally and Teddy stay with us while they await their relatives. Oh my, yes. Florrie and Ben, wouldn't thee like to take Cally and Teddy out back to play in this lovely sunshine? I'll call thee, *weans*, when yer relatives arrive."

Cally and Teddy looked at each other, bewildered, but followed two children close to their own ages out the open door.

"Now, Paudeen, are we quite certain Cally and Teddy are meant to go with these relatives? I feel a block in my spirit." Nathanael chuckled at Paudeen's confused expression.

"That's Quaker talk, Paudeen, I do apologize. Probably thee can't answer my question. Be at peace. Cathleen writes thee must pick up young Charlie from his lesson. Godspeed, and we thank thee for thy help to our family."

"Thank ye, sir. I'm a God-fearing man too, sir, and I'm praying for the best decisions to be made for wee Cally and Teddy. I've grown fond of them, sir."

"I can see that. God bless thee for it. Godspeed."

"Goodbye, sir."

CHAPTER 18

KEEGAN

Luck o'the Irish Tavern, New York harbor, Wednesday, July 15, 1891

KEEGAN KELLY WALKED INTO THE BAR, waved at the other customers, yelled "I'll have my usual, Seamus," and sat down at the corner table. He pulled a pencil from his ear and began scribbling on a pad. His head came up and twisted around when a woman raised her voice, speaking with a southern County Cork accent.

"Ain't I always told ye, Malachy Quinn, that yer man Frank ain't worth trustin'? How many times did I tell Maureen ever since she was a girl, but she was so taken by those blue eyes and the dancin' and the singin'. And now we've been here two whole days spendin' money, and we know the ship's come in—what's its name again, the *Lion III*—but still no sign of Frank Donnelly. And after we drove the wagon a day and a half to get here, and had to pay that no-count Finnegan to look after our animals back on our farm, and don't know whether he has or not, and—"

Seamus set Keegan's ale on his table. He took a sip, still tuned to the conversation a few tables away. The man's reply was steady.

"Roisin, we've gone over all this already, over and over, so we have. We must be patient a little longer. Ye know the steerage passengers'll be the last off the ship, and maybe the wee ones can't walk fast. And there's no point worryin' about the animals, seein' as we can't do nothin' about it from New York City. Besides, Frank will have to go through immigration, won't he? Who knows how long that may take? Just settle down, Roisin. We may yet have a long while before we see him."

The tavern door banged, and a ragged boy walked in yelling, "Roisin McCarthy, Roisin McCarthy, I have a message fer Roisin McCarthy and I'm to take it to every tavern on the wharf and I don't get paid until I find her. Roisin McCarthy, Roisin—"

Roisin stood to her feet, her legs wobbly, and Malachy stood beside her. "Sure I am Roisin McCarthy, so. Wha—what is the message?"

"It's on this paper here."

The boy handed the paper to Roisin, who looked around desperately. "Sure this does me no good, since I can't read it."

"And ye have to write yer name on this other paper, here, so I can get paid."

"Sure, how will I do that? I can't write."

Before Keegan could offer his skills and his pencil, the tavern door banged again, and a crew of sailors flooded in, laughing and talking. Seamus raised his hand. "I'll serve ye in just a wee minute, sailors. I can tell by yer blue and yer green that yer from the *Lion III.* Can any of youse read and write?"

"That would be Tully here." The sailors pushed forward a skinny sailor with hair even brighter red than Roisin's.

"All right then, Tully. See that paper the lady is holdin'? Read it out loud to her."

"Fancy writin', this is," Tully opined.

"Never mind that. Just read it."

"To Roisin McCarthy: In the matter of Frank Donnelly and his children, please meet me at 353 East 53rd Street at your earliest convenience. Captain Peter Malcomson of the *Lion III.* Why, that's our own captain! And—"

"353 East 53rd Street. Ye got that, ma'am? Then, Keegan, loan us yer pencil. Tully, sit down and take the lad's paper. Write, 'Roisin don't know how to write, but she got yer message.' Then give it back to the laddie and he can be on his way."

"*. . . but she . . . got . . . yer message.* Here ye go, lad." The tavern door banged again, admitting more sailors. The boy pushed through them out the door, declaring "A whole quarter, he's givin' me, so."

Keegan leaped to his feet, ran around the sailors and out the door. He pulled the boy back into the tavern in time to hear Malachy say, "Thank ye, sailor Tully" and then Seamus said, "Don't ye worry none, ye will all get served, sailors. A half 'un fer each of youse?"

"Let me go!" The urchin struggled under the hand Keegan clamped on his shirt.

"Hush! See this quarter? It'll be yours if you keep still for a moment. I want to hear this."

"Where the dickens is 353 East 53rd Street? Why is Frank makin' us go there? And when did he start talkin' so fancy? 'In the matter of Frank Donnelly . . .'"

"Hush, Roisin. The message is from the captain, not from Frank. Ye were just wonderin' what we should do and now we know. 353 East 53rd Street is easy to remember. Let's finish our food and then we'll look fer a hansom cab. Don't ye worry none, we'll make Frank pay fer it."

The lad, seeing his captor focused on the conversation, slid his hand toward the quarter still sitting in the man's open hand. Tobacco-stained fingers closed over it. "It will be yours, I promise, if you keep still and quiet for a wee minute," the man whispered.

Seamus was speaking. "And there is the matter of payment fer the food and drink and bed and care of yer mule the last two days, Mr. Quinn."

"Yes, sir. Now before ye start fussing, Roisin, Frank will have to give us the money fer this, since we're here fer his sake. So payin' our bill is just a temporary loss."

Malachy sat down and took a drink of his ale. Roisin opened her mouth and looked around. Seeing no one to complain to, only sailors scrambling to give Seamus their orders, she sat down to finish her pasties.

Keegan was about to free his captive when Tully said to his mates, "Ain't Frank Donnelly the name of that man what went overboard? Sure his lassie's the spittin' image of that woman there, ain't she. Captain Malcomson had her and her brother right beside him at the prayers fer the dead."

Roisin was on her feet and banging on her table before the sailor finished speaking. "What are ye sayin', there, sailor? Frank Donnelly went overboard, and he's dead? Is that what yer sayin'?"

Tully ducked his head, and the other sailors looked at each other. "Come on, speak up. Frank Donnelly is my cousin's husband, so he is. I have a right to know what ye were sayin'."

Malachy had his hand on his wife's arm, urging her to sit down. The new group of sailors pushed a man forward. "Ma'am. I was on the crew fer the main sail. Frank Donnelly tried to help us battle a storm. The wind was so strong we couldn't hold on to the clew when we were tryin' to take down the sail, and it knocked Frank overboard. Our mate Cathal went right in after him, tryin' to save him, ma'am, but the sea was so rough both of them drowned, and Cathal was a powerful swimmer, so he was, the best of us all. There wasn't nothin' else we could do, ma'am. I'm right sorry fer yer loss, ma'am. We were about to drink in memory of Cathal. We could add Frank Donnelly to our toast if ye would like to drink with us, ma'am. Sir."

Malachy cut off whatever Roisin was going to say. "That's very kind of ye, sailor, but I think we need to be gettin' on to 353 East 53rd Street. The message said go as soon as possible. There's the *weans* to think of, now. Here's yer money, barman. Can ye tell me how to find a cab? And can ye keep our mule and wagon one more night?"

Keegan put the urchin on the other side of him next to the wall so he couldn't escape and pulled a fresh paper from his pad. He wrote, "Got a lead on a story related to my street children series. Asking permission to proceed. Keegan," folded it, wrote a name on it, and handed it to the lad. "After ye deliver Captain Malcomson's message, take this round to the *New York World* offices, In the new World Building, you know it? The tallest building in New York City, did you know that? Give it to the lady at the front desk. Tell her it's from Keegan and you'll wait for the answer. I know her. She'll give you a sweetie while you wait. Then come back here, give me the answer, and I'll give you your quarter *and* your supper. Now run as fast as you can."

The lad leaped for the door, eyes shining. Keegan shifted so he could watch the stairs leading to the sleeping rooms, where the bereaved couple had gone to gather their things. While he waited, he noted on his pad details he might forget later. *I'll hire a cab of my own and follow the Quinns. I can't wait to see how this story plays out.*

∞

Roisin's voice carried easily from the open hansom ahead. "Well, ain't this cab a fancy way to travel. And look at them houses! Them as live at 353 East 53rd Street must be rich, Malachy. Are ye thinkin' we're to take Frank's *weans*, now they're orphans? The laddie can work with ye on the farm, bein' farm-raised himself. And the lassie can help me in the house. Sure, this may be a windfall, Malachy. Not meanin' to speak ill of the dead."

Malachy's voice was harder to hear. "Let's wait until we get there, and listen to the captain, and meet the lad and lassie before we decide anythin', Roisin. We know nothin' about the *weans*. Do ye even know how old they are?"

"I know they are Cally and Teddy and they're my cousin Reeny's *weans*. That's all I need to know. There'd be another lassie if Reeny hadn't died and the *babby* with her. But then these two wouldn't be orphans, would they, and fer sure they wouldn't be here in America."

"Well, don't set yer heart on anythin' just yet, Roisin. Aren't ye even a little bit touched by Frank's death? His wee ones must be grievin', missin' their father and Ireland and all."

"Oh, pshaw. If they're in with rich people, they're sure to be happy as clams. I won't have any fussin' and mournin' in *my* house, so. I think the good Lord planned this, so we could have our own laddie and lassie, Malachy. It would be a stretch to be sad about that."

Malachy sighed and leaned his head back. Soon he was snoring. His snores were louder than his speaking voice.

☙❧

Keegan stopped his cab a few houses before 353 East 53rd Street. He paid his driver, ran across the street and around that house and through two back yards, and slipped into the bushes on the side of the front porch of 353 East 53rd Street. He could hear Roisin arguing with the driver of their cab. "No, we ain't got any money. The people at this house will pay ye."

Roisin turned and stopped for a moment, surveying the house. Then she straightened her clothes, walked up the front steps, and banged on the door, her husband trailing after her.

From his place in the bushes, Keenan could see Roisin, but couldn't see the person who opened the door and said, "May I help thee?" Roisin spat and made the sign of the cross. "So ye are *that* kind of people, are ye? Do-gooders. Thinkin' ye are better than the rest of us."

"Roisin, stop that at once," Malachy said. "The Quakers were good to my grandparents at the time of the Great Hunger. Soup kitchens every day, and good soup too, so I was told. Sure, I wouldn't even be alive if it weren't for them, because my grandda and grandmammy'd a died from hunger."

"That's as may be, Malachy, but our priest in Cork warned us against the Quakers' devilish ways. 'Don't be taken in by their kindness,' he said. 'They're after convertin' ye away from the true church.' So I never have been friendly to a Quaker and I don't mean to start now."

Roisin turned back to the woman at the door. "Bring out Frank's *weans* and we'll be on our way. No, we won't be goin' in. They're our kin and there's nothin' to discuss except the matter of payment fer the days we been waitin' fer them here in New York City and a pretty penny it cost us, and worry too, not knowin' why they didn't come to our agreed-upon meetin' place. And then to hear the news about poor Frank. I never did like him, but now his *weans* are orphans, I mean to do right by them, so I do."

Keegan crawled to a different position so he could see the front door head on. Roisin was peering around a Quaker woman trying to see inside. A man walked up to stand behind the woman. Keegan watched his face change from friendly, to concerned, to stern, and back to friendly. The man stepped around the woman onto the porch and indicated two rocking chairs. "Please, be welcome. Sit with me on the swing, Sarah, so we can know our guests better. I am Nathanael. This is my wife Sarah. And you are?"

Malachy took a seat, but Roisin remained standing. "Like I said, there's nothin' to discuss. Now if ye will give my husband the money ye owe him, and fetch the lad and lassie, we'll not trouble ye further. We've a long way to go towards home, and it's too late to start tonight, so Malachy will be asking ye fer two more days lodgin' and food for this trip. Tell the man, Malachy, how much to pay us."

The cab driver walked down the sidewalk and up the steps to the porch, interrupting brusquely. "Ahem. Speaking of payment. I'm waiting for payment for your ride here. Which of you is going to pay me? It will cost you more for every minute you make me wait."

"This man will pay ye," Roisin said, pointing to Nathanael.

"Roisin, we don't even know who he is! He don't look like a captain. I will pay the man, and we can add that to the total we'll settle with Captain Malcomson once we have the *weans*. Here ye are, sir, and I apologize for the long wait."

The cab driver looked at the coins Malachy put in his hand, opened his mouth, shrugged, walked back to his cab, and drove away.

Keegan could no longer see faces, but he could clearly distinguish one speaker from another. Sarah had not said a word since her initial greeting. Now she whispered to her husband, and he replied audibly, "Yes, Sarah, I understand supper won't cook itself. Thee may go." The swing creaked, and Keegan saw her walk in the front door.

"Roisin, is it? And from thy conversation, I understand thy name is Malachy, sir? Sarah and I welcome thee both to our home. Now, Captain Malcomson should arrive within the hour, and thee are welcome to wait for him, here or inside."

"We've no need to talk to the captain. If the *weans* are here, and ye pay us, we'll take them and go."

Nathanael gave the swing a gentle push. "I'm sure thee both can understand Frank's wee ones have suffered a great shock, on multiple levels. Not only have they lost their dear father, but they are in a strange land among people they don't know. My cousins who were on the ship with them are concerned to make the best decisions possible on the children's behalf. Please accept our hospitality until the captain and his family arrive, and then over supper we can discuss what may be best for Cally and Teddy. We would be glad to offer thee beds for the night, since thee will have a long road home, but for now, will thee accept refreshments?"

"Thank ye" said Malachy at the same time his wife said, "We won't eat yer food or drink yer drink." She spat again and was making the sign of the cross when a group of children ran around the house, shouting and in hot pursuit of an older child. The two in fancy clothing stopped short when they saw the adults on the porch. The girl reached for the boy's hand and backed away a couple of steps.

"So, these are the poor orphans? They don't look poor to me! Where did ye get those rich-people clothes, *cailín*? I ain't taking ye home lookin' like that!"

The girl pulled closer to the boy and took another step back.

"Cally, Teddy, come here, children. These are thy mother's cousins, Roisin and Malachy. I'm sure they would like to say hello to thee."

Cally looked around wildly, seeking an escape. Nathanael gazed at them, smiling, and finally she and Teddy ran up the steps, past Roisin and Malachy to the refuge of his arms.

"She's a skinny wee thing, ain't she, probably not good fer much, though I do see my cousin Reeny in her face. And Malachy, did ye see the limp on that lad? Frank didn't say nothin' to us about his *weans* bein' damaged goods! It's clear we'll have to raise our price fer takin' them off yer hands, ye Quakers, since they won't be as much good to us as we had hoped. But it's the Christian thing to do, carin' fer our kin, so if ye will—"

Nathanael interrupted. "It's well thee understand I won't pay thee anything for taking these precious children, ma'am. Now if thee wish to wait for the captain, thee can discuss the matter with him. Won't thee come in the house to wait until he arrives? Surely we can reach a good solution for everyone if we are patient and ask God for his direction."

"God! My God would not have me leave my kin to Quakers, I can tell ye that! What say ye, Malachy? Ye have been awfully quiet."

"The man has a point, Roisin. We won't be travelin' this late in the day anyhow, so why not eat supper and learn what we can about Cally and Teddy from people who know them better? And if we sleep here, it will save a night's lodgin' at the tavern. What harm could it do?"

"Well, I ain't goin' in that house, that's fer sure and certain! I'll wait out here, and the *weans* can wait with me." Roisin flounced into a chair and held out her arms to Cally and Teddy. "We can start gettin' acquainted, can't we. Cally, is it?"

Cally shrank even further back against Nathanael, while Teddy, yelling, "No! I won't!" ran down the steps and around the house. He stopped when he saw Keegan's leg sticking out from the bushes, but Keegan put his finger to his mouth and made his eyes smile. Teddy, sensing a game, smiled back, and continued his run to the back yard.

Cally whispered to Nathanael, who stood and held out his hand. "Cally thinks she should change out of these clothes. Will thee excuse me while I ask my daughter to help her do that, and perhaps Teddy too?"

Without waiting for an answer, Nathanael walked into the house. As soon as they were through the door, Cally burst into tears, which soon became a wail, which faded slightly for Keegan as Nathanael called his eldest daughter from the kitchen, explained what Cally needed, and the two of them went up the stairs.

"So, he has a temper, and she's a crybaby. Well, I won't have that, Malachy. But we'll whip them into shape, so we will. And it won't take long, either."

Nathanael, returning to the porch, said, "Ma'am, I beg thee to remember what these wee ones have been through in the last few days. They need love, and patience, and kindness, and time to heal. Their wee hearts are broken into pieces."

"Humph, what nonsense. Hearts broken into pieces. Ain't ye somethin', tellin' us how to treat our own kin. Tell him, Malachy, we won't be havin' any more of that!"

"He's right, though, Roisin. Didn't ye see the lassie's face? And the lad's? They are sufferin', so they are."

"I'll show them what sufferin' is, so I will! I've a mind to take them and go, Malachy, without waitin' fer any more rich people to tell us our business."

"Ma'am, I implore thee . . ."

"No more of yer sermonizin', Quaker. Call us a carriage and bring us the *weans*! The fact they'll go hungry tonight will be on yer head, being as yer too stingy to pay what is due us, we who are willin' to sacrifice out of Christian charity to orphans."

"Roisin, stop and think. . ."

"I'll have no more 'Roisin, stop' out of ye today, Malachy Quinn! We've made up our minds. We'll have the wee monsters in their own clothes here and ready to go by the time the carriage arrives. And waste no more time sittin' around yappin'."

Nathanael walked in the house to send his oldest son for a carriage. After a while, Keegan heard the back door close. He squirmed from the bushes, ran to the corner, and crawled into another set of bushes by the back porch. Nathanael sat on the step and raised his hands to heaven as he watched Teddy and his children play. "What am I to do, dear Lord? I need thy wisdom here," he said aloud.

What an expressive face he has, Keegan thought. As Nathanael sat there perfectly still, Keegan saw his face relax. "I see," Nathanael said softly. "Yes, I will consult a lawyer, to know our options before the law. I'll send Tobias for Mr. Shea when he gets back with the carriage. I thank Thee."

Nathanael stood, called Teddy, and walked with him through the back door. Keegan stood, surprised at his own boldness but half wanting to be discovered. He watched the Quaker set out a washtub and pour warm water into it. He seemed in no hurry, letting Teddy play in the tub and murmuring all the while what a fine lad Teddy was. An older Quaker lad appeared, reporting the carriage was out front, and the people were impatient.

"I thank thee, Tobias. Now run to Mr. Shea's house. Ask him to come to our back porch for a few minutes if he can."

Keegan squatted into the bushes as Tobias ran out the back door, then stood again. Banging could be heard on the front door, but Nathanael paid no attention.

Since Roisin refuses to enter, the children are safe while they are inside the house, Keegan realized. *Perhaps it's time for me to meet Nathanael. I would love to be part of his conversation with Mr. Shea.*

Nathanael was singing to Teddy now and pouring more warm water into the tub. Keegan stood, brushed off his clothes, walked up the steps, and knocked on the back door. "Sir, my name is Keegan Kelly. I'm a reporter for the *New York World*. Do you have time to speak with me? I'm writing a series of articles about the rights of children, sir. I was sitting in the Luck o' the Irish tavern, when . . ."

CHAPTER 19

NATHANAEL

Manhattan, Wednesday, July 15, 1891

"IT IS GOOD OF THEE TO COME, Mr. Shea. May I present Mr. Keegan Kelly, journalist for the *New York World,* and my young friend Teddy? Tobias, please help Teddy dress and take him to supper. I thank thee, son."

"I'm pleased to meet you, Mr. Kelly."

"So, we have a situation here, Mr. Shea, and I need to know what the law may say about it. Mr. Kelly is writing a series of articles for his paper exploring the rights of children. We may have half an hour together before the adults eat supper."

"Your household is quite full presently!"

"Yes. Cousins from Ireland, their children, and grandchildren. We are eight adults and ten children. And two guests on the front porch who refuse to enter our home."

"Describe your situation, Nathanael. I will help if I can."

"I thank thee, Mr. Shea. In short, two children, Cally, seven years old and Teddy, six, emigrated from Ireland with their father on my cousin's ship. A storm swept their father overboard. Their mother died some years ago. So Cally and Teddy are now orphans."

Nathanael stopped, took out a large handkerchief, and blew his nose.

"Their mother's cousins are on our front porch demanding the children. They want Cally and Teddy for labor on their farm. Their manner of treating the children is intolerable. I could not live with myself were I to allow these cousins to take them."

"Are there other options?"

"Indeed, they have a loving uncle and aunt in Ireland. Teddy wants to return home to them. Cally, however, insists she cannot go back to Ireland, for reasons Teddy does not understand."

"It does seem a return to loving relatives in Ireland would solve everything."

"Indeed, sir. My question is this, Mr. Shea: If the children remain here, does the law require them to go with their relatives, or could someone else adopt them—my family, for example? I am not certain we should, but I wish to know whether it's possible."

"The law leaves great discretion in such matters to the judge assigned to the case. The courts strongly favor blood relatives. Despite recent sentiment that the best interests of the child should prevail, the guiding principle is what will allow the child to be the most productive, that is, contribute the most to society. Helping relatives farm would fit well into this concept of what is best for the children."

Keegan wrote as fast as he could. "When you say, 'recent sentiment,' you refer, I suppose, to the Adoption of Children Act passed in Massachusetts in 1851, but slow to be adopted in other states, including our own."

"Yes, Mr. Kelly, that Act was the first time the 'best interests of the child' was codified."

Mr. Shea turned to his neighbor. "Should this case go to the courts here in New York, Nathanael, the children will be awarded to their relatives, with little consideration of how they may be treated.

Immigrant children, especially, have no 'rights' under our law. Our streets are overrun with homeless, orphaned, or abandoned children, though Charles Loring Brace's so-called orphan trains or mercy trains have helped."

"Oh, yes!" Keegan exclaimed, while Nathanael blew his nose once more. "I have just completed an article about the thousands of street children gathered up from the crowded cities here on the east coast, put on trains and sent west. Look for it Sunday in the *New York World*."

"I will do that, Mr. Kelly. Your articles may help sway public opinion. Significant change is needed in the way our society views and protects its children. But I must go to my own supper, Nathanael. Call me if I can help further. Good night."

"I must go too. Nathanael, I want to use Cally and Teddy as a case study for my next article. I will use pseudonyms, of course, and won't include details that would allow anyone to track them. May I bring a draft by for your approval once I have it written?"

"Of course. That is considerate. You are welcome here any time, Mr. Kelly. I am grateful for your work."

"Thank you, sir. Enjoy your family reunion!"

CSSO

On his way to the sitting room, Nathanael found his oldest daughter Matilda re-setting the dining table to serve the adults. "The children have all eaten and gone upstairs, Father. Tobias will read stories and play with them while the adults eat. You're just in time."

Nathanael kissed the top of her head and stepped into the kitchen. "Thee hath done wonderfully well, my dear wife. Shall I invite our guests to the table?"

"If Matilda is ready, yes. I thank thee, husband."

Peter rose as Nathanael entered the sitting room. "I see you are looking toward your porch, Nathanael. After some discussion when we arrived, I persuaded them no decisions were forthcoming tonight and sent them in our carriage back to their tavern to sleep. I can well imagine what this afternoon has been like for you and your family!"

"You did well, Peter! Now we can enjoy catching up with one another. Cathleen, what a delight to see thee again after such a long time. Let me see whether I can name all thy family. How good to see thee again, Charlie. Was thy piano lesson with Mr. Paderewski satisfactory? Good, good. And thee must be Daniel, and thy beautiful wife Meghan. Thy dear children Martin and Molly are upstairs? I look forward to meeting them."

"We're pleased to meet you, Cousin Nathanael."

"And this wee one must be Sally, sharing a name with my dear Sarah, so thee art Margaret, and thy husband Percy. Consider this thy home away from home while in New York City. May I invite thee all to our table? Sarah advises me our supper is served."

As they moved toward the dining room, Nathanael continued, "How fares Thomas since completing his studies at Oxford, Peter? We had interesting discussions when he was here last summer, did we not? Have thee all met my dear daughter Matilda? She hath inherited her mother's generous heart."

Sarah served huge bowls of fragrant stew and fluffy biscuits straight from the oven, with homemade jellies, and fruit pies for dessert. The chatter was lively. No one referenced the two orphans upstairs who, related Tobias later, fell fast asleep before the stories ended.

At the door, Peter told Nathanael, "Cathleen and I will leave Charles at the church tomorrow morning to practice, then come to discuss what we should do regarding the Quinns and the Donnelly orphans. Thank you for caring for Callandra and Theodore overnight."

Nathanael climbed the stairs and laid a hand of blessing on the head of each sleeping child. He lingered over Cally and Teddy. "Father, source of all wisdom, guide us into thy plan for these thy beloved ones."

 C380

"We agree, then. Returning the children to their relatives in Ireland seems the best solution," Peter said. "Does anyone understand why Cally seems reluctant to do so?"

"Cally said she can't tell me why. 'It wouldn't be right'—those are her exact words."

"Yes, Cathleen, but that woman on the ship, Mrs. O'Shay—O'Shanty—"

"Mrs. O'Shanahan."

"Ah yes. Mrs. O'Shanahan told us she thinks Cally had dealings with the faeries, and that's why she's afraid to go back."

"Do people still believe in faeries?" asked Sarah. "I thought that was historic Ireland, not present day."

Cathleen's brow puckered. "Those beliefs are still very real in some parts of rural Ireland, Sarah. I grew up hearing the stories, and many of my playmates believed in and were afraid of the faeries. My father told us it was ignorant superstition, but I saw things that made me wonder. I can imagine Cally's fear."

Nathanael sighed. "Perhaps with a little more time, Cally may yet confide in you, Cathleen. Or in Charles."

"I do hope so. Peter, tell Nathanael and Sarah the good news about Teddy!"

"Teddy has an appointment tomorrow afternoon with a well-regarded orthopedic surgeon here in Manhattan. Perhaps something may be done to repair the damage to his leg."

Sarah stood. "Will thee excuse me for a moment, please? I want to check on Cally and Teddy. They are playing in the back yard while my children do their lessons. Will thee take Jimmy for me, Nathanael? He's fallen asleep."

"Of course, Sarah. Here thee go, sweet babby. So, Peter and Cathleen, will thee both accompany Teddy to this doctor's appointment?"

"Nathanael! Come quickly!" Laying Jimmy on the carpet, Nathanael ran through the house and out the back door, Peter and Cathleen at his heels.

"They are gone! I have looked everywhere. They aren't here."

"Perhaps they are attending to necessities, Sarah?"

"No. I already checked. Oh, Nathanael, I feel this as a knife in my heart!"

"Why don't thee two women search the house, every room, while Peter and I run through the nearby streets. I don't believe the children would go far on their own. We mustn't leap to conclusions, Sarah. Meet back here in five minutes."

❦

"They truly seem to be gone, though their bag and their father's duffle are still here," Cathleen said. Ought we alert the police, Nathanael? I suspect Roisin and Malachy."

"From what Mr. Shea told me, I doubt the police will be sympathetic, Cathleen. They will think we should have let the children go with their relatives yesterday."

"Peter, have we any idea where Roisin and Malachy's farm is located? That would give us a clue what roads they may take. If they are in a farm wagon with one horse or mule, we may be able to overtake them."

"And then do what, Cathleen? Play tug of war with the children? If the law is not on our side, there may be nothing we can do."

"We must at least try, Peter!"

"I have the impression the farm is north, dear, near Albany. Shall we pursue them, Nathanael?"

"I am willing to try, Peter. There is only one main road north to Albany, along the river. At the least, if we find them, we can take the children their things."

Sarah sank to the back steps, threw her apron over her head, and sobbed. "How could I have been so careless? I never imagined—"

Cathleen sat beside her. "None of us imagined this could happen, Sarah. I am as upset as you, but all we can do is pray Peter and Nathanael overtake them. They can't have been gone more than half an hour, because Peter and I greeted the children when we arrived. Let us pray together, then I can help you make lunch for your children. Charlie will practice the rest of the morning. The others wanted a slow start to their day. So, tell me how I can help you."

"Father God, we entrust to thee Cally and Teddy. Keep them safe. And whether the children return to us or not, wilt thou teach Roisin some measure of love and compassion. Amen."

CHAPTER 20

CALLY

Somewhere north of New York City, Thursday, July 16, 1891

CALLY BLINKED HER EYES OPEN. Darkness. *Wh—what happened? My head hurts. It's so dark and stuffy I can't breathe! I can't move! Where's Teddy?*

"HELP!" Cally tried to yell, but something was stuffed in her mouth. *I can't move my hands. Or my feet!* She jerked her body, trying to break out of what confined her. Something heavy pinned her and she heard a voice. She frowned as she focused on making sense of the words.

"None of that, ye hear? Lie still and hold yer *wheest*. Ye must learn obedience, ye and yer brother both."

My brother . . . "Teddy! Where is Teddy?" Cally tried to yell, her body trembling. *I think that was Cousin Roisin. I'm scared. What can I do? That heavy thing is still on top of me. I must think. Where am I?*

Unable to move, Cally focused on listening. *I hear wheels. I can tell I'm moving. Is Teddy here too? Where are we going? OW! We must have hit a hole in the road. My head hurts so much! I can't breathe. Where is Teddy? OW! When will this stop? I'm so thirsty.* "HELP!"

Tears ran down her cheeks but Cally could do nothing to wipe them away. The heavy thing lifted. Immediately she threw her body again, as hard as she could, just as the wagon hit another bump. Everything went black.

CR&O

Cally forced open her eyes. *Nothing has changed. I'm still trapped. I'm still moving. Oh, my head! I can't breathe! I wish I could turn over. Oh. I hear talking.*

"Enough is enough, Roisin. I must find out why our mule is limpin'. And while we're stopped, I'm lettin' those *weans* out of them bags. We're far from the city. No one will find us."

Cousin Roisin laughed. "It was clever of ye to hide for the first few hours, Malachy. In soul, them rich do-gooders won't exert themselves this far fer two homeless orphans."

I feel us stopping! Something next to Cally was pulled away.

Is that Teddy? Is he all right?

She heard him wailing, and the sound of a slap on skin. Then a shuddering breath. *It is Teddy! He's alive! We're together! It will be my turn next. I won't cry, I won't.*

The light was blinding at first, but the air! Cally gulped it in, tears streaming down her cheeks despite her vow. Before she could open her eyes to the light, the gag was pulled from her mouth, and water trickled in. It was hard to swallow at first because her throat was swollen and scratchy.

Oh, that feels so good. More, please. Squinting, she opened her mouth.

Teddy! She looked from one side to the other. "Where's Teddy?" It came out like a frog croaking.

"There now, lassie. Better? Roisin, ye should be ashamed of yerself. Look what ye've done to these poor *weans*. They've bumps on their heads where ye knocked them out. I'm freein' their hands and feet now, poor *crayturs*."

"Don't act the goat, Malachy Quinn. They'll run away."

186

"Not likely, Roisin. Look at them! They're injured, weak, hungry, and thirsty. Ye've subdued them, so ye have. They'll not love ye fer it. Ye might get work from them, but ye won't get love."

He talks like we're not even listening.

"Such *blether*, Malachy, ye *eejit*. Untie their hands, then, but not their feet. We must keep goin.' Tis a long road still to Peekskill. If we're late fer the ferry, we'll have to sleep there."

"Use yer head, Roisin. It's been hours. Don't ye think they need to do their necessaries? I'm untyin' their feet. I'll help Teddy and ye can help Cally. What, ye want them to do it in the wagon? Ye are insufferable, woman!"

I can't feel my hands. Cally rubbed her wrists together where the rope had bound them, catching Teddy's teary eye as Malachy lifted him from the wagon.

Does Cousin Roisin have to be so rough? Cally jerked away when her numb feet touched the ground, but fell flat on her face, jarring her aching head. Roisin carried her a short way from the wagon, pulled down her pantaloons, and held her upright. "Hurry up, then!"

I don't think I can do it. Cousin Roisin raised her hand to strike. Cally felt herself let go.

Cousin Roisin dumped Cally back in the wagon beside Teddy. She reached for him.

"No funny business, ye two. Ye already know what I can do to ye, and I will, so." Roisin gave each of them another drink of water and a piece of bread.

"Roisin, look at this. I found our poor mule's problem."

While she chewed, Cally drank in Teddy's fear, and relief, through his eyes.

"We must stop at the next town. The farrier in Glenmont didn't do a good job. I think he'll need a new shoe."

"More money! And more delay!"

Cally turned to look at the mule.

Malachy squinted at the sun. "We might still make the ferry, Roisin. Climb up."

Cally grabbed the side of the wagon as it jerked forward. "Which direction are we goin'?" she whispered to Teddy, her finger to her lips.

"That's easy. Look at the sun. We're goin' north."

"Then New York City is south. Do ye still 'member the address?"

"353 East 53rd Street. Three-five-three-five-three. And East is where the sun rises."

"We must keep repeatin' it, so we don't forget."

"No talkin', ye two!" Cousin Roisin yelled. "Teddy, move to the other side of the wagon. Or do ye want to go back in the sacks?" She turned back to Malachy. "Can't we go faster?"

"That's a village ahead, Roisin. While the farrier's workin' ye can stretch yer legs."

Cঙৎ♡

Alone in the wagon, Cally scooted over and hugged Teddy. He looked around. "We don't have our bag, Cally! Or Da's!"

"They're safe in New York. Once we escape, we'll get them back. Feel this." Cally guided Teddy's hand to something round and hard in her waistband. "It's my treasure! I sewed it into my dress while we were still on the ship."

Roisin appeared. Cally moved back to her place. Soon Malachy and Roisin climbed onto the bench and the wagon rolled on. She grew drowsy and lay her head on a sack. Teddy yelped as they hit a bump and his head banged the side of the wagon. Cally sat up and looked around. Roisin and Malachy were talking and waving their arms. Cousin Roisin's face was red and angry.

Cally moved over by Teddy. "Look at them," she whispered. "Do ye think we could jump out of the wagon without them seein'?"

Teddy's eyes brightened. Cally pointed. The road followed a huge river a short distance away, with trees along its bank. "Can we run fast enough to reach the trees before they notice we're gone? Let's stretch our legs out first. Tell me when ye feel ready."

Roisin seemed to be dozing now, her head against Malachy's shoulder, her mouth open. Cally pumped her legs, getting the stiffness out of them from being tied up. Teddy did the same, then looked at Cally and nodded.

"If we stand on that bag there, we can jump over the side. Ye can't yell, Teddy, no matter how much it hurts. Go first, and I'll jump right after."

Teddy stood precariously on the bag. With a frantic look at Cally, he jumped. Crumpled on the ground, he jammed his arm against his mouth, tears streaking his face.

Cally didn't let herself register the pain as she hit the ground. She ran to Teddy, pulled him up, and half-carried him, rushing toward the trees. Blundering behind a bush, they collapsed, panting and sobbing.

Cally rubbed Teddy's leg, then peered around the bush toward the road. "I don't see them, Teddy. They must not have noticed yet that we're gone. We must start walking south through the trees."

"But my leg hurts, Cally."

"I know. I'll help ye. We can't stay here. They might find us!"

Teddy got to his feet and took a few tentative steps, leaning on Cally. "I can do it, Cally. I don't want them to grab us again."

"I don't either. You were so brave, jumping out of that wagon and not crying."

"It hurt, Cally. My leg still hurts." Tears filled Teddy's eyes.

"I know it does. Let me rub it a little bit more. Is that better?"

"A little."

"When we get farther into the woods we can rest a little longer. Oh Teddy, look! What's that little gray creature with the bushy tail?"

"I don't know. I never saw animals like that in Glenbower Wood. There's another one!"

"Stay here a minute. I'm going to look at the road again." Cally made her way through the trees until she could see the road, then returned to Teddy. "I didn't see the wagon. Only a carriage going south."

"While you were gone, I saw a rabbit."

"I wonder what else we'll see in these woods. Let's pretend we're on a treasure hunt, Teddy. I wonder if American woods have berries we can eat."

"This is an adventure, isn't it, Cally? Do ye 'member Cousin Louise read to us about adventures?"

"Yes, and when we get thirsty, we can drink from the river. Have ye ever seen such a big river in yer life?"

"Cally! Look at those big blue birds by the river! With the long necks!"

"They're not blue. They're gray."

"Blue."

"Gray. Oh! What's that? Up in the sky! It has a white head and a hooked beak."

"Wouldn't it be fun to fly like that?" Teddy ran ahead, arms outstretched, swooping and diving in the breeze.

ɔ৪৯

The children walked through the woods all afternoon, stopping now and then to rub Teddy's leg. As sunset shone in oranges and pinks over the broad river, the trees suddenly ended. Squinting, Cally noticed a few buildings ahead of them to their left, and several boats tied up to a wharf on their right.

"I 'member this place! It's Sleepy Hollow, where Cousin Malachy got a new shoe for his mule. Cousin Roisin said it was haunted." Teddy pulled back into the trees. "What shall we do?"

190

"I don't know. Let's sit on that rock while we think. Do ye have any berries left?"

"Oh, look, they made my pocket purple," giggled Teddy. "They're squashed, but they still taste good. I'm still hungry, though, Cally."

"That's yer own fault, now, ain't it."

The voice came just before two arms grabbed Cally from behind. A moment later, two hairier arms pinned Teddy. "No!" he screamed, and bit Cousin Malachy's arm as hard as he could just before a bag over his head plunged him into darkness. Cally squirmed and kicked as hard as she could even after Cousin Roisin threw a bag over her too, pulling the drawstring tight at her feet.

"Fight as hard as ye like, ye tramp. If ye wear yerself out, ye'll be easier to manage. That's what ye get for running a way. Did ye really think to escape us? Ye can't escape. Ye belong to us now. So get that idea out of yer heads. The sooner ye accept us as yer new da and mammy, the less ye'll suffer. Now will ye go quietly, or does Malachy have to knock ye out? That's the choice ye have, yer only choice. I ain't going to carry ye kicking and throwing yerself about, Cally."

"Nor I carry ye until ye stop yer caterwauling, Teddy. It'll go better for ye if ye be quiet," said Cousin Malachy.

Once Cally stilled and Teddy quieted, the adults picked them up and threw them over their shoulders. "Ye had to realize we'd know ye would walk south," said Cousin Malachy. "Ye'd have to come out of the woods sooner or later. We've been sitting here just waiting for ye to show up."

"It's too late now for the ferry," said Cousin Roisin. "But I don't want to sleep in this haunted town, in soul I don't. What shall we do, Malachy? Drive on to the next town?"

"I'm knackered, so I am, Roisin. And hungry. There's no reason we can't sleep here. There's no such thing as ghosts. We got the children.

That's what ye wanted. Now it's yer turn to do what I want. I ain't driving any farther today."

Cousins Roisin and Malachy argued until they dumped the children into the wagon. Then they started arguing over whether to eat the last of their bread or try to find a tavern in Sleepy Hollow. Their voices faded as they walked away from the wagon.

Both children burst into tears, and sobbed until a young voice said, "Hush. I want to talk to you and I gotta do it quick."

"Who are ye?" asked Cally.

"I'm Buck. I live here. I was in the woods and heard a woman say, 'They won't escape this time. We'll keep them tied up until we get home to our farm.' She spoke so mean I waited to see what would happen. I saw you come and then I saw them put you in those sacks and carry you here. So tell me quick, do you want to go with them or do you want to be free?"

"Free!" said both children at the same time.

"But we don't know how soon they'll be back," said Cally. "They'll be angry if they see you talking to us."

"I'll watch and see what happens. I'll help you if I can. I have to go now," said Buck.

The evening was long, hot, stuffy and scratchy inside the sacks. Cousins Malachy and Roisin came back from their supper arguing over whether they should spend the money to sleep at the tavern. They offered no food to Cally and Teddy. "After what they did today, they don't deserve to eat," said Cousin Roisin.

"We must at least give them water," insisted Cousin Malachy. "What, do ye want them to die overnight of thirst, after all the trouble it took to get them back? And they need to do their necessaries."

In the end, Malachy and Roisin decided to sleep at the tavern. Malachy drove the wagon to the stable. "No one will know these two sacks are children," he told Roisin on the way. "We'll sleep and then set out for home early tomorrow morning."

"I'll care for your mule," said a voice Cally recognized as Buck's. "My pa's the owner of the tavern. I sleep here in the stable. No one will bother yer things."

"See to it that's true," said Roisin. "Stop fussing, Malachy. Let the lad do his work. We should get as much sleep as we can for the money we're paying. If the ghosts let us, that is."

"There's no such thing as ghosts," said Malachy, his voice fading as he and Roisin walked away.

Buck immediately began loosening the ties on the children's sacks. He had a jug of water ready for them when they were free, red-faced and sweaty.

"Oh, thank you, thank you, Buck," Cally said, to a dark-haired lad who looked about the same age as Charlie. "This water is the best thing I ever tasted. It feels good on my face, too."

"I have a meat pie for you to share. It's leftover from yesterday, but I didn't think you would mind."

"*This* is the best thing I ever tasted," said Teddy. "Buck, will ye get in trouble for helping us?"

"If I do, it will be temporary. Those people might cause a ruckus while they're here, but they won't be staying. My pa knows what I'm doing so that part is all right. I'll stuff the sacks with straw. If they leave early like they said, they might think you're just sleeping in there and drive a while before figuring it out. You'll have all night, I think, to get away from those mean people."

"Why are you helping us?" asked Cally.

"I didn't like the way they were treating you, that's all," said Buck. "Now listen. It's too dark now to walk through the trees. You better follow the road, until it starts to get light. Then you'll have to go back into the trees. If you walk all night, you'll be miles away before those people wake up."

"I'm scared to be out in the open like that," said Cally.

"No one travels that road at night. You'll be fine. And you'll be able to walk much faster than you can in the trees."

"I guess so," said Cally.

"I have something else to tell you. My father is Irish, but my mother is Oneida. I sent a message to her people across the river. They always travel south on Fridays to sell their wares in the big markets. They'll watch for you along the river. They look like me but with skin a little darker."

"I don't understand," said Cally. "Why will they watch for us?"

"To take you with them in their canoe. Here's what you need to do: After you're back in the trees when it first starts to get light, go down to the river when you come to a clearing—another town like this one. Stay there until they come for you. They can take you safely on the river many miles south. Those mean people will never think of that, will they." Buck grinned, so Cally and Teddy smiled back. *But I still don't understand.*

"It's a great plan, don't you think? They will be kind to you. Now you should get started. If you're thirsty, you can drink from the river. If you're hungry, you can eat these cakes." Buck handed each of them a small parcel. "I'm not sending much food with you because it will be too much to carry. And my uncle will have something for you to eat in the morning. He's a good man. You can trust him."

"Thank you, Buck," said Cally. "I hope you won't get in too much trouble."

"Don't worry about that. Go now, as fast as you can. I hope you'll never see those mean people again in your life."

"We hope that too. Goodbye," said Teddy.

"What's a canoe?" Teddy asked Cally as they walked to the road.

"I have no idea."

⋯

The children walked south until they were too tired to walk any more. A grassy place beneath a large tree barely registered in Cally's mind before they fell fast asleep.

⋯

Cally woke to the rustling, cooing, and chirping of birds, her face creased by grass and leaves. A crescent moon hung among a blaze of stars. She eased away from Teddy and walked to the edge of the woods toward the road, the direction she knew to be east. The sky in that direction was lighter.

As she returned to Teddy, she heard the far-away hoot of an owl and the rustling of a small creature in the woods behind her. "Teddy," she whispered. "Wake up. It's time to go."

He moaned and turned over, nestling again into the grass. Cally shook him gently. "Teddy! Remember our plan? We must find the next town and go down by the river while it's still early and the people there are sleeping. We don't know how far away that is."

Teddy sat up, rubbed his eyes, and slowly stood. "I dreamt we were back on the farm in Killeagh. Da was singing to me." Tears welled, and Cally hugged him.

"He's still singing, Teddy. He's singing with the angels now, so he is. If we're quiet enough, we'll be able to hear him. Are ye ready?"

Teddy sniffed, rubbed his nose on his sleeve, and nodded. They walked to the edge of the wood, staying in the grassy space close to the trees so they could duck into safety if anyone came along the road. They heard only the faint lapping of water against the shore on the river side. The owl hooted again, closer this time, and both children jumped. Hardly breathing, they ran until they were tired.

The stars were fading when they came to another clearing. They zigzagged through the trees until they came to the edge near the water. Cally peeked out. No one moved. The village was still quiet.

"I'm thirsty, Cally. Can we go down to the river and get a drink?" whispered Teddy.

"Good idea. We can wash too. Yer face is dirty!"

"Yers is dirtier than mine!"

"Can't be."

"Is too."

"Teddy, hush!"

The children froze. They had reached the river, with no place to hide. A long, thin boat glided silently through the water. Cally made out two people paddling. The boat turned toward the shore. Two tall men, with long dark hair, oddly dressed, left the boat and walked toward them, speaking in a strange language.

"You lost children?" one said.

"No."

"You need help?"

"No." Cally put her arm around Teddy. Close up, the men looked even stranger.

"You hungry?"

"Yes!" Teddy said, before Cally could stop him. The speaker said something, and the other man turned back to the boat.

"We give food."

"Th—thank ye," Cally stuttered.

"You know Buck?" the speaker asked.

"Oh. Yes. You are his people?" Cally was so relieved she sat down, hard, on the sand by the river.

"Buck tell us help you." He opened a packet brought by the other man. "This corn cake. Good. You eat."

"Th—thank ye." Teddy took a huge bite of corn cake. Cally turned hers over and over and took a bite too. *I can't tell if it's salty or sweet.* While the men watched, she ate it all.

"We go Yonkers. Trade there." The man pointed south. "You go?"

"New York City," Teddy said. "We don't know Yonkers."

"New York after Yonkers. We take you Yonkers. We go now."

"Yay! Let's go, Cally! What fun!"

Cally opened her mouth, but Teddy was already running toward the boat. The men shifted some parcels to make space. As they pushed off, the sun rose, sparkling on the water.

"We're flying!" Teddy yelled, stretching his arms as the boat caught the current.

It's fast. Cally gathered her long hair against the breeze. *Faster than we can walk. Roisin and Malachy won't look for us on the river. We're safe.* As the realization hit her, she began to cry. *Thank you, God. Thank you for Buck and his people and this boat.*

Teddy turned around. "Be happy, Cally. This is fun!"

Cally wiped her face on her sleeve. It was fun. Birds flew over the water, even faster than the boat flew. The steady dipping of the men's paddles in the water soothed her. *The men are kind. Buck said they are good. They won't hurt us. I hope, hope, hope Buck won't get in trouble for helping us.*

Teddy's body slumped. Cally felt for her treasure and said out loud, "Three-five-three East Fifty-third Street." *This is my third boat. Cousin Micky's fishing boat, the ship, and now this one.*

⊙≫⊙

"Cally, wake up! We're at Yonkers. Yer face is red."

Cally sat up and touched her face. *It feels hot and hurts.* The boat was tied to a dock. The two strange men weren't there, and their parcels were gone too. She looked around. *Yonkers must be a big, important city. So many boats! So many people and buildings. I wonder how close we are to New York City.*

"The men gave us more corn cakes. Do ye want one?"

"I do, and I'm thirsty."

"I already ate one. I'm thirsty, too, but this water looks dirty. I wonder where all these people find water to drink."

"Ye could ask someone, I guess. And ask how far to New York City. I'll stay here while ye find out. Don't go far, though. Ask the first person ye see."

Cally watched Teddy stop a man in a top hat. *Cities squeeze and confuse me. I told Teddy I would wait here, but I need—oh, good. Teddy is running back. But the man is following him!*

Cally clambered out of the boat and walked down the dock toward them. "It's about fifteen miles to Mr. Nathanael's house. Do we want a ride in his carriage?" Teddy yelled.

Why would he want to give us a ride? I'll ask him. "Why would you give us a ride, sir?"

"My name is Reverend Maguire. As I told yer brother, I work for a Catholic charity that helps children like ye two find new homes. I can take ye to our office in New York, and we can talk about it on the way."

"We don't need a new home, thank ye, sir. We're goin' to our cousins' house in New York City. They're expectin' us." *That was just a wee lie, wasn't it? Mrs. Malcomson said to pretend we're Charlie's sister and brother. At least he speaks Irish so I can understand him.*

"Wouldn't ye like to hear more about it while we drive to the city? I won't make ye go if ye don't want to. But it's hard being small and alone and homeless in New York City, so it is."

"No, thank ye, sir. We're not homeless." *Especially since we got to come all that way in that boat with those strange men.*

"Well, if you change your mind, you can go to the address on this card, and tell them Grady sent you."

"Yes, sir. Thank ye, sir. Put the card in your pocket, Teddy."

The man turned and walked away. "Did he tell ye anythin' about water we can drink?"

"No. He just wanted to give us a ride. Let's start walkin' south, Cally. Maybe we'll get away from all these boats makin' the river dirty."

The children walked a very long way, and still there were buildings and people and boats in the river. Finally, they came to another river, blocking their path. "Look, up there farther into the city. There's a bridge. And across the river it looks like woods. Come on, Cally. Let's go see. I'm so tired, and my leg hurts, and the sun is goin' down."

"This river looks as dirty as the big river."

"It's because we're still in a city. Maybe Yonkers is bigger than New York City. What does the sign say?"

"Har—Har-lem River. Pri—private. Keep out. We can't cross this bridge, Teddy."

"But no one is watchin' us. I think we can climb over that gate."

"Hurry, then, Teddy, before someone comes."

The gate was fancy, with swirly patterns around a big letter "S."

"It's easy, Cally. There's a road, with woods on both sides."

Cally lost her footing and tumbled. She stood and brushed herself off. "Oh, I'm so happy to be back in the woods." The road curved around and up a hill.

"Come on, Cally. I'm goin' down this path into the trees."

"It's getting dark in here."

"Cally, come quick! There's water comin' out of that hill! It made a little pool. Mmm, so good. Hurry up, Cally."

Cally plunged her whole head into the bubbling water. *Oh, that feels wonderful!* She took a long drink, and then, laughing, flicked a handful of water into Teddy's face. He splashed her back. By the time they tired of the game, they were both thoroughly wet. They flopped onto the grass side by side, breathing deeply. Sunset colors faded in the sky. *The world seems still. I feel quiet inside too.* A scent of honeysuckle gave

Cally a deep sense of yearning.

"Let's explore some more. The path keeps goin', Cally."

She scrambled to her feet. Teddy disappeared. "Teddy, where are you?"

"Cally, I found a cave! It's dry! We can sleep here tonight."

"But what if animals use this cave—"

"What if they don't? I'm goin' to sleep. I'm hungry, but more tired. My leg hurts. Sing me a song, Cally."

"Just one. I'm tired too." Cally rubbed his leg. She heard Teddy's light, whiffling snore before she finished her song. Finding a comfortable contour for her body on the cave floor, she fingered her treasure through the cloth of her dress. *Three-five-three East Fifty-third Street...*

CℰℬO

Nathanael sat on his porch swing singing an off-key tune to Jimmy, waiting for James to bring the brougham. *How grand to hear the famous Mr. Paderewski play in the new concert hall!*

Tobias wandered out holding the hand of his brother Ben, faces scrubbed, hair still wet.

"Father, look! Is that—"

Nathanael leaped to his feet, thrust Jimmy into Tobias's arms, and ran down the street, his arms open wide.

Cally and Teddy were filthy. It didn't matter.

CHAPTER 21

CHARLIE

Carnegie Hall, Saturday evening, July 18, 1891

CHARLIE PACED BACKSTAGE. *Will Mr. Paderewski even call me? He's already played three encores. Oh, but I've never imagined such glorious playing as I heard tonight!* His thoughts were interrupted by a stagehand who gestured him through the curtain. *Here we go . . . I hope I don't embarrass Mr. Paderewski.*

Charlie bowed to the audience as he heard Mr. Paderewski say, "My young friend Charles Malcomson will play with me Mozart's Sonata in D for Two Pianos. This will be the last encore of the evening."

Charlie knew which piano was his—the one wheeled in after Mr. Paderewski completed his scheduled program. That had been his cue to walk backstage. He flipped the tails of his tuxedo behind him as he sat on the bench, then looked across to catch Mr. Paderewski's nod.

After that, nothing mattered but the music: twenty-four minutes of concentrated collaboration.

೮ತ೩೦

Charlie felt himself flush as the applause went on and on and on. Eyebrows raised, he looked sideways at Mr. Paderewski. *Enough is enough, don't you think, sir?* He moved his eyes and angled his body slightly toward the stage exit but Mr. Paderewski grasped his hand and lifted his arm high. The applause strengthened, and Charlie bowed once more. Finally, Mr. Paderewski began walking toward the exit and Charlie gratefully followed.

"Water, sirs?" *Nothing has ever tasted so good. I'm exhausted—and I only played one piece, not a whole concert!*

"You did well, Charles. I'm proud of you. Don't worry, dealing with the audience gets easier with time and experience. Don't let it discourage you from walking into the bright future you have as a concert pianist. Here, let's sit for a minute before we face our admirers." Mr. Paderewski laughed, and Charlie grinned despite the tension he still felt. *He has such a gift for putting people at ease—including me!*

"I have a question for you, Charles. Mr. Tretbar just informed me he scheduled a concert in Albany my one free day next week, Tuesday. Would you like to go with me? We could play the Two Pianos sonata not as an encore, but as part of the program."

"I—I don't know. I would like to, of course, but I'll have to ask my parents. I don't remember their plans for next week. Can I leave a message for you at the hotel?"

"Of course. And don't feel pressure about this—assure your parents it's completely optional, not meant to upset family plans. Now, do you see that anxious Carnegie Hall official hovering in the doorway? Shall we make him happy by greeting the folks waiting for us?"

"You mean for you, don't you, sir?"

"I mean for us. You can't play so beautifully and then escape without some deference to those who cheered so loudly for you! Stick by me, smile, shake hands, and give short responses to any questions they ask. You'll be fine."

Mr. Paderewski steered Charlie through the door. As they emerged into the reception area, patrons pressed forward, clapping and cheering. Charlie's head swiveled. Finally, he located his family in a far corner. He caught Mummy's encouraging smile and noticed that James stood out from the crowd. After that he had no time to do anything but smile, shake hands, and give brief, courteous answers to the many questions thrown at him. Staying by Mr. Paderewski proved impossible.

When Charlie thought he could not bear it one more minute, the lights dimmed briefly, and the Carnegie Hall gentleman who had escorted them from backstage announced the hall would close in ten minutes. The crowd dispersed, and Charlie once again looked for his parents. They waited in the same corner, alone. *The others must have taken the children to bed.*

As Charlie made his way through the lingerers to his parents, he looked for Mr. Paderewski. *He must have escaped already. Good.*

"Our carriage is waiting, son. Are you ready to go?"

"Oh yes, please, Father. I've been ready for a long time!"

"We have news for you, Charlie. We'll tell you on the way to the hotel." Mummy's eyes sparkled, but Charlie was too spent to imagine what she might mean. He followed her into the night and into the carriage, the horses held quiet by the coachman.

"What is it, Mummy? Did Mr. Paderewski talk to you already about Albany?"

"No, son. It's about Cally and Teddy."

Charlie caught his breath. "They've been found?"

Mummy laughed. "Yes! Well, not exactly. They escaped from their cousins and made their way alone back to Nathanael's house. Can you believe that? What bright and resourceful children they are! We don't know the details yet, because they arrived just as the family was ready to leave for the concert. Nathanael and Sarah stayed home with them and their two little ones, leaving James to escort their other children. We'll go there tomorrow to learn what happened. But what were you saying about Albany?"

"Mr. Paderewski invited me to play with him there next Tuesday evening."

"Perfect! That's the day we plan to travel to Albany. If you want to play, we'll invite my O'Connell cousins. The next day we'll float on the Erie Canal to Schenectady and then catch the train to Niagara Falls."

Charlie let out the breath he hadn't realized he was holding. "Thank you, Mummy. I learn so much from hearing Mr. Paderewski perform. And playing with him is a great honor."

"It certainly is, son," Father inserted. "What a magnificent concert! I am proud he chose to end his performance with you, Charles. I could feel the audience's pleasure. Congratulations!"

Charlie glowed. "Thank you, Father." *Father's words make me happier than all the applause from that huge audience.*

☙

"Good morning, son. I'm glad you were able to sleep in after such a late and exciting and exhausting night."

Charlie yawned. "Good morning, Mummy. I'm still tired, but I couldn't sleep any longer. And I want breakfast."

"Charlie, let's talk about today. After early mass at St. Patrick's Cathedral, you have three options. Daniel, Meghan, Margaret, Percy, James, and all the children will go to the menagerie and a picnic in Central Park. Your father and I will visit Nathanael and Sarah to learn what happened to Cally and Teddy. If you need time to yourself you may return to the hotel, though since it's the Sabbath, you won't be permitted to practice. Nathanael's children must be home in time for their Quaker Meeting at 4:00, so we'll all return to the Windsor by then to rest."

"Oh, Mummy, how can I choose? I didn't see the menagerie when I was here before. More than four hundred animals! But I want to know what happened to Cally and Teddy. And a quiet day sounds delightful."

"You have until the end of mass to decide, son. We'll all go together from the church to Nathanael's house, and the menagerie expedition will leave from there. The hotel is packing plenty of food for the picnic, so you needn't worry about that."

"Mummy, I bet Cally and Teddy would love the menagerie and picnic. You can tell me what Nathanael and Sarah say. I'll rest this afternoon after we get back."

"I'm not sure Cally and Teddy will be ready for an outing, but you can go yourself in any case. It's time to leave for mass. Won't it be splendid to worship God at St. Patrick's? I plan to light a candle for Cally and Teddy, asking God for wisdom."

 CஜOJ

Charlie sat with Mummy and Father across the room from Cousin Nathanel and Cousin Sarah, with Cally and Teddy wedged between them on the couch.

"I'm sorry we missed Mr. Paderewski's concert last night, but James exchanged our tickets for tomorrow night. The maestro will play almost every night for the next week, did thee know that, Charlie? My children told me thee played with Mr. Paderewski at the end, and the crowd was appreciative."

"Yes, sir. Thank you, sir. I'm glad you will hear him play."

"And Mr. Paderewski has invited Charlie to play with him at a concert newly scheduled for Tuesday evening in Albany," Mummy offered. "You missed last night for the best of reasons. We want to hear all about your adventures, Cally and Teddy."

Nathanael and Sarah looked at each other and down at the children. "Cally and Teddy have been reticent to talk, Cathleen. Their journey in both directions was difficult. I surmise they traveled almost thirty miles to return to us, all the time fearing recapture. They are still afraid their cousins will return and snatch them again. I believe their safety must be our primary concern today. As the children feel safer, they may then be able to tell us more about what happened to them."

Charlie watched the children's eyes track this conversation, but even Teddy was silent. He sat gripping his sister's hand, his body tense. *They've borrowed Quaker clothes from Cousin Nathanael's children, minus the girls' cap. Cally looks sunburned. I wonder how Teddy made that journey with his bum leg. It's too bad he missed his appointment with the bone doctor. I wonder if Father can make another one.*

"What do you suggest, Nathanael?"

"Much as we love them, Sarah and I believe Cally and Teddy cannot stay here. Logically, Roisin and Malachy will look for them here first. Could they stay with thee at the hotel, and travel to Albany and Niagara Falls with thee? Perhaps by then Roisin and Malachy may give up pursuing the children."

Father glanced at Mummy, who nodded. "I believe that makes sense, Nathanael. I still think it best for the children to return to their loving relatives in Ireland."

Cally stiffened, while Teddy cried out, "Yes!" before his sister pinched him. "Ow!"

Father continued. "What do you think, Cathleen? Can we care for them until the *Lion III* is ready for our return voyage?"

Mummy gazed at Cally, who looked up at her briefly and then down to her lap, fingering her white apron.

"I think Cally and Teddy must have a voice in this decision, Peter. They have shown an amazing ability to fend for themselves. I can't imagine Martin and Molly accomplishing what they have done in the last two days. I promised Cally we will not make them do anything they don't want to do, and I mean to uphold that promise."

Cally's eyes were fixed on Mummy during this speech. *Ah, a sign of life in her face, for the first time since we walked in.*

Father frowned and opened his mouth, but Mummy put her hand on his arm. "May I ask the children a question, Peter?"

Father looked at her for a moment, then gave a small nod. *He's used to being in charge. This is hard for him.* Charlie sat back, surprised at this insight into Father's world.

"Cally and Teddy, remember when we talked together on the ship? I told you we wouldn't make you do anything you don't want to do."

Cally nodded slowly, while Teddy said, "Yes! And I want to go home to Killeagh, but Cally doesn't want to. And she says we have to stay together."

"Well, you don't have to decide yet. It's still two weeks until the ship will sail back to Waterford. But we need to know how to care for you in the meantime. We want you to be safe."

Teddy pulled back, sliding his hand around Nathanael's arm. Sarah hugged Cally against her. "What are thee thinking, Cally? Can you tell us?"

Tears filled Cally's eyes and she rubbed them away with her free hand, never letting go of Teddy's. "I—I'm afraid Cousin Roisin will find us again." Cally's whisper was so soft Charlie had to lean forward to hear it.

"I don't want to be hit on the head and put back in that sack." Teddy cried, then sobbed, then wailed. Nathanael pulled him into his lap, hugging him until the tempest eased. Cally pressed her hands into her eyes. *She wants to cry but won't let herself. She doesn't know whether she can trust us. Those people must have treated her and Teddy terribly.*

No one said anything for a while. Then Mummy spoke again. "Cally, do you think you would feel safer going with us to the hotel? I don't think your cousins can find you there. They don't know where we're staying."

"Wh—what's a hotel?"

"It's a big building with many rooms where people pay to sleep when they're away from their homes."

Sarah said, "If thy cousins come here again, Cally and Teddy, we will not tell them where thee are. We will just encourage them to return to their farm." She turned to Mummy. "The children would stay with thee at the hotel for two days, before thy family leaves for Albany?"

"But I heard Cousin Roisin say their farm is near Albany," Cally blurted, then pulled back against Sarah.

"That is important for us to know. Thank you, Callandra." Father said gently.

"That's right. It's north. They were goin' to cross the river on the ferry at Peekskill. Cousin Roisin didn't want to sleep there. She kept tellin' Cousin Malachy to hurry up. But we jumped out of the wagon." Teddy spoke in a rush, his eyes flooding again.

"You were very brave, Teddy. That must have hurt."

"Yes, ma'am, Mrs. Malcomson. It hurt a lot. My head still hurts. And my leg. We walked such a long way. But those strange men took us in their boat to—what was that place, Cally?"

"Yonkers."

"Yes. We saw them early in the mornin' near the haunted place, and they took us in their long skinny boat. The sun was shinin' on the water. But Cally and I both fell asleep. We had to walk in the woods at night so no one would find us. I was scared."

"Thee are both very brave. I am so thankful thee came back to us." Cousin Nathanael wiped a tear and settled Teddy more firmly in his lap, massaging his sore leg.

"Father, do you think we could make another appointment for Teddy tomorrow?"

"I can try. The doctor was not pleased that we cancelled, after he rearranged his schedule for us. I will explain the circumstances, but this may not be possible, son."

Mummy turned to Cally. "Can we make one decision at a time, Cally? The first decision is whether you want to stay at the hotel with us for the next two days. I know it will be strange for you, but I think it would be safer than staying here."

Cally looked at Teddy, then at Nathanael, then Sarah, then Father, then back to Mummy. *I wonder what thoughts are going through her head.* She gave a big sigh, and said in a small voice, "We'll go to the hotel." Then she could no longer hold back her tears. Sarah gathered her in, while Charlie spoke to Mummy.

"I want to go with them back to the hotel. I can see the menagerie another time."

"You are their first friend from our family, Charlie. I imagine they will both want a long nap after lunch. It will be good for them to find you there when they wake up."

Sarah spoke. "Cathleen, there is the question of clothes for the children. They are welcome to these clothes of Ben's and Florry's, but they may be more comfortable in something familiar. The clothes they wore on their long journey were not salvageable. I could guess some of their story from what I saw and smelled on those garments."

"You are so sensible, Sarah. I hadn't thought of that. They could use Martin and Molly's clothes, I suppose, but it would be nice for them to have their own. Do they not have another set of clothes they could change into now?"

"They do, but when I took them from their bag, I realized they probably had not been washed since they set out on their journey from Ireland. I washed them this morning, but they are still drying. I didn't want to put the clothes out on the line as an advertisement of their presence with us, so they are draped on chairs in the dining room."

"I see. Well, how about this. If they can use Florry's and Ben's clothes for today, I will go to the shops when they open tomorrow morning. I'm used to buying clothes for Martin and Molly, whose clothes fit Cally and Teddy well, so I know their sizes."

"Why don't thee share our luncheon, then, before thee take the children to the hotel for their naps. I'll shift their clothes to Nathanael's study to make space for us to sit. I have soup simmering, and fresh bread. We can eat in just a few minutes."

"The aromas from your kitchen make your home so inviting, Sarah. Thank you."

Father stood and stretched. "I'll take those few minutes to walk around the block. Would you like to go with me, Charles? Nathanael? I'm not used to sitting so much. Give us a whistle, Sarah, if the cousins show up in the next ten minutes. I almost wish they would. I relish the thought of giving them a piece of my mind."

Sarah laughed. "Ah, Charlie hath told thee about my whistle! A useful thing it is, with so many children. Go on then. We'll eat when thee three return. Will thee help me set the table, Cally? Teddy, I know thee likes to play with Ben's wooden animals."

I made the right choice, but I still hope to see the menagerie someday! While Cally and Teddy nap, I'll read that Tom Sawyer book Mummy bought me.

CHAPTER 22

CALLY

Train to Albany, NY, Tuesday, July 21, 1891

THIS IS SO DIFFERENT from our last trip north. Cally stared out the train window as fields, houses, and trees flicked by. *I feel safer than if we were going by road. But will Cousin Roisin see us in Albany? She never came to Mr. Nathanael's house in New York. Maybe she's given up on finding us. I hope so, but I just don't know . . .*

Cally sighed and opened the book Charlie had loaned her, *The Blue Fairy Book. I didn't tell him I have the Red Fairy Book. I wonder if he knows somehow.* She soon lost herself in "The Bronze Ring." She was starting "Prince Hyacinth and the Dear Little Princess" when Mrs. Malcomson gently touched her shoulder and said "We're almost to the station, Cally! Albany is one of New York's most important cities. I hope you will enjoy our stay there."

"Thank you, Mrs. Malcomson."

"My cousin John will meet us at the station. I played with him when we were children, but he emigrated to America as a young man and married an American lass. I wonder how much he's changed since we used to call each other Johnny and Cathy?"

Cally only half-listened to Mrs. Malcomson as she watched the city

211

emerge from the farmlands. *I don't want to meet any more cousins. My mammy and Cousin Roisin were friends but she hurt me and Teddy. What if Mrs. Malcomson's cousin is like that too?*

Cally startled as she realized Mrs. Malcomson had asked her a question. "Par—pardon me, ma'am?"

"Your thoughts were far away. I wondered what you were thinking about."

"About the stories in this book Charlie let me read. Do ye think in real life there's a happy ever after? Seems I just know somethin' else will go wrong."

"Life can bring us many challenges, Cally, you're right about that. Have you ever thought of asking God to protect you and provide for you?"

"That sounds like something Aisling would say."

"Aisling is your aunt in Killeagh?"

"She's married to my uncle, yes."

"So, what would you answer if Aisling asked you that question?"

Cally blushed. "I wouldn't answer, ma'am. I would turn away or talk about somethin' else."

"Ah, so it's not just with us you're evasive."

"Evasive, ma'am?"

"Evasive means you avoid questions or ideas you don't want to talk about. You are especially evasive about your own thoughts and worries, Cally."

"Yes, ma'am. Oh, the train is slowin' down. We're pullin' into the station!"

Mrs. Malcomson laughed. "See what I mean? What you just did, Cally. That's being evasive. But I won't pressure you." Mrs. Malcomson was quiet, and Cally turned her head from the window to glance at her face. She looked serious.

"I do want to say this, Cally. Life is too hard for any of us to handle by ourselves. We all need help. I do, and you do too."

"Ye need help, ma'am?"

"Oh yes. I ask for help all the time, from my husband and children, from my friends, and especially from God. That's the only way I know to make it through the hard things."

"There are hard things in yer life? To me yer life seems easy and perfect."

"Right now, we need to get off the train. But let's talk more about this another time, Cally, all right? I'll tell you some of the hard things in my life. And then, if you like, you can tell me some of the hard things in your life.

"Yes, ma'am."

"My cousin Johnny used to be funny and make me laugh. I wonder if he's still like that."

The rest of the family appeared, lurching down the aisle from a snack in the dining car. They laughed and talked, even Teddy. Cally felt something inside her relax when she saw him. *I don't like him out of my sight, so I don't. Da told me, take care of Teddy. How can I take care of him when I can't see him? But he doesn't like being stuck to me all the time. I wonder if he'll run away someday. Like we ran away from Cousin Roisin.*

Cally tucked that worry away while she accepted their bag from Charlie and shared its weight with Teddy. With her other hand, she smoothed the new dress Mrs. Malcomson had bought for her, savoring its softness and its beautiful green print. She glanced at Teddy as they walked slowly behind Charlie toward the exit. *Mrs. Malcomson found a blue shirt exactly the color of his eyes. It makes me feel happy.*

A loud laugh and booming voice startled Cally as they climbed carefully down the steps from the train. Without thinking, she slid her hand into Mrs. Malcomson's as she looked up to see the source of this rowdy cheerfulness. As the man met and hugged each family member in turn, she studied his broad, happy face and twinkly eyes. "We are so delighted all ye are here to visit us! We've been lookin' forward to this day ever since we received Cathy's letter! Cathy, there ye are! It's been much too long, cousin! Let me look at ye. Why ye've grown up even more beautiful than I remember! And that's sayin' a great deal. Ye've done well, Peter! And who is this? More *weans*, Cathy, at yer age?"

Mrs. Malcomson laughed. "May I present our friends Cally and Teddy. They have joined our family for these vacation days. Children, this is my cousin Johnny O'Connell. Or should I say John now?"

"No, no. Everyone calls me Johnny. I guess some people never grow up, do they, Cathy? Or are ye Cathleen now?"

"Well, yes. Most people call me Cathleen. But I'll make an exception for you. Oh, it's good to see you. How is Amelia? And your children?"

"They're all anxiously waiting at home, all but my big lad Henry. Now let me get a count. I ordered two carriages in addition to my own. Will that be enough? Could the little ones sit on laps, perhaps? I've sent Henry to fetch yer luggage."

"We are six adults and five children and Charlie. An even dozen. I think we'll have to count Charlie as an adult, don't you? Unless you want him on your lap, Johnny."

Cally looked curiously at Mrs. Malcomson. *I've never heard her talk that way. She must remember being with her cousin when they were weans.*

Cousin Johnny laughed, and Cally saw heads turn their direction as the big man pushed his way through the crowded station to the street, talking all the way. "Well done, Henry, my lad. If it weren't fer the luggage we wouldn't even need these carriages, we could just walk. Ye'll see how close we live. Come meet yer Irish relatives, son, the best of the best they are. Malcomsons, this is my Henry, a sound man, so he is. Henry, we'll wait fer introductions of this crowd until they all get to our house fer supper, so we can do it but once fer ye and yer mother and

214

the young 'uns at the same time. Now, folks, don't worry about gettin' into the carriage that has yer own bags in it, since they're all goin' to the same place. May I help ye with yers, little lassie? I see yer worried about gettin' separated from it, so let's put it right here and ye right there on top of Charlie, and ye can keep an eye to it all the way to the hotel. All right, is everyone ready? Off we go! Now Cathy, I'll have the carriages return to the hotel in one hour to fetch ye all fer supper. Henry will come with our carriage and guide ye to our house. What's that ye say?"

"Charlie must go right away to the Cathedral of the Immaculate Conception to meet Mr. Paderewski and prepare for the concert tonight."

"Go way on out of that. Comes from me flaffing too much. Out of this carriage, everyone. Charlie, my man, why did ye have to get in first? Lassie, ye must find another lap to sit on. Henry, go fetch that brougham there. We'll have to send ye separately, Charlie, since ye are goin' the opposite direction. We'll see ye at the concert tonight. Fair play to ye. What's that? Speak up, lad."

"I'm sorry, sir, but I need that black bag there."

"What, ye have a miniature piano all tucked away in there? It doesn't feel quite heavy enough to be a piano, but who knows what they're inventin' these days in New York City."

Cally giggled at the droll expression on Cousin Johnny's face as he hefted Charlie's bag. "All right then, we'll see ye this evenin', lad, and we're lookin' forward to it. Sorry ye'll miss our supper. Tell Mr. Paderewski Johnny says to buy ye somethin' nourishin'. Now, Cathy, any more convolutions or complications? We'll follow Henry to the Delavan House right here on Broadway. The hotel's not a mile from the Cathedral, so if it's a fine night some of ye might enjoy walkin' back after the concert. It's just a bit longer walk to our house."

Does he ever stop talkin'? And laughin?

☌

I need to relieve myself. I should have asked at the house, but I was too embarrassed. I wonder how long the concert will take. Cally looked around. Mrs. Malcomson, beside her, was caught up in the music. Captain Malcomson kept time, drumming his fingers on his knee. Beyond him sat the rest of the Malcomson family.

On her other side, Cousin Amelia struggled to keep her eyes open. From time to time, she gave up and let her head sag, her light snore blending with the notes of the piano. Beside her, Cousin Henry and his brother and sisters, and their da, quiet for once, all had their eyes fixed on Mr. Paderewski.

What shall I do? I'm going to wet myself! Wearing Molly's pretty dress, too. Oh, why didn't I stay at the hotel with Teddy and Sally and her mother? Why did Mrs. Malcomson sit in the middle and pull me in with her? What shall I do?

To her immense relief, Mr. Paderewski stopped playing, and the crowd stirred. "It's intermission, Cally. Do you want to go with me to the ladies' room?"

"Oh yes, please, ma'am."

"Let's hurry and see if we can get toward the front of the line. Follow me so you don't get lost."

Cally felt even worse standing up. *I can't wait in any line at all. Oh, there's a door. I wonder if it goes outside.* She tested the door, and it opened to a light breeze. She hurried down the steps and behind a tree. *Oh, what a relief.*

She stayed for a moment savoring the thankfulness that swept through her. When she walked back around the tree, though, she stared, frozen, into the startled face of Cousin Roisin. As Roisin moved to grab her, Cally ducked under her arm, scampered up the steps and through the door into the safety of the crowded church. Lightheaded, she weaved her way through the crowd to the row where Mrs. Amelia still dozed, scooted in, and scrunched down on the floor in front of her seat, panting.

As her fright eased, tears came, silent tears coursing down her cheeks. Her whole body trembled. She tucked her head down and tried to still her wildly beating heart.

"Cally, there you are! I've been looking everywhere for you. What happened? What's wrong?"

"Cou—cousin Roisin. She's here!" was all Cally could manage. She put her head down again and wept as the intermission ended, the row filled with people, and Mr. Paderewski introduced the sonata he would play with Charlie. Cally knew Mrs. Malcomson was whispering with Captain Malcomson but couldn't hear what they were saying. Too frightened to rise and take her seat, she huddled there, Mrs. Malcomson's hand on her head, until the piece was over. As applause exploded over her head, she looked up and saw Mrs. Malcomson speaking, but couldn't hear her words. When the clapping lessened, Captain Malcomson leaned over.

"Callandra, we won't let anything happen to you. I promise. I want you to sit in your seat. I want Roisin to see you, so she will come, and I can talk to her. I will explain we are taking you and Teddy back to your uncle and aunt in Ireland, who have a clear prior claim on you. I will tell her that tomorrow I will send Dugan and Aisling a telegram to let them know briefly what has happened and when to expect you in Killeagh. And I will tell Roisin there will be consequences for her and Malachy if they try to oppose this plan or harm you in any way."

Captain Malcomson sat back and looked toward the stage. Mrs. Malcomson said, "Come, sweetheart. Sit with me and let the music soothe you. You are safe. I promise."

Piano music swelled again, filling the cathedral. Still shaking, Cally carefully stood and let Mrs. Malcomson pull her into her lap. Her arms and the music were so warm and comforting that Cally relaxed. Through half-closed eyes she noticed Charlie slip in beside his father, who smiled and shook his hand. Cally suddenly missed her own father so much she was breathless. Mrs. Malcomson reached for a handkerchief and Cally pressed it to her eyes, helpless to stop her tears.

After that, she slept. She only knew she had slept because she woke up. All around her, people were standing and clapping. "Charles, Charles, we want an encore by Charles."

"Do you have a piece you could play, if Mr. Paderewski calls for you, Charles?" Captain Malcomson wasn't even trying to speak quietly. He would not have been heard over the roar. Charlie nodded, his eyes fixed on Mr. Paderewski. The maestro raised his hand, asking for silence. "Charles, are you willing to play?" he asked.

Cally watched as Charlie stood, made his way past his family to the aisle, and walked to the front of the room. *I don't understand what is happening, but it seems important.* Charlie bowed to the audience, sat at the piano, raised his hands over the keys, and began to play. Not European classics, but Irish lullabies, the music Da had sung to her for as long as she could remember. "I see your broken heart. I know your grief and your fear," the melodies seemed to say. "You are not alone. Don't be afraid. Open your heart to peace and safety."

Gradually, Cally noticed others weeping. She sat up on Mrs. Malcomson's lap to look around. All through the great cathedral people were crying. And then someone began to sing, and others took up the melody, and soon people were standing, arms around each other, swaying and singing as Charlie led them from one Irish song to another. Finally, he modulated into Cally's favorite of them all, the one Da had sung to her and Teddy so often, *Sure a little bit of heaven fell from out the sky one day . . .*

Cally mouthed the familiar words and thought *Sure a little bit of Da fell from out the sky today.* For that moment, she was not afraid.

⊗⧉⊘

Cousin Roisin and Cousin Malachy stood one at each end of their aisle filled with Malcomsons and O'Connells. Captain Malcomson sat calmly, waiting, so everyone else sat down too. When the crowds around them had dispersed, murmuring their hopes of greeting Mr. Paderewski and Charles at the door, Captain Malcomson spoke, loud enough for both Cousin Roisin and Cousin Malachy to hear.

"Choose one side or the other, and stand together, Roisin and Malachy. You must free our families to take their children home to bed. Cathleen and I and Callandra will sit here until that is accomplished. Then we will talk."

Cally felt a thrill go through her. *This strong, important man is protecting me.* She looked into Mrs. Malcomson's eyes as she said again, "You're safe, Cally."

Cally stilled. *This time, I'm not alone. This must be what Mrs. Malcomson meant on the train. It's like when Da went with me to talk to Miss Hilda.* Cally sat as calmly as Captain Malcomson beside her and Mrs. Malcomson hugging her.

When Captain Malcomson began to talk, Cally was so focused on Cousin Roisin's face she scarcely heard the conversation. She watched it turn red and her mouth open, but what she yelled didn't seem to matter. She saw Cousin Roisin grab her husband's arm and point at her. She saw Malachy shake his head, remove Roisin's hand from his arm, and walk away. She felt more than saw Roisin yell some more, and then stomp after Malachy.

The three of them sat quietly a little longer. A man in a white robe approached them from the front of the cathedral. *He's like Father Michaelson.* The man stopped at the end of their row, gave a little bow, and asked whether he could be of any help. Captain Malcomson stood and walked down the row toward him. Cally heard him say all was well and thank him for allowing the cathedral to be used for the concert.

"Amazing. I've never heard anything like Mr. Paderewski's playing. And what that lad Charles did at the end—why it was a touch of heaven for this Irish congregation."

"Thank you. I will tell him. Your words will encourage him."

"Then you are—you must be his parents. What an honor to know you, sir."

"The honor is mine, Father—I'm sorry, I didn't catch your name."

"Father Callahan, Mr. Malcomson. I will bid you good night. I'm sure both your son and this wee lassie are longing for their beds."

"Good night, Father Callahan. And thank you."

Mrs. Malcomson stirred, set Cally gently on her feet, and gathered her wrap and her clutch. Without another word, they walked past stained-glass windows and stations of the cross and out the door of the cathedral. Beside Charlie, another white-robed man waited to lock the door.

The four of them climbed into the waiting carriage, rode to the hotel, entered their rooms, prepared for bed, and lay their heads on their pillows, all without saying one word. *Every one of us is too tired to speak. Or maybe we need a break from Cousin Johnny's constant chatter.*

Cally felt for Teddy, and then remembered he had his own bed, across the room from hers. Yet one more strangeness in this day of new experiences. *How can I sleep all by myself?*

○ॐ○

Cally dreamed of building a castle in the sand with Da at Youghal while Shep and Teddy chased and splashed each other at the edge of the waves. She lay savoring every detail, the delight of Da's laughter, the star shell he always placed at the top, the sun warm on her back, until she heard an uneven gait. Teddy flung himself on top of her, yelling "Wake up, sleepyhead!"

Suddenly Cally understood an emotion at the edge of her dream that had confused her. *Captain Malcomson said he would take me and Teddy back to Killeagh.*

"Teddy, stop tickling! We need to talk."

"No, ye need to get dressed. Everyone else is ready to go."

"Go where?"

"Don't ye 'member? We're floating on a boat down the Weary Canal to see where Nagra falls. Hurry up! They're all waiting downstairs."

Cally laughed. "Teddy, they're only floating to Sheneckady. Then they're taking the train."

"Why did ye say 'they'? We're going too! Hurry up and get dressed!"

"I'll get dressed, but listen carefully. We're not going on the boat."

"But Cally—"

"Hush. Pay attention. The Malcomsons are good and want to help us. But they'll make us go back to Killeagh, and we can't. Da meant for us to live here. He made us say goodbye to Uncle Dugan, Aisling, Cousin Micky, Louise, Shep, and Simon, and he brought us all the way here on that big ship."

"Not all the way," said Teddy. His voice trembled.

"Not all the way," Cally agreed. "But don't ye see, Teddy? The best way we can remember Da is to live here. Goin' back to Ireland would be goin' backwards, away from what Da wanted for us."

Cally paused to fasten the new shoes Mrs. Malcomson had bought for her, then turned so Teddy could button her dress up the back.

"Do ye understand, Teddy? Now listen. This is our chance to get away. Yesterday I saw a back staircase and a back door. We can go out that way. Are all yer things in our bag? Close it then while I use the bathroom."

"What about Da's bag?"

"We have to leave it. It's too big fer us to carry."

"But Cally, where will we go? What will we do? What if Cousin Roisin—"

"We don't have to worry about her or Cousin Malachy anymore. I'll tell ye why, but first we need to get out. Stick yer head out in the hallway. Is anyone there?"

"No. But—"

"Hush, Teddy. Walk as quietly as ye can. No, not that way. Down to the door at the other end. No more talkin' now til we get out of the hotel."

"But—"

Cally laid a finger against her lips, looking at him sternly. He screwed up his face, but he followed her down the long hallway, through the door, and down four flights of stairs. The door at the bottom led to an alley with garbage bins lined up along it. They stopped, not knowing which way to go. A barking dog raced in front of them chasing a cat. Cally watched them go by, then turned the other way.

At the end of the big hotel building, were other buildings, and then a street. To their left Cally saw the river. *That's the street in front of the hotel.* She pulled Teddy the opposite direction into a stream of people. *It will be harder for them to find us in the middle of a crowd.*

They walked for a long time, twisting and turning through the city. Cally chose the busiest streets, keeping a close eye on the sun. She knew which way would lead them back to the hotel and the river and turned always west, away from where the Malcomsons might be looking for them.

Without warning, Teddy sat down, pulling their bag and Cally down with him. "I'm not walking one more step. I *want* them to find us, Cally. I *want* to go back to Uncle Dugan and Aisling. I think yer wrong. Da wouldn't want us to be alone. He 'spected to be with us in this country. I think there's some other reason ye don't want to go back to Killeagh, because this story ye told me isn't right."

Cally stared at him. *How did Teddy learn to think and talk like that? How can he suddenly sound so old? Am I wrong?*

She sat beside him, confused. *He's right about everything. Da wouldn't want us to be alone. He didn't know Cousin Roisin and Cousin Malachy would be mean and kidnap us. Uncle Dugan and Aisling love us. But—no. No. I can't. The faeries will know I'm back and they'll hurt the people I love.*

Cally imagined seeing Uncle Dugan and Aisling. *They'll look at me and know Da died because he stood up to the Dubh Sidhe for me. They won't love me anymore. I couldn't bear it. Maybe they already know it was my fault Mammy and the babby died. Mammy even knew it would happen.*

Cally cringed inside as she remembered Mammy's voice, "Callandra Mae Donnelly, ye'll be the death of me yet." *And I wished the babby would die, so Mammy wouldn't love her more than me. And that's exactly what happened. And Teddy's accident was my fault, too. I wasn't paying attention, and the faeries noticed.*

People swirled around them on the sidewalk, hurrying on unknown errands. Teddy sniffed and rubbed his eyes, trying not to cry.

Aisling will still love Teddy, but she won't love me, so neither will Uncle Dugan. I can't bear that, I can't. I can't go back. And Teddy must stay with me. Da said, "Take care of Teddy." That's the clearest, strongest thing he ever said to me. I can't let him down.

Teddy kicked pebbles in the road, sniffling and waiting. *He's waiting for me to see he is right, and I'm wrong. But I'm not wrong.* She stood up.

"No, Teddy. There's no way back for us. We have to go forward, not backward."

Teddy stopped kicking and looked at her in a way she had never seen before, his face hard, his voice intense. "Sure, just like we ran away from Cousin Roisin and from the Malcomsons, I can run away from ye too, Cally, so I can. Someday I will."

He stopped and took a deep breath. "Someday I'll go back to

Killeagh, so I will. Going home isn't backwards. It's forwards. Ye can make me go with ye now, but ye can't keep me forever. I'm already bigger than ye are. Ye won't be the boss of me much longer. Someday I'll sail back."

Cally stared at her brother in confusion, tears filling her eyes. *What has become of him? I don't know who he is anymore. What will I do if he leaves me?*

Cally nearly crumpled. *It would be so easy, to let the Malcomsons be in charge, and then let Uncle Dugan and Aisling be in charge. So easy to pretend I'm just a wean.*

Cally turned away from Teddy and paced to the end of the block. *It would be easy in one way, but hard in another. The Malcomsons and Uncle Dugan and Aisling think I'm a good girl. But I'm not a good girl. I make bad things happen to the people I love. I must stay away from them. I don't know where Teddy and I will go or what we'll do, but I know we can't go back.*

Cally took a deep breath, blew it out, clenched her fists, and set her face into a stern expression. She walked back to Teddy, pulled him to his feet, picked up their bag, and said in a voice as intense as his, "We can't go back. There's nothing more to say."

Teddy pulled away, leaving her to carry their bag alone. He muttered and stomped and kicked the ground. But he followed her.

CHAPTER 23

UNCROSSING

Albany, Wednesday, July 22, 1891

"I AGREE, DANIEL! Charlie was fantastic last night." Percy turned to Charlie. "Who knew I was marrying into the family of a prodigy?"

"Thank you, Percy, but please don't use that word. I'm just me, not a prodigy."

"What gave you the idea of playing Irish songs, Charlie?" Margaret wondered. "You had the whole crowd in the palm of your hand!"

"Good question, Gritty. I didn't plan it. Being in that church made me homesick. I played what I would have played if I was alone, feeling like that. I'm glad people enjoyed listening in."

Mummy hugged him. "You gave a grand gift to the people of Albany, and to us too, Charlie. Your music touched something deep inside wee Cally. She wept and wept."

"Where are those children? What's taking them so long? We'll miss our train!" Margaret shifted Sally on her hip.

"I'll go find out," Charlie offered.

Soon he was back. "They're gone! I searched everywhere. There's no trace of them or of their things, though their father's duffle is still there. Do you think Roisin and Malachy . . ."

"Calm down, Charles, and let me think."

"Sir, I—"

"Percy, ask at the hotel desk about the next train out of Albany. Daniel, consult this map of Erie Canal stops and tell me which one comes after Schenectady. I'll notify the packet not to wait for us. We'll catch up with it further on."

"Amsterdam, then Canajoharie, Father, then Little Falls. The guidebook says there's an aqueduct across the Mohawk River at Canajoharie and the scenery is 'romantic and grand.' It recommends floating from Canajoharie to Little Falls. That would take us through two locks, Fort Plain and St. Johnsville, with interesting things to see at both ends of the float. That's eighteen miles and takes four to five hours. We could spend the night in Little Falls, then take the train tomorrow morning the rest of the way to Buffalo."

"That sounds good, Daniel. Is everyone all right with that plan?"

"Father—"

"Wait just a minute, son, while I write."

Meghan, at the other end of the lobby supervising Martin and Molly in a game, looked up curiously as Charlie stomped back and forth, his fists clenched, while Father dispatched an errand boy from the hotel with his message.

"Now, Charles. I am confident we need not worry about Roisin and Malachy. After our confrontation at the concert, they won't attempt anything more."

"Peter, I've been thinking. I felt uncomfortable at the time, but thought I was imagining things. Now I think I was right."

"Right about what, Cathleen? You're making no sense."

Mummy took a deep breath. "Peter, I was watching Cally's face when you assured her you would see her and Teddy safely back to Ireland. I know you had—and have—the very best intentions, but I could tell Cally didn't see it that way. She's told us clearly she doesn't want to go back. I think she's taken Teddy and run away."

Daniel frowned. "After their unbelievable escape and trip back to us? That hardly seems possible. Obviously, they wanted our care and protection."

"Yes, I believe that's true, Daniel. But for some reason, Cally believes she can't return to Ireland. I promised her we would not make her. Yet you told her, Peter, you *would* take them back. I suspect Cally felt she had no recourse against Captain Malcomson. She's chosen, I think, to risk living on her own with Teddy rather than be forced to go back to Ireland."

"Father!"

"Just a minute, Charles."

Margaret sat down with Sally on a nearby sofa.

"I can't imagine, Mummy . . . a child of seven and a child of six, on the streets on their own?"

"I know, Margaret. It makes no sense to us. But that's because we don't understand Cally's story and the marks it has left on her soul. We don't understand the resilience of a child who has lived in difficult circumstances all her life, and without her mother since she was five. Martin and Molly give us no context for understanding Cally and Teddy."

"Then what do you think we should do, Cathleen?"

"Father—"

"I need to hear your mother's answer to my question, Charles."

Cathleen opened her mouth to speak, but Martin and Molly rushed up, with Meghan trailing behind them. "Is it time to go, Grandfather?"

Peter smiled. "Almost. Would you two like a snack? If that is all right with you, Meghan."

"Sure, but—"

"A wee problem has come up, so we'll leave later than we thought. I'll explain it to you—"

"I'll take them, Meghan," Daniel interrupted. "Stay so you can understand what's going on."

Mummy smiled warmly at Martin and Molly before they skipped away with their father. "Cally and Teddy are missing, Meghan. We're trying to figure out what to do."

Meghan's eyes widened, but she asked no questions. Charlie saw his chance.

"Father, the longer we stand here talking, the harder it will be to find Cally and Teddy. May I, at least, go look for them? They can't be too far away yet."

"We'll be more effective if we organize. Who else is willing to look for the children?"

"Father, shouldn't we just let them go? Obviously, that's what they would prefer."

"I'm not sure that's true, Margaret. I think if I could apologize and tell them I will keep your mother's promise not to make them return to Ireland if they don't want to, we might have the chance to figure out something better for them than the streets of Albany. Perhaps Nathanael and Sarah would take them. After all, they adopted wee Jimmy. I need to try. I couldn't live with myself if I did not. The streets of a city are no place for children."

"I still don't understand why you've gotten so attached to these orphans, but oh well. Do as you must. Obviously, I will stay here to care for Sally."

"I'll help look, sir, but I think we should put a time limit on it, for the sake of the train and the packet and all our plans. As Charlie said, the children can't have gone far. What do you say we meet back here in half an hour?"

"That sounds reasonable, Percy."

"I'll help look too, Peter," Cathleen offered.

"And I'll stay with Martin and Molly so Daniel can look."

"Thank you, Meghan. All right, that makes five of us. Cathleen, go to the left out the main door of the hotel. They might be hiding by the river. Stay on this street and start back in fifteen minutes. Meghan, please ask Daniel to do the same thing, but walking south. Charlie, walk to the back of the hotel and head west. Percy, angle southwest, and I'll angle northwest. If any of us sees a policeman, alert them we're searching for missing children, and enlist their help. And if you find the children, please assure them on my behalf I won't force them to return to Ireland."

"Precious Father, please help us find Cally and Teddy."

"Amen. Thank you, Cathleen. Successful or not, meet back here in half an hour."

It's like searching for a needle in a haystack. They have a half hour lead on us already.

CR&&RO

Charlie rounded the corner just as Father pulled open the hotel door, alone. *I bet no one found them.* He walked slowly to the hotel entrance, reluctant to face what he already suspected.

Mummy welcomed him with a hug, worry spread across her face.

"If I may, sir?"

"Certainly, Percy."

"I think our best chance is to turn this over to the police. We could spend all day hunting and never find them, sir. And there's the family to consider."

"I agree, Percy. I will go to the police station to file a missing persons report while all of you make your way to the train station. I will meet you there as soon as I can."

"May I go with you, Father?"

"Yes, Charles. Daniel, here are our 9:00 train tickets to Schenectady. Please exchange them for the 12:00 to Canajoharie. We'll catch up with our packet there, or rather, the packet will catch up with us. I'm sure

Charles and I will finish at the police station in time to board the train."

"Son, I know this is difficult for you. It is for me as well. I feel doubly responsible," Father said as they walked out the door with directions to the nearest police station.

"Doubly, Father?"

"My folly on the ship resulted in Mr. Donnelly's death, And if your mother is correct, my hubris in thinking I knew what was best for the children resulted in our present situation."

"Cally does have a stubborn streak."

"That may work in her favor if the police fail to locate the children. I'm glad you're coming with me, son. You can help me give an accurate description of the children."

"I'll do my best, Father."

ﾂ 茶 0

As the packet floated away from the Canajoharie dock, Charlie found a place at the rail near the officer at the helm, away from the family. *Too much has happened since we left home. I need time just to be still. I wish I had a piano to help me untangle my feelings. Cally and Teddy, where are you? Why did you run away? Can't you understand we just want what's best for you?*

Charlie watched the town gradually fade into farmland, and then countryside, until trees on both sides of the canal limited the world to a sort of sky-roofed tunnel. The speed limit on the canal, four miles per hour, suited his desire to slow down.

I would love to float all the way to Niagara. I'm glad we get at least a taste of this world apart, with its own gentle rhythm so different from the big cities. One week. One week of Niagara sightseeing. One week for the police in Albany to find Cally and Teddy. Will they? Even if they do, Cally may still decide not to go back to her home and family. She's so stubborn about that. Will we ever know why? Will we ever see them again? Oh, Cally . . .

230

Charlie stretched his arms high, toward the bit of sky he could see through the canopy of trees, and then wide, rolling his shoulders and savoring a release of tension. *I wonder what has happened inside of Father. He surprises me at every turn. Hugs, conversation, encouraging words . . . Sometimes he even calls me Charlie! I don't know who he is anymore. Which is the real man: the stern, demanding, distant captain, or this new one who can cry when I play Irish songs at a concert? Does Mummy notice the changes, I wonder? I hope there will be a piano at the hotel in Little Falls or at least the one in Niagara. . .*

Familiar voices interrupted Charlie's reverie. He looked around to see Margaret and Percy approaching, pointing to something across the canal. Walking quickly around the curve of the rail away from them, he found another place at the rail among passengers he didn't know. *I need this time to myself! Will the Niagara Falls be as spectacular as we've been told? Please, no more disappointments right now. Or big events. I wish I could have had more lessons with Mr. Paderewski, though. No idea when our paths will cross again.*

Martin and Molly ran down the deck, yelling "Charlie! Charlie!"

Well, that quiet time didn't last long. Charlie sighed, but turned toward his niece and nephew with a smile as Molly grabbed his hand.

"Charlie, we're almost to the Fort Plain lock! You can see better from the other side. Come quick!"

It's just as well. I'm too tired and sad for any more thinking.

Debra Kornfield

CHAPTER 24

CALLY

Albany, Thursday, July 23, 1891

"OW!"

Cally jerked groggily away from whatever had hit her in the ribs.

"Get up or I'll kick you again!"

In one motion, Cally sat up and scooted back against the wall. A candle threw shadows on a lad's scowling face. "I—I don't understand ye."

"Ah, ye speak the Irish, do ye?" The lad switched smoothly into language Cally could understand. "Where are ye from, then?"

Teddy jumped up. "We're from Ireland. What do ye think, the moon? Where are ye from?"

"A feisty one, are ye? I meant, where in Ireland are ye from?"

"Killeagh, in County Cork. What about ye?"

"Sure, I'm a County Kerry boy, so I am. What are ye doin' here in this country?"

Teddy looked at Cally. She replied, "Our da wanted a new life, but he died on the ship."

"Ah, I know all about that. My mammy and da died on the ship, too. Cholera. I know what those nasty, dirty ships are like. Hundreds died on our ship, so they did."

Teddy leaped toward the boy and pummeled him as hard as he could. "Ye take that back! My da was a hero! He didn't die from no collar."

Cally jumped up and inserted herself between Teddy and the lad. She threw her arms around her brother. "Teddy, he didn't know. How could he know? He's just tellin' us what happened to him and his parents. He's not talkin' about Da."

Teddy pulled away, sobbing, and crumpled against the wall. Cally crouched next to him, crooning, until he calmed down, and then turned back to the lad.

"Why did ye kick me? It's still nighttime, isn't it? We weren't doin' ye no harm. We were just sleepin'. No call for a touslin'."

"Don't get yer nose out of joint. This is my place, so it is. How did ye get in here, anyway?"

"I—we—the door was open. We came in to get out of the rain. We were tired and we went to sleep. That's all."

"Well, this is my boxcar. Everyone knows that. Get out."

"Can't ye let us stay til mornin'? We don't know where to go. This is our first night in this city, 'cept for the night we slept in the hotel. Look, there's plenty of room. Please. Tomorrow we'll find somewhere else."

"What are yer names, anyway?"

"I'm Cally and my brother is Teddy."

"How old are ye?"

"I'm almost eight and he just turned six."

"But he's bigger than ye."

"Yes, but I'm older. What's yer name? How old are ye?"

"I'm Patrick—Saint Patrick, everyone calls me. I'm the boss of my gang, that's why this boxcar is mine. Since ye are Irish, ye can call me Paddy. And I'm twelve, so I am. I was ten when Mammy and Da died on the ship. I didn't like New York City so one day I jumped on a train that came here."

"What's a gang?" Teddy's voice still held a trace of tears.

"Ye can meet them tomorrow. They are other lads on their own like us."

"Are there lots of them?"

"In my gang there are ten. I've been thinkin' I should have two more to make twelve, so I have, to match my age. But I ain't never had no *cailín* before. The lads wouldn't like it. I could keep ye, Teddy, maybe, but not yer sister."

"If ye want Teddy, ye have to keep me too. We stay together."

"Turn around."

"What?"

"Turn around."

Cally frowned, but she turned slowly until she faced Paddy again.

"Cracker. We could make ye into a laddie."

"What?"

"If we cut yer hair, and put ye in lad's clothes, no one would know. Ye would look like a laddie with curly hair and freckles, like me. I could even say ye are my long-lost cousins shown up from Ireland."

Cally's hand flew to her head. "Cut my hair?"

"Are the other lads Irish?" Teddy asked at the same time.

"No. They are from all over. Some were born here but most came from some other place. Everybody in my gang must learn the English, that's the rule. Otherwise we don't know what each other is sayin'."

"Are ye the only one who sleeps in this train car?"

"Mostly, yes. It's because I'm the boss."

"Where does everyone else sleep?"

"Here and there. Mostly under the bridge. The German lads on one side, the Dutch lads on the other. But enough *blether*. It's late and I'm knackered. I'll let ye sleep here tonight, but by mornin', Cally, ye need to decide whether ye'll change to be a lad. If not, ye must go away and be on yer own. I won't help ye then."

Teddy, his cheeks still stained with tears, said, "But I want to know—."

Cally put her hand over his mouth and pulled him down beside her. They were in the corner of the boxcar furthest from the door, on the other side of several stacks of large boxes. Paddy slept in the opposite corner. She could hear him moving around, but soon he blew out his candle. Almost immediately she heard him snoring. A short time later Teddy made the whiffling sound that told her he was asleep.

Cut my hair? Become a lad?

Cally felt in the dark for their bag, opened the clasps, and reached into the little pocket for her treasure. She had pulled it out of her dress before her bath at Mr. Nathanael's, and a good thing, too, because the next morning Madam Sarah told her she had burned the dress and Teddy's clothes.

Cally lay back beside Teddy, the comforting curve of the little mirror in her hand, remembering. *Just in time, before Madam Sarah came back into the kitchen with clothes for me, I hid my treasure inside a pot on a shelf. When Madam Sarah ran to check on one of her* weans *taking a tumble, I put it into a pocket in the Quaker dress. After the others were asleep, I hid it inside my bag. What will I look like if I let Paddy cut my hair? Will I still be me?*

With one hand grasping her mirror and the other a long curly lock of her hair, Cally finally fell asleep.

ɔʒ∞

Sunlight streamed through the boxcar's partly open door when Cally woke. Easing away from Teddy, she sat up and looked around, but couldn't see past the stacks of boxes in the center of the car. She tucked her treasure back in their bag and peered around the boxes. Paddy wasn't there. Needing to relieve herself, she smoothed her hair and her dress and walked to the door.

Cally scanned what she could see through the door, not opening it further lest she wake Teddy. In the dark and rain of the night before, she hadn't realized this boxcar sat by itself as if forgotten. The main tracks led to a jumble of trains some distance away.

Turning the other direction, Cally noticed scruffy wild rose bushes, still blooming red. She jumped from the boxcar and darted behind the bushes. Almost back, sniffing a rose she had plucked, she heard whistling. Paddy appeared carrying a bag.

"Come on then, Cally, ain't ye hungry? Look what I found behind the bakery! Is yer *eejit* of a brother awake yet? We could sit out here to eat breakfast."

Cally boosted herself into the boxcar and saw Teddy beginning to stir. "Teddy! Paddy has food fer us. Come on! I'm hungry."

"Me too!"

Cally felt her first flash of admiration for Paddy as he shared the delicious rolls he had found for their breakfast. She lay her rose beside the bag of rolls. Between bites, Paddy chattered about his plans for the day.

"Did ye decide, then, Cally? I can't take ye with me if ye ain't a lad."

"I—I don't know. I've never been a lad."

Paddy laughed as if that was the funniest thing he had ever heard. "It ain't so bad, is it, Teddy. 'Course, I can't truly make ye a lad. Ye'll hafta pretend. But we can teach ye, right, Teddy? Hmm, what shall we call ye then? It's gotta be a lad's name. I know, Calvin. I knew a Calvin once. Then if Teddy fergets and calls ye Cally, it will just seem like a nickname fer Calvin. Ye do still look wee enough to have a nickname. So that's settled. Nice to meet ye, Calvin."

"But I didn't decide yet."

Paddy laughed as if that was another funny joke.

"Ye don't have to decide, Calvin. I'm the one who decides things around here. Now, how will we cut yer hair?"

"Cally has scissors in her sewing kit," Teddy volunteered, his mouth full of bread. "But she won't let me touch them."

"Well, I'm yer boss now, not Calvin. Go get the scissors, Teddy."

Teddy eyes and mouth opened wide. He looked at Cally, who stared back as shocked and scared as he was. Paddy burst into laughter once more. "Go on. I ain't plannin' to hurt ye. Ye'll see. Didn't I tell ye I'm called Saint Patrick? That's 'cuz I'm the best gang boss in Albany. All the lads want to be with me, 'cuz I treat them so good. Didn't I get ye a nice breakfast, then? I only keep the lads I like. Ye should feel honored that I invited ye two. But I won't ask ye again. If ye don't want to be a lad, Calvin, ye and Teddy can go on yer way, and I won't begrudge yer breakfast. Bring yer bag, Teddy, not just the scissors. It looks like yer sister ain't stayin'."

Teddy disappeared into the boxcar, and Paddy said nothing more, just stuffed the last roll into his mouth. When Teddy reappeared at the door of the boxcar, dragging their bag, Cally went to help him maneuver it to the ground.

"What should we do, Teddy?" she whispered. "It seems like if we're not in Paddy's gang, we'll be on our own. Maybe he'll be mean to us then."

"We don't have to stay in this city, do we? We could keep walkin'."

"It's a big city. Maybe we could find another place to sleep, far away from here."

Paddy began whistling, a familiar Irish tune, one Da used to sing to them. Tears sprung to the eyes of both children. They turned around and to their amazement, saw Paddy jigging.

"Come now. It's a beautiful day. Don't ye want to spend it havin' fun, 'stead of worryin' about runnin' away from me? Who else will understand yer Irish? Who else will help ye learn to live on the streets? We need to hurry now, 'cuz the other boys from the gang will be here soon. I already told them to come meet their new brothers. I told them ye are my cousins, and that's why ye are going to stay with me in my car. It's the reason I can treat ye special. Now, Calvin, get me yer scissors. It's a grand day in Albany, New York. Let's not waste it."

Cally looked again at Teddy. He looked back at her wide-eyed and shrugged. Hesitantly, not sure this was right, she opened the clasp of the bag, took out the sewing kit Aisling had made for her, and found the scissors. Paddy, hanging over her shoulder, glimpsed the doll Aisling had given her.

"Ye can't keep that doll, Calvin. Why would a lad have a thing like that? Now then. Do ye have some lad clothes she can wear, Teddy? Yer clothes are as fancy as Cally's dress. Where'd ye get those fancy clothes, then? I bet ye didn't wear them on the boat from Ireland. No, never mind. We hafta hurry. Ye can tell me later. Yes, those look more like clothes ye should be wearin'. But we'll hafta give them to Calvin fer today til I can find her—him—lad clothes of her—his—own. Now let's cut yer hair, Calvin, and then ye can change to a lad back there in those bushes."

"I—I'm not sure I want to. God made me a lassie." Cally held the scissors behind her back.

"It's just hair. Ye can let it grow back if ye don't like being a laddie. But come on—ye don't want the others to see. Teddy, pick up the hair I cut and throw it in the bag from our breakfast. And throw that flower in too."

Reluctantly, Cally proffered the scissors, and Paddy began snipping. Long, shiny auburn ringlets fell to the ground. Teddy grabbed them as they fell and stuffed them in the bag.

I mustn't cry. It can grow back . . .

"There now. Run behind those bushes and change into yer brother's clothes. Leave yer fancy dress hidden there for now. And leave the doll with it. They'll both bring a pretty penny later, or maybe we'll trade 'em fer street clothes fer Teddy. Did ye steal these fancy—no, tell me later. There come the lads."

My doll . . . what am I doing? "Teddy! Help me undo my buttons!"

Cally peeked around the bush and saw a ragtag group of lads, some as young as Teddy and some older. None were as big as Paddy. She fastened Teddy's pants around her waist, then pushed her dress as far as she could under the bush. *I wish I had time to look in my mirror. What if I still look like a lassie?* She peeked around the bush and saw Paddy watching his gang approach. Teddy, beside him, glanced back and forth from the gang to the bushes.

"Cally, ye do look like a lad! I think we both need hats. See—all the gang has hats. Maybe Paddy knows where we can get some." Teddy's whisper was loud enough that Paddy turned to look, gesturing for him to be quiet. Paddy pulled them both forward, positioning one on each side of him.

"Watch how we greet each other. This is only for our gang, understand? Ye don't use this greeting fer anyone else."

Cally and Teddy gazed in surprise as the lads made a line and greeted Paddy one by one. Each one extended his right hand, palm up. Paddy slapped the open palm, then the lad bowed. *I wonder what that means. I don't want to bow to Paddy.*

After each of the ten lads performed the ritual and took his place in a semi-circle around their boss, Paddy said something in English that Cally and Teddy didn't understand. *I hear the words Calvin and Teddy so he must be talking about us. I wish I knew what he is saying. We must learn the English as fast as we can. Can those lads tell I'm a lassie just pretendin' to be a lad?*

"I told them yer my cousins just arrived from Ireland, and since ye don't know the English yet, ye need to stick close by me while ye learn. Now, to join our gang, ye need to swear an oath. Repeat after me, Calvin: I, Calvin, swear to follow ye, Patrick, as my leader, do what ye tell me, and treat all my brothers with respect."

Cally started to protest, but at the look on his face, she crossed her fingers behind her back and repeated what Paddy told her.

"Now Teddy, same thing."

"I, Teddy, swear to follow ye, Patrick, as my leader, do what ye tell me, and treat all my brothers with respect."

Paddy turned to his gang. "They said it, just in Irish. Ye all need to help them learn the English." Turning back to Cally and Teddy, he switched again to Irish. "Now the greeting. Yer open hand and me slapping it means ye work fer me and I provide fer you. The bow means ye pledge to obey me as yer boss."

Teddy readily followed Paddy's instructions. *He thinks this is all a game. I'm not sure. What if I don't agree with what he tells us to do?*

But with twelve pairs of eyes watching, Cally did as she was told. *In my heart yer not the boss of me, Paddy. My job is to take care of Teddy, not to work fer ye, boss that ye think ye are.*

"Anything to report?" Paddy said this first in English and then in Irish, so Cally and Teddy could understand. The biggest lad stepped forward and bowed again. She couldn't understand what he said, but all the lads laughed, and Paddy did a little jig before responding.

"What are ye sayin'?" Teddy demanded.

"There's a ship in port with work fer all of us today, so we'll go there now. We'll have a good supper tonight! Maybe ye two are good luck fer us."

If only ye knew. I'm not good luck fer anyone.

"Ye two need hats. It ain't safe to work without one."

Paddy consulted with the lad who had given the report. He nodded and gestured to Cally and Teddy to follow him. The children looked at Paddy.

"Go with him to get yer hats, then ye'll join us on the wharf. His name is Jeb. He don't know Irish, but a hat is a hat and Jeb's a sound man with a dab hand."

Teddy had already started walking after Jeb. Cally ran to catch up. *One thing I know fer sure. I can't let Teddy out of my sight.*

⋙⋘

Cally lay in the corner of the boxcar beside Teddy, listening to his light whiffling blend with Paddy's deeper snore, comforted by the fragrance of another rose she had sneaked in without Paddy seeing. *I'm tired. I haven't worked so hard since we left the farm. But Paddy made us laugh, too. I've never met anyone like him. I wish I could see what I look like. I wonder. Is there enough moon?*

Cally eased her treasure from their bag and crept to the door of the boxcar. A bright moon gave enough light to see her reflection in the wee mirror. She choked back a sob as she turned the mirror this way and that, careful not to reflect light into Paddy's corner. Tears blurred her vision as she made her way back to Teddy. *What have I done? Who am I now? Will I ever be a lassie again? What would Da think, and Aisling? Now I know fer sure we can never go home.*

Cally tried to remember Aisling's bedtime prayer, but the words twisted around each other in her mind. Peace? Safe? She buried her face in her arm, clutching her rose in one hand and her treasure in the other, weeping until finally she fell asleep.

⋙⋘

I lik Sundays. This is are forth Sunday in the gang. Paddy takes us al to cherch, in the same cherch where Charlie playd in a consert and I saw Cousin Rosheen. Its almost the sam as going to cherch in Killeagh.

Cally set down her pencil, sighed and stretched. She looked out over the water, then located Teddy, playing in the sand by the river with another laddie from the gang. *Writing is hard. I don't know how to spell all the words. I think more than I know how to write. I don't even know why I'm doing this. I just know I must try.*

242

She took up her pencil again and smoothed the brown paper on the stump beside her. *After mass, there's a diner and Paddys gang and other gangs can eat. Father Calahan maks Paddy promis we wont werk on Sunday afternuns. He says childrun need tim to play. And they need homs and famlys. He keeps telin Paddy we shud all go on the orfun trans, just lik that man in Yonkers sed. Paddy lafs and says Albany is ar hom and the gang is ar famly. I ben tokin to Teddy about it. I want to lern more about the trans frum Father Calahan. I think goin away is a gud idea. What if Cusin Rosheen sees us again? Even Paddy wud not be abl to help us agenst her.*

☙

Cally looked around in alarm. *Where is Teddy? He was just here!* She ran to the end of the block, looked up and down the cross street, then ran the opposite way to do the same. *Not just Teddy, but everyone is gone! Where did they go? How did I miss them? I know I was thinking about how Killeagh feels when the leaves start changing. But I should have heard them! I have no idea which way to go. Da, I'm sorry. I'm sorry, Da.*

Crying now, Cally walked aimlessly, down one street and up another. Stumbling past a smelly alley, she stopped short. *What is that sound?* She scrubbed tears from her eyes and started into the dim alley. *That whining sounds like my heart feels.*

Behind a pile of trash, she saw a mother dog, dead, and beside it a wee, trembling pup, eyes large in its wee face. She climbed around the trash, picked up the puppy, brushed it off, and cradled it close to her heart. "Oh, ye poor wee thing! I lost my mammy, so I know how ye feel. And my da, too. Don't worry. I'll take care of ye. Ye are safe now, so ye are."

Back on the street, Cally looked at the sun to get her bearings. *It's afternoon, so the river is that way. So I'm not lost, and sooner or later, Teddy will show up with the rest of the gang. Why did I get upset?*

243

Crooning, Cally walked east until she reached the broad avenue fronting the river. Then she turned south, watching for a place along the riverbank where she could give the pup a drink and a bath. *Don't worry, wee one. If Paddy won't let me keep ye, I'll leave the gang, so I will.*

⊂⊱⊃

Fith Sunday. The only tim I can rite is Sunday afternun. More than a hol month being a lad. Hardest is when they swim and take of all ther clos. Paddy sends me on erunds. I wonder if Uncle Dugan and Aisling went to cherch today in Killeagh. We named the puppy Cash. Teddy wanted Frank, for Da. But that dusnt seem rite. Finly, we used Das midel name, Cashel. But everyone calls him Cash, even me. Paddy lafs and says if he brings the gang cash he can stay.

Cally stood, located Teddy, throwing a stick for Cash to fetch, then sat again by her stump and labored on. *This is my speshul ritin plas, in the shad under a prety tree. I see Charlies mammys bruthr, the one who toks so much, evry Sunday at church, but he dusnt see us. Today he brushed my shert carryin a table sayin owt of the way lads if ye plez. We don't mach how we loked when he met us. Father Calahan teeches skool lessons Sundays after mass after dinner. Teddy runs away with the yunger lads but I lik it. I want to lern everythin.*

⊂⊱⊃

"Cally, nach dtiocfaidh tú agus spraoi liom?"

"Say it in English, Teddy."

Teddy sighed. "I'm tired of English."

"We're in America now. English is the language of this country. We have to keep practicin' until we can speak it as well as the other lads."

"Won't ye come and play with me and Cash? The others went somewhere else."

"I will. Just let me finish what I'm writin'. I'll be quick."

"Ye always say that. And then ye write and write."

"I think it's important. Why, I don't know. But I hafta do it. I'll write

244

as fast as I can."

"When are ye goin' to teach me to read and write?"

Cally looked up, eyebrows raised. "Ye want to learn? I didn't know that! Why don't ye stay fer lessons with Father Callahan?"

"The other lads would laugh at me. Please. Let's start today."

"All right. I'll try to remember how Cousin Louise taught me. Just let me finish this first. Go walk along the street and see if ye can find any paper to pick up. But don't turn any corners. Stay on this street by the river."

"I will!" Teddy jumped to his feet, scanning the ground as he ran, Cash trailing after. Cally sighed, watching her brother's limp, and turned back to her writing.

Yesturday was the furst day Paddy askt me to steul sumthin. We wer at the city market, and he wanted a per. They hav so many, they wont even notis, he sed. I sed no. I walkt up to the wuman and said, "I want a per, but I dont hav any muny." And she gave me one, and I gav it to Paddy. See? Ye dont hav to steul, I told him.

"I found paper!" Teddy yelled. "Show me how to write my name."

∞

Cally frowned as she looked from her writing place across the broad river. She wrote, My tree's leevs are turnin red. Sunday number 8 in Albany. Paddy is mad at me and Teddy becus we wont steel. Da sed we shud werk fer what we hav, not take what is not ars. Paddy says we tuk an oth to do what he tells us. My ferst oth is to my Da and to Teddy. I wont steel. Paddy says then we haf to leev the gang. I dont know yet wher we shud go. Paddy is nis and hes fun and funny. But he dus things that are rong. He says its what he must do to car fer his lads. I stil feel like a lassy insid. I decided its a game, bein a lad. But I cry evry nit after Teddy and Paddy and Cash ar asleep. I cant help it. I cant remember Aisling's prer.

Debra Kornfield

CHAPTER 25

CHARLIE

Mayfield House, Wednesday, August 19, 1891

CHARLIE JUMPED AS THUNDER CRASHED and wind rattled the drawing room doors. He had tried to distract himself with *Roughing It*, a book Mummy had bought him at a Niagara Falls bookshop. But from the first rumblings of the storm as he finished his afternoon practice, he had felt headachy and sick to his stomach. *What's wrong with me? I know I'm safe in my house. But my body is afraid, and I can't seem to control it.*

Drenched with sweat, Charlie loosened his collar and settled back on the sofa. But even Mark Twain's rowdy humor was no match for the panic that coursed through him with the next rumble of thunder. He heard squeals from the barn. *Oh! That's Midnight! Should I go to her?*

He peered into the rain, falling so fast he could hardly see the barn. *I'm alone. Mummy's at the school, Father is sailing, and Lillian is visiting her sick mum. Cook is on her fortieth anniversary trip. Rory went home when the sky turned black. I know Evan will comfort the horses, but . . .*

Lightning flashed, silhouetting trees dipping and swaying in the wind. Charlie heard a sharp crack as a branch tumbled to the ground. He raced down the hall, up the stairs, and into Mummy's room, leaped onto her bed and pulled the covers to his chin. His body shook so much his teeth rattled. But he couldn't stay. He barely made it to her washbasin as his stomach heaved.

Trembling, Charlie pulled Mummy's drapes closed and lit every lamp in the room. Then he sought the comfort of her bed once more, closing his eyes against the pain in his head.

Forever later, Charlie heard Mummy downstairs, calling his name. He started from the bed, but a gust of wind pounded rain onto the windows, sending him deeper into the bedclothes. Mummy's voice came closer. "Charlie! Charlie! Where are you, son?"

And then she was there, solid and warm. Charlie threw himself into her arms, soaking himself with the rainwater dripping from her clothes. "Charlie, Charlie, it's all right, sweetheart. We're safe. It's only a storm. It will be over soon. I came as soon as I could. Oh, Charlie. Let me get out of these wet things. Don't worry, I'm right here. I'm not going out again today."

Mummy's voice faded as she disappeared into her dressing room, but he could still hear her. "I'm sorry you were alone, Charlie. I know you planned to ride Midnight today after your practice time. I don't think the storm will cause much damage. Mostly to the garden, I expect, but Evan can help Rory put it to rights. Just a minute, son, while I pull on this dress."

Mummy's voice stopped. Charlie felt panic rising inside him, but soon her voice once more anchored him. "I know you'll want to check on Midnight as soon as you can, but it's getting dark now. Evan has a way with the horses, as you know. Take some deep breaths, Charlie, and open your eyes. I'm here now."

Charlie sat up, gripping her hand. "What's wrong with me, Mummy? My brain knows I'm safe, but my body seems separate from my mind. I couldn't convince it not to be terrified."

"I don't know for sure, son. But you acted the same way during the storm on the ship. I think your body learned that storms aren't safe.

That's why I rushed to come home as soon as I could. It seems being alone is a large part of your fear."

Tears pooled in Charlie's eyes. "Will it be like this the rest of my life, Mummy?"

"I don't know, son. Let's not worry now about the rest of your life. I got a bit chilled running over from the school. Does hot cocoa sound good to you? And then, will you play for me the Chopin Mr. Paderewski asked you to learn?"

⋘⋙

Charlie looked up from the piano as the drawing room door opened. "Father! I didn't think you'd be home until tomorrow!"

"I wanted to surprise you." Mummy walked in close behind Father, her eyes sparkling. Behind her Mr. Rory carried a crate.

"You did surprise me, Father!"

"I have another surprise. Come and see."

Mr. Rory opened the door of the crate, and at first nothing happened. Then a shiny black nose appeared, and two bright eyes and floppy chestnut ears. The puppy rushed from the crate directly into Charlie's lap. All four observers laughed.

"Oh, you cute wee thing! Who are you? Let me see you properly." The puppy squirmed as Charlie lifted it for inspection.

"Before I sailed, Charles, I deputized Rory to find just the right puppy for you. Ah, Evan! Come in! Charles will need your help to train this pup."

"That will be a delight, sir. No doubt she'll soon want to race alongside Charlie and Midnight. A *modder rhu*. Good choice, sir."

"Rory made the choice, knowing I'm partial to Irish setters. Perhaps Charles doesn't know we once had three."

"We did?"

Father laughed. "Have your brothers and sister never talked about them? Your mother and I bought three setters to celebrate our third wedding anniversary. Rory selected those *modder rhu* for us way back then. Sadly, all three got old and died before you were born."

Charlie glanced at Mummy and back again. "No one ever told me this! Sometimes it seems I grew up in a different family from my brothers and sister."

"In some ways, I guess you did, Charles. What do you think of your pup? You'll have to give her a name."

"I'm a little overwhelmed. I never imagined . . ."

"We waited until you were old enough to train and care for a puppy yourself, Charles. Irish setters are energetic, but they take patience and consistency to train properly. Rory thinks he's too old, so he recruited Evan as your chief trainer. But you can count on Rory's advice when your puppy gets feisty and opinionated."

"This lassie is eight weeks old, so she is," Mr. Rory said. "The ideal age to begin learnin' her manners. She'll test yer patience, Master Charlie, but she'll be devoted to ye the rest of her life. She needs exercise. She'll love havin' so much space to run, but she's a house pet and won't want to be away from ye any more than she must."

"Thank you, Mr. Rory. Look how she's checking the place out! We'll have to be careful what we leave within her reach."

Mr. Rory chuckled. "That ye will, Master Charlie. At least while she's learnin' what she can and can't do."

"Her color reminds me of a sunset I saw last week. I think I'll call her Rosy."

Father raised his eyebrows, but said, "Rosy she is! I'll leave you two to get acquainted while I settle in and rest a bit. It's been a long day for me."

"Oh, yes, Father. Thank you! I'm delighted! And I'm glad you're home a day early!"

Father chuckled. Mummy took his arm as they left the room.

"Now, Master Charlie, where do ye want me to set up Rosy's bed?

Will ye want her to sleep in yer room, or would ye prefer she settle into the kitchen or another place?"

"I don't know. I've never had my own dog before. Will she wake up during the night?"

"She's a baby, so she'll sleep as long as ye do, Master Charlie. She'll take daytime naps, too, so she'll probably want another bed in the main part of the house."

"And what will Miss Rosy be eatin', I'd like to know," a familiar voice chimed in. "That will fall to me until Cook returns. I see ye've enough work to keep ye from the taverns, Rory. A storm, was it, that leveled the garden?"

"Lillian! You're back!" Charlie ran to give her a hug. "How is your mother?"

"My mother passed, Master Charlie, I'm sorry to say. But she was ready, and it was a peaceful passin'. I'm grateful your mother let me stay to attend to everythin'. I see ye all have saved some chores fer me, so I'd feel needed here, is it? Not to mention this wee scallywag. She'll give us a run fer our money. A pup is as much work as a baby, so it is. But she'll be a grand friend to ye, Master Charlie. What is she yappin' about now?"

Charlie ran to pull Rosy from under the sofa. He hugged her and laughed as she licked his face and wagged her wee tail. *I'll never be all alone ever again.*

CRSO

Mummy smiled when she saw Rosy snuggled against Charlie rather than in her own bed. "I see you two are grand friends already. I'm glad, Charlie."

"Mmhmm," Charlie replied sleepily.

"Charlie, are you still awake enough for me to tell you something? I've been thinking about the name you chose for your puppy. The sunset you mentioned reminds me of a verse from the Psalms, *From the rising of the sun to the going down of the same, the Lord's name is to be praised.* We praise the Lord because he is with us always. He never sleeps. He watches over us day and night. Even in storms."

"Mmhmm."

Mummy laughed. "All right, good night, Charlie. When you look at Rosy, remember God too is your constant companion and friend. Sweet dreams, dear son."

Charlie turned over, cuddling his already-sleeping puppy. "Day and night. Good night, Mummy."

෧৪৮

"So, how did you two sleep?" Father greeted Charlie at the breakfast table.

"We slept well! Thank you, Father. How long will you be home?"

"For several weeks this time, to supervise the overhaul of *Lion III*. I've been thinking, Charles, we've let too much time go by without visiting Callandra and Theodore's relatives in Killeagh. They may not even know Frank has died, much less that the children have disappeared. It's not happy news we take them, but it must be done."

"And we need to take them Mr. Donnelly's bag."

"You're right! I had forgotten we have it. We'll go Saturday and return Sunday. Do you want to go with us, Charles? We'll need an early start. It will take all day to travel the forty-five miles to Killeagh."

"Hmm. I planned to ride with Liam Saturday. May I think about it and tell you tomorrow?"

෧৪৮

Waking from a nap, Charlie pressed his nose against the carriage window, seeing only fog and drizzle. *It wouldn't be fun to ride Midnight in this. I'm glad I decided to go with Mummy and Father. But it's hard, taking Cally's family such bad news. I wonder if they will know why Cally refused to come back to Ireland. That's why I'm going, to ask them that question.*

Mummy touched his arm. "Lost in your own head, are you, son? I asked whether you talked with Lillian about Rosy."

"I'm sorry, Mummy. Yes. Since Evan is driving us, Mr. Rory will train Rosy today with Lillian watching so she knows what to do. If the rain keeps up, Rosy won't be able to run outside."

Father spoke. "We may not make it all the way today. The muddy road is hard on the horses."

"Where will we stay, Father?"

"We'll watch for a place as we approach evening. In Killeagh, I'm told I should inquire at the Old Thatch Pub."

Oh. Two days—maybe three—with no practicing. I didn't think about that. But I guess it doesn't matter, since I'm not preparing for any events.

As if she could read his mind, Mummy said, "Charlie, we received a letter yesterday afternoon you will be interested in hearing. Shall I read it to you?" She pulled an envelope from her satchel and removed a single sheet of official-looking paper.

"Dear Captain and Mrs. Malcomson: I greet you from the Royal Irish Academy of Music in Dublin. We have undertaken a series of concerts to raise money for the Rotunda Hospital, to be held in the Rotunda Concert Rooms in March of next year. We invited Mr. Ignacy Jan Paderewski, but he is unable to come. He recommended your son, Charles. He said Charles performed brilliantly in concerts both in Vienna and in New York.

"Would you wish to bring Charles to Dublin for an interview and evaluation? We are most interested in pieces by our own Irish composers, John Field, George Alexander Osborne, and William Vincent Wallace.

"Yours sincerely, Cara Martin, Executive Assistant."

"Oh my." *March. That's . . . seven months away. The only pieces I could play right now are Wallace's Midnight Waltz and John Field's*

Nocturne in E major. Oh, and maybe his Nocturne No. 5. Will that be enough?

"What are you thinking, Charlie?"

"I don't think I have enough pieces ready to play right now, Mummy."

"But would you like to do this?"

"Yes. But it will take a lot of work. Already today and tomorrow I'm missing practice."

"Why don't we consult Mr. Pearse when he comes for your lesson on Monday, Charles. I don't want you to live under undue pressure for the next seven months, son."

Charlie stared at his father. *Where did this man come from? He's never been concerned about me before! Not like this.*

Mummy too gazed at Father. "That sounds wise, Peter. We must also consider when I will be free to take Charlie to Dublin. Our school is busy with the new term beginning."

"Well, perhaps I can take him, while the *Lion III* is being repaired. I have never been to Silas and Priscilla's home in Dublin, even though my mother lives with them. You and Charles stayed there in June for the piano competition, Cathleen. Would they welcome Charles again, and me with him?"

Mummy smiled, a bemused expression still visible in her eyes. "Why yes, I believe they would be delighted. Would you like a trip with your father, Charlie?"

"If you have time, I would love that, sir."

"First, we'll consult Mr. Pearse, then contact Miss Cara Martin about a date, and then check with Priscilla. Meanwhile, you can practice, Charles. I'm confident the interview will go well. I can arrange the *Lion III's* schedule to allow me to attend the concerts."

Mummy glanced at Charlie and their eyes caught in a moment of shared wonder. Never had Father adjusted the *Lion III's* schedule around family interests.

C880

As they entered the Old Thatch Pub, Charlie caught his breath. *I feel like I've been here before.* He said, "Mummy" at the same moment Cathleen said, "Peter, I know this place! Charlie, do you remember?"

"Yes! Our carriage wheel broke, and we stopped here while it was repaired! I remember a wee lassie. You showed her your mirror. . . Do you think—is it possible—"

"That was Cally? Yes, I think it was, Charlie! Can you believe it?"

"Whoa, Cathleen. I'll ask for a table and then you can tell me the story from the beginning. I have no idea what you two are talking about."

"She had a basket, Mummy. Lots of freckles."

"She was fascinated by my wee mirror."

"And with you, Mummy. She kept watching while we walked into the pub. She was with a man."

"A young man, who looked like her. Not her father. Frank had dark hair, like Teddy."

"Maybe her uncle?"

Father returned and escorted them to the table the bar lad indicated.

"Peter, do you remember a trip I made to Cork when Charlie was, maybe seven or eight? Our carriage needed repairs on our way home. We stayed overnight here, in this pub."

"What a coincidence, Cathleen. You met Cally back then?" Father sipped his warm ale.

"We didn't know it was Cally, Father," Charlie began. An older gentleman appeared beside their table.

"I am Colin Sweeney, owner of this pub. I'm told ye are inquirin' about Dugan and Aisling McCarthy? May I ask the nature of yer business, sir?"

255

"I am Peter Malcomson, captain of the *Lion III,* sailing between Waterford and New York City. This is my wife Cathleen and my son Charles. I must speak with the McCarthys about events that occurred while Frank Donnelly and his children were passengers on my ship in July."

"Sir. Ma'am. Bad news, then, is it? Ye must know they will take it very hard. Aisling is my daughter. She loves Cally and Teddy. Frank was like a father to Dugan when his parents died."

"I understand. I am heartbroken by what has happened. We all are. That's why we made the trip personally to talk with them. Can you give us directions to their home?"

"Ye've driven a long way in this rain. Why don't I send for Dugan and Aisling to come here to talk with ye? I can give ye a private room in the back. And I have a guest room available upstairs, if ye wish to rest fer an hour or so until they arrive."

"Thank you, Mr. Sweeney. We will keep the room overnight, if we may. Our horses need a good rest before starting home tomorrow."

"I'll send a lad to care fer the horses, and another to fetch Dugan and Aisling, and then I'll show ye to yer room. We have stew and fresh-baked soda bread. Would that warm ye?"

"Thank you for your courtesy, sir. We will freshen up and then come back down to eat."

᎒Ꮗ᎒

Charlie exchanged an excited glance with Mummy as Dugan and Aisling approached their table. *Yes! That's the man I remember who let the lassie look at Mummy's mirror!*

He watched Dugan grip Aisling's hand during Father's long telling of what happened on the ship and after. *Dugan looks just like Cally! And like her cousin Roisin.*

Though tear-filled, Aisling's brown eyes never left Father's face. *She loves them. How awful to hear that Cally refused to come back to her and Dugan.*

Aisling's soft weeping into Dugan's handkerchief accented a long silence when Father stopped talking. Charlie lifted his hand. "Father. Mr. and Mrs. McCarthy. May I ask a question?"

They nodded. Charlie took a deep breath. "Do you know why Cally refused to come back to Ireland, even when Teddy insisted? I know Cally loves you. And she knows you love her."

Dugan and Aisling looked at each other, eyes brimming, and shook their heads.

Mummy spoke. "On the ship, a woman named Mrs. O'Shanahan befriended Cally when she was not allowed to berth with her father and brother. After Frank's death, she told us Cally sometimes cried out in her sleep, in fear of the Dubh Sidhe. Might Cally be afraid to return to Ireland because of the faeries?"

Dugan glanced at Aisling, who shook her head. Dugan spoke. "Sure, she never told us. But if Cally had dealin's with the faeries, Miss Hilda would know."

"Could we consult Miss Hilda today, while we are here?" Mummy asked.

Aisling looked at her father. He had hung about more than necessary for serving them coffee and apple cake. "Can ye send someone fer her, Da?"

"I can, but better to wait until mornin', I'm thinkin'. Hilda's helpin' Mrs. Byrne with her birthin'. Twins, it is, so I've heard."

Mummy sighed, and Father put his arm around her. "My mother died birthing twins," she said. "I will pray for Mrs. Byrne and for Miss Hilda helping her."

I never knew that. I never thought to ask Mummy much about her family. How sad.

Father said, "Miss Hilda will be tired, then. Dugan and Aisling, could you consult with her at a better time, and write us a letter about anything you learn? I must get an early start tomorrow morning back to Waterford."

"Of course, sir. We will do that. Can ye leave yer address with Mr. Sweeney?" Dugan looked at Aisling and continued. "Of course, our first thought is to travel to Albany, New York to search for Cally and Teddy. But Aisling is six months pregnant."

"Oh, I am so happy for you both! May I call you Dugan and Aisling?"

"Of course, ma'am. I wonder whether Frank's cousin Micky and his wife Louise might go. They too love our Cally and Teddy. Do ye think Micky and Louise might have success in findin' the weans in Albany, New York, America, sir?"

"I truly do not know, Mr. McCarthy. The Albany police are to notify me if they locate the children, but of course they have many other concerns. If Mr. Donnelly's cousins wish to travel to New York, I will gladly give them free passage on the *Lion III* and a letter to the police, reminding them to continue their search. My ship will sail again in one month. If your cousins wish to go, they can contact me."

Aisling spoke for the first time. "We are that grateful fer all ye have done, Captain Malcomson, Mrs. Malcomson, Master Charles. Our hearts are broken, but it helps to hear the tale directly rather than through a letter or telegram. Thank ye fer makin' the long trip here from Waterford, in the rain yet. Ye are always welcome at our home. And should there be any way at all we can be of service to ye, please let us know."

Dugan put his arm around Aisling's shoulder. "Indeed, we are deeply grateful. I wonder how many ship captains would take the trouble ye have, not just in travelin' to tell us, but all yer efforts to care for the *weans*. We thank ye sincerely."

"You are most welcome, Mr. and Mrs. McCarthy. May this story yet reach a happy ending, with Callandra and Theodore restored to your love and care."

"This is Mr. Donnelly's bag, Dugan," Mummy said. "We opened it once, in the presence of the children, hoping to find identity papers for them. Otherwise, the contents are intact."

"The *weans* are alone in America without papers? As if they have no family, no connections?" Dugan rose from the table in agitation, while Aisling blew her nose.

"I'm afraid so, Dugan. Another reason we must pray for them. May we do so now?"

"If ye will, ma'am."

Cathleen stood, and extended her hands. Mr. Sweeney included himself in their circle. "Dear loving God, we don't know what has befallen Cally and Teddy in Albany, or what has frightened Cally so much she has chosen not to come home. Oh, Father, care for these dear children, send thy angels to guard them, and if it please thee, may we one day witness a joyful reunion with their family. In the name of Jesus, Amen."

Everyone sniffed and wiped their eyes. "Amen. Thank ye, ma'am."

"It is a pleasure to know you, Mr. and Mrs. McCarthy," Father said. "We will await word of your conversation with Miss Hilda, and your relatives' decision about travel to Albany. May God comfort your hearts in the loss of Mr. Donnelly and the temporary loss, as we hope, of Callandra and Theodore."

Dugan and Aisling bowed and walked out, carrying Frank's bag. Mr. Sweeney went with them, his arm around his daughter.

I wish I could have visited their farm. I wanted to see where Cally and Teddy grew up. I wonder whether I'll ever come here again.

Debra Kornfield

CHAPTER 26

CALLY

Albany, September 22, 1891

WITH CASH RESTING IN HER SHADE, Cally sat with the gang on the edge of the wharf eating leftovers from a ship's galley. *We worked hard carrying all those heavy boxes off the ship for this supper.* Swallowing a piece of stale bread as she fed half to Cash, she saw Paddy stand up and shade his eyes. A comical figure walked toward them between two animals. *Not horses. Maybe mules, like Cousin Malachy's.* The man's skin was burnt dark by the sun, his clothes a patchwork. He walked with a limp like Teddy's. *I don't like the way his eyes look. But I don't know why. He's smiling, and Paddy seems glad to see him.*

"Lads, look who's here! It's our friend Captain Flannery!"

The boys leaped to their feet and surrounded the odd man, Teddy with them, all chattering at once in the English. Cally went straight to the mules, petting them and murmuring in Irish. *Oh, I miss Simon so much!*

"I see ya like Carson and Harry, my mules," Captain Flannery said. "Are ya good with animals, then? I need someone ta ride 'em on the canal and feed 'em and take care of 'em. My bum leg's been hurtin' me and I ain't gonna do the walkin' no more."

Cally brightened. *Maybe this is what Teddy and I should do! But what's a canal?*

"What's yar name, boy?"

Cally continued petting Carson.

"Is he some daft, then, Patrick?"

"No. Just not good with the English." Paddy kicked Cally's leg, and she jumped. "*Labhair leis an bhfear, ach is féidir leat do dhearthái a fhágáil anseo liom.*"

Cally glared at Paddy. "I'll talk to him, but no, I won't leave Teddy with you." She turned to the man, speaking in Irish. Paddy translated. "My name is Calvin. That's my brother Teddy. We stay together. If ye want me, ye have to take him too."

"Teddy's a good worker. Ye won't be sorry," Paddy added. Cally looked at him in surprise. *He let Teddy go so easily! All right, then.*

"If ye take me, ye have to take my dog Cash, too," Teddy said in Irish.

Paddy passed this on in English. "Ya call this a dog? Why he ain't bigger'n a kitten. I'm stayin' over the night at the tavern. Ya knows the one, Paddy. Bring me the two boys and the pup in the mornin' when ya wake up. I'll be waitin' for 'em. Good night, then, all ya boys. Ya can see yar mates whenever we dock here in Albany."

Captain Flannery bowed, turned, and walked away between his mules, whistling.

"This calls fer a celebration!" Paddy yelled. "What's good fer my boys is good fer me, too. Pull our yer harmonica, Henry, and let's have a jig."

Cally smiled when Teddy pulled out his harmonica too. *He's catching on fast to Henry's teaching.* Her smile faded. *Paddy does want to get rid of us. Have we been that much trouble? I guess he's not used to his lads speakin' their own minds. He doesn't like "no."*

CRLF

Paddy gave up waiting with Cally and Teddy for Captain Flannery. "Enough of this! We've work to do, lads. Off we go. Calvin and Teddy, ye know where to find me when next Cap brings ye to Albany. Come fer dinner and tell us all about workin' on the canal. Fair play to ye both."

Cally sighed and followed Cash as he trailed Teddy, who limped back and forth on the sidewalk outside the pub, playing an Irish tune on his harmonica. *So, we're out of the gang now. Am I doing the right thing? I don't know this man, or what is a canal, or how much mules are like horses . . .*

Teddy stopped so abruptly Cally bumped into him, almost stepping on Cash. "What is it, Teddy?"

"I don't think we should do this, Cally. Maybe the man fergot us or changed his mind. Maybe he's already gone. He doesn't seem re—re— what's that word Paddy always says we should be?"

"Reliable."

"Anyway, nor ye nor Paddy asked me what I think. Ye two made all the plans and I don't like them. I like Paddy. I want to stay here. I know he'll keep me. That's what he said when the Captain first asked fer ye to go with him."

Cally sighed again. "Teddy, ye know I can't leave ye. And Paddy made it plain he doesn't want me anymore. So do ye have a better idea of what we should do?"

"Go back to Killeagh."

Cally glared at him. "Besides that. Which we are not talking about anymore."

"Well, I think about it all the time. Every time I'm cold or hungry or my leg hurts, or people don't listen to me or I miss Uncle Dugan and Aisling so much I can't hardly breathe."

Cally stared as tears welled up in Teddy's eyes. *He wants things I can't give him. I never saw that before.*

"Uncle Dugan doesn't know I've learned to play the harmonica he gave me, or that the lads and I play with my train when it rains. The lads in Paddy's gang—they don't have anyone else. But we do, Cally. We have people who love us. It ain't right. Soon as I can, I'm goin' back home. Even if ye don't."

The tavern door opened with a bang, revealing the strange figure of Captain Flannery carrying a worn satchel and leaning for a moment on the doorpost. He pulled his hat down over his eyes. "Egad, why did the Almighty hafta make the sun so bright? Oh, my head. . . There ya are, ya little scamps! I thought ya had abandoned me. Did ya feed Harry and Carson yet? Come on! We ought ta be floatin', not standin' here all day."

"Yes, sir. We'll just grab our bag."

"Aha! Ya do speak English! That rascal Patrick was foolin' with me. Hurry up then."

Pulling their bag from under a table in the back of the pub, Cally whispered to her brother, "Don't worry so much. If he's mean to us, we'll leave him. Maybe it will be all right."

Teddy made a face, but he grasped the handle on his side of their bag. Outside, they saw Captain Flannery disappearing around the corner by the tavern. Scooping up Cash, Cally left Teddy with the bag and ran to catch up with him. At the side of the tavern was a stable. Cally threw her arms around Carson's neck and nuzzled his mane, while Cash barked and Teddy lumbered in hauling their bag.

The captain laughed. "Ya are smitten for the animals, aren't ya! All the better for me. I couldn't run my business without them mules. Now, while ya two feed 'em and brush 'em down, I'll go see ta my supplies at the store in the next block yonder. Ya two can bring Carson and Harry and we'll load 'em up and go ta my barge. I'll expect ya at the store in ten minutes. Don't make me wait."

"After he made *us* wait half the mornin'," muttered Teddy when the captain was out of sight.

"Never mind that. He's our boss at least for now, so we must do what he says. There's a bucket, Teddy. Fetch water. I'll brush the mules while they eat their hay."

Carson and Harry willingly followed the children down the block and across the street. They showed no fear of Captain Flannery. *If he's good to his mules, maybe he'll be good to us, too.* The captain finished haggling with the shopkeeper, shook his hand, and turned. Cally saw a pleased smile spread over his face when he saw the children standing there with his mules.

"Help me get these supplies loaded, then, boys. We must get the balance right so it's easier for the mules ta carry. Here, give me that bag. Harry can carry that for ya. And ya can call me Cap. Now I know one of ya two is Teddy and one is Calvin, but I don't remember which is which. My memory ain't what it once was. And what do ya call that poor excuse for a dog?"

Cap whistled as they walked toward the wharf. Cally, snuggling Cash, led Carson with a rope around his neck, Teddy and Harry following. *Maybe this will be a good thing fer us. I used to not know any captains, and now I know two! Both like being the boss. But inside I am the boss of me. And of Teddy, like Da told me. We'll stay with ye as long as it's good fer us, Captain Flannery."*

"Thar she is. Ain't she a beaut? I call her the *Mabel Lee* after a lady I once knew. I've had her since I was seventeen, half ma lifetime. Thar ain't nothin' like the freedom of the water, the breeze coolin' yar face, wavin' at the people ya have known yar whole life. One big family, that's what the canal is, and ya'll see, they'll adopt ya two also. Back and forth, back and forth, Albany ta Buffalo, Buffalo ta Albany, surrounded by friends and the Almighty sendin' sun, shade, rain, or snow, just so we don't get bored. The only thing I was needin' was help with Carson and Harry, and the Almighty done sent me two boys what love my mules. I'm a happy man. Now, help me with the gangplank and we'll take

Carson and Harry aboard ta unload them. Then I'll show ya 'round and tell ya yar jobs."

Cap leaped from the pier over the railing, opened a gate, and pushed a broad board toward the dock. Cally and Teddy grabbed a corner each and pulled until Cap yelled, "That's good! Bring Carson across, and Harry will follow."

Carson walked confidently across the plank and turned right, Harry trailing after. "Attaboy, Carson. Ya know exactly what ta do, don't ya, ya old lug, and ya'll teach the boys as well as ya taught Harry. Come on, boys, help me get the weight off 'em."

The mules walked past what seemed a mountain covered by thick, oiled cloth, and stopped beside a shed. Cap waved at the mountain. "That's our cargo, tools and machines, mostly, for the farmers shoppin' in Buffalo. I got it all loaded yesterday. On our way back ta Albany, we'll bring grain, meat and vegetables for the city dwellers' tables."

While he talked, Cap unlocked the door to the shed. "Unload here, then take Carson and Harry ta their stable. Carson'll show ya the way. Did I tell ya I named Harry after our President, since I got him the same day Benjamin Harrison was elected? But Carson's been my buddy and pal since I first got this barge. I'll meet ya at the stable after I clean up the cabin for ya two."

"This is no worse than what we would be doing with the gang in Albany, Teddy. At least so far. And we have Harry and Carson! And he let us keep Cash!"

Teddy just grunted.

CR80

"So ya see, I'm goin' ta let ya two sleep in the cabin and I'll sleep in the wheelhouse. That's cuz I don't trust ya yet with my *Mabel Lee*. And so ya can fix my breakfast while I'm still sleepin' and I can stay up as late as I want after ya two go ta dreamland. I'll do most of the cookin' ta start and ya two'll do the washin' and take care of Harry and Carson. I'll show ya what ta do ta make breakfast. Durin' the daytime while we're travelin' ya two can ride or walk, I don't care. Ya'll take all yar orders from me about startin' and travellin' an I'll show ya what to do at the locks. Ya'll like it soon enough, but don't set yar hearts on becomin' bargemen yarselves cuz more and more people are shippin' by rail and runnin' the barges out of business. A darn shame, that's what it is, disruptin' a whole way of life. But I have people I've been servin' for years, so I'm not worried. I'll be a bargeman the resta my life and happy ta be nothin' else."

How does that man have enough breath to say so many words in a row?

"Ya need to know that the packets—them's the passenger barges— have the right a way over us line boats. That means if we need ta pass another mule-pulled packet comin' the other direction, ya need to pull over on the towpath away from the canal, stop an drop the towline ta the ground. The mules or horses of the packet will keep on comin' on the canal side of the path an they'll step over our towline while the packet floats right over our line dropped inta the canal. Once ya see it happen a few times ya'll understand how it works." Cap pulled a flask from somewhere in his clothes and took a swallow.

"Now let's get *Mabel Lee* floatin'. Here are the ropes we use. See how I'm attachin' this one ta Carson, boys? Now, I'll take it off. Let me see ya do it, Calvin. And now Teddy, attach this part right here ta Harry. That's it. Ain't it a wonder of the Almighty that two mules can pull such a heavy load? They could never do it if *Mable Lee* didn't float on water, could they now. The mules walk about four or five miles an hour, same as the speed limit on the canal."

Cap swore as Harry lifted his tail and took a dump on the deck of the barge. "Couldn't ya have waited a few minutes, Harry? Have ya no sense of propriety? Ya don't see Carson doin' anythin' like that, now, do ya? Well, let's get goin' and I'll clean up yar mess before we reach the

Federal Lock. Let's get the gangplank in place again, boys.

"I do my trips the slow way, cuz I don't work at night, so it's nine or ten days ta Buffalo an nine or ten days back ta Albany, an nobody cares if there's an extra day or two or three thrown in between for restin' me and the mules or takin' a side trip. Our first job today is travelin' north up the Hudson River to the Troy Lock, then three more miles to the Erie Canal itself, climbin' up through sixteen locks ta reach Waterford. We'll eat lunch some time in there, whenever I get hungry. Seventeen miles west from Waterford to Schenectady. We'll tie up there for the night. On our way back to Albany, remind me ta stop in Waterford ta show ya the Mohawk Falls. But we don't have time for that taday."

"We have a city called Waterford in Ireland," Teddy volunteered.

Cap took another swig from his flask. "Is that so. It's gonna be a hot one taday, sure enough. Indian summer, though I never did know what the Indians have ta do with it. Calvin, take Carson across ta the towpath an wait for Harry an Teddy. I'll close the gate and push off. Then Carson an Harry will walk, so if ya want to ride, ya need ta jump on in a hurry. Ya know how to ride bareback? That's good. Off we go! Ya two are hoggees now! Just don't fall asleep an fall off the mules. Stay with them when we reach the first lock. They know what ta do. Ain't this the life?"

"Cally, what is a hoggee? What is a lock? Why would we fall asleep and fall off the mules?"

"I have no idea."

CHAPTER 27

CHARLIE

Mayfield and Waterford, September 28, 1891

"COME ON, YOU WEE RASCAL." Charlie pulled Rosy out of the flower bed near the drawing room door. "We're going to see Father off on his voyage and meet Cally and Teddy's cousins. They live in Youghal. We went to the Youghal beach once, Mummy says, but I don't remember."

Rosy licked Charlie's face until he placed her in her carrier.

"The *Lion III* is shipshape again, and it's a beautiful day for sailing," Father said. "The lads worked hard."

"I'm praying for no storms on this voyage, Peter."

"Thank you, Cathleen. I count on your prayers."

I don't like disappointing Father, but I'm glad I'm not going. I'm his last hope that one of his sons will take to sailing.

"Father, thank you for taking me to Dublin for the interview. I liked seeing Mummy's Grandfather Daniel O'Connell's monument."

"It was a pleasure, son. Your mother will telegraph the news from the Academy of Music. I've already scheduled next March home so I can attend the concerts."

"I thought we would know by now. It's been three weeks since we were there."

269

"They planned to interview two other candidates before making a decision, Charles. But don't worry. You played well."

"Speaking of Dublin, Peter, wasn't it a surprise to learn from Priscilla and Silas that Thomas has been in touch with them, and is learning about Silas's work in America?"

"Indeed. One never knows with that lad. I bought a copy of John Woolman's *Journal* to read on this voyage, just so I know what Thomas is thinking about!"

"One thing he's thinking about, Peter, is a wedding date. He and Cora are anxious to pin that down. What would you think of a Christmas wedding? We know you'll be home then."

"That would be convenient. When is your Waterford Christmas concert, Charlie?"

"There will be two concerts this year, Father, December 18 and 19."

"Then I vote for December 26, but Cora and her parents can decide."

"I'll let them know. Have you heard, Charlie, that Thomas and Cora want to emigrate to America? They want to see Niagara Falls, so they will delay their honeymoon until spring. Apparently, there's a major railroad hub called Kansas City. Thomas is sure they need someone with his training and experience."

Father laughed. "Doubtless Thomas will convince them he's invaluable to their enterprise. My knowledge of America is limited to New York, but Thomas says new train routes are developing in the interior of the country, now that the major cities are connected."

"Thomas is such a charming blend of little-boy-playing-with-trains and Oxford-trained philosopher. Cora will never be bored, I dare say."

"His charm is all from you, my dear. Update me on your plan for London, Cathleen."

"What? You're going to London, Mummy?"

"Yes, she is, to study at the University of London. Isn't that grand? I'm so proud of her!"

"Mummy! You didn't tell me! Are you going to be an artist like Cora?"

"No, son!" Mummy laughed. "I want to study education, so I can expand our school's curriculum and reputation. The University of London has admitted female students for several years already, a dream coming true for me. Don't worry, Charlie. It won't happen until after Thomas's wedding, and maybe not until next fall."

Why am I only hearing about this now?

"Well, here we are. I see a couple I take to be Micky and Louise Donnelly waiting exactly where I asked them to meet us. I'll tell Evan to hold the carriage, since it won't take you long to greet them, Cathleen."

"Leave Rosy in her crate, Charlie. Evan will take her to the vet for her check-up after he drops you at home and me at the school. I wonder whether Micky and Louise are as lovely as the other Donnellys and McCarthys we've met."

"I see someone else, Charles—"

Charlie leaped from the carriage and rushed to hug a tall, burly sailor walking toward them. "Paudeen! I didn't know I would get to see you!"

"How are ye, Charlie? All recovered from our adventures, are ye? I'm to escort some friends of yer father's to their cabin on the ship. Ah, that must be them, the ones yer parents are talkin' to. Shall we go meet them?"

"Yes, sir. This is the first time for Louise, but I was in the navy," Mr. Donnelly was saying. "I'm familiar with the workin's of a ship. But none so beautiful as the *Lion III*, sir."

"It's kind of you to say so. Mr. and Mrs. Donnelly, may I present my son Charles and my right-hand man, Paudeen?"

"Oh, please, sir, we're not great ones for ceremony. Just call us Micky and Louise. We're grateful fer yer provision of this trip fer us, sir, so we are."

"Sailor Paudeen will escort you to your cabin on the *Lion III.* I may not see you often aboard ship, but Paudeen will check in daily to be sure you have everything you need. Before we go, my wife wishes to pray for God's favor on your journey."

The men removed their hats.

"Lord God, master over the seas and the skies, protect these your beloved ones as they embark. Thou knowest where Cally and Teddy are this very minute, and what trouble or need they may be facing. Provide for these precious children, guide Micky and Louise in their search, and may we one day rejoice in their return to their dear family."

Tears flowed from Louise's eyes. She dabbed them with Micky's handkerchief. "Will—will ye pray fer us every day, ma'am? We are that needy of God's favor, so we are."

"I will indeed, Louise. The children's welfare is never far from my thoughts."

"Paudeen will take you to your cabin, now. Are these all your things? Oh my. What makes this bag so heavy, may I ask?"

Louise blushed and curtsied. "They are books, sir. I am a librarian in Youghal, and wee Cally does love books so. I hope we'll read them together on the voyage home, sir."

"It's a good thing Paudeen is strong, then," Father laughed. "Oh, and I see you have brought fishing equipment, Mr. Donnelly."

"I'm a fisherman by trade, sir. I hope to share what I catch with the galley, sir."

"Off you go. Let me know whether you will return with me on this voyage or wait until the next. I understand you're considering a visit to Niagara Falls. You know how to reach me?"

"Yes, sir. The telegraph information is tucked away in Louise's satchel. Thank ye, sir." With Paudeen's assistance, the Donnellys gathered their things and started toward the *Lion III*.

"I must go too, Cathleen. Thank you for your prayer. With or without Callandra and Theodore, I hope to see you by October 17 at the latest."

"October 17? That's Cally's birthday! She'll be eight years old. Remember, Mummy? She told us when she was going through her father's papers, after—" Charlie's eyes filled. "Won't it be grand if she can celebrate her birthday back here in Ireland with all her family?"

"That would be grand indeed, son. Goodbye, my dear."

"Goodbye, Peter. I love you. God go with you."

"Mummy, on our way back to Mayfield, please tell me more about studying in London."

"I'll be glad to, son. I began thinking about this after meeting Olga Wisinger-Florian in Vienna. She helped me articulate the unfairness of so few educational and vocational options available for women in Ireland, especially at more advanced professional levels. Then I started thinking about my own desire for more education. Cora's courage in leaving her family and traveling to another country to pursue her dreams has shown me it can be done."

"I never knew you weren't happy just being my mummy."

Mummy hugged him. "It may not seem so to you, Charlie, but I'm still young, just forty-nine. I married your father at nineteen and gave my whole life to this family. I don't regret that, but after thirty years, I want to do something more. Can you understand that, son?"

Charlie stared at his mother as she delivered this speech. *It's like I pushed a button, and all this poured out. I never thought of Mummy as anyone other than, well, Mummy. There's so much I don't know about her.*

"What are you thinking, Charlie?"

He blushed. "I was thinking I don't know you very well. I never knew your mother died with twins, like you told Mr. Sweeney. What else don't I know?"

She laughed. "Oh, there is so much you don't know, Charlie. Sometimes I think people see me only in the roles I play in our family, not in who I am, myself. It was hard for your father to understand that, at first. I hope my doing this will encourage Margaret, and Meghan, and Cora as she marries Thomas, and all the girls in our school, to value their dreams for themselves too, not just for their families."

"Mummy, um, well, what will happen to me if you go to London?"

"You must help us decide, son. One possibility is for you to go to London with me. You could attend a school there and have a different experience educationally than you've had so far at home with Mr. Hobbs. I think it would be good for you to be with other children, not by yourself so much of the time. I know Mr. Paderewski would support that idea."

"But—what if they don't like me? Do English children like Irish children? And will I have enough time to practice? And would I study the same things I'm learning now? What kind of school would it be? Would I live with you, or would it be one of those boarding schools like in Vienna? Would I even see you? Could Rosy go with me?"

Mummy hugged him. "Whoa, Charlie. Those are all good questions, and I don't know the answers to most of them yet. Before you get too anxious about the idea of going to London, there are other options."

"Other options?"

"Well, you could stay at Mayfield, with Lillian and Cook and Evan and Rory and Rosy."

"I think I would feel lonely, even with all of them, with Father sailing and no family at home." Tears once again filled Charlie's eyes, and he brushed them away.

"Yes, I can see how that would be hard for you, Charlie. You could attend Foxwell School in Waterford, where Thomas studied. Or you could live with Margaret and Percy and Sally and continue to study with Mr. Hobbs and Mr. Pearse. Or you could live with Daniel and Meghan in Belfast, with Priscilla and Silas in Dublin, or with Nathanael and Sarah in New York City. Think how many people love you!"

"My head hurts, trying to make sense of this."

"Well, son, we have plenty of time, more than three months to figure this out, and more than that if I delay until autumn. So, let's not worry more about it now. As your father often says, we'll take it step by step. I hear Rosy stirring. Would you like to take her out of her crate for some play time until we get home? I'm sure she would like that."

"Sure, Mummy."

I never ever ever ever imagined Mummy would leave me and our home. Or that Father would want her to. Why can't life just hold still for a while? Why do things always have to change? Can't Mummy wait until I go to university? I'll ask her that, some time when Rosy isn't— jumping—all over me.

∞

"Liam, let's practice jumps today after our run. Evan set up some challenges for us. Would Firebrand be up for that?"

"You bet! Come on—I'm going to beat you in our race today!"

"Not a chance! Midnight has been waiting for this all week!" *So have I—so much pent-up energy I could burst!*

∞

"Ma'am, there's been an accident. Mr. Evan asks you to send for the doctor and I'm to drive the wagon to the jump by the creek." Liam rubbed his sleeve over his anxious, sweaty face.

"Charlie? Oh my, Liam. Lillian! Run to the school and ask Zeke to ride as quickly as he can to fetch Dr. Fisher. Liam, I'll ride in the wagon with you. Cook! Heat water and prepare bandages. I don't know what we'll need."

As the wagon trundled down the hill, Cathleen saw Evan bending over the crumpled figure of her son. Midnight hovered close by, while Rosy pressed her body as close as she could to Charlie's, whining anxiously. Evan had torn his own shirt and wrapped it around Charlie's thigh, but he was looking at her son's right hand. Charlie grimaced with pain.

"Oh God, not his hand," Cathleen breathed. The wagon stopped. She set her face into a calm, confident expression as she walked toward Charlie. "The doctor is on his way, sweetheart. No, don't try to talk. You can tell me later what happened. Evan, is it safe to move him? Shall we take him to the house to wait for Dr. Fisher?"

"I believe so, ma'am. Charlie didn't hit his head. The gash in his thigh looks worse, but the greater pain is in his wrist. Liam, would ye help me lift Charlie into the wagon?"

"Of course, Mister Evan. I want to help any way I can. This is my fault, ma'am. I dared Charlie to make the jump when he wasn't sure Midnight was ready for it."

"Thank you, Liam. We can talk about the details later."

"Mrs. Malcomson, could ye support Charlie's wrist while Liam and I lift him? No, here's a better idea. I'll use the rest of this shirt to bind his wrist to his chest. There ye are, Charlie. That will be more secure and less painful for ye. Ma'am, can ye open the back of the wagon?"

☙❧

"That's the last stitch. I believe this thigh wound will heal nicely, Charlie. Thank you for holding so still." Dr. Fisher gave Charlie a moment to stretch. "Now let me examine your wrist. It was brilliant of Evan to bind it to your chest. I'll be as gentle as possible, Charlie."

"Ye—yes, sir. Ow. Oh, please stop, sir." Charlie could not contain his tears.

"It's clear you've broken the radius. That in itself is not serious. A cracked wrist is the most common of fractures. But you've broken the bone in several places, Charlie. I believe you will need surgery."

"Sur—surgery, sir?"

"Mrs. Malcomson, please hold Charlie's arm—yes, just so—while I wrap it to reduce the pain. There we are, Charlie. That's the best I can do for you."

"Tha—tha—thank you, sir." Charlie glanced at Mummy and saw tears in her eyes too.

"Ma'am, I recommend you take Charlie to the hospital in Waterford. The surgeons will determine whether they can manage this or whether you should take Charlie to Dublin. Do you have access to ice, Mrs. Malcomson? That will help with the swelling."

Charlie interrupted. "Dr. Fisher, will I be able to play for the Waterford Christmas concert?"

"That's—let's see—how many weeks away?"

"Eleven weeks, sir. But I must practice."

"I would only be guessing, Charlie. Even the surgeons may not know until they see how your wrist recovers from surgery. It will require careful exercising to restore full function once the bone has mended. I'll alert the orthopedic department in Waterford, Mrs. Malcomson, but I want you to ice Charlie's wrist for twenty minutes before you go, and then several times a day for the next week."

"Yes, Doctor."

⊂੪⊃

"I will set the bones and bind the arm again. Once the swelling decreases, take him to Dublin, ma'am, to the Richmond Surgical Hospital in Grangegorman. Be careful to protect the arm and rigorous in containing the swelling, as Dr. Fisher instructed."

"Yes, Doctor."

"Charlie, you must move your arm, wrist, hand, and fingers as little as possible. Your mother will examine your fingers twice a day to be sure the circulation is good. If they turn blue or cold, ma'am, return here at once. You may use laudanum for pain, but as sparingly as he can bear. A week from today, take him on the train to this address in Dublin."

He mostly talks as if I'm not even here. Oh God, how could you let this happen to me?

"Mummy! Why did God let this happen to me?"

"I don't know, son. Let's talk with him about it on our way home."

CHAPTER 28

CALLY

Albany, October 17, 1891

TODAY IS MY BERTHDAY and I am ate yeers old. Fer my berthday Cap cut my her and Teddy's to. I got out my tresur to see if I luk difrent sins I am older now but I think I luk the sam. I am surprized peple think I am a lad. To celebrate, we are staying in Albany fer the weekend, and tomoro we will see Paddy and the gang. It seems lik a long time sinse we saw them.

Cally flexed her wrist and fingers and gazed out over the river, enjoying the play of sunlight on the water.

I am sitting in my old riting place by the river while Cap and Teddy take car of the mules at the tavern. It is a wee bit cold today. I told Cap Teddy and I wil need warmer clos to wer. He ses to find sumthing whil we are her. I wil ask Father Calahan tomoro. And I want to ask him fer books. The ones we hav are worn out. I no he wil tok about riding the orfan tran to hav a famly to car fer us. But Teddy and I are good at caring fer areselvs.

It's strang I haven't ritin anything since we joined Cap, but I hav ben to tired to rit at nite. Teddy and I ride or wak the mules all day

279

and tak car of them at nite and wak up erly to cuk brekfust and wash are clos if we want to so they can dry during the day. We only hav one set of clos to chang into. Cap never washes his clos. He just jumps in the canal and swims around and then his clos dry on his body. That's efishunt, he says. When he gets a hole he just sos anuther pece of cloth over it.

I like Cap, mostly. He has a hart of corn, but he drinks a lot frum his bottle and if he drinks to much wont stop flafin and he dus silly things lik woking on the raling and faling in the canal and fergetin wher he's suposd to go next. We hav to keep an ey to him. Sometimes he sings rilly loud and bothers peple on other barges. He's never meen to us. He likes us. Somtimes he fergets to giv us food, but we always find somthing. Teddy wants to argu with him about food but I say let the har sit. Cap liks to here Teddy play his harmonika after super.

We no the anser now to most of are qweschuns about the canal. A hogee is

"Calvin! Come on now! Let's go eat yar birthday dinner!"

෦ඊ෧ඊ෭

We ar in Rochester. Cap had a big delivery here. It is a munth sinse my berthday but I still don't feel any older. A wunderful thing hapend tho. I was sittin on the whorf reedin to Teddy whil Cap unloded with the men frum this toun. Cap sed we cud tak a brak. An old lady cam by and sed, do you lik books? O yes, I sed. We just finishd the last book we hav that we must giv bak to Father Calahan in Albany. He let us borro sum books. The lady sed, I hav many books. Wud you lik to borro sum? You cud bring them bak next time you are in Rochester. Ask yer father if you can cum to my hous to chus what you lik.

I sed thank you but Cap is not our father. Our father is ded and our mammy to. I dont no if we will be bak befor winter. She sed, o ther is time fer yer barge to mak one more trip. Go ask if you can cum to my house. It is clos by. Tell him my nam is Susan B. Anthony. I no how to spel it becus it is in all the books she let us borro. We tuk ten books. One is Five Little Peppers and one is Light Princess. I am copying so I spel them rite. I am goin to pay attenshun to the werds in the books so I lern to spel better. I never had so meny at one time in my lif! I think the lady must be famus becus Cap sed mind yer maners at her hous. She sed next time we cum to Rochester she wil help us lern to spel and do sums. I am so hapy and Teddy is to. Cap ses yes we wil cum to Rochester agen befor winter. Winter is stil a munth away. I don't no yet what we wil do in the winter when the canal is frozen.

On my berthday, I decided I must rit at leest wuns a munth so I dont ferget things. I am tird but I think this is important. I dont no why.

❦

After we met the old lady in Rochester we went to Bufalo and I saw Cousin Micky and Louise gettin of the train. I was so shokd I almost faynted. They wokd rite by me and didnt see me becus I hid behind a barel. Teddy was stil on the barg with Cap. I herd Cousin Louise say she wud try not to cry eny mor about not finding the weans sins she new Cousin Micky wants her to hav a nis time at Niagara Falls. I think Teddy and I are the weans they wer looking for. I almost ran out to hug them, I luv them so much. But they wud mak me go bak to Ireland and I cant do that. I didnt tell Teddy and I hop he will never reed my ritin. I hav been holdin my tresur and cryin evry nite after Teddy gos to sleep, rememberin Cousin Louise tellin the story about tresur to Da. He never got to find his new lif and its my falt because of the faries. I no how to cry quietly so Teddy dusnt wak up. I hav no one to tel me if I am doin the rite thing for him.

I hav to mak a decishun. I dont no how to spel that word. The old lady, her name is Susan B. Anthony, askd if Teddy and I want to stay with her in Rochester fer the winter and Cap sed thats a good idea becus he has no way to tak car of us whil the canal is frozen. I askd him what he wil do and he didnt rily anser me. In the spring when the canal melts we wil go back to Cap.

I dont no what it wil be lik to liv in a fansy house with the old lady and her sister. Teddy wants to and we dont hav eny other plas to go, so mayby we wil. But she ses we must werk hard evry day on skool werk and all three of us (Teddy and me and Cash) must clen up befor we can go in her house.

Cash is gettin big now. A boy cald him a mut and Teddy hit him, and he ran off cryin. Its alredy cold and Cap ses the canal wil freez soon. We wil be in Rochester next wek and if I say yes Susan B. Anthony ses she will order clos made fer us befor we cum bak. We hav red all the books and started over agen.

୦୫୨୦

The old lady Susan B. Anthony ses we must call her Miss Anthony and call her sister Ant Mary. She never got meryd and has no children. She askd me to rite about her hous and told me my spelin is atroshus but my persepshun is good and I notis things. I no I wil lern a lot frum her and Ant Mary. But we must keep her owers and do whut she ses al the time. I told Teddy to stop his slaging and tak a grip becus we may never hav a chans agen to lern so much. We are yousd to werkin hard and this is just anuther kind of werk. I hop he wil lik it becus I am eksited to lern all I can. Miss Anthony burned are clos as soon as her made mad us new wuns, to sets of clos fer ech of us. One to wash one to wer she sed. I am glad she didnt mak me tak my clos off but sed I wil meshur the bigger one and mak a siz smalur fer the other. She dusnt no I am older but Miss Anthony nos becus Teddy told her. Miss Anthony stil thinks I am a lad. I think. I dont no what wil hapen if she finds out I am a lassie. We slep in the bedrum at the end of the hal and Miss Anthony never gos in there. She ses she respeks are privasy. Teddy and I tak terns woking with Cash, so we are lerning mor about Rochester. I lik the river mor than the canal. It's lik this: canal rod river tran all runin besid each other with the town in between and around and briges across the canal and the river. A big lak is clos by.

CREO

I am surprisd to say I mis Cap. And of corse I miss Carson and Harry. Miss Anthony traveld on the tran to tel pepul women shud be abl to vot. She liks to travl in winter becus mor pepul are at home. She wil chek are progres when she gets bak. Ant Mary spends evry mornin with us. We hav to wash areselvs evry morning in cold water and et brekfust at 7:30 and then we stay at the tabl to do are werk. The tabl is butiful oke. It was a gift frum ther frends. She givs us werk to do and then dus her own werk until we finish then she cheks what we did and gives us mor werk. She ses Teddy lernd as meny bad habits as I hav, but she can tel I am inteligunt. Evry day she givs me a new list of werds to lern the rite speling. Then if I spel eny of them rong in my riting asinement she givs me a hol new list to lern. I dont mind. I no I hav a lot to lern. Sumday I want to rite books. Miss Anthony gave me this notebook to rite in after I lernd to spell notebook.

After are skulwerk Teddy and I shuvle snow and col fer the stov and then we can red any book we lik. Teddy is lerning to red sum buks by himself. I lik that becus then I can red my own books.

CRELO

For Christmas Miss Anthony gave Teddy and me warm coats, mittens, scarves, and boots. She made us spell the words corekly before she let us wear them. And she gave Cash a bone. She says my spelling is impruvin but I have a long way to go. She has so many books. I want to read them all. We have never eaten so much food. She says we have a long way to go before we or Cash will get fat.

We had such a surpriz yesterday. It was New Year's, and she took us in our new coats to see fireworks. We never saw fireworks before. Many other people were waching and gess who we saw? No, you will never gess. It was those men dressed funny who took us in their boat to Yonkers when we were going bak to New York City after Cusin Rosheen and Malaky stole us. They were there with wimen and children too. They got excited and pointed to us and talked fast in their langueg. We didn't understand. We just smiled. I said yes, Teddy cud go talk to them. But I stayed with Miss Anthony and Aunt Mary and wached.

She askt how we knew those people. She said they are Oneida and told me how to spell it. She said, very seryus, Calvin, their lands were stolen by the state of New York and ther people were scattered. It's not rite. They live now in small family grups. I want to help them get their land back. I said how will you do that? She said, well, I don't give up on justus matters. I have been fiting for women's rites my whole life. She told me she voted in an elecshun even tho women can't vote! Later they arested her and told her to pay a fine, but she never did. And the city stopped botherin her about it. She says sumday, maybe after she is ded, women will have equal rits with men.

When he came back, Teddy said the Oneida invited us to visit them by the lake north of Rochester. I hope we can go.

⊂⊱⊰⊃

Miss Anthony is back from her last trip. She says we must learn useful skills, not just books. So now, instead of reading so much in the afternoons, we must learn carpintry. We go to the carpinter shop and we work for him, doing whatever he tells us. We are helping make a bookcase for Miss Anthony. She says a person can never have too many bookcases because new books are written every year.

I just showed her this paragraph and she corrected carpintry (carpentry) and carpinter (carpenter) and said I spelled every other word correctly. She is proud of Aunt Mary's work with me and Teddy. Now I am reading more at night and writing less in my notebook because I can take the notebook with me when we go back to Cap, but I can't take all these books.

⋈

Today, February 15, 1892, is Miss Anthony's birthday. She was born in 1820, so she is 72 years old. I don't think I ever knew someone so old, but she says she is still spry (she taught me that word) and doesn't intend to kick the bucket any time soon. That means she doesn't plan to die yet because she still has work to do. Next week she will travel to many cities to talk about women's right to vote. She says it's not fair we don't have to worry about voting, because we are boys, and she hopes we will always treat people of the female sex fairly.

So, I guess she still thinks I am a boy. Sometimes I think her eyes aren't very good but she notices everything. I asked if the B in her name is Beth or Beatrice. She told me it doesn't stand for anything. When she was young, she wanted a fancier name than Susan, so she decided to add B. She thinks it's funny to watch people guess, like I just did.

It is very cold, and we have so much snow it is hard to go anywhere. Teddy and I worked hard to shovel a path for taking Cash outside. I don't think we ever had this much snow in Killeagh. Teddy asked Aunt Mary if Miss Anthony's handyman, Jake, could help us. But Aunt Mary said no, Cash is our dog, so we must take care of him ourselves.

⋈

It is almost the end of March. Miss Anthony wasn't here for Teddy's birthday, but Aunt Mary made a cake for him and gave him marbles. Now he wants me to play marbles with him all the time.

Mírliní we called them in Ireland. My little brother is seven years old. I wish for his birthday I could give him a leg that doesn't limp.

We have had enough sunshine to melt the snow and everything is one big messy mud puddle. Miss Anthony says if we have another freeze without more snow, so her carrige can move on the roads without getting stuck, she will ask Jake to take us to visit the Oneida. We only have three more weeks here before Cap comes to get us and Miss Anthony travels again. She wants to visit her friend Elizabeth Cady Stanton. She says if we want to, we can come back to live with her and Aunt Mary to continue our education next winter. I want to and I think Teddy does too. He says he likes having enough food to eat so he doesn't feel hungry all the time.

I wonder how it will be, going back to life on the canal. I miss Cap and Carson and Harry, but some things are hard, like riding or walking so many hours on the towpath. Miss Anthony says we can borrow books as often as we come through Rochester, as long as we bring back the ones we took the last time. Aunt Mary will write down what we take and check off her list when we bring them back in good condishun. So, Teddy and I can take turns reading to each other on the towpath. That will make the time go faster. I wonder if the mules will understand what we read. Mules are smart.

◌⊰⊱◌

The canal is almost all melted, so Cap will show up for us any day. Miss Anthony says it's now or never for visiting the Oneida. If it's not raining, we'll go tomorrow. Teddy is excited. If the Oneida have dogs, I hope Cash will behave.

The bookcase we helped make was instaled today in Miss Anthony's library. We are proud of it. Teddy said, wheekers, stickin' out a mile! Miss Anthony said, is that good? And he said, absolutely the best! Miss Anthony said if we like woodworking, we could consider it as a trade for the future. A trade is work a person learns to do well so people will pay money for it. She laughed and said Teddy can make bookcases for me to fill up with the books I will write. I can tell she is proud of both of us.

I told Miss Anthony thank you for inviting and teaching us, and she said pshaw, she and Aunt Mary liked our cumpany and she hopes when we are men, we will remember her lessons about the equality of all people, men and women from every ethnicity. She says that means any color of skin, any language and culture. Culture is what people believe and how they live. She says we will learn something about Oneida culture when we visit them tomorrow, and we should look for what is beautiful in the way they live.

෨

Yesterday we visited the Oneida and now Cap is here. He came this afternoon and said he will expect us at the barge tomorrow morning bright and early. He said he hardly recognizes us in our fancy duds and wonders if we are too soft now for the work we must do, and did we eat so much the mules won't like carrying us. He laughed, but he didn't look good to me. I wonder what he has been doing all winter. When I asked him, he just shrugged and turned away and said see you tomorrow.

We will try to visit the Oneida whenever we are in Rochester. We are friends now. They love Teddy. They call him Blue Eyes. They taught us some Oneida words. I said thank you for helping us get to Yonkers in their canoe. They said some day the spirits will give us a chance to help them. I wonder how. Their spirits seem different from Irish faeries but I don't really know. The Oneida make beautiful things out of beads and gave us a pretty wee basket. I wanted to try on a bracelet, but I must pretend I am a boy. They trade at the markets in Yonkers and other cities.

Today, April 20, is Charlie's birthday. I wonder if he's having a party with his family. I think he is turning 13. So old.

I told Miss Anthony more power to your wheel about getting the vote for women. She laughed and said that was charming and yesterday Aunt Mary told Teddy, you have a heart of corn, that I taught her earlier in the winter, after Teddy helped her clear the table after supper. Don't ever lose that, Miss Anthony said, no matter what happens in life, don't lose your own language. Then later, she told me, you have a soft hand under a duck in caring for Teddy. I taught her that too. It made me happy.

CHAPTER 29

CHARLIE

Dublin, October 17, 1891

CHARLIE TRIED TO FOCUS on the subjunctive declension of the Latin verb *velle*, to want, wish or desire. *This word makes me feel angry. I wished so much for Cally and Teddy to come home with Micky and Louise. I prayed for it. What good did that do? Cally and Teddy could be anywhere. No one knows whether they are still alive. It's all Cally's fault! Why is she so stubborn? Why couldn't she tell someone what made her afraid to go home?*

He shifted his right arm on the pillows, seeking a more comfortable position. *Oh, what's the use. It hurts no matter where I place it.*

Maybe God doesn't listen to prayers like mine. Maybe God doesn't care about children. Maybe God doesn't even exist! Maybe the whole idea of God is as made up as the fairy tales Mummy used to read to me. After all, he didn't keep me from breaking my wrist. And here we still are in Dublin so the surgeons can oversee my convalescence. I learned that word from listening to them talking to Mummy. Father is coming to Dublin tomorrow or Monday. I want him to take me home. I'm tired of this rented house. Martha and Abigail try to cheer me up but I'm tired of them too.

And Mummy still wants to study in London. What will I do? All the options upset me right now. Why do things have to change? Why does Mummy have to do this?

Charlie wrote as well as he could with his left hand on a page in his Latin notebook:

The Abandoned Lad's Options
1. Stay at Mayfield and see Father between voyages
2. Go to London with Mummy
3. Stay with Margaret and Percy in Waterford
4. Stay with Daniel and Meghan in Belfast
5. Stay with Cousins Priscilla and Silas and Grandmother Charlotte and Aunt Jemima in Dublin
6. Go to New York to live with Cousins Nathanael and Sarah
7. Find out where Mr. Paderewski will be and go to school there— Paris? Vienna?
8. Go to Thomas's school in Waterford (Foxwell)

Blether. This is no help. I know what I should do—write to Mr. Paderewski and ask his advice. Mummy might know where he is. I haven't heard from him for a long time. I wonder how his son is doing. The newspaper says his son is sicker. It's sad, after he already lost his wife.

Charlie stared at the paper for a while, and then turned the page and wrote at the top:

Events I can't play for
(said the doctors yesterday. Are they right?)
1. Christmas concert with the Waterford Chamber Orchestra (December 18 and 19)
2. Thomas and Cora's wedding reception (December 26)
3. Rotunda Hospital Benefit Concerts (March 18, 19, 20) PROBABLY. MAYBE.

Blimey, there's the doorbell. Mr. Hobbs. Mummy thinks it's grand he came to Dublin to continue my tutoring. But I can't focus.

Charlie threw his Latin notebook as hard as he could across the room, and then yelped with pain as the motion jerked his right arm. The crash brought Mummy running, Mr. Hobbs close behind her.

"Volo ire in domum suam! (I want to go home)*"* Charlie yelled as loud as he could. "Father will take me. I know he will!"

◌◦◌

Charlie sat in a corner of the Mayfield drawing room, his face sullen, surveying the happy faces of his family gathered around the Christmas tree. He flexed his fingers. *Last Christmas I played while everyone sang. Last year I played for the Waterford Christmas concert. At Margaret's wedding I played for the reception. What do I have this year? Nothing.*

Molly ran over and grabbed his left hand. "Come on, Charlie. Don't be grumpy."

For a moment, Charlie smiled at Molly's hopeful face. Then he glanced at the merrymakers and resistance surged in his soul. "I can't, Molly. I'm sorry. You go on. Have fun."

Her face fell, and Charlie felt a twinge of regret. "I'm sorry. I just can't do it right now."

Molly hesitated, then scurried back to laugh at the funny story Thomas was telling, with gestures and different voices for each of the characters. Charlie watched as, from time to time, members of his family glanced over at him, expressions of worry crossing their faces.

What is wrong with me? I have always loved this time of year. And I'm glad Thomas is marrying Cora, truly I am. He glanced at the perfect wee Rosy dog she had carved for him for Christmas. He pushed it under the couch cushion and turned over, away from his family.

◌◦◌

Gradually, Charlie became aware that the room was quiet. Then he heard Mummy's voice. "Should we wake him? I think he would be disappointed to miss Christmas supper."

"I leave that to your judgment, my dear. He seems fast asleep. He's been like this for weeks, hasn't he. Ever since we came home from Dublin."

"Yes. Every morning I wonder whether this will be the day he comes back to us."

"This has been so hard for you, Cathleen. For all of us. With time and work, he will be able to play again, but it's hard to keep that in perspective when one is twelve years old. Come, my dear. The rest of the family and our guests are waiting for us."

Tears seeped from Charlie's eyes as he heard his parents close the door behind them.

⋘⋙

"Charlie? Are you awake?"

Whose voice is that? I don't recognize it. Charlie lay still and kept his eyes closed.

"Charlie, I'm Louise, who married Cally's father's cousin Micky. Remember? We met at the wharf before we boarded the *Lion III* to search for Cally and Teddy."

Charlie made no sign of being awake. *Why is she talking to me? Where is everyone else?*

Louise took a deep breath. "Well, Charlie. I told your mother I needed to use the powder room, but it was an excuse to come to you. In my grieving over not finding Cally and Teddy, I've been thinking about you, too. And praying for you. I didn't know until we came as your parents' guests for Christmas that you suffered an accident with your horse. But I felt in my spirit that you were in trouble."

To his surprise, a sob burst from Charlie's throat. Sobs became howls. Louise gathered him in as if he were a small child. "Yes, Charlie, yes. Let the pain flow out to God. He's been longing for this day, when you could open your heart to let him comfort you."

How long he wept, Charlie could not later remember. He was vaguely aware of the drawing room door opening and then closing again. And a sense of peacefulness in the room. And, oddly, the scent of honeysuckle.

He did realize later that a huge, strangling weight in his chest had disappeared. He never talked to Mummy about it. Strangely, she never asked.

CRED

"Helping the Rotunda Hospital raise money is a good thing, Mummy. So why wouldn't God want me to do it?"

"I don't know, Charlie. I'm disappointed too. You've worked so hard to recover the strength and dexterity of your fingers. And you've made good progress, son! I'm proud of you!"

"But the doctors still don't think I'm ready. They say I might hurt my wrist with the hours of practice I need, even though it doesn't hurt anymore. Most of the time."

"We have to do what's best for the long run, son, frustrating as that is. Oh Charlie, I'm so very sorry this has happened to you."

"'It will take hard work for some time yet'" Charlie said, mimicking the doctors. "I'm so tired of hearing that over and over."

"They're doing the best they can for you, Charlie."

Tears suddenly filled Mummy's eyes. They made his own eyes water. *She's always so strong and cheerful. I didn't know—* He threw his left arm around her neck. For a few moments they wept together. Then Mummy drew back.

"It's been many weeks since I've seen you cry, Charlie. I think this is a good thing. I've been so worried you would let your heart grow bitter."

"I've been angry about many things, Mummy. I still am. But you gave up your dream of going to London this semester, to stay home with me. And you didn't fuss about it. I've been whining about every little thing. I'm sorry, Mummy. But don't you ever feel angry? Aren't you disappointed not to be in London?"

"I am, a little. The right time for that will come, though, I know. And I love you, Charlie. I'm glad I can help you through this very hard and long recuperation."

"I love you too, Mummy."

CB∞

"What would you like to do for your first teen birthday, Charlie? What would be special for you? We could invite Liam, and Abigail and Martha from Dublin. Maybe Martin and Molly could come from Belfast—you're not listening to me, are you . . ."

They've never asked me that question before. They always wanted to surprise me. Hmm. What would I like? It would be fun to go somewhere . . .

"I know, Mummy! I want to go to Killeagh to meet Aisling's baby! Can we do that? We could invite their Donnelly cousins, too. Or go to their house in Youghal and have a beach birthday party! Do you think Dugan and Aisling would want to do that?"

"I love that idea, Charlie! We haven't seen Micky and Louise since they joined us for Christmas. I'll write to them and to Dugan and Aisling."

"Mummy, I never heard what happened when Dugan talked to Miss Hilda. Do you know? Did she think Cally was afraid of the faeries?"

"Yes, she did. That is probably why Cally is afraid to come back to Ireland. I'll tell you the story while you do your arm and finger exercises."

CB∞

Stuffed so full of salmon he thought he would burst, Charlie stroked Rosy, wiggled his toes in the sand and looked one at a time at the happy faces surrounding him. *I hope I never forget this.* Mummy with baby Caoimhe on her lap, Father, his cap pulled down against the sun, Dugan with Shep at his feet and Aisling holding her father Mr. Sweeney's hand, Cousin Louise laughing at something, and Cousin Micky managing the

294

grill. *It's like having a second family. I'm glad they all wanted to come today. How could Cally give this up?*

Aisling unwrapped the gifts Mummy had brought for the baby, two beautifully carved rattles. "She'll be reaching for these soon, ma'am, so she will. Thank you."

"Oh please. Won't you call me Cathleen? Thank you for letting me hold her. She is like her name. Precious." As if she understood, Caoimhe giggled and kicked her wee legs.

Aisling blushed with pleasure. "Thank ye, Cathleen. She looks like Dugan, don't ye think?"

Dugan nudged Micky. "So, cousin. Is thirteen too big fer bumpin'?"

Micky looked at Charlie appraisingly. "The two of us together could manage it, strong as ye are, mate. But let his dinner settle first. I've no wish to see again all that salmon he ate."

"I have a toast for Master Charlie, so I do." Mr. Sweeney stood to his feet, glass in hand. Everyone raised their own. "May ye live a long life," he began, and the others joined in. "Full of gladness and health, with a pocket full of gold as the least of yer wealth. May the dreams ye hold dearest be those which come true. May the kindness ye spread keep returnin' to you."

"Sláinte! To your health!" Everyone yelled. Then Dugan pulled his harmonica from his pocket and started playing a jig. They all cheered, jumped from the table, and danced on the beach. Wee Caoimhe laughed and kicked her legs, her whole body radiating her excitement.

Oh, there go Shep and Rosy running for the waves! I'm after them. Charlie gasped as a cold wave smacked his face. *Anything to escape the bumping!*

CHAPTER 30

CHARLIE

Mayfield, April 20, 1893

"YOU MADE A GRAND CHOICE for your birthday last year, Charles, but your mother and I want to surprise you this year." Father looked him up and down. "Come stand next to me, son. I believe you're almost as tall as I am."

Mummy lined them up against the wall. "You are indeed, Charlie! Another inch or two and you will overtake your father. We're so proud of you, son. Fourteen. How could time pass so quickly?"

"Come on, Mummy. You're stalling. What's the surprise?"

Mummy looked at Father, eyes sparkling. "You tell him, Peter."

"All right then. I have a letter here from Thomas and Cora. Let me read it to you:

London, April 1, 1893

Dear Mummy and Father,

Are you sitting down? We have news! We are finally going to America! Uncle James has written a letter of recommendation for me to the railroad in Kansas City, and I'm to begin a three-month trial period there August 1. Cora says she knows I'll sweet talk them into hiring me, so we mean to go bag and baggage as if it's a done deal.

Now here's the truly fun part: Cora's friend and mentor Olga Wisinger-Florian from Vienna will be participating in the world art exposition at the Chicago World's Fair and has invited Cora to display three of her sculptures! We are thrilled beyond words! The Fair runs from May 1 through October 30, but Cora wants to attend with Olga the World's Congress of Representative Women May 15-22. They expect over 100,000 women from all over the world! Imagine that! We have tickets to sail from London May 6 and plan to spend a month in Chicago before traveling on (by train, of course) to Kansas City. We want time to settle in there before I start work. Won't that be a lark?

So, would you three join us in Chicago for part of our time there? I'm sorry for the late notice, but could you come whenever best fits Father's sailing itinerary? The World's Fair is not to be missed! Even a week or two will be an unforgettable experience. There will be so much to do and see that a month will fly by for Cora and me. Think about it and let us know!

Don't come to Kansas City yet. Give us a chance to find a home and get acquainted with life there first. But it would be a lark to enjoy the Fair and tour the city of Chicago with you!

With all our love,

Thomas and Cora

"Oh my." Charlie felt his stomach tighten. *It means sailing again.* He stood up and began pacing, looking more like his older brother than he imagined. "Where is Chicago?"

Father laughed. "That was my first question too. I have a map right here. Chicago is eight hundred miles inland from New York, on the edge of a huge lake called Lake Michigan. That's four times the distance from Waterford to Belfast, think of that!"

"It's about the same distance as Paris to Vienna, Charlie," Mummy chimed in. "We don't know details yet, but I'm sure it means an overnight on the train from New York."

"Another grand adventure, Mummy. You can see Mrs. Wisinger-Florian again! Will you go with us, Father?"

"I wouldn't miss it, son. I'm enchanted by the descriptions I've heard of the technological innovations to be on display at the Fair. The *Lion III* is scheduled to sail from Waterford day after tomorrow, as you know, and then May 29. That's five and a half weeks from now. We'll join Thomas and Cora for their last week at the Fair, then stay another week on our own before sailing home."

"Five and a half weeks! So soon!"

"Yes. But I have another letter. This one is from your old friend, Mr. Paderewski."

Charlie gasped. "Will he be there? Will I get to hear him play?"

"He'll be there, but sadly, he'll leave before we arrive. He will play a few times for the opening of the Fair the first week of May, but he has a full schedule in Europe thereafter. Listen to what he says:

Herr and Frau Malcomson, I hope you and Charles are well. My assistant has presented me with articles from the Waterford News about one Charles Malcomson, 13, playing in the Waterford Christmas Concert and for Belfast's anniversary celebrations. I am delighted to know Charles is playing again!

I sail for America this evening. My friend and fine musician Mr. Theodore Thomas, director of the Chicago Symphony, is helping organize the musical offerings at the upcoming World's Fair in Chicago. I suggested to him that Charles Malcomson would be a delightful addition to his roster, playing Irish classics, and he has agreed. Would it be possible for Charles to travel to Chicago? The Fair, I am told, will be unforgettable. Sadly, I can only be present there for the opening days, so if you go, I will not see you.

If you and Charles are interested, please write directly to Mr. Thomas.

I must run to catch my train. Please greet Charles for me. I look forward to any opportunity God may give us to see each other again.

I remain sincerely, your most devoted friend,

    Ignacy Jan Paderewski

Father looked up. "What do you think, Charles?"

Charlie flexed his fingers, frowning. "Since the surgeons released me six months ago to play again, I've only performed in concert twice. Do you think I can do it, Mummy? I have almost no time to prepare."

"I think you could play the Irish classics in your sleep, Charlie!"

"It may open doors for the future, Charles. The whole world, it seems, will be attending this Fair, including the classical music artists."

Charlie sighed. *I'm just turning fourteen. Must I already be concerned about opening doors for my future?* "May I think about it overnight, Father?"

"Of course. But we must write Mr. Thomas one way or the other very soon. We'll arrive in Chicago just over six weeks from now."

"I'll decide by tomorrow evening, Father."

"All right, Charles. Shall we go in for dinner?"

Mummy took his arm and whispered, "Don't worry, Charlie. Enjoy your special day!"

As Father opened the dining room door, "SURPRISE!" startled Charlie from his reverie. Liam was there, and Martha and Abigail, Cousin Priscilla, and Margaret and Percy and Sally. And, to his great pleasure, Cally's family from Youghal and Killeagh. Charlie grinned and hurried to greet everyone, letting the decision he must make fade into the background.

03&80

"What is this dessert called, Thomas?"

"It's an invention called a brownie, Father. Isn't chocolate grand? Cora and I have eaten one almost every day since we arrived. They're all the rage, not just here at the Hotel Burnham."

300

"Delectable!" said Mummy.

"Speaking of chocolate," Cora said, "we met a man from Pennsylvania named Mr. Hershey. He has a caramel business, but he's thinking of adding chocolate to his candies!"

Thomas smiled at her and said, "We've chattered about so many topics, but I'm curious. After one day at the Fair, how would you summarize your impression, in one word? I'd love to hear from each of you."

"Only one word?" Father protested. "Let me at least have a sentence to explain."

"All right, then. One word and one sentence. Are you first, Father?"

"Intriguing. I've never seen so much innovation displayed in one place, while still acknowledging our debt to history."

"Exhilarating! Seeing what women from all over the world are accomplishing, particularly our Cora, has inspired me to think about what my own contribution can be and whether I should reconsider my abandoned plan to study in London, and—"

"Mummy, you can't just go on and on by using the word 'and'!"

"Well, once we've complied with the rules of your game, Thomas, I have more to say!"

"What about you, Charlie?"

"You and your games, Thomas! My word is overwhelming. I'm exhausted, and since I must play tomorrow, may I be excused? I need time to myself and a good night's sleep."

"Of course, Charles. Is there anything you need?"

"Thank you, no, Father. I did like your sculptures, Cora, especially the mermaid. I'm proud to possess some of your earliest pieces, my beautiful horse family and my Rosy. After I play. I want to hear your words and sentences too, Thomas and Cora. Tomorrow. Good night."

As Charlie left the room he heard Cora tell Mummy, "Yes, we're to have lunch with Olga the day after tomorrow. In the end, more than

150,000 women attended the World's Congress of Representative Women." At the same time Father asked Thomas, "You went to the top of that Ferris Wheel?"

I've never seen Mummy like this, so excited and—and fired up. Thomas manages to make a game out of everything. Cora, though, seems—what's the right word? Subdued, somehow. She didn't eat much at dinner. I wonder if she's truly well from the cholera. Whew. I am so tired. And I still must do my wrist and finger exercises before bed.

ເຊ≫ອ

Charlie wandered around the Manufactures and Liberal Arts Building, reviewing in his mind the Irish classical and dance music he had just played. *Why did so few people come to hear me? Those who did come seemed to like my playing. But I feel alone. Everyone is off doing something somewhere else. I didn't want to go with them, but still . . . I wish I had a friend here.*

After viewing the art displayed on the second floor, Charlie wandered outside to the long, tumultuous midway. Piano music wafted toward him. *What is this rhythm? I've never heard anything like it!*

Charlie pushed through the crowd, focused on the strange, syncopated melody to a small stage surrounded by people dancing exuberantly. *I can see why. This music begs for participation, for movement.* A placard said, "Scott Joplin and the Texas Medley Quartette, Ragtime Blues."

Charlie wove his way through the dancers close enough to watch the pianist's hands, frolicking over the keyboard. *Ragtime? Wait. What was that chord progression?*

Still maintaining an um-pah rhythm with his left hand, the pianist looked up to wipe his brow, and grinned at Charlie's intent expression as his right hand fell back into the off-beat melody. *This is complicated music. It can't be easy to play. I haven't heard anything so delightful in— well, I guess, ever!*

Mr. Joplin finished the piece, stood for a quick bow, and then began another. A cornet joined him, then a clarinet, a tuba, and a baritone horn, as the four men playing these instruments pranced onto the stage, to the cheers of the swelling crowd. "Ladies and gentlemen, the Texas Medley Quartette!" announced the pianist without missing a beat. The crowd clapped and swung. *No wonder not many people were there to hear me play! This is so much more fun! I think I'm starting to understand what Mr. Joplin is doing.*

By the time the musicians finished their set, Charlie felt bold enough to say, "Mr. Joplin, my name is Charlie Malcomson. I've never imagined anything like what you just did—ragtime, you call it? Could you show me the chord you used in the second-to-last piece?"

"I know exactly the chord you're asking about. This one, right?"

"Amazing! It makes me happy."

"You must play too, Mr. Charlie."

"I do, yes, a bit. But nothing like this."

"You've been watching me for quite a while. Try doing your own ragtime, Mr. Charlie."

Hesitantly at first, then with more confidence, Charlie let the rhythms and chords take over his hands, creating his own rendition of ragtime. Mr. Joplin watched and listened for a while, then put his hands on either side of Charlie's, adding both soprano and bass voices, their distinct rhythms combining in a way that excited Charlie so he thought he would burst. "That is the most fun I've had in forever! Thank you, Mr. Joplin!" he exclaimed.

"Show me a bit of what you usually play."

"Really?" Charlie looked around. Only a few people still gathered around the stage, talking to each other. He thought for a moment, and began to play an Irish folk song, then modulated into Wallace's "Midnight Waltz." Mr. Joplin caught the melody and turned it into a syncopated version of itself in the piano's upper register. The onlookers clapped.

"We're starting to gather another crowd, Mr. Charlie, and I need a break."

"Mr. Joplin, what would you think of playing with me tomorrow? I'm scheduled to play at 3:00 in the concert hall. You could add your magic to some of my pieces. Wouldn't that be fun?"

"Hmm, 3:00. That could work, before I start here again at 4:00. Turnabout is fair play, though. I'll join you if you'll then join me."

"I would love that, Mr. Joplin. You've opened a new world to me."

"In that case, Mr. Charlie, let's try reversing roles. I'll play the base rhythm. Let's see what you want to add to it."

Charlie no longer noticed the spectators, until the cornet joined what he and Mr. Joplin were creating, followed by the other instruments. When they finished, breathless, spectators clapped and cheered as Mr. Joplin took a bow, then pulled Charlie to his feet. "Join us at three o'clock tomorrow in the concert hall," Mr. Joplin shouted.

"Then four o'clock back here!" yelled Charlie. *Oh no. What time is it? I was supposed to meet Mummy and Father at 5:00.*

"I'll see you tomorrow, Mr. Joplin!" Charlie said, then pushed through the people and hurried back to the Manufactures and Liberal Arts Building. Mummy and Father stood on the steps, frowning and looking around.

"Here I am! I've had the best time today!" *I had no idea music like that even existed! And I get to play it again tomorrow!*

"Charlie, what a relief! We had no idea how to find you. You're glowing, son."

"Are you ready for supper, Charles? You can tell us all about what has you fired up. I know your mother has had an interesting day as well."

CRSO

"I met the most extraordinary woman," said Mummy after they ordered their food. "Her name is Susan B. Anthony. She has devoted her life to bettering women's lives and is deeply engaged in the quest for suffrage. 'Not for ourselves alone' was the theme of her talk. Just imagine if women in Ireland could vote!"

"Ireland's problems are more complex than can be solved by women voting, my dear," said Father.

"I know that's true, Peter. But Miss Anthony claims issues are resolved more peacefully and expediently when women vote, because they have always been problem solvers at home. She will speak again tomorrow. Won't you come hear her with me, Peter?"

"For you, Cathleen, I would do almost anything. It will be like our old days protesting together for nonviolence. What time will she speak?"

"That's the difficulty, Peter. It's at three o'clock, the same time Charlie is scheduled to play. And we already missed his performance today."

"Oh Mummy, don't worry about that! You've heard me play almost every day of my life. Go enjoy Miss Anthony, both of you. It makes sense to me that women should be able to vote!"

"If you're sure . . ."

"It is too bad you won't hear Mr. Joplin playing with me. But perhaps you can find us on the midway after Miss Anthony's lecture. And after, shall we ride the Ferris wheel? I want to see Chicago from the top."

"A wonderful idea, Charles," Father said. "My head is spinning from all I've seen and heard today. I covet a quiet evening at the hotel."

"I want another of those brownies, first, Peter," Mummy laughed. "I must get the recipe before we return to Ireland!"

ᘒᘙ

At the top of the Ferris wheel, while they admired the city and the lake, Mummy suddenly said, "I'm bursting with news! I found out nothing is wrong with Cora at all. Peter, you and I are going to be grandparents again! I'm sure she'll want to tell you herself, so will the two of you promise to act surprised?"

"I'll try, Cathleen. I know what we should do for Cora! Let's offer her parents free travel to Kansas City when the baby is born. Doesn't every new mother wish for her own mum to support and guide her?"

"In this case, yes! Nothing will please Cora more. You could suggest this at our final supper together this evening—*after* Cora tells us about the baby."

"Perfect."

"You are so thoughtful and generous, Peter. I knew I married well, and you keep showing me how true that is."

Charlie looked from Mummy's face to Father's. *Oh well.* "Look! Look at the size of that ship! How could a ship that size get into this lake?"

"She must have been built here, to spend her life plying Lake Michigan waters. She is a beauty!"

"Oh, here we go, heading back down. Can we ride the wheel once more before we leave Chicago, Father? There are other rides, too, on the Midway Plaisance. I want to experience the travellator. And see the moving pictures of animals at the Zoopraxographical Hall. I invited Mr. Joplin but he said he couldn't go with me."

"Mr. Joplin?" asked Father. "Is he the pianist you were just telling us about, with the new kind of music? Hmm, someone handed me a pamphlet." He reached in his pocket and pulled out a crumpled paper. "I haven't read it yet, but come to think of it, for the most part I have only seen dark skinned people in support roles at this fair. Odd, isn't it? Their accomplishments are not featured at all, that I've seen. Except for a minstrel group called the Creole Show. I did see them. Quite entertaining."

"But what is a travellator?" asked Mummy. "And what is the Zoo— what did you call it?"

"A moving walkway. Zoopraxography is the study of animal locomotion. It's so popular it has its own building" said Charlie.

"I love seeing you excited, Charlie, even when I have no idea what you're talking about. Moving walkways? Moving pictures? Oh, Peter! Do you know what I want before we leave?"

"Please enlighten me."

"I want to buy one of Olga Wisinger-Florian's paintings. I know just where to hang it in our drawing room. You could help me choose, Peter! When will we have a chance like this again?"

"I agree, they are lovely. She captures the soul of the flowers she paints—if one can say flowers have souls. One could almost lift them out of the painting and smell their fragrance."

"Oh, thank you, Peter. What do you want to take home from this Fair?"

"A happy wife and a happy son. That is all my heart needs."

CঙৎO

At supper on the second-to-last day of *Lion III's* voyage home, Charlie pulled from his pocket a ragged piece of paper titled "The Abandoned Lad's Options." "Mummy, I've been thinking about your wish to study in London. I've never seen you so excited as when you were talking with Mrs. Wisinger in Chicago. I want you to go to London and follow your dream."

"Are you sure, son? What will you do?"

"I wrote this list of my options when I was in Dublin. I think they are still valid. I've thought about each one, and I want number eight, Foxwell, Thomas's school in Waterford. I need friends. More than just an occasional Saturday gallop with Liam. Since Liam is a student at Foxwell, I already have a head start. And Margaret will be nearby if I need her."

"I'm listening, Charlie. Go on."

"The wonderful time I had with Scott Joplin at the Fair showed me how lonely I am, basically doing life by myself. I want to know other boys my age. You can visit me, Father, whenever you're in port at Waterford, but then you can go see Mummy in London."

"I'm quite sure the school has rules about how often parents can visit, Charles. But what about your music?"

"In Vienna, Mr. Paderewski told Mummy I must develop naturally, not under pressure. Honestly, I don't care about my music very much right now. The long recuperation after my accident was horrible, but it showed me I can survive without playing the piano. I want to play for pleasure, because I love it, not because it's required of me. Do you understand?"

"I'm trying to understand, Charlie," said Mummy. "Are you sure you're not doing this just for me, so I can go to London? I haven't regretted postponing that idea, truly. I didn't want to be anywhere else during the hard time following your accident."

"I know, Mummy. I know I needed you. But I'm well now, and this is what I want for me. I'm happy thinking it can allow you to do what will make you happy too."

Father frowned. "Are you saying, Charles, you won't take piano lessons and you won't practice or perform this next year?"

"I don't know yet, Father. I want to find out what school is like without lessons and practice. I want time to do whatever the lads do. I don't even know what they do when they're not in classes or studying. If I miss it too much, I can always go back to the piano, can't I? I promise I will keep up my wrist and finger exercises."

"You've caught us by surprise, Charles. I believe you're on a good track, but I need space to absorb it when I'm not also managing the *Lion III*."

Charlie grinned. "Of course, Father. I know it's a change. But when you think about it, you'll see it's a grand plan for all of us."

"Charlie! You looked and sounded just like Thomas when you said that!"

Debra Kornfield

CHAPTER 31

CALLY

Erie Canal, July 1894

"CALLY, I DON'T FEEL GOOD." Teddy coughed and rubbed his eyes.

"Climb back on Harry and ride for a while. Maybe ye'll feel better."

"I'll try." Teddy did try, but instead of leaping onto Harry's back as he usually did, he sunk to the ground. Cally stopped Carson and ran back even with the barge, yelling "Cap, Cap! Help!"

Cap emerged from the wheelhouse and shaded his eyes with his hand. "What's wrong with ya, Calvin?"

"It's not me, it's Teddy! He fell and won't get up. And his skin feels hot!"

"Well, it's a hot day, ain't it. I feel hot too. But help me with the gangplank and I'll go check him out."

Grumbling that his men probably already waited to unload at the dock in Rochester and he would have to pay extra for their time, Cap stumbled across the gangplank and down the towpath. *Usually he's not this shaky until later in the day. He's drinking more and more from that bottle. I don't like it. And he stinks.*

"Ya are right, Calvin. This boy is sick, sure enough. I never felt no one with such hot skin. Help me get him onta the barge. We're about two hours out from Rochester, I reckon. It's closer than going back ta Palmyra. Teddy, what a big boy ya are for a nine-year-old, skinny as ya are." Cap grunted, Teddy groaned, and Cally supported his legs.

"Go on back ta Carson, now, Calvin, and take us ta Rochester as quick as ya may. I'll do what I can for Teddy. We have some clean water left from Palmyra. I'll try ta get his fever down."

"Maybe the Anthonys can help him."

"Well, it won't hurt ta ask. He needs help, that's for sure and certain. Go on now. Use yar mule-speak. Tell Carson and Harry ta go as quick as they can."

"But—I—"

"I know ya don't want to leave him, boy. Ya treat him like ya was his mother. But the best thing ya can do for him now is get us ta Rochester. Go."

It's my fault, I know it is. I let him play with that Irish boy when we spent the night in Canandaigua. He was coughing like Teddy is now.

ဆ႘ာ

"Do ya see which one is the biggest and strongest, Calvin? Hey there! Abner! Yes, you! Come here. This boy is sick. I want ya ta carry him to Miss Anthony's house. Ya know where it is? Calvin here will go with ya. Then come right back ta help with the unloading. I'll know if ya dawdle and I'll dock yar pay. Understood?"

Cally registered only with a corner of her mind the red roses blooming by the Anthonys' front porch. She pounded on their front door, yelling "Miss Anthony! Miss Anthony!" Aunt Mary opened the door.

"Calvin, what is it? What's wrong? Oh my. Is Teddy sick?"

"Yes, ma'am. He's terribly hot, and coughing, and—"

But Aunt Mary had already turned away, leading Abner to the couch. "Hold him a minute longer while I get a sheet to lay under him. Calvin, you know where the sheets are. Run! And you—Abner, is it?

After you lay the boy on the sheet, please go buy me a block of ice. You know where to go?"

"But ma'am—"

"Don't fret, Abner, I'll pay you for your time. That's right, spread it out, Calvin. A sheet will feel nice on his skin. Now please hurry for the ice, Abner. Here's the money. Calvin, get a pan of cool water and a rag from the kitchen. I want you to give Teddy a sponge bath."

Aunt Mary pulled off Teddy's shirt and loosened and removed his pants. "Now, wet the rag, Calvin, wring it out, and begin washing his body with the cool water. Rinse your rag often. Don't worry about drying him. Start with his face and work your way down. When you reach his feet, get clean water, and start over. I need to write a note for the doctor before Abner gets back."

Teddy's body shook, and his skin looked purple. He moaned and talked between his coughs but didn't seem to see Cally even when he opened his eyes. Cally couldn't make sense of what he said. She worked as quickly as she could, humming one of Da's lullabies.

After what seemed to Cally a long time, Aunt Mary walked in, saying "Where is that Abner?" just as a knock sounded at the door.

"Abner, put the ice in the sink in the kitchen. Now run as fast as you can to Dr. Hempfield's office on Twelfth Street. You know where it is? Give him this note and tell him it is urgent. Come back here with the doctor or you won't get paid."

"But, ma'am—"

"Saving this child's life is more important than whatever I'm keeping you from, Abner. I'll speak for you if need be. Now please, bring the doctor as quickly as you can."

"Yes, ma'am."

"Good job, Calvin. Keep bathing him while I chip some ice. We'll keep this up until Dr. Hempfield arrives and tells us what to do next."

"Yes, ma'am."

Cally exhausted her repertoire of Irish lullabies and started over before Dr. Hempfield walked in. "Where is our young patient? He's cooler now than he was, you say? Let's see, young man. Hmm, 105. Still plenty warm. Yes, ice packs under his arms and in his groin is exactly right. Keep going with the bathing, boy. You are—?"

"His brother. Calvin, sir. His name is Teddy."

"Do you think you can get Teddy to drink this powder, Mary? Mix it with half a glass of cool water. He needs the fluid in any case. Here, I'll help you lift him. Ask him to drink it, Calvin. He may hear you even if he can't respond right now. Ah, that's it, good boy, Teddy. This will help bring down the fever, Mary, but the ice and the bathing are even more important. You did right to call me. I suspect it's the measles, going round up and down the canal, and he's higher risk than most because he's undernourished. We'll have to keep an eye on you too, Calvin. You'll likely be the next one sick."

"Me, sir?" *Oh no. If she treats me as she did Teddy, Aunt Mary will discover I'm a lassie! But I can't worry about that right now.*

"Now, Mary. Give him a dose of this powder every six hours until his fever is below 102. By then he should be back to himself, out of immediate danger. If I'm right about the measles, you'll see a rash start on his face and spread over his body a couple of days from now.

"Yes, Doctor."

"Our next concern is dehydration. A high fever on a hot day dehydrates a body quickly. Do you have any broth? That would be good for him. And you can mix some sugar and salt with water. He may not like it, but I want him to drink a cup of liquid every hour until he goes to sleep tonight. Can you help us with that, Calvin? Teddy seems to listen to you."

"I'll try, sir."

"All right, then. I must attend another patient. Send for me if you need me, Mary."

"Thank you, Doctor."

Aunt Mary sighed and stretched, saying to herself, "I didn't know when I woke up this morning, I would be fighting for a little boy's life instead of packing for the women's convention." She gave herself a little shake and became all business once more.

"Now, Abner. Take this message to the post office and ask them to telegraph my sister, Miss Susan B. Anthony, at this hotel in New York City. Then go to Captain Flannery. Tell him I must keep Calvin here to care for his brother, so I want you to take Calvin's place as Cap's hoggee until both boys are able to return. Ask Cap to come to my house as soon as possible so we can agree on this arrangement. Here is your pay for the last hour. Thank you for helping us."

"Yes, ma'am. Should I come back with Captain Flannery, ma'am?"

"Yes, that's a good idea. Bring me the receipt for the telegram when you come with Cap."

"Yes, ma'am."

"Now, Calvin. Get fresh water and I'll chip ice. I do think Teddy is better than he was when you arrived, don't you? But we mustn't take anything for granted. It may be a long night."

"That doesn't matter, ma'am. Thank you for helping us."

"It's good you showed up today, because if you had come tomorrow, I wouldn't be here. I was to join Susan at a women's convention in New York City. But no matter. I'm more suited to this work than to Susan's, truth be told, though I believe passionately in what she's doing and try to support her every way I can. Now, Calvin. Replace the ice packs with these fresh ones, and call me if there is any notable change, for better or for worse. I'll be in my office."

"Thank you for helping us, Aunt Mary."

ೞ

"Measles usually runs its course in 7-10 days, Captain Flannery. But there's every chance Calvin will get it next, and then I'll need Teddy to

315

care for him. And they will both need time to get strong again. So why don't you check in on us the second time you're back in Rochester, and we'll evaluate the situation then. That will be about three weeks from now, am I right? Are you willing to play hoggee for three weeks, Abner?"

"Yes, ma'am. Though I may have to ask Captain Flannery here to take a bath."

"I agree, Abner. Is there some reason, Cap, you have let yourself go to this extent? How can you care for two children when you're not caring for yourself?"

"It's the drink, ma'am. It's gotten hold of me. I've no power over it."

"Well, that's no proper environment for two children. You must think about letting them go, Cap, if you can't take yourself in hand. It's not right. Every time I see these boys, they're scrawnier. You're not giving them enough food."

"No, ma'am. I'll try, ma'am."

"You could start by throwing all your spirits overboard. You can't drink what you don't have, can you."

"No, ma'am. But I tried doing that one time and I like ta went crazy."

"I know what that's like, Cap. I can help you through the shakes," Abner intervened.

"Well, I won't keep you. Abner, please move our block of ice to the ice box. Will you do that for me? And Cap, take Calvin back to the barge with you to collect all the boys' possessions, including the books we've loaned them. Calvin, I'll bathe Teddy while you're gone."

"Yes, Aunt Mary. Thank ye, ma'am."

"You can check in tomorrow morning if you like, Cap, to see how Teddy is doing before you leave town. Thank you, Abner. I'll expect to see you both in about three weeks."

"Yes, ma'am. I thank ya for taking them in, ma'am, and for asking

Abner ta help me in their place."

"I hope to see you in better shape than you are right now, Cap. Don't disappoint me."

"Yes, ma'am."

❦

Teddy is better, but his rash is still itchy. I showed him his funny face in my mirror. What if Aunt Mary hadn't been here? I think Teddy would have died, because Cap didn't know what to do and neither did I. Now I'm starting to feel sick. I haven't told Aunt Mary yet because I'm scared of what will happen if she discovers I'm a lassie. Will she keep our secret? Cap won't want us anymore if he learns I'm a girl. Oh. Aunt Mary is calling me.

❦

It's been ten days since I wrote that. When I felt a fever getting hold of me, I decided to tell Aunt Mary I'm a lassie so she wouldn't be shocked. I was surprised how surprised she was, but she said the important thing was to take care of me and then we could talk about why I became a boy. Then Teddy was surprised when he found out I told Aunt Mary. He wasn't well enough yet to take care of me, so Aunt Mary did all the work. Teddy is starting to eat now. He is so happy to have good food. Should we go back on the barge with Cap? I don't know what else to do. Soon Aunt Mary will want to talk about me being a girl. She started calling me Cally like Teddy does. I like it. And she put a vase of red roses on a wee table by my bed. They remind me of Cousin Micky's house, and Da saying "Red rose, proud rose, sad rose." I wonder if Miss Anthony has a book of Mr. Yeat's poems.

❦

"So, Miss Cally, how old are you now? Wait, let me figure it out. You were eight when we first met you, and Teddy turned seven that winter. Now we're in July 1894. So, Teddy is nine. Your birthday is in October, do I remember that correctly? This next birthday you will be eleven, but you're ten now."

"Yes, ma'am."

"So, how long have you pretended to be a boy? Start at the beginning and tell me the whole story. I need to understand why you made that decision."

"I'll try, ma'am, but ye might not like it."

"Don't worry about that. Just tell me the truth."

"Our da died on the ship coming to America and the only way Paddy would let us in his gang was if I became a boy."

"I see. Where is your mother?"

"She is in Heaven, ma'am. She died in Ireland, birthing our baby sister."

"So, you and Teddy arrived in America as orphans. Was Paddy's gang in New York City?"

"No, ma'am. In Albany. One day Cap showed up and wanted Teddy and me to be his hoggees and Paddy didn't want us in his gang anymore because I wouldn't steal and wouldn't let Teddy steal. So we left the gang and started living on the barge. Paddy is still our friend. We visit him when we're in Albany. He likes talking Irish with us."

"How old were you two when you became hoggees?"

"I was seven and Teddy was six. We met you and Miss Anthony that same year, Aunt Mary. Can I ask you a question?"

"*May* I ask you a question. Yes, you may."

"Miss Anthony hasn't been here the last two times we traded our books. Where does she go?"

"The last few months, she has been tromping up and down the state of New York collecting signatures on an amendment to the New York constitution that would allow women to vote. She spoke in all sixty New York counties and collected 332,000 signatures. This very week there will be a vote at the constitutional convention in Albany. We will soon find out whether our work has been enough."

"But she's an old lady! How can she do so much work?"

"Susan is 74, but she is old in years only. She has more energy and determination than anyone I have ever known. But let's get back to you and Teddy. My guess is Cap won't know what to do with you if he finds out you're a girl."

"I'm afraid of that, Aunt Mary. If he finds out and doesn't want us, we have no place to go."

"I see. Well, he won't hear it from me. The time will come when you won't be able to hide it, but you may have a couple of years yet, especially because you're undernourished."

"What does that mean, undernourished? The doctor said that word too, talking about Teddy."

"Undernourished means you don't eat enough food. Cap isn't feeding you well enough. I mean to talk with him seriously about that before I let him take you back."

"Teddy will be happy about that. He's always hungry."

"And you're not?"

"Well, I guess I am sometimes. But I worry more about Teddy."

"You've taken good care of him, Cally. But sometimes I think you need someone to care for you, too."

Cally looked down, unsure how to respond to this idea. "I—I don't know, ma'am."

"I understand. For you, caring for Teddy is more important. Is that right?"

"Yes, ma'am."

"Cap should be back in the next couple of days. Do you and Teddy want to go back as his hoggees? Until winter, that is, when you can come back here for more schooling."

"I think so, ma'am. I don't know what else to do."

"All right. We'll see whether Cap has decided he wants you enough to start taking care of himself. I mean to check up on him every time you and Teddy stop by for books this summer and fall. Now, I've been wondering whether you would like to visit your Oneida friends tomorrow. Teddy has been asking me about that."

"He'll be very happy. Thank you, Aunt Mary."

"Cally."

"Yes, ma'am."

"Don't worry. Your secret is safe with me. I won't even tell Susan."

"Oh, thank you." Impulsively, Cally threw herself into Aunt Mary's arms for a hug that surprised them both.

CHAPTER 32

CHARLIE

Foxwell School, Waterford, Fall, 1893

Sept. 17, 1893

DEAR MUMMY,

I'm sorry I haven't written much. I've been too busy. The Quakers think we should learn many things besides class work. I tried to carve wood like Cora but I'm not good at it. Instead, I am learning to make furniture! I already made a simple children's table. My teacher says it is good enough to give to the Waterford orphanage. Now I want to make chairs to go with my wee table. I'm learning about beekeeping and honey. The bees seem to like me. I haven't been stung once. All the students must help with housework and gardening. I wish I had paid more attention to Lillian's and Mr. Rory's work at home. I've never done any of this before.

My woodworking teacher, Mr. Darby, told me Thomas didn't know anything either. Everyone here talks about Thomas.

A nice young teacher, Mr. Barrow, talked to Margaret when she brought me the new clothes you asked her to buy for me. She told him I play the piano. He said, Oh, is Charles the boy who plays at the Waterford Christmas concerts? He told her he's been trying to convince the board at our school to buy a piano, and now he has one more justification for his request. So maybe that will happen!

Mr. Barrow told me the Quakers who founded Foxwell thought playing musical instruments was frivolous. That's the word he used. But most Quakers don't believe that anymore, and Mr. Barrow thinks musical instruction should be part of Foxwell's curriculum. See how many new words I am learning?

Also, Mr. Barrow decided Margaret can pick me up on Saturday afternoons so I can practice and not get too rusty. I think rusty means not being able to play well anymore. She takes me home to Mayfield, so I can have a romp with Rosy and a gallop on Midnight, too. I get a hug from Lillian and walk around and just look at everything and notice how empty the house feels without you, Mummy.

I tried to convince Mr. Barrow that Rosy should live here at Foxwell with me. He laughed and said that can be his next campaign, once he succeeds with the piano. But if I can bring Rosy, all the other students will want to bring their pets too, so he is not optimistic. That's another Mr. Barrow word. I said, then I guess I shouldn't even think about bringing my horse Midnight.

It's time for Meeting. My opinion, not growing up Quaker: Meeting takes more patience than I possess. But perhaps I will learn to like it better. Liam thinks so, and he's not a lad who likes to just sit around in silence.

I hope you are having a wonderful time in London!

Love, Charlie

꿍

October 29, 1893

Dear Mummy,

I was happy to get your letter this week. I'm glad you are enjoying your studies. I can't wait to see you at Christmas!

You asked me about friends. Liam is my best friend, of course. He's been nice enough to share his pals with me. Morgan is funny, Owen is grand at the running games, Philip has a telescope and knows everything about the stars. Patrick is the assistant gardener— he can make anything grow. Conor is odd, but in a good way. He's gentle and talks to the birds and animals living in the woods beside the woodworking shop. I know you would like them all. This school doesn't try to make everyone be alike.

Mr. Barrow succeeded in getting a piano for the school! A sweet Mansfield baby grand. I can play whenever I wish, but I can no longer spend my Saturday afternoons with Margaret and Sally and baby Cate at Mayfield. I miss Rosy and Midnight and Lillian and Mr. Rory and Evan.

The secret is out that I play the piano. Having a piano here is such a novelty, the boys often want me to play for them. The headmaster asked me to give lessons to five young boys he thinks have aptitude. Yes, another word I have learned. Three of them do. I'm not sure yet about the other two. But I must spend time preparing for each lesson, plus the lesson time itself. I am busier than ever and have more appreciation for Mr. Pearse. I brought some of my early lesson books from home the last time I was there.

Mr. Barrow is still my favorite teacher. He is teaching us Irish classics. Right now we are reading Gulliver's Travels. I never realized it is a satire. I always thought it was just a fun story. We must learn the history and current events of the early 18th century when Mr. Swift wrote it. I'm good with languages and mathematics. But I'm not so good in philosophy and rhetoric. Thomas's best subjects, as the teachers often comment.

Once again, since I only write to you on Sundays, it is time for Meeting. I am starting to understand a wee bit what goes on during this time, even though I don't receive any revelations. I never thought I would say this, but I miss the rhythms of the Catholic mass.

Please bring me a surprise from London for Christmas! Can we invite Cally's family again? I thought about her on her birthday. I wonder where she is—if she's still alive.

Tell me what you are learning in your classes and whether you are happy to be there.

Love, Charlie

ᘓᔓᘔᘓ

December 3, 1893

Dear Mummy,

Friday I received your telegram saying Thomas and Cora's babies have been born. Twins! Both Shane after Cora's brother AND Shauna! But they came early, didn't they? I thought they would be born around Christmas. I hope they are all right. When will we get to meet them?

We had our first snow yesterday, enough for a grand snowball fight. Everyone got into it, even the teachers. My piano lessons—the ones I'm teaching—started late and I could tell the boys wanted to be outside, not sitting on a piano bench. So I made the lessons short and everyone was happy.

When will you be home?

I'm to play in the Waterford Christmas concert again, so I am practicing every chance I get, remembering how to play Mr. Handel. I will practice with the orchestra next week. It feels good to have something to work toward, but I'm happy not to have the pressure of regular lessons. Sometimes I can pretend I am just an ordinary lad like every other lad. I like that.

I think I made the right choice coming here.

Love,

Charlie

☙

January 14, 1894

Dear Mummy,

Here I am back at school. It felt strange that you left before I did, but Lillian spoiled me rotten (her words but it's true). It looks like we will have more snow than usual this winter.

Mr. Barrow invited me and three other new boys to take tea in his room yesterday, but I couldn't because of the piano lessons I teach. He said, never mind, there will be another opportunity. Since he was new here last year, he knows how it feels and he wants to be sure we are happy here.

It was fun to have the whole family together at Christmas, except Thomas and Cora and the twins, of course. I'm glad Shane and Shauna are all right after their rough start, and that Cora's parents are with them. Hasn't wee Sally a grand sense of humor? Baby Cate is the same age as Caoimhe's baby brother Cathal. Martin and Molly are so big I hardly recognized them.

I'm tired and want a wee nap before Meeting, else I will fall asleep and receive a reprimand from the headmaster. I loved catching up with you at Christmas time, Mummy. Now I'm looking forward to Easter in London exactly three months after Christmas, March 25! It will be fun to travel with Margaret and her family.

Love,

Charlie

☙

April 22, 1894

Dear Mummy,

I like being able to imagine you there in London! It was grand celebrating Easter there in "your" world, with Father and Margaret and her amusing family.

Thank you for your telegram wishing me a happy birthday, which came Friday. For my birthday, I received permission to cancel piano lessons and spend Saturday afternoon with Margaret, Percy, and the children. They surprised me by driving out to Mayfield. I was delighted to see Rosy and Midnight, Lillian, Mr. Rory, and Evan. Sometimes I worry they will forget me.

The house and gardens look grand, ready for you to come home the end of June. Two whole months at home with you! I heard Father's idea of traveling on the continent, but all I want is to be home, and I'm glad to know from your letter that's what you want too.

I received a letter from Mr. Paderewski last week. Now that I am fifteen, he says he will deal directly with me. He assumes I will consult with you and Father about any decisions. The big news: He has been invited for an Irish tour next February. He accepted on the condition that I travel with him and play occasionally, and "teach him all things Irish."

The thing is, to play at that level again would require giving up most of my freedom at school. I would have to start practicing seriously, several hours a day. And I would need guidance—that's what Mr. P calls taking lessons again.

Do I want to make those sacrifices?

Mr. P says I am at a crossroads. He is happy I've had these months to "pretend to be an ordinary boy," but he says we both know I am not ordinary. Am I willing to throw away my gift to enjoy the comforts of being ordinary? Only I can decide. By your decisions and provisions, you and Father have opened the door for me to pursue an extraordinary life, but only I can choose to walk through it. (Most of these are Mr. P's words.)

Mr. P believes walking through the door labeled "professional pianist" will require a choice: (1) return home, with a tutor for my academic studies as I have had for most of my life, (2) negotiate with

Foxwell to have every afternoon free for practicing, or (3) spend my last two high school years in Dublin, with a teacher Mr. P recommends (see #2).

As well, he says I must prepare to take on regular concert performances, in Ireland and abroad, beginning with Mr. P's Irish tour next February. This would require hiring an agent to promote and manage what he calls my career.

(I would have to make more ocean voyages. You know how hard that is for me.)

I have just turned fifteen, Mummy, yet Mr. P expects me to decide now how I will live the rest of my life. I wish you and Father were here to discuss this with me. I will pray for revelation at the Meeting, to which I must run.

Mr. Barrow invited me to tea at a time that works for me, since I can never go on Saturdays with the other boys. Perhaps I can discuss all these decisions with him.

Perhaps you can tell I am somewhat angry with Mr. P. I cherish being ordinary.

Love,

Charlie

CRBO

May 27, 1894

Dear Mummy,

I have gone twice to Mr. Barrow's rooms to discuss the decisions weighing on me. Each time, he has been attentive and has asked me good questions. He pays me a great many compliments and asked me to play for him so he would understand better my "extraordinariness." I found that odd, but he said how can he advise me if he doesn't really know me?

I have not yet made any decisions, either about the Irish Tour or about my future. I hope to wait until I am home in June and can talk to you about it. I sent Mr. P a short note saying I am thinking hard and will advise him when I have made my decisions.

I have been practicing whenever I can and once again wish for a nap before Meeting. Everything else seems less important than it was: whether my beets are growing well, or receiving highest marks in class, or the hallway properly cleaned, or my piano students preparing well for their recital at the end of term.

I have not received any revelations in Meeting.

Don't be alarmed if you don't hear from me again before we see each other the end of June. I am busy.

Your ordinary son,

Charlie

❧

July 1, 1894

Dear Mr. Paderewski,

At Foxwell Academy, I got into the habit of writing my letters on Sunday afternoons. Today it is your turn, finally, to hear from me. My parents are both home so I have been talking with them about what I should do. I asked them to speak frankly, but afterward I half wished they had not.

My father is convinced I have a gift, and to throw it away would be to spit in the face of the Giver. I have never heard him talk like that and was quite startled. He thinks we must serve the gifts we are given. My mother, in her gentler way, believes this as well.

Part of me wished they would say "Yes, Charlie, we agree it's more important for you to be free and happy than to sacrifice all the other things you love for this one purpose, to serve the gift of music." Then if I made the other choice, I could consider myself noble, rather than just doing what my parents expect of me.

A teacher at my school named Mr. Barrow advised me at the end of May, "Charles, for one month, live an ordinary life. Try it out. Do not play the piano, except to help your students. Use your free time as the other lads do. Don't try to evaluate. Just enjoy each day."

I respect Mr. Barrow, so I agreed. The first couple of days were grand. But by the third day, I longed for the piano. I even looked forward to seeing my students, so I could partake in music in that small way. I found myself touching the piano, wanting to stroke it. Can I say that without sounding odd? I felt physically connected to it.

In short, by the end of the second week of this experiment, I knew I could not live like other lads and be happy. I am captive to my instrument and how it can sing through me.

So, I accept your invitation to travel Ireland with you in February and will take joy in preparing for your tour. I believe I will spend the next two years, when not touring, in Dublin, living with my father's cousins. Please send me the name and address of the piano teacher you recommend there.

Thank you for your confidence in the gift God has given me. Each time I learn someone is moved by my music, I will know it is due to your investment in me.

Gratefully,

Charles Malcomson

Pianist

Debra Kornfield

CHAPTER 33

CALLY

Albany, October 16, 1896

TOMORROW IS MY 13TH BIRTHDAY. Cap likes to celebrate my birthday in Albany and his in Buffalo ten days later. Teddy's birthday comes while we're wintering at Miss Anthony's in Rochester. I like that word, wintering. I read it in a book. We'll have dinner with Paddy and the gang and stay tonight at the tavern. I don't like it because Cap gets drunk. Between my birthday and his he'll probably be drunk most of the time. When we stop in Rochester to pick up books, he'll have to be sober or Aunt Mary will scold and threaten to take us away from him.

I'm getting tired of living with Cap. There, I said it. So is Teddy. We take care of Cap more than he takes care of us. But we don't know what else to do. Teddy talks about running away, going home to Killeagh. He might do it, too. He has become stubborn and says he's tired of walking back and forth from Albany to Buffalo, Buffalo to Albany. He's growing fast and acts a little crazy sometimes. He's much bigger than I am and doesn't like me telling him what to do. I wonder if I will always be small.

I'm sitting in my writing place by the Hudson River. The stump is still here, the fall leaves are lovely, and Teddy is showing Cash the old places where he liked to play. This riverside doesn't seem to change. But every time we come back, Teddy and I are different.

It's been more than five years since we left Ireland, since Da died. I wonder if he can see us. Can he watch us growing up? When I look at the moon, I wonder how Uncle Dugan and Aisling are, and whether they have any children. Does Aisling still think of us when she looks at the moon? Sure Cousin Micky and Cousin Louise have forgotten about us by now, but I think Cousin Louise would be happy Teddy has learned to read and write so well. And I have learned to spell most of the words I know.

I wonder if someday there will be a library in Rochester, like Cousin Louise's library in Youghal. I have read most of the books at the Anthonys' house, at least the interesting ones. I want to find more books about science and about history. Miss Anthony has books about New York history, but I want to learn about the rest of the world. I don't even know much about Ireland, my own homeland. And the Anthonys aren't very interested in science. I think I might want to be a doctor.

Aunt Mary told me a long time ago, when Teddy and I had measles and I told her I'm a girl, that later it would be harder to pretend I'm a boy. I wonder what she meant. I never found a good time to ask her. So far no one else knows. Only Teddy, and Paddy, who made me into a boy to be in his gang, and Aunt Mary, who has kept her word not to tell.

Teddy is calling to show me something. I hope I will have time to write more tomorrow.

 C3&O

I didn't have time to write on my birthday because one of the men Cap hired to load the barge was sick, so he asked Teddy and me to help. It was hard work and took all day. We met Paddy and the gang at the tavern for supper. Paddy is almost a man now, and so is his right-hand boy Jeb. I talked to Paddy by himself after supper and told him I didn't like the way Jeb looked at me.

Then I had a terrible shock. Paddy told me the reason he sent Teddy and me away with Cap wasn't because we refused to steal. It was because Jeb saw me one time doing my necessaries and saw I was a lassie. Jeb didn't like that. He told Paddy either I left the gang, or he would. So Paddy sent us away to keep Jeb. Now Paddy says I shouldn't visit the gang for a while, until Jeb settles down, whatever that means.

I will be glad not to visit the gang for a while. I feel scared of Jeb. I wish I had someone to help me understand why he looks at me like that. Maybe I can ask Aunt Mary this winter. And ask her if she thinks it will be hard to keep on being a boy.

This is my last writing in this notebook because it is full. I hope no one ever finds and reads it. Aunt Mary says Miss Anthony is bringing a new notebook for me back from California, with a picture of Yosemitty on it. I can pick it up next time we are in Rochester. I wonder what Yosemitty is.

∞

Teddy did it. He ran away. And I think Cash went with him. When it was time to leave Albany, we couldn't find either of them. I think Teddy went to New York City to find a ship to Ireland. He might even look for the Lion III. I don't know what to do. How can I find one eleven-year-old boy in New York City, without Cash to help me?

Teddy's been telling me for a long time he would do this, so I'm sure he doesn't want me to find him. I have failed at doing what Da asked me to do, care for Teddy.

And now I am by myself. All I know to do is keep on with Cap until the canal freezes and then go to the Anthonys for the winter.

What else can I do? I am brokenhearted. When I'm by myself I can't stop crying. But I don't let Cap or other people at our stops see me cry. I don't want to have to explain or listen to people's opinions about my situation.

For the first time in my life that I can remember, I have to sleep by myself. I couldn't sleep last night. Not even Cash was there to comfort me.

I wonder if the Malcomsons were sad when Teddy and I ran away from them. But it can't be the same. They all have each other, and we weren't part of their family. But Teddy is all the family I had left. Now I have no one.

What should I do? I tried to pray, but I couldn't think of any words. It's so long since I thought of Aisling's prayer. I remember the last time I said it: in the boxcar in Albany before Paddy cut my hair and made me a boy and I lost myself.

Please, God. Take care of my brother. And Cash.

⊰⊱

Something strange is happening to my body. Is this what Aunt Mary was talking about? Next week I will begin my wintering in Rochester.

⊰⊱

I can't believe it. I went to the Anthonys and no one was there. I knocked and knocked, and called, and walked around the house. But I could tell no one had been there today because there were no footprints in the snow except my own and Cap's. Did I come sooner that they expected?

Cap says he'll stay over one more day to see whether they show up, but after that I'm on my own. What will I do? Find a corner somewhere to sleep, I guess. Or maybe try to find the Oneida. I've never gone there by myself, but I can try. I have nothing left to lose. My bag is heavy with books from the Anthonys. Maybe I can find a safe place to put them, so I don't have to lug them around and maybe lose them.

CRISO

The Anthonys still aren't home. Cap gave me a bag for their books. I wrapped them in one of Teddy's shirts that he left behind and tucked them under their porch. There might be animals under there, but I don't think they'll be interested. At least the books will stay dry.

Cap is gone. He said he had to leave before the canal freezes over. He never has told us where he goes in the winter or what he does. But every spring he looks the worse for wear. That's a phrase I learned from him. He said I looked the worse for wear after I had the measles.

So, I am going to try to find the Oneida. Every other time we have gone to their settlement in a wagon or carriage. It will be a long walk, and I'm not sure I know the way. I wish I knew someone to ask. But I don't know any of the people walking in the streets. Most people are tucked away in their homes because it is cold.

The coat, mittens and boots the Anthonys gave me are all small for me now, but I'm glad I took them with me along with the books last month.

CRISO

I haven't written for a long time because I have been busy learning to live like the Oneida and helping them smoke meat for the winter. It's hard work. The men do the hunting and the women butcher, skin, cut, and smoke the meat. Oh yes. When I got here, I was frozen and hungry and I passed out. The women took my clothes off to rub snow on my body and found out I am a girl. So now the whole Oneida clan knows I am not a boy.

It took me two days to find their settlement but when I finally recovered, they seemed happy to let me stay with them. One of the men who took us in the canoe to Yonkers, River Rider, has learned a lot of English because of his trading. He said one more day in the cold without food might have been too much for me. They are calling me Short Hair because all the other girls and women have long hair.

River Rider says I can go with him next time he goes to Rochester, to find out whether the Anthonys are back and whether they want me to stay with them. I hope so. I like the Oneida and they are very kind to me. But I have so many questions to ask Aunt Mary. The Oneida women don't speak English and I don't know very many Oneida words yet. I am trying to work hard so they won't mind that I am here.

◌◌◌

You will never believe what has happened. I don't believe it myself. Today another group of Oneida joined this one. With them they brought a boy with blue eyes. Yes! My brother Teddy! I was so surprised and happy to see him! I yelled and laughed and cried and ran to hug him, while Cash jumped all over me. But Teddy pulled away from me. The sting of it hurts me still. I'm sure he's afraid I will try to make him come back to me. I told him I won't, he can do what he wants. But I don't think he trusts me. He just called Cash and turned away and went to another place on the edge of the settlement where the new Oneida were setting up their teepees. I cried and cried. I couldn't help it. I still don't know what he has done or where he has been since he left us in Albany.

I failed at the one thing Da asked me to do. But at least I know he is alive and well.

Tomorrow River Rider is going to Rochester and I will go with him. I hope the Anthonys are back, or at least, Aunt Mary. If she will have me, I will stay with her. It hurts me too much to know Teddy, Blue Eyes as they call him, is here but doesn't want to see me or talk to me.

All this time I thought Teddy went back to Killeagh. I wonder if in the end, he felt like he couldn't show up there without me.

ೞ

Besides Teddy showing up and not wanting me, I had another scary thing yesterday. Blood started running down my leg. I was so scared I yelled for help. Three squaws came running and when they saw it, they laughed and got me some rags for the bleeding. But I still don't understand what is happening to me. I hope, hope, hope Aunt Mary is home in Rochester and will want me to stay with her. I have been wearing Oneida girl clothes but now I am dressed in my boy clothes for the long walk to Rochester.

Please God, help me. Keep my brother safe.

ೞ

I only have time right now to say: Yes. Aunt Mary is back. Miss Anthony is not. I will stay in Rochester with Aunt Mary for the winter. She explained things to me. It seems very strange, but she says I am normal. I am glad for that at least. I secretly looked in my mirror and I think I look the same, though I feel different. Aunt Mary thinks we should reconsider whether I go back with Cap in the spring. For now, I am still a boy. Next week is Christmas, my first Christmas without Teddy.

She is calling me.

Debra Kornfield

CHAPTER 34

CHARLIE

Dublin, August 31, 1894

"MY LESSONS WILL BE ON TUESDAY and Friday afternoons. There will be a recital tomorrow evening to conclude the summer music term," Charlie told the family at supper. "Mr. Esposito says we are all welcome to attend. He wants me to meet the other students."

Cousin Priscilla looked at her husband and daughters. "We are free, are we not, Silas? Would thee like to go, Abigail? Martha?"

"Will they all be piano students?" asked Martha.

"No. They will play various instruments, some pieces as duets or in a chamber orchestra," said Charlie.

"Priscilla and I have been thinking about Sunday," said Cousin Silas. "Thee hast attended Meeting at Foxwell, yes? But would thee wish to attend mass in the morning as well?"

"I would, yes. Thank you, Cousin Silas."

"We know thee will have many adjustments living with us, Charlie. We want thee to feel at home with us. Are thee comfortable in thy room?"

"Yes, thank you, Cousin Priscilla."

Priscilla turned to her husband. "We have a letter from Aunt Charlotte, Silas. Jemima's tour is going well—the Americans appreciate her poetry, and she has sold almost all the books she took with her. Charlotte says this will be her last grand adventure."

"Well, she is, what, 85? Amazing woman. I'll read her letter later. Thee may be excused, Abigail, Martha, Charlie."

ভঙ

The family found their seats just as the lights dimmed and two students walked onto the stage and bowed. The boy slid onto the piano bench. The girl bent her dark head for a moment, then lifted her violin. Charlie held his breath. *Will she be good? I hope—*

The girl's violin swept him into "Méditation" from *Thaïs*. The duo waited for the applause to die down, then began *Sonata for Violin and Piano in E Minor*.

"My teacher composed this!" Charlie whispered to Abigail beside him. *I'm beginning to understand why Mr. Paderewski sent me to the Royal Irish Academy of Music.* He glanced at his program. *Laoise Murphy, 15. And her accompanist is Ciaran O'Brien, 17. Might that be me someday?*

As Charlie went to sleep that night, his thoughts were filled with a slim girl's sapphire eyes, dark hair, and magic in her fingers.

ভঙ

Laoise stopped by Charlie's desk on her way out of the music theory classroom. "Charlie, I didn't understand what our professor said about quartal chords. Would you have time to explain it to me?"

ভঙ

Charlie stepped into Mr. Esposito's room thinking about the complicated fingering he would shortly have to perform. He looked up to see Laoise sitting in a chair by the piano, her violin on her lap.

"I'm sorry. Am I in the wrong place? Or do I have the time wrong?"

"No, no, Charles. You must practice accompaniment, not just solo playing. I asked Laoise as a favor to help me teach you today. She is willing for you to practice with her during this next week as well."

"It's my pleasure, Charlie," said Laoise. "I owe you for all your help to me with theory class."

◌◌◌

"Charlie, a group of us are going for a picnic on North Bull Island Saturday. Do you want to go? Please do." Laoise's smile so dazzled Charlie that for a second, he didn't connect with what she was saying.

Perhaps I can have friends again. That was the hardest part about leaving Foxwell.

◌◌◌

"Charles, you have done well accompanying Laoise. She complements you on your sensitivity to her leadership," said Mr. Esposito. I want you to try accompanying the Academy's string quartet. If you do well, you may serve as their accompanist for the Christmas recital."

◌◌◌

Laoise hung back after the string quartet practice. As Charlie gathered his music, she said, "Charlie, my family will host an end of term party after the Christmas recital December 15. Will you come? I would like that very much."

Charlie watched her fingers trail up his arm. Face warm, he looked up. "I would like that very much also. Thank you."

"I'm glad. I won't see you over the holidays because my family will be in France. But I want you to meet my parents."

Laoise gave him a brilliant smile as she left the room.

◌◌◌

"A letter for thee, Charlie. From thy mum, I think. I can't believe it is December already! What are thy plans for Christmas?"

"Perhaps this letter will tell me. Thank you, Cousin Priscilla."

341

London, November 20

My precious Charlie,

I hope all is well with you, son. I have missed hearing from you, but I know you are frightfully busy with your music and your schoolwork. I hope you are finding time for fun with your cousins and friends as well. And helping at home from time to time.

My studies are going well. I enjoy them immensely. There is so much I am eager to put into practice at our school when I complete my degree.

I have given a great deal of thought to our Christmas plans this year. Daniel and Meghan will be with her family, and Margaret and Percy have planned a trip on the continent with his parents. Father suggests we travel to Kansas City to visit Thomas and Cora and the children. Would you like to go with us if we decide to do that?

"An ocean voyage on winter seas? No, thank you," Charlie said out loud to the empty room. "Besides it would take too long. I can't take that much time off." He walked into the kitchen. "Cousin Priscilla, Mummy and Father are thinking of spending Christmas with Thomas and Cora. Might I stay here with you?"

"Of course, Charlie. We will be delighted to have thee."

⊂ℬ୫⊃

December 23, 1894, Dublin

"Charlie, you have a visitor. He's in the drawing room."

"Thank you, Abigail. I'll be right down." *A visitor? Me?*

"Mr. Barrow! What a surprise! What are you doing in Dublin in the last days of term?"

"Charles, it's so good to see you. Are you well? Is there a place we can talk?"

"We can go to my room."

"Splendid. You are living with your aunt and uncle?"

"My father's cousins, though they seem like aunt and uncle. And their two girls. They have been grand to take me in. Here, let me clear

342

some space. I have been practicing so much I haven't kept my room in proper order."

"So I see. Let me help you. I'm a master at making things look good."

Charlie stopped, and stared at his mentor. *What can he possibly mean by that?*

"Charles, you have always honored me by sharing your thoughts and struggles. Now I need to honor you in the same way."

"Me, sir?" *Every part of this is strange. Why would an adult come to a boy, a teacher to a student?*

"That's enough straightening. Come sit by me, Charles."

"Sir?"

"Charles, I always felt you looked up to me."

"Indeed, sir. I—yes, I did, sir."

"The fact is, Charles, I used the other boys, inventing those Saturday afternoon teas, as a pathway to you. I loved you from the moment I first met you. Then you left. By then I was too involved with the other boys—was found out—fired—thrown away. Beastly things said. But I knew you would understand my heart."

Charles backed toward the door.

"Sir, I don't understand what you are saying. Perhaps Cousin Silas . . ."

Mr. Barrow suddenly crossed the room and put his mouth on Charlie's, gripping his shoulders. Charlie jerked his head away. Feeling for the doorknob behind him, Charlie managed to throw open the door and yell, "Help! Cousin Silas! Help me!"

Footsteps pounded on the stairs. Mr. Barrow released his grip and Charlie fell backwards through the door. He leaped up and slammed the door, shaking so much he almost fell again into Cousin Silas's arms.

"What is it? What has happened? Talk to me, Charlie!"

"Th-there's a man in there who tried to—" Charlie could not complete the sentence.

"What do thee need me to do?"

"I do-don't know. C-call for the police, I think."

"What will happen if I just open thy door?"

"I-I do-don't know."

"Charlie, I think that's what I should do. Can thee tell me what thee are afraid of?"

"I-I-I—N-No. C-Cousin Silas!" *I sound like an idiot. I don't know what to say.*

Cousin Silas opened the door. The room was empty and chilled. A curtain fluttered at the open window. He walked over, trailed by Charlie reaching toward him, wanting to stop—.

A man lay crumpled on the sidewalk, blood spurting from his head.

"He's still alive, Charlie! We must run for help!"

Charlie couldn't move. He opened his mouth, swayed, and crashed to the floor.

CʒꝵꝊ

February 5, 1895 Dublin

"Charles, you must talk to me. Your playing last night and tonight was flawless, technically. But the beauty, that unique purity which drew me to you like a bee to honey—the beauty is gone. In its place I feel—hmm."

Mr. Paderewski tapped his cheek with his finger. "I feel fear. And grief. Grief, yes. But something more. Anger. And something beneath that . . . betrayal, I think. What has happened to you, Charles?"

Charlie shook his head, staring at the floor. *Is that what this terrible weight is inside me? I have no words, just darkness. I am numb. Empty.*

"You have had a great shock?"

Charlie looked up and slowly nodded his head.

"Can you tell me?"

Charlie shook his head no. To his surprise, he felt a tear on his cheek. He rubbed it away.

"Does playing help you feel better?"

Charlie nodded yes.

"Then we will continue the tour. Let the anguish bleed out into the music, Charles, so the beauty can find space in your soul to return."

Mr. Paderewski stood and walked to the door. Turning, he said, "It may be no one else will notice. The applause these two nights was thunderous. How did it make you feel? Happy?"

Charlie looked back at the floor. He shook his head no.

Cؤ

April 19, 1895, Royal Irish Academy of Music

"I brought you a birthday present." Laoise, smiling brightly, extended a gift. "You have time to open it before your lesson. Happy sixteen, Charlie!"

Charlie gazed at her, entranced as always by Laoise's blue eyes and silky dark hair. Her gentle spirit that turned to fire when she lifted her violin.

Then he remembered. He pulled back. His face closed.

Laoise sat next to him. "Charlie, what happened just then? Please, please tell me. You've been so different since Christmas. I'm worried about you."

"I'm fine. Just—busy. A bit worried about the concerts in Londonderry. 'Get your act together, lad,'" said Charlie, mimicking Mr. Esposito.

"Before Christmas, I thought—well, I thought—we—"

"There is no 'we,'" said Charlie, his voice hard. "You're mistaken. Take your gift and go home."

Tears flooded her eyes. She jumped to her feet and ran from the room.

"Sixteen. What a baby. The child prodigy. Teacher's pet," said his one-time friend Ciaran from a chair by the window. "You could have destroyed her with more finesse, don't you think, little virtuoso?

Sarcasm is my domain, not yours. It does not become you, baby Charlie."

Charlie glared at Ciaran and pretended to be absorbed in his music until Mr. Esposito's assistant called his name.

"I guess this means she's fair game, eh, baby Charlie? She needs a *man*. Like me." Ciaran's mocking voice followed him out of the room.

CHAPTER 35

CALLY

Rochester, NY, March 14, 1897

AUNT MARY THINKS I should not go back on the barge with Cap. She says his drinking has consumed him. I have been thinking long and hard about this because I don't know what else to do. Aunt Mary says I can stay here to help with Miss Anthony's biography, but the girls working on that are all friends and I am left out because they think I am a boy. Aunt Mary says, then why don't I switch to being a girl.

I try to imagine myself doing that, and how surprised the other girls would be. But being a boy feels safer to me for some reason I can't explain. I think I can get away with it for another year at least. I read in a book about a girl disguising herself as a boy by binding her breasts. I could do that if I ever get enough to worry about. Aunt Mary says I'm too skinny and if I ate better regularly, I would look different. Who knows. The thing is, I can always switch to a girl later, but once I do it, people will know. It will be harder to go back.

Anyway, I must decide, because the canal ice is thawing, and Cap will come for me soon.

I hardly saw Miss Anthony this wintering. She turned 77 last month but still travels and speaks about women's right to vote.

When she is home, she seems anxious and upset about what is happening with the suffrage movement. She looks at me but doesn't really see me. She goes on and on about Populists opposing immigrants, her disagreement with Mrs. Stanton about that and about educated suffrage, the failure to get the vote in Kansas despite all her efforts, the confusion of suffrage with temperance in the California campaign, white men setting up white women against black women, her anger at the way people treat her friend Miss Ida Wells, and on and on. I don't understand most of it.

Miss Ida came to visit and stayed even after Miss Anthony traveled again. I like her. She is gone now.

Another Ida, Mrs. Ida Harper, is living here, trying to organize trunks, boxes, and bags of letters and papers and diaries and convention reports and scrapbooks into something useful for writing Miss Anthony's biography. I help with the sorting for two hours every afternoon, along with the girls who don't want to be my friends. The diaries have dates with every entry, so I am going to start adding dates to what I write.

CB80

April 4, 1897 Aunt Mary says, laughing, it's a good thing my wintering is ending because I have learned all she knows to teach me and if I come back next winter, I will have to teach her. She is joking, of course. I still have so much to learn. Just last week I found out there are places in the world that don't ever get snow or cold. They are hot all year. I would like to visit a place like that. I wish I could see Aunt Mary's roses bloom.

I think I want to be a doctor. I want to learn biology and chemistry and everything there is to know about the human body. Yesterday I learned the words anatomy and physiology from reading a book about Elizabeth Blackwell, the first woman to attend medical school in America. I want to be like her.

I have decided to go back with Cap. I know that without Teddy's help with Harry, being Cap's hoggee will make me very tired, so I probably won't write much for a while. I haven't heard anything at all from or about Teddy.

Please, God. Take care of my brother. Since I cannot.

⊂⊃

October 17, 1897 We are back in Albany for my 14th birthday, a whole year since I lost Teddy. I feel sad and empty and lonely. I saw Paddy today near the tavern, but when he saw me, he turned around and walked away. I dread the next days, because Cap will use my birthday and his as an excuse to go on a binge.

⊂⊃

October 31, 1897 I went with Cap to check in with Aunt Mary as he promised. He was mostly sober. Aunt Mary looked at me and shook her head. Later she told me, as I was choosing books, "We will talk about Cap in a few weeks when you come for your wintering. I promise I will be home this time." I was so relieved, I laughed. It felt good to laugh.

While we were still at their house, a message was delivered. It was from my Oneida friend, River Rider. The message was not easy to read, but it said "We go south. Oklahoma. Blue Eyes with us." I cried. I am so thankful River Rider let me know. What if I had gone to visit the Oneida and found them gone? It would be like losing my brother all over again. At least I know he is alive. I don't know where Oklahoma is, but I intend to find out when I return.

⊂⊃

November 21, 1897 At breakfast, Aunt Mary greeted me with the Rochester Post-Express open to an article about Cap. Yesterday he was found frozen in the canal, between Rochester and Pittsford. He must have been drunk and fell off the barge and the canal froze around him. Poor Cap. My first thought was for Carson and Harry.

Aunt Mary sent a note to Abner's house asking him to take me to find the barge, which must be frozen in place. I'll write more when I get back.

⊂⊃

We put Carson and Harry in Abner's shed because the Anthonys have no place to keep them. They were so happy to see me. I will visit them every day.

It's strange. Now that Cap is gone, I miss him. I didn't miss him during my winters here while he was still alive. "Such a tragedy," Aunt Mary says. But I think it's for the best. Cap was a kind and generous man in his way, but he had no power over the drink. He knew it and it made him sad, sad enough to drink more. He was never mean to me or to Teddy, but he never let us really be friends. He showed everyone a cheerful face, but the drink ate him away inside until he was hollow. What would we have done if Cap hadn't taken us from Albany, though? Six years we spent with him, watching his slow dying. I wonder if Paddy knows his friend is gone.

Having Carson and Harry close by makes me miss Teddy terribly, all the hours and days we spent riding and walking from Buffalo to Albany and back, reading books, talking, making up stories we told to the mules. Oh God, please take care of my brother.

⊂⊃

January 2, 1898 I had a shock Friday night at the New Year's Eve celebration in downtown Rochester. I saw Jeb. I was holding Aunt Mary's arm to steady her and turned to look for the safest way to walk, and there he was, staring at me. I pretended I didn't see him and took Aunt Mary the opposite direction, telling her it was because of the ice. It upset me terribly. Now I am afraid to go out, but I must go see Carson and Harry. Carson is getting feeble and Abner doesn't think he will live long. Harry is still strong, but how will he live without his friend?

How did Jeb find me? I am terrified. And I don't really know why. I think he wants to hurt me.

⊗⊗

January 4, 1898 I saw Jeb again. When he looks at me, I think he wants to hurt me. Why? What did I ever do to him? I took a long way around coming home from seeing Carson and Harry. I don't want Jeb to know where I live. Abner says Carson will die any day now. I must prepare for this loss. Carson has been such a good friend to me.

Should I tell Aunt Mary I'm worried about Jeb? I wonder why he left Paddy and left Albany. I don't know how to explain how he makes me feel. His eyes cut right through me.

⊗⊗

I lost track of the date. It might still be March or maybe April. It's cold but no more snow. I've been running, running, running south. I don't know how far I still have to go. All I can think about is finding Oklahoma and Teddy. I'm sick and so, so tired. But when I try to sleep, I see Jeb's eyes. Every sound wakes me up. I dream about what he did to me, over and over until I wake up screaming. I throw up and make Harry run some more. But Harry is weak and lame and hungry and exhausted. He might be dying. I'm scared. I don't know what to do.

I went south by the sun from Rochester and after days and days came to a place called Derry Church. I asked a farmer how to find Oklahoma. He told me to follow the road west through the mountains to Columbus. He said Oklahoma is more west than south. If I reach Columbus, I will ask again. The man's wife gave me and Harry food and let us sleep in their new shed. They put straw down for us. I decided to let Harry rest today. I don't feel good.

⊗⊗

I woke up to rain. The farmer's wife brought breakfast and said I should rest today. My body agreed with her. I took Harry out when I went to the outhouse and saw this is a dairy farm. A huge barn is near the shed. I stayed out in the rain for a long time. I scrubbed and scrubbed my skin, but I still feel dirty, inside. I changed my clothes for the first time since I left Rochester and lay my wet ones one the hay to dry. Perhaps I can go back to sleep. I am so alone, with no one but Harry to hold on to. Sometimes I feel emptiness inside that twists into panic that makes me scream even when I am awake. I don't know how to get away from the pictures in my mind.

○३≿○

I didn't know I was so tired. Today is my fourth day in this shed. I couldn't make myself move. The farmer's wife feeds me three times a day, but I feel too sick to eat very much. I give it to Harry and to the farmer's dog who wanders in when the door is open. Last night the farmer and his wife invited me to supper in their house. It is a plain and comfortable house, full of peace and solid gentleness. Can I say, "solid gentleness"? That's how it seems to me.

The Woolseys (I finally asked their name) asked me why such a well-mannered boy was traveling alone to Oklahoma and crying out in the night. I said my father died and I needed to find my brother. To my relief they did not press me. I can't talk about what set me off on this long journey. I didn't know they could hear me at night. I must be more careful, but I don't know how.

They told me Oklahoma Territory is more than a thousand miles away. I don't even know where in Oklahoma Teddy is. Mr. Woolsey said my mule does not have one thousand miles left in him. Maybe not even one hundred miles.

I told them thank you for their kindness. I must go to Oklahoma or die trying. My brother is all the family I have left. I will rest one more day, then begin my journey again. What else can I do but try? I do feel sorry for Harry.

○३≿○

April 3, 1898. This morning when I woke up, I felt too sick to eat the breakfast Mrs. Woolsey brought me. I fed it to Harry, then ran outside and threw up.

Later, Mr. Woolsey came to the barn and told me he had bought a train ticket for me from Harrisburg, a city near here, to Kansas City. He said he didn't know what trains run from there to Oklahoma, but Kansas City is a major train city, and I can find out there. He gave me an envelope with my ticket and some money for food on the train and for what he thinks it will cost to travel from Kansas City to Oklahoma. The ticket says April 4. That's how I know today is April 3. I missed Teddy's birthday. He turned 13 on March 13th. I couldn't stop tears coming to my eyes.

Mr. Woolsey asked if I was all right. I told him I missed my brother's birthday. Saying so out loud made me start crying. He handed me his handkerchief. When I stopped crying, I said thank you for the ticket, but what about Harry? I think thee should leave Harry with us, he said (that's how he talks). I promise we will take good care of him for as long as he lives. I started crying again and ran over and hugged Harry until I could make myself stop.

I didn't notice when Mr. Woolsey left the barn. So now I am writing all this down. My notebook is full. Maybe I can use some of Mr. Woolsey's food money to buy a new one, and a new pencil too, since I'm not eating much. This one is just a stub. I will try to buy them before I get on the train, since it will be a long ride. I think best when I can write down my thoughts.

Two nights on the train, Mr. Woolsey said. But it would take me weeks to walk that far.

I haven't done anything today, yet I feel worn out. I am going to take a nap. That's how soft I am getting with the Woolseys' kindness. I still wake up every night with nightmares.

⊂ℨ⊰

April 4, 1898 I am on the train writing in my new notebook. We are going through mountains. It was hard to say goodbye to Harry. Mrs. Woolsey gave me a basket of food for my first day of travel. Folded at the bottom I found a new shirt and pants. She must have made them for me. I hope I will remember their kindness always, and someday be as generous to someone else.

Mr. Woolsey drove me in his wagon to the train station in Harrisburg. I told him I didn't know how to thank him and Mrs. Woolsey. He said they received kindness from strangers once and were happy they could do this small thing and they would pray for me. He told me they are Quakers. I don't know what that is, but it must be good. He told me he hopes I find Quakers where I am going because I can be sure they will be kind to me.

When I took my nap yesterday, I dreamed I was back in Killeagh, back at that place in Glenbower Wood where there was a stone cross and I felt someone holding me and singing to me. It was so lovely I lay there for a long time after I woke up, letting myself feel the peace the dream brought me.

I remembered feeling that peace another time, on the ship after Da died. I dreamed then too that someone held me and sang to me. It is strange to think about that, almost as if it really happened. I wonder why I am thinking about it now, so many years later.

This is all I can write for now. I feel like I did when I had the measles, like I am getting a fever, and my stomach hurts. I don't think I will be able to eat Mrs. Woolsey's good food.

ଔଓ

I gave Mrs. Woolsey's food to the man beside me. He gobbled it down. He doesn't like my cough, though. He asked the train man for a different seat. I am glad he's gone.

During the night I threw up on my clothes, so I changed to the ones Mrs. Woolsey made for me. They fit nicely but I rolled up the pant legs and sleeves because I feel so hot. I didn't know what to do with my smelly clothes. I couldn't take them back into the passenger car, so I threw them out the bathroom window. I feel like I am burning up.

The train man walked through our car and announced we will arrive in Kansas City in half an hour. I don't remember much about the last two days. It's all a haze. It is a huge effort just to keep my balance on the way to relieve myself. What will I do when I get to Kansas City? I guess I will pick the cheapest train to Oklahoma.

CℬEO

I am in another barn, somewhere on the south side of Kansas City. I chose Bartlesville, Oklahoma as my destination because I liked the sound of it. But when I pulled the envelope out of my bag to pay, my money was gone. I think the man next to me stole it. I didn't notice anything else missing. I'm sad that I didn't take better care of the Woolseys' gift to me. I started walking south, until I couldn't walk any more, and crept in here. I made friends with the horses. There are three. It is dark but there is a bright moon shining through a small window. I have no energy to write more.

CℬEO

April 7, 1898 I can tell I am getting sicker. If I don't leave now, before the farmer comes in and finds me, I may not make it to Oklahoma and Teddy. I must borrow one of the horses because I am not strong enough to walk. I will write the farmer a note saying I will bring her back as soon as I can.

Debra Kornfield

CHAPTER 36

CHARLIE

Dublin Academy, June 26, 1896

CHARLIE GAZED AT THE FAMILY gathered on the Dublin Academy lawn following his graduation. Even Cally's family had come, all the way from Killeagh and Youghal. And Mr. Hobbs! *They seem to think this is a big deal. It matters more to them than it does to me. I feel—what's the word? Detached, like this is happening to someone else and I'm just watching.*

"I'm proud of you, son. Graduating with honors from a school like Dublin Academy is no small feat, especially while practicing and performing in Belfast and Londonderry."

As Father spoke, Laoise and her family walked by. She looked straight at Charlie, then turned her head and made a comment to her brother beside her. He laughed.

It took Charlie a second to realize Father waited for a response. "Oh. Thank you, Father. You can credit Cousin Priscilla. She kept me on task. She and my grandmother Charlotte."

Everyone laughed. Abigail and Martha said at the same time, "That's true!" and Mummy gave him a hug, a pleased smile on her face. *Good. A little humor will distract them. And Mummy will be reassured that I'm*

357

fine. What she doesn't know won't hurt her.

"May I introduce my tutor, Mr. Hobbs? He too deserves credit for all the years he put up with me as a child. Thank you, Mr. Hobbs, for coming so far. I am honored."

Mr. Hobbs bowed. "It is my great pleasure to be here, Charlie. I am gratified by your accomplishments."

"What do you plan now, Charlie?" Micky asked.

Good. I can tell everyone at once and get it over with.

"I've persuaded Father to let me delay Oxford for a year, so I can focus on the piano. He's not yet convinced I can support myself through music. I hope to show him—and myself–that I can. Then maybe he'll let me skip Oxford altogether, though he's been hoping for a hat trick. That's why my parents had a third son."

Everyone laughed again.

"Will ye be based here in Dublin, then, Charlie? Or will ye return to Mayfield?"

"I expect to travel a great deal, Dugan, but now that Mummy has completed her own course of studies in London, I expect to be home in Mayfield whenever I'm not engaged elsewhere. Allow me to introduce my agent, Terrence Baldwin of Waterford. Now all of you know: if I fail to make enough money this year to satisfy Father, it will be Terry's fault."

A third round of laughter. *Hat trick.*

Ɂ

Charlie looked over his notes from a 10/18/1896 planning session with Terry.

Schedule:

10/27-11/29 Cardiff and England

Christmas concerts, Waterford

March-June, 1897 Continent—Bday (18) Mr. P Switzerland

Have I thoroughly bled out? Mr. P will know. I can fool

everyone but him.

Terry w me Mar-Apr; Mummy May-June?

Terry says I get moody when alone

7/10/97 Play Terry/Julia wedding reception

Mid-Sept or early Oct—Begin long American tour (until Aug 1898)

Christmas Kansas City, Thomas/Cora, Mummy/Father

April 1898 Bday (19) KC with Thomas and Cora – 4-6 wks rest

Priorities:

Some large events to pay bills; rest small towns/cities for fun

Relatives in NYC, Albany, Detroit, KC?

Brainstorming:

Music/lecture series w Cousin Silas (Thomas?)

∞

"The reviews are fantastic, Charles. I'm so proud of you. See— Helena is keeping a scrapbook for me. She clips news about each of my protégés." Mr. Paderewski proffered a beautiful book, opened to a page featuring in large letters, Charles Henry Malcomson, Ireland.

"But?"

"But there's an undertone of sadness, Charles. Can you tell me about that?"

Charlie sighed, and set the scrapbook on the table. "I've been half dreading, half hoping for this conversation. Thank you for caring. Most people, even in my family, don't notice."

"I too have experienced great sadness. Tell me."

Charlie fidgeted, staring out the window at Lake Geneva. "Where shall I start . . ."

"With the first thing that comes to your mind, and then the second, and then the third . . ."

So Charlie talked. The first storm on *Lion III* when he was ten. Father's anger that he disobeyed. The second storm that claimed the life of Cally's father, Frank. Intense fear, since then, of sailing. His family trying to help Cally and her brother Teddy, and their disappearance. The accident with Midnight and long convalescence. Mummy going to London. The loneliness that took him to school at Foxwell. His friendship with Mr. Barrow.

Along the way, Charlie began sobbing, which grew in intensity as he spoke the name of Mr. Barrow. He hardly noticed Mr. Paderewski asking his wife for handkerchiefs, "a whole stack, please, my dear."

By the time he reached Mr. Barrow's visit to him in Dublin, Charlie could hardly breathe. "I—I don't think I can tell this part. I've never talked to anyone about it."

"I know this is difficult, Charles. But I'm here with you. You are safe. You can do this. Sit back, take a few deep breaths, and a drink of water. Better? Now, you were saying Mr. Barrow paid a surprise visit to you at your cousins' home in Dublin. Tell me what happened."

Hesitantly, with steady encouragement from Mr. Paderewski and more tears, Charlie told, leaving nothing out. After the telling, he sobbed for a long time. Finally, he blew his nose, wiped his face, and gulped some water. *What will Mr. Paderewski think of me? It's my fault Mr. Barrow died, just because I couldn't handle—*

"Charles, when you're ready, tell me how Mr. Barrow's death made you feel."

"I—I can't." Tears sprang to Charlie's eyes once again. "I'm sorry. I thought I had cried all the tears that were in me."

"It's all right, Charles. But we need to do this one last part."

"I-I'm afraid of what you will think of me."

"I will think what I have always thought since I first met you in New York, that your musical capacity is extraordinary, you are extremely sensitive, and you will bless the world through both of those gifts."

"Bu-but you see, it's my fault Mr. Barrow died."

Charlie didn't sob. He howled, burying his face in his arms. Mr. Paderewski stood and placed his hand on Charlie's shoulder, ignoring the tears running down his own face.

Finally, Charlie coughed, and rubbed his eyes. Mr. Paderewski gave him a fresh handkerchief.

"Charles, I want to ask you something. If the very same thing happened to me, would you think it my fault if the person chose to commit suicide? Think about it for a moment, with me in the picture instead of you."

"Oh."

"You see, Mr. Barrow was a very troubled man. That is tragic. But it wasn't your fault. His decision to end his life was none of your doing. It was his own choice."

"Oh."

"Now let me ask you another question. How do you feel about his attempt to kiss you?"

"I feel confused. Shocked. Dirty. Disgusted. Angry. It frightens me away from wanting to even think about love."

"In a sexual way, you mean?"

"I-I guess so. I feel upset even when I see my father kiss my mother. Or my sister kiss her husband. That part of life has become obnoxious to me." *Oh, sweet Laoise, I hate myself for what I did to you. Something is wrong with me, terribly wrong. It's better for you that you're free of me.*

"I understand, Charles. It was forced on you, it bears no relation to real love, and it's linked in your mind and emotions to the horror of the suicide."

"Yes. I don't see how I can ever get past this. I badly hurt someone I care about deeply."

"Ever is a long time, Charles. Let's not worry about that now. As your heart heals, some things may shift in your soul. Tell me, how are you feeling now?"

Charlie stood, stretched, and walked to the window. A breeze had come up, ruffling the surface of Lake Geneva. *It feels like I've passed an eternity in this room. Like I've re-lived my whole life but come out different than I did the first time I lived it.* He turned toward Mr. Paderewski. "I feel lighter. Like the breeze on the lake is blowing through me, relieving a pressure I've been feeling for as long as I can remember."

"That's good. I am glad to hear it. Now, Charles, I have a student coming for a lesson in fifteen minutes. Would you enjoy a walk along the lake?"

"I would, sir. Thank you."

"Off you go, then. I'll see you at dinner. You have another week with us before your mother arrives, isn't that right?"

"Yes."

"Then we must consider the fingering of your interpretation of Chopin's *Piano Concerto No. 2.* Enjoy your walk."

Charlie laughed as the door closed behind him. *That was clever. He put music back into my mind instead of all we just talked about. Hmm, I wonder which passage he's concerned about?* As he walked along the shore, Charlie played through the entire concerto in his mind. *Ah! I think I found it!*

Cঐর∞

"Charlie, I'm delighted you invited me to travel with you. It reminds me of our trip to Vienna, so long ago. We're visiting places I've never been."

"Yes. Didn't Terry choose fascinating little cities? This tour has been grand, even more so since you joined me, Mummy."

"Charlie, you seem different to me than when you left Mayfield in March. Lighter. Happier."

"I am lighter, Mummy." He gave her a warm hug.

CHAPTER 37

CALLY

Somewhere south of Kansas City, April 7, 1898

ON A PAGE TORN FROM THE BACK of her new notebook, Cally wrote in large letters as carefully as she could, "Don't be alarmed. I am not stealing your horse. I am borrowing her because I must." She stopped, fighting nausea as a spasm of pain gripped her abdomen. "I will bring her back as soon as I can. Calvin."

Cally softly greeted the mare she had chosen, the one with *Felicity* printed on the stall door. Easing the bridle from its hook so she wouldn't disturb the other horses, she fastened her note on the hook, and led Felicity out of the barn and through the gate of the corral. The sun's first rays glimmered on the horizon.

She returned to the barn for her bag, hung it over a fence post, and closed the gate. She adjusted the bridle in the horse's mouth, then, suddenly dizzy, leaned against her. Her heart pounded, her head hurt, and the pain in her stomach was intense. Her whole body ached with fever. *Can I do this? Soon the farmer will be out for his early chores.*

Cally took a deep breath, which set off a fit of coughing. She summoned all her strength to heave her bag onto Felicity's back. Balancing the bag and holding the reins, she climbed the fence to mount. *Good thing I know how to ride bareback. No way could I manage a saddle right now.*

Breathless, she collapsed across her bag against Felicity's neck. *I must go now, or not at all.* She signaled the horse and walked slowly toward the road.

The door to the house banged. Startled, Cally looked straight into the eyes of an angry man. "Stop, thief!" he shouted. A shot whizzed over Cally's head, spooking Felicity into a gallop. Pounding toward the road, Cally's hat flew off as more shots trailed them. *All she could do was hold on.*

Some distance from the farm, Felicity's gait eased to a trot and then a walk. Cally lay across her bag, completely spent, giving the mare her head. Felicity walked on, and Cally lost track of time, vaguely aware by the sun shining from behind her that they were traveling west. *My fever is going up. I might throw up. How long can I do this?*

"Oklahoma. Teddy," she said out loud as they came to an intersection. "South, Felicity."

Felicity obediently turned left and walked on.

Cally woke to bright sunshine. *Oh. I must have passed out. I am burning up. So thirsty. No more—* She felt herself falling, her bag tumbling after her.

◦◦◦

"Heigh ho. Home we go, Reuben. We'll overnight at the Williams farm near Olathe. You remember staying there before, don't you? Very kind people. Good food!"

Dr. Tann continued talking companionably to his horse as they traveled south from Kansas City. He glanced back to be sure the medical supplies were well-balanced in his wagon. "One hundred forty miles home to Independence. I'm getting too old for making this trip twice a year. Truth be told, so are you, Reuben. How long have we been doing this? I'm not sure I can count that high." He chuckled. "Mind if I take a nap? Just keep going south and wake me if you need me. No detours, hear? I am tii-red."

Dr. Tann pulled his cap over his eyes and snoozed in his seat, his dreams shaping themselves around the rhythm of Reuben's hoofbeats. Suddenly the rhythm stopped, and he woke with a start.

"What's this, Reuben? Another horse? Ah, I see. A mare. I agree, she's a beauty. But we must be on our way. No time for dilly-dallying today."

Reuben didn't move. "What's this about then, friend? Stone in your shoe? Well, let's have a look." Dr. Tann heaved himself off the wagon seat and bent to raise Reuben's first hoof. "This one looks fine to me, Reuben."

The lovely chestnut mare nickered, and Reuben responded. Dr. Tann looked up from Reuben's second hoof and saw something in the ditch near the mare. "What do we have here? Let me fetch my specs. My vision isn't what it used to be."

Spectacles in place, Dr. Tann slid down the bank into the drainage ditch at the side of the road and approached a crumpled heap beside a bag of some sort. A boy. Not in good condition, by the looks of it. He squatted and touched the boy's forehead. Burning hot! And a rash.

"Typhoid fever, I reckon, Reuben. Dehydration, certainly. And too long without good nourishment, though the clothes look new. What is a boy like this doing with a horse like that? A runaway? A theft?"

The mare gave a soft whinny.

"Can we save his life? Too soon to tell, ma'am, too soon to tell. Now how am I going to get this child up that slope and into the wagon? Let me look at you again, boy. Skinny and small, you are. But old and tired am I. Perhaps I can drag you to road level? Oh, someone is coming!"

Dr. Tann struggled back up the slope to the road and waved his arms to halt the oncoming carriage. The driver slowed, looking annoyed.

A female head popped out of the window of the carriage. "What is it, Max? Oh, let's see what this man needs."

"Ma'am, I am Dr. Tann. We have a boy in the ditch, critically ill, and I without strength to lift him into my wagon. Might Max be able to help us?"

"Of course! Where will you take him, sir? He would ride more comfortably in my carriage than in your wagon."

"How far are we from Olathe, Max? I'm headed to a farm near there, the Williams farm."

"About five miles, I believe, sir."

"Thank you, Max. Five miles. We could do it in a little over an hour if we push the horses."

"I'm headed to Olathe myself, Dr. Tann. I live in Kansas City, but I have an art show in Olathe this weekend. Max, give the bag to Dr. Tann and bring the boy into the carriage. There you go. Oh my. His skin is burning hot."

The boy groaned and muttered "Oklahoma. Teddy."

"I believe he has typhoid fever, ma'am. It is contagious, so I must ask you not to touch him if you can avoid it. Do you have a way to wash your hands? You too, Max."

"Max, give me some of that water in the jug you have up front. Thank you. Now, what will you do with the mare, Dr. Tann?"

"I'll tie her to the back of my wagon. May I ask your name, ma'am?"

"Oh, I'm sorry! My name is Cora Malcomson. Here is my card. Let me just write on the back the address where I'll be staying in Olathe, with my friends Celia and Sheridan. If we can help in any way, please let me know. I will return to Kansas City on Monday."

"Thank you, ma'am. Now, if we mean to try to save this boy's life, we best be on our way. Are your horses up to a trot, Max?"

"Certainly, sir. Lead the way. I'll be right behind you."

Reuben seemed to sense the urgency of the situation. He trotted without stopping all the way to the Williams' columned front entry.

"Mommy! He's here! Dr. Tann is here and has other people with him!"

Dr. Tann looked around and spied a young lookout scrambling down from a tree.

"Dr. Tann, why do thee have an extra horse and an extra carriage?"

"Oh, there's your mother. I'll explain as soon as I can, Benjamin. But right now, I need to speak to her. All right, my friend?"

"George, thee look concerned." Athena Williams took in the entourage with a glance and hurried to his side.

"Athena, I have a boy with typhoid fever in that carriage. I can't risk taking him into your home. Might he stay in your barn while I give him emergency care?"

"Nonsense. We have spare rooms, thee know that. We can keep him separate from the family. Bring him right this way, sir. Florence! We have a situation! Bring water and rags and then chip some ice, please."

Max, followed by Dr. Tann, climbed the grand staircase, and walked down the hall to the third bedroom on the left. Athena opened crimson drapes.

"Now then. I'll pull down the bed clothes and thee can lay him right here, sir. Thee are?"

"Max, ma'am."

"Well then, Max, there is a pump outside, and soap, where thee can wash your hands and face. Ask Florence or my son Ben to show thee."

"Thank you, ma'am. Will there be anything else, Dr. Tann?"

"No, thank you, Max. Please tell Mrs. Malcomson I thank her for her aid."

"I will, sir. Goodbye."

But when Max turned to go, he bumped into Cora coming in.

"Ma'am, it's best that thee—"

Cora gave Athena a quick curtsey but turned to Dr. Tann.

"Doctor, I'll talk fast so you can tend to the boy. I don't understand it at all, but he muttered the names of members of my husband's family during our ride here, and Irish phrases I understood because I also am Irish. I am perplexed and troubled. Will you allow me to stop by Monday on my way home to learn how he fares? And—and would it be a terrible inconvenience for all of you to write down whatever the boy says?"

Dr. Tann looked at Athena, who nodded.

"Of course, Mrs. Malcomson, though we don't speak Irish. Since you are here, there is one other thing you and Max could help me with, if you and he are willing, ma'am."

"Anything."

"Could you send a telegram to my wife, advising her I have been delayed? Mrs. George Tann, Independence, Kansas."

"Certainly, sir. Come, Max."

"Thank you, Mrs. Malcomson. Goodbye."

Taking a deep breath, Dr. Tann turned to the tasks required to reduce the boy's fever and rehydrate him. Athena and Florence shared his surprise as, together, they stripped off the boy's clothes and discovered he was a she.

"Pregnant," observed Dr. Tann.

CR80

"How did she fare during the night, George?"

"She's still alive, Athena, but despite all our efforts, the fever has not broken. She's still delirious. Thank you for allowing Florence to take a shift so I could get some sleep."

"Well, it's my turn now. There's breakfast ready for thee in the dining room. I believe Richard may still be finishing."

"Thank you, Athena."

"George—before thee go—"

"Yes?"

"Yesterday, I heard thee refer to the woman with the carriage as Mrs. Malcomson. I assume she is Cora Malcomson, the painter and sculptor? I had planned to attend her exhibit this afternoon. I hear her work is remarkable. Everyone in Olathe is talking about her."

"You know more than I, but she did reference an art show this weekend."

"Don't thee find it extraordinary that this boy—I mean girl—spoke names of people in Mrs. Malcomson's husband's family?"

"Perhaps they are common names in Ireland. Most of what I heard in her delirium through the night was Irish, so I have little more to offer."

"Fascinating. I think I will attend the exhibit this afternoon if thee and Florence can handle things here. Perhaps I can learn more about Mrs. Malcomson."

"Certainly."

"Well, go on then, George. Eat and sleep while thee can."

Entering the dining room, Dr. Tann found his host, Richard Williams, staring at a piece of paper, a partially eaten breakfast in front of him. "No, no, don't get up, Richard. Good morning. Thank you for welcoming a mystery child into your home."

"The plot thickens, George. Look at this. It came with today's newspaper."

Richard proffered a flyer with HORSE THIEF in large letters across the top, saying "And the newspaper article is fascinating—it made the front page! I wondered how the girl managed to escape with Felicity. Didn't thee? So, according to the paper, the owner did try to give chase on another of his horses, wearing only his pajamas and his boots. In his haste, he went bareback, fell off the horse and broke his leg."

"Oh my, what a story!" George read out loud, "$500 reward for capture of red-haired boy, alive or dead, and return in good health of prize chestnut mare, Felicity." He looked up at Richard. "That's serious money. The photo does look like the mare—hmm, receiving a prize for dressage. And the drawing of the thief bears a remarkable resemblance to our patient."

"Indeed. We can return the horse, certainly. She seems none the worse for wear. But what about the boy?"

"Well, the 'boy' is captive in your home, Richard. What do you think should be done? I'm sure you're not thinking about the reward."

"I've been thinking . . . It seems only right to give the boy a proper burial."

"What?"

"Consider, George. The flyer asks for return of a boy. The child lying upstairs may be a horse thief. All evidence points that direction. But she doesn't qualify as a boy."

"So . . ."

"So. What if we get a simple coffin, weight it with the girl's approximate weight—she can't be ninety pounds, do thee think?—seal it, and send it back along with the mare, accompanied by a letter from thee."

"What would my letter say?"

"Tell the truth. Thee found the boy and the horse, but the boy was critically ill with typhoid fever and dehydration, and, sadly, did not survive. Thee do not recommend opening the coffin because of the contagious nature of the disease."

"Did not survive . . ."

"The boy did not survive, isn't that right? It's a girl we're dealing with now. As well as the child within her womb."

"I have never propagated untruth, Richard."

"Nor will thee now, to my way of thinking. Clearly, the person who wrote this flyer just wants his horse back. He doesn't care whether the thief is captured alive or dead. The boy's 'death' will look to him like justice, and that will be the end of the matter. The girl then, if she survives typhoid fever, will be freed from facing an outlaw life or almost certain execution if she is caught."

"I certainly favor an outcome which can give the girl choices. If she survives."

"Why don't thee think about it for a few hours, George, and decide after your nap? If thee conclude my idea is good, I will prepare the coffin. Thy part will be writing the letter. I can also see to returning the horse and coffin to the address on the flyer. Not until Monday, of course, because tomorrow is the Sabbath. But we'll have time today to prepare everything."

"I have always found you to be innovative, Richard, ever since we met on the shore of Elk City Lake."

A shadow crossed Richard's face. "Maybe the loss of our little daughter motivates me to save this girl, George."

"I honor that, Richard. Let me sleep a while, to clear my head, and then I'll give you my response. The girl has a fractured radius, on top of her other troubles. She must have fallen on her arm. I missed it in my first examination. It became apparent during the night as swelling of her wrist increased."

"Well, she's in the best of hands. If thee missed it, any doctor would have."

"Thank you, Richard. It will take all of my skill and a large dose of God's mercy to bring her and her baby through this."

"Then we will pray to that end."

CR&O

Despite his fatigue, Dr. Tann could not sleep. Finally, he rose and wrote a letter exactly as Richard had suggested. At the end, he said, "This boy was but a child who met a tragic end. I would be grateful if a photograph of his gravestone could be sent to me, so I can know he received a proper burial. Yours sincerely, Dr. George A. Tann, Independence, Kansas."

After that, the doctor slept, dead to the world until awakened by a soft knock on his door. "Dr. Tann, Mrs. Williams asks me to tell you the girl is waking up. Her fever has broken."

"Thank you, Florence. That is good news. I will be right there."

૭૪૪

Blinking her eyes fully open, Cally tried to sit up but cried out in pain when she pushed on the bed with her left hand. *Where am I? Who are these people?*

A woman bent over her and said calmly, "My name is Mrs. Williams, child. Thee are in my home. Dr. Tann, the man walking in now, found thee unconscious beside the road and brought thee here."

"Felicity! Where is the horse?"

"She is in our barn. We are taking good care of her."

"My bag! Where is my bag?"

"Thy bag is there on the dresser. Can thee see it there? We have not opened it."

Cally rolled over to use her right hand to push herself up to sit on the edge of the bed. Her head spun, and she toppled over. "What's wrong with me?" she whispered as Mrs. Williams caught her and eased her back on the pillows.

The doctor approached the bed, and Cally shrank back. "I am Dr. Tann. I have been taking care of you. You have typhoid fever and a broken wrist. You have been very sick, but you are getting better. You must rest for a while yet, but your strength will come back."

"I can't rest! I must go to Oklahoma!"

"What is in Oklahoma, dear?" asked Mrs. Williams.

"My brother! I must find him! He is with the Oneida. He is the only family I have left."

"I may be able to help you with that," said Dr. Tann. "I worked among the Osage and Cherokee in Oklahoma for some time, and I have friends there. I could write and ask for their help. Whom should I say they should look for?"

Can I trust this man? It seems like he wants to help me. Maybe he's Quaker. That farmer, Mr. Woolsey, told me to trust Quakers.

Cally lifted her eyes. "Are you a Quaker?"

The doctor threw a glance at Mrs. Williams. "No, but Mrs. Williams is."

Cally looked back and forth from the doctor to Mrs. Williams. Finally, she said, "His name is Teddy, but the Oneida call him Blue Eyes. He is thirteen but he is bigger than me, even though I'm older."

"And what is thy name, dear? Dr. Tann must be able to say whose brother he is looking for."

Cally lifted her hand as a fit of coughing racked her. "My—my name is Calvin. Oh!" She stared at the lace edging the sleeve of the nightgown she wore and began to tremble. "You—you know . . ."

"Yes, dear. We had to undress thee to reduce thy fever. I am sorry."

Cally pulled the covers up to her chin. "You—you looked at me?" Her teeth chattered. Dr. Tann placed his hand against her forehead. "Your fever is climbing again. I will give you something to drink, and then you must rest. We will talk more later. All right, Calvin?"

"C-C-C-Cally," she whispered. Tears filled her eyes and dripped down her cheeks. "My name is Cally. Callandra Mae."

"That is a beautiful name. Now drink this medicine and let yourself fall back to sleep. We can talk more when you wake again."

Mrs. Williams placed a hand gently on Cally's shoulder. "Thee are safe here in our home, dear Cally. We want only to help thee and bless thee."

"B-b-bless me?"

"Yes, dear. May I ask Florence to sing thee a song to help you sleep? She has a lovely voice."

"Yes, please." Cally closed her eyes, tears still seeping from her eyelids.

"In peace I will lie down and sleep," Florence sang. "For thou alone, O Lord, will keep me safe."

"Aisling. Aisling's prayer," whispered Cally. And then she was asleep. In her dream, she walked into church, her hand warm inside Aisling's. Aisling said, "The kingfisher has a little cave in the bank under the bridge. I shall go in to the altar of God, to God who giveth joy to my youth. . . Our help is in the name of the Lord. . . Thou wilt turn, O God, and bring us to life. . . Thou alone, O Lord, will keep me safe." A breath of honeysuckle wafted over her, and in her dream, for that moment, Cally relaxed.

CHAPTER 38

CALLY

The Williams farm, Olathe, Kansas April 10, 1898

"ATHENA, YOU'VE OUTDONE YOURSELF. Thank you for this lovely meal."

"Thee are so very welcome, George. I'm glad we have this chance to talk before Meeting this afternoon. Thee will join us? Yes, Ben, thee may be excused. Remember thy Sabbath manners."

"I will, Mama."

"I think not, Athena," George said. "I will attend our patient so Florence can attend."

Richard laid his napkin beside his plate. "It seems to me we have a number of decisions to make, George. I have the coffin ready to go north tomorrow, along with thy letter and the lovely Felicity. So that aspect is well in hand. What is thy prognosis for Cally?"

"She has made progress, certainly, Richard. But I can't say she's out of the woods yet. Typhoid fever can get complicated, especially in cases as severe as Cally's. I don't think it would be wise for her to travel for another month, but I have patients waiting for me in Independence. Could she stay here for a few weeks? She will need careful nursing. Perhaps we could hire a private nurse to attend her?"

Richard glanced at his wife and visibly relaxed. "That's just the solution we need, George. Yes. With the help of a nurse, we can keep her as long as she needs."

"Perhaps two nurses, one for days and one for nights."

"That makes sense. Athena, can thee pursue that tomorrow?"

"Yes. I know who to ask."

"Thank thee, my dear. Now, George, what happens to the girl once she has recovered? Athena says her primary concern is to find her brother, but she has no idea where in Oklahoma to look. Do thee truly think thee can help her?"

"I do. We know he is with the Oneida, or at least was, last Cally knew. My friends with the Indian Bureau will know where the Oneida have settled. He's a white boy with blue eyes. He will stand out. In the time it takes Cally to convalesce, we'll find him if he's there."

"So, once Cally is strong enough, we'll send her to thee in Independence?"

"Yes, that makes sense to me. We can be in touch meanwhile by letter. Or telegram, should you have an urgent concern."

Athena said thoughtfully, "Physical convalescence is one thing. Emotional healing is another. Cally is alone and pregnant. She found it necessary to travel as a boy and to commit a capital crime. Those four facts conjure a story filled with pain and loss. Will she live with the Indians as her brother has done, I wonder? What will be our ongoing responsibility, if any, once she is well physically? We have more questions than answers, George."

"I appreciate the predicament I have placed you in, my friends. These questions will be good ones to place before the Lord in your Meeting this afternoon. Though I must leave tomorrow, I will keep you in my prayers and stand ready to help in any way I can. Thank you, Richard and Athena, for taking Cally in. Now, if you will excuse me, I must check on our patient and give Florence a break."

"Of course, George."

Cally was asleep, a chestnut curl resting against her flushed cheek, her broken arm cushioned on a pillow. Though still fevered, her breathing was steady and even. Dr. Tann released Florence, and sat beside the bed, praying and thinking. *Might Eliza welcome Cally into our home, at least until her child is born? She needs a safe place to learn to be a girl again—a young woman, I should say, as well as a mother. We have no idea where she has come from, her habits, her abilities, her emotional disabilities. We know very little, really. I will tell Eliza what I know and don't know. She may offer refuge to this homeless little waif.*

Cally stirred and cried out in her sleep. "No, Jeb! Stay away from me! Stop! Help! Help! Someone help me! Please, no! Stop!" And the girl was awake, wailing and shouting "No! No! Ye are hurting me, Jeb!"

Athena ran into the room, gathered Cally's flailing limbs into a warm embrace, and rocked her like a small child, saying softly, "Cally, Cally. Thee are safe. It was just a dream. Thee are safe. No one is hurting you now. Thee are safe."

Gradually, Cally's violent sobs eased into whimpers. *"Thee can trust Quakers," that farmer told me.* She clung to Athena until, exhausted, she fell asleep again, soothed by her soft murmur. Athena lifted her eyes, filled with tears, and across the bed met George's, also teary, and in the doorway, her husband wiped his face with a handkerchief.

"I believe God has sent this child to us, George. Perhaps he means to use her to help heal the deep brokenness still inside Richard and me from Chrissy's death. Please, will thee pray for us, George, right now?"

"I will, Athena." And he did.

ᘓᘔ

Dr. Tann woke at dawn, dressed quickly, and went to check on his patient, freeing Florence from her overnight vigil. Cally woke as he examined her head to toe. "Good morning, Cally. I must leave today. You still have fever, but that is to be expected. Tell me, how did you come by this scar on your forehead? How old were you when that happened?"

Cally's hand flew to her forehead. "I was five. My brother—" Cally's mind flashed to her treasure flying through the air and into the river, then a series of images. *Teddy. Uncle Dugan. Mammy. Miss Hilda. Da.* She burst into tears.

"I'm sorry, child. I shouldn't have asked. It doesn't matter. Forgive me. I was too curious. Here, take this." The doctor handed her a handkerchief and continued talking. "Better? Now, Cally, to get well you must rest. Eat and drink as much as you can. Rest some more. Do you understand?"

"Ye—yes, sir."

"Leave it to me to find your brother. I believe I can do so by the time you are strong enough to travel. Now, Cally, tell me what I want you to do to get well as quickly as possible."

"Rest. Eat and drink. Let you find Teddy."

"That's right. You will stay here with Mr. and Mrs. Williams until you are well enough to travel by train to my home in Independence, Kansas. Then I will take you to Oklahoma to see your brother. All right?"

"Yes, sir. Thank you, sir."

"Goodbye until then."

"But Doctor, I'm worried about Felicity, the horse. How can I return her to the farm where I borrowed her?"

"Ah, you borrowed her. You didn't steal her?"

"Oh, no, sir. I would never steal anything. I left a note saying I needed to borrow her and would return her as soon as possible."

"Ah. You know how to write."

"Yes, sir."

"Well, Mr. Williams has arranged to send Felicity back to her owners today."

"Oh, thank you, sir. That is a great relief."

"Don't thank me. Thank Mr. Williams."

"I will, sir."

"All right then. Will you obey Mrs. Williams and Florence and anyone else who may come to care for you?"

"I will try, sir."

"Then I will expect to see you in about a month."

"Thank you for taking care of me, sir."

Dr. Tann hummed as he prepared Reuben for their day's journey toward home. *Another week and I'll be with you, Eliza, my dear!* He eyed the rising sun. "Looks like good weather for travel, Reuben. You should be doing well after the unexpected rest you've had." *Ah, there's Athena.*

He climbed down from the wagon seat. "Good morning, Athena. I hoped to leave quietly so as not to wake you."

"Not to worry, George. I always wake early."

"Cally seems better this morning. I believe she'll do well. She needs nourishment, fluids, and rest more than anything, though she may have fever for another week or so. But should she take a turn for the worse, do call a doctor here. Keep me appraised, please. On the nightstand you'll find a list of my intended stopping places, and you know how to reach me once I'm home."

"Have a good trip, George. It's always a pleasure to have time with thee."

"It's a pleasure for me, too, Athena, and one of the reasons I've continued to make this trip by horse and cart. But this will be the last time. From now on, I'll take the train. That means I don't know when I will see you and Richard again."

"But George, thee hath always said thee would not submit to being treated as a second-class citizen on the train."

"That I have, Athena, and the thought of being treated so when the whole reason for my travel is to procure medicines for my white patients—it rankles, I can't deny that. But Reuben and I are both too old

379

to keep making the trip this way. And it consumes too much of my time."

Richard emerged from the house in time to hear George's last statements. "There may be another way, George."

"Ah, my friend the innovator. What is your fertile brain concocting now, Richard?"

"Send me a list of what thee would purchase and all the necessary scripts and a letter authorizing me as thy agent. I'll go to Kansas City to buy the medicines and ship them to you by train."

"Perhaps," Athena said with a glance at her husband, "Richard and I could accompany the shipment so we can visit thee and Eliza."

"Even better," Richard agreed. "Give Eliza our love."

"We'll be in touch about sending Cally to thee, George. God bless thee, dear friend. Goodbye."

Dr. Tann climbed back onto the wagon seat and lifted the reins. Just then a carriage pulled into the circular drive.

"Ah. I think that's Mrs. Malcomson, Reuben. I believe I'll just be a minute." He climbed down once more.

Athena waited on her porch. "Mrs. Malcomson, how nice to see thee again. I was delighted by thy art show and couldn't resist buying a small sculpture."

"Oh, thank you! Which one did you choose?"

"The bird in flight. It is exquisite. Richard immediately claimed it for his study, so if thee come to Olathe again, I'll look for another for me." She laughed. "Do thee know, my parents would be shocked to see a 'graven image' in our home. I am glad our religion is more relaxed than that now."

"Oh my. It's not meant as an object of worship, but as a celebration of the beauty of the Creator's work. Good morning, Dr. Tann. Can you tell me how your patient is faring? I couldn't go home without knowing."

"Better than I hoped, Mrs. Malcomson. I expect a full recovery. Thank you again for your help, and Max's. It was invaluable for saving this child's life. I wish you Godspeed."

"That is wonderful news! Thank you, Dr. Tann. It appears you are departing as well."

"Yes, so I will say goodbye."

"And so will I. I am anxious to see my husband and children. Goodbye, Dr. Tann. Goodbye, Mrs. Williams, Mr. Williams."

The Malcomson carriage followed the Tann wagon around the circle and out the long driveway to the road, where Dr. Tann turned right to drive south, and Max turned left to drive north.

☙

A few days later, Cally woke to the smell of hot food on a breakfast tray beside her bed, tried to sit up and immediately threw up. "Oh, Florence. I'm so sorry. I've just caused you so much extra work."

"Let me help," Mrs. Williams said as she appeared in the doorway. "I see we'll have to be more careful regarding food in the mornings. I remember those days so well."

"Remember, ma'am? Did you have typhoid fever also?"

Cally noticed a glance pass between Florence and Mrs. Williams. "No, I never had typhoid. But I felt that way when I was pregnant with my son."

A memory of Mammy's rounded abdomen popped into Cally's mind. She saw Florence give Mrs. Williams a quick shake of her head as she walked toward the door with her arms full of soiled bedding. *Hmm. What aren't they telling me?*

"Was your son born well, Mrs. Williams?"

"Yes, he was. He's busy with his lessons now, but I could bring him to thy door to meet thee at luncheon time, if thee like. His name is Ben."

"I would like that. I have a brother named Teddy. I am on my way to

Oklahoma to find him."

"Yes, Dr. Tann says he will help thee find Teddy. We've just received word the doctor is home safely. It's a long trip by horse and wagon, though not far by train."

"That's good, ma'am."

"Well, Cally, rest a while. When thee feel thee could eat, ring this little bell. Florence and I will be close by."

Cally turned away from the door, repositioned her left arm, and closed her eyes. For a long time, though, she couldn't sleep. The memory of Mammy pregnant made her feel sad and alone. Tears seeped from her eyes. Someone eased the door open briefly and closed it again. Cally felt more alone than ever. *They think I am asleep. I must get well so I can go find Teddy.*

◌৵৵

Kansas City, April 18, 1898
Dear Mrs. Williams,

I hope this letter will not be an imposition. Despite knowing the child under your care for such a short time and under such a dire circumstance, I feel a bond with him and find I think of him often. Could you tell me how he fares?

When I stopped to inquire upon leaving Olathe, in my relief that the boy was improving, I neglected to ask whether he said anything further that might be of interest to me. Of course, I understand you don't speak Irish.

I found the beautiful mare's solicitousness toward the ill child so endearing, I decided to carve her as a gift for the boy. I am sure by now you know his name. Could you tell me, so I can write a note to him to enclose with the package?

My husband's mother has been here helping with our children for several weeks, and his brother will arrive for a visit this evening. That

fact reminds me of the boy's concern to find his brother. I pray he may
have success.

Sincerely,
Cora Malcomson

Athena set the letter on the sideboard after reading it aloud to her husband. "Richard, what do thee think? Shall I tell Mrs. Malcomson our patient is a girl?"

"There's no harm in being cautious, my dear. Cally is so reticent to tell us about her life, I would say no. Once divulged, there's no way to unsay it."

Olathe, April 20, 1898
Dear Mrs. Malcomson,

I was surprised and pleased to receive thy letter. I too feel a bond with this child which comes, I suppose, from having seen him close to death and having a small part in bringing him back to life. Besides telling us his name is Calvin, he has divulged little else. Doubtless he will be delighted with thy gift! I am sure it will disappoint thee to know we have nothing more to offer except the name Jeb, which is always accompanied by great distress. Does that name mean anything to thee?

Our patient is making progress. Once well enough to travel, we plan to send him by train to Dr. Tann in Independence, who will accompany him to Oklahoma to find his brother.

I hope thee will have a lovely time with thy husband's family.

Sincerely,
Athena Williams

☙❧

Cally took deep breaths of the warm spring air coming through the bedroom window. The day nurse had helped her dress and then walk to a chair. She watched Ben playing with other boys in the garden beyond the driveway. *It feels good to be out of that bed! And this dress is so pretty! It was kind of Mrs. Williams to have it made for me. Everyone here has been kind.*

With her right hand, she fingered her curls, longer now than they had been for many years. *Cap was good about cutting our hair. I wonder what I look like now. Can I really be a girl again, or is "boy" stamped on my face, after so many years as Calvin?*

She studied the distance between her chair and the dresser, where her bag still sat, unopened. *Can I do it? I just want a quick peak, and then I'll hide my wee mirror away again. And I would like a book to read.*

Taking another deep breath, Cally pushed on the arm of the chair with her good hand, and slowly rose to her feet. She stood there a moment as her head swirled, and then took one step at a time toward her bag. Leaning against the dresser for support, she fumbled to open it and pull out her treasure with her one good hand. Finally succeeding, she gazed at her face. The same green eyes and freckles. The same chestnut curls. The same small turned-up nose. *I guess I'm still me.*

She held the wee mirror so it reflected her new dress, coppery brown with a lighter floral design and ivory lace edging the sleeves and neck. *I like it.* Something relaxed inside her. *On the inside, I've been wound up tight for all these years, pretending to be what I'm not.*

Through the open doorway, Cally heard someone climbing the stairs. Hastily she put away her mirror and pulled a book from her bag.

Mrs. Williams appeared in the doorway. "Cally! How lovely to see thee on thy feet! And that dress is so becoming. Can I help thee with anything?"

"I wanted a book to read."

"Let me help thee back to thy chair."

"Thank you, ma'am. I do feel a bit wobbly."

"*Huckleberry Finn*. That's not one I've heard of, Cally."

"It's a good story. Ben would like it. I've read it so many times I practically memorized it."

"I have just read a charming book by Louisa May Alcott called *Little Women*. Would thee like to try it?"

"Thank you, Mrs. Williams. That would be wonderful. I haven't read a book for a long time. May I give *Huckleberry Finn* to Ben?"

"Why, he will be delighted, Cally! I thank thee. I'll go get *Little Women* for thee now. Perhaps thee would like to drink this tea while thee read. Florence sent strawberries she grows herself, and some of her sweet biscuits."

"Yes, ma'am. Thank you. I'm eating too much though. My tummy is getting fat. I've never been this fat in my life."

Mrs. Williams laughed. "My dear, thee are a long way from fat. Remember, the doctor said eating is important for thee to get strong again."

"Yes, ma'am. I'll try. Thank you for the dress. It makes me feel happy to be a lassie again."

☙

May 1, 1898

Dear George,

I hope thee and Eliza are well. Thank thee for the news that Teddy has been found. Cally is eager to see him and asks me every day whether she is strong enough to travel.

Cally has been with us three weeks. She has had no fever the last week, and her rash has faded. She can sit in a chair and walk short distances. How will we know when we can safely send her to thee?

Gratefully,

Athena signed and folded her note and wrote Dr. Tann's address on the envelope. She glanced at Cally, sitting across the table writing a thank you to Mrs. Malcomson for the lovely little horse adorning the table between them. Beside it rested a carving of a bird's nest with three fledglings, mouths open, awaiting their feeding.

Athena began her own thank you note.

May 1, 1898

Dear Mrs. Malcomson,

I was overcome when I discovered the darling bird's nest tucked into the parcel containing Cally's beautiful mare. I thank thee. This one is NOT going to Richard's study, though he made a laughing move to take it from me. I will treasure it always.

Gratefully,

Athena Williams

"There. Can you read this and tell me if it is all right?"

"Certainly, Cally."

May 1, 1898

Dear Mrs. Malcomson,

I was surprised to receive your gift. I love it! It reminds me of how kind Felicity was to me when I needed her. I am happy she is back home.

I am sorry to say I don't remember you. Mrs. Williams told me you helped Dr. Tann rescue me from the side of the road after I fell off Felicity. I guess I was too sick to remember that. It's strange to have a piece of my life just—gone. But maybe one day I will be able to meet you and Mr. Max. I was surprised to learn your name is Mrs. Malcomson, because long ago I knew a Malcomson family.

Mrs. Williams told me you think I am a boy. I had to pretend to be a boy for a while, but I am happy to be a girl again. Soon I will go to Dr. Tann's home in Independence, Kansas. He has found my brother Teddy in Oklahoma and says he will take me there.

My name is not Calvin. It is Callandra. Most people call me Cally.

Thank you for your beautiful gift.

Cally

"That is lovely, Cally. Here is an envelope. We will mail all these letters tomorrow."

Cউৎৎ০

May 8, 1898

Dear George,

I will send this letter to thee tucked into Cally's bag. We will take her to the train station tomorrow afternoon. I am gratified by her return to health, yet troubled by her ongoing nightmares. I am quite sure Jeb, whoever he is, must be the father of her child. I am asking God for the grace to forgive him, and for the grace Cally will need for the long road of healing lying ahead of her. Despite her suffering, somehow, she has retained a delightful sweetness.

We have not talked with Cally about her being with child. We believe you, as a doctor, will do so with less shock than the news would give her coming from us. But she does need to know soon. She told me yesterday she felt she had butterflies in her stomach. Her morning sickness has subsided. She attributes that to her recovery from the typhoid fever. She tells me she must be eating too much because her tummy is getting fat.

I have just received an intriguing letter from Mrs. Cora Malcomson, asking whether, since she is a girl, Cally might consider going to live with them to help care for her twins and baby. Her mother-in-law has been with them for some time but will return to her own home soon. Cora doesn't yet know Cally is pregnant. I have no idea how that may affect her desire for Cally to join them. I include here the Malcomsons' address in Kansas City. I hope I am not asking too much of thee to follow up as thee and Cally think best, once thee tell her of this offer.

I will inform Mrs. Malcomson of Cally's departure from our home

*and ask her to communicate with you. Richard and I thank thee for
understanding why we cannot keep Cally ourselves, though she will
always have a place in our affections.*

We are grateful for thy friendship.

Athena

"Why won't Richard and Athena keep Cally, George?" Eliza asked
after reading the letter. "I would think she could be a God-sent comfort
to them."

"Had she lived, their Chrissy would be the same age as Cally. Her
presence reminded them every day of what they lost. For Richard
especially, it has been too hard. It stirred up all his grief."

"I remember that day very well—the emergency summons you
received to Elk City Lake, the little girl already dead. The remains of a
picnic, the parents beside themselves. I'm glad I was free to go with
you."

"You were such a help to them that day, Eliza, and to me. Their grief
was vastly complicated by their guilt over the accident—Richard's,
because he was driving the wagon that ran over Chrissy, and Athena's
because she briefly lost track of the child. As you know, they traveled a
long, dark road that almost broke them and came close to breaking
their marriage. Ben's birth, by God's grace, was their salvation. A new
little life to love and cherish."

"And you faithfully supported them through all those long years.
That's one thing I love about you, George Tann."

CHAPTER 39

RECROSSING

Olathe, Kansas, May 21, 1898

"THANK YOU, BEN." Athena smiled at her son as he brought her the mail. She opened the one from Independence first, a letter from Cally and one from George in the same envelope.

Independence, Kansas May 15, 1898

Dear Mrs. Williams,

You and Florence and Mr. Williams and Ben and the nurses were so kind to me that I want to let you know what has happened since I left you. The train ride was fine. Dr. Tann and his wife were there to meet me at the station in Independence. You know already how lovely they are. They gave me one day to rest from the trip and then took me to Teddy in Oklahoma Territory.

I was so happy to see Teddy well and strong that I hugged him and cried and didn't want to let go. But he seemed a little afraid of me. I quickly realized he is happy with the Oneida. Once I told him I would not make him leave them, I could see him relax. I can visit him again. I am sad, but I must plan for my own future without counting on Teddy being with me.

The day after we returned from Oklahoma, Dr. Tann and Mrs. Tann told me I am pregnant. I am going to have a baby in the fall. I was very surprised, and I still don't know how I feel about it—all different ways, I guess. How can I be a mother? I have not had a mother since I was five. But I understand now why my body feels strange and the butterflies in my tummy and why I am getting fat.

Dr. Tann told me about Mrs. Cora Malcomson's invitation for me to live with her family and help care for her children. But we haven't heard back yet whether she still wants me, since I am pregnant.

I told you before how strange it is for me to think of meeting another Malcomson family, since I once knew a Malcomson family from Ireland. It must be a more common name than I realized.

Dr. Tann showed me exercises to do with my wrist twice a day to make it strong again now that the bone is healed.

Thank you for caring for me while I was so sick. And for the beautiful dresses and nightgowns. I will remember your kindness to me the rest of my life.

With love,
Cally

Athena smiled, brushed away a tear, then smiled again and said softly, "Oh Lord, be merciful to Cally and to her child. Show them their way, step by step."

She picked up George's note. Hastily written, she could tell.

Richard and Athena, a quick note to tuck in with Cally's letter. I received the photograph I requested of the grave. The coffin was buried in the New Santa Fe Cemetery, some thirteen or fourteen miles east of you, I believe. It is marked by a plain stone that says simply, "Horse Thief 1898." Thus concludes one chapter and begins another, as young Cally feels new life stirring within her. I have not yet told her about the burial of the horse thief we found so ill beside the road. Have you?

Enclosed with the photograph was the reward money. I have pondered and talked with Eliza about what to do with it. Her suggestion is to place it in trust for Cally and her child, against some time when they may need it. Please let me know what you think about this, since rightly, the money is yours—it was your idea, Richard, and you carried it out. I await instructions. Thank you again for taking in the boy and bringing the girl back to life.

Fondly,

George

Athena smiled, wiped away a tear, then smiled again. She returned both letters to the envelope, walked to Richard's study, and placed it on his desk, where he would see it when he came in from the dairy.

❦

Independence May 22, 1898

Dear Mrs. Williams,

Tomorrow Mrs. Malcomson is coming for me. Dr. Tann told her I could travel by myself, but she wanted to come, to get to know me a little bit, she said. I am glad since I don't know her at all. Dr. Tann believes her to be a fine woman. Had she not stopped to help him I might not be alive. Her mother-in-law and brother-in-law are there to care for her children while she travels. They will leave the day after we get there.

Dr. Tann says Kansas City is not far from Olathe. I hope I can visit you.

With love,

Cally

Cally lay her head for a moment on the table, trying to still a surge of fear. *What if the Malcomsons don't like me? What if I don't like them?*

She gently caressed her tummy and began another letter.

Independence, Kansas May 22, 1898
Dear Aunt Mary and Miss Anthony,

I am sorry I left without saying goodbye. Something terrible happened and I had to escape. Then I got sick with typhoid fever. I am well now. Kind people are helping me. I found Teddy with the Oneida in Oklahoma. He is happy there. I will try to write more soon, from Kansas City where I am going next.

Thank you for your kindness to me and Teddy and all you taught us. I miss you.

Oh—I am Cally now, no longer Calvin. I guess Carson is yours, if he is still alive.

Love,

Callandra Mae Donnelly

ஏண

Cora read the telegram from Dr. Tann and caught her breath. *I am really doing this! Thomas and I are taking into our home a homeless, orphaned, pregnant girl we know almost nothing about except those three facts. How does this make any sense? Yet I feel so clearly, it's what we are to do. I'm not sure I've ever felt anything so strongly, other than how right it was to marry Thomas. Well, here we go. I don't know how Cathleen and Charlie will react. I expect they will think we are out of our minds.*

Cora walked into the dining room, where the family laughed at wee Josie's antics. "You will teach her bad habits, Charlie!"

Charlie looked at his mother and wiped his eyes. "Was I ever this funny when I was a baby?"

"What do you mean, when. You're still a baby, baby brother."

"Even at nineteen you won't let me grow up, Thomas?"

Cathleen looked attentively at her daughter-in-law. "Cora, you look serious. And at the same time, excited. Is there something you wish to tell us?"

"As a matter of fact, there is. Thank you for asking, Cathleen." Cora took a deep breath and looked across the table at Thomas as Charlie's eyes swiveled to hers.

"Thomas and I have decided to do something a bit—unusual."

"This sounds intriguing."

"Well, you may not think it wise, Charlie, so let me first say I feel strongly it's the right thing for us to do. And Thomas has chosen to support me." Cora looked from Charlie to Thomas. "Thank you, Thomas."

He smiled. "You know I would do almost anything for you, sweetheart. I'm all about adventure."

"More and more mysterious."

"All right. I'll just tell you. I am going to catch a train this afternoon to Independence, Kansas. It's about 160 miles south, just a few miles north of the Oklahoma Territory."

"And—"

"And tomorrow I will bring home with me a fourteen-year-old girl. Just fourteen years old, orphaned and homeless." Cora swallowed. "And pregnant. I have hired her to help me care for our children. Perhaps Thomas and I can be of help to her as well."

Charlie's and Cathleen's eyebrows shot up and their mouths opened.

"How—"

"Why—"

"Before you start asking questions, let me tell you I hardly know anything about this girl. I met her briefly when I went to Olathe for the art show. She was seriously ill at that time from typhoid fever and a broken arm, but she has recovered. That's all I can tell you right now. This morning I need to prepare for her coming. I know you must go to work, Thomas. Cathleen and Charlie, can you help me with the children both this morning and while I am away? I am so grateful you are here."

"Of course, Cora. Sit down and eat some breakfast. While the baby naps and Charlie entertains the twins, I'll help you however I can."

"Thank you, Cathleen. Frankly, I have no idea what I am getting us into."

"Clearly you desire to bless this girl, Cora. It occurs to me that our Lord's mother may have been about the same age when she became pregnant out of wedlock. Shall we treat this girl as we would want to have treated Mary had she come to us?"

"Only you would think such a thing, Mummy," Charlie inserted. "Mary or no, I must leave day after tomorrow. I play that night in Wichita, and then three concerts in Denver over the weekend, and then travel to Chicago. Don't forget Father expects you to sail home with him a week from now, Mummy."

Cora exhaled a breath she didn't realize she was holding. "I've told you, haven't I, Charlie, how your Kansas City concerts delighted our friends?"

"You told me, Cora. Eat your breakfast. I'll deal with squirmy Shane—yes, that's you!—and sticky Shauna while you manage Josie, Mummy. You're better at the diaper thing."

ભ્ર

"Oh, that may be Cora now!" Thomas hurried to open the door.

"Thomas, may I introduce Callandra Donnelly? She—oh, there you are, Charlie and Cathleen."

"Charlie?"

"C-C-Cally?"

"Mrs. Malcomson?"

To Cora's amazement, Cally threw herself into Cathleen's arms. Charlie hugged them both.

All three burst into tears.

EPILOGUE

New Santa Fe Cemetery, October 17, 1903

THE OLD CARETAKER leaned into the shade against the church wall, breathing heavily, gnarled hands trembling on his rake. As he rested, he watched a beautifully dressed young woman, holding the hand of a little girl, wander up and down the rows of graves until they came to the one in the far corner, the simple flat stone engraved "Horse Thief 1898." There they stopped, gazing at the stone, and talking to each other.

Why just yesterday I cleared away honeysuckle growing all over that gravestone.

Curious, the old man raked his way close enough to hear what they were saying. He remembered the day—five, six years ago?—when he had dug that grave. Everyone in New Santa Fe remembered. The story had caused a stir. A boy's brazen theft of the famous Felicity, and the owner falling off his horse as he gave chase, would not soon be forgotten. God Himself had rendered judgment on the thief.

So, at first, hearing the young woman say "Felicity" did not surprise him. Nor hearing the words "typhoid fever" and "Dr. Tann." He knew the story by heart. Dr. Tann's letter had been published in all the papers and he had a copy of the reward poster tucked in his box of keepsakes.

But as the caretaker watched and listened, it seemed the young woman addressed the little girl as Felicity. He edged closer. There it was

395

again, "I love you, Felicity Rose," as the woman hugged the child, then turned and smiled at him, her green eyes warm, the sun shining on an auburn curl escaping her hair pins and hat.

The old man gasped and took another step. *It's the face—the face on the reward poster! I'm sure of it!* He reached out and opened his mouth, but the woman was already walking away, the little girl skipping ahead of her.

Leaning on his rake, the old man looked from the woman to the grave, back and forth, until she and the child were out of sight. Then he walked to the grave and stared at the stone, as she had done, thinking about the reward poster.

How hard would it be to dig up the coffin?

Historical Figures

Author's note: I read extensively from what has been written both by and about these remarkable people, until I felt I knew them, and could weave their personalities into my story with confidence. Although a framework of facts undergirds their roles—I've noted when for the sake of the story I departed from their history in some way—the rest, of course, comes from my imagination.

David, Joseph, and other members of the Quaker Malcomson family built a multifaceted shipping and commerce empire unequalled not just in Ireland but in the world until its gradual decline to an 1877 bankruptcy due to mismanagement after Joseph's premature death at age 60 in 1858. Malcomson wealth helped finance extraordinary efforts to feed, clothe, and educate desperate victims of the Irish potato famine, most of them Catholic. The intense animosity between the Society of Friends, only 8,000 strong in Ireland at its peak, and the Catholic majority population makes these social efforts amazing. Finding common ground between Quaker and Catholic families in my characters Peter Malcomson and Cathleen McConnell gave me pleasure.

Jan Ignacy Paderewski (pronounced *Paderevski*), 1860-1941, Polish pianist and composer, conquered America in the late 1890s and early 1900s not only through his music but through his charm. A man who suffered intensely from his earliest childhood due to injustices in his homeland, Paderewski left his musical career for a time at its peak to serve Poland as Prime Minister, seeking independence and healing from the atrocities of World War I. *Author's note: I invented the Paderewski concert in New York City in chapter six, which Peter refers to on the first page of chapter eight. It is not historical. I also invented the concert at Schönbrunn Palace in Vienna in chapter ten, though such a concert could have taken place. And in fact, Paderewski's first American tour began in November 1891, not in July of that year as in this story. As he expressed to Charlie* *in chapter seventeen, Paderewski was initially scheduled for eighty concerts on that first tour. In the end, Paderewski played 107 concerts in 117 days. In so doing he seriously damaged his arm and the fourth finger of his right hand and never fully recovered. For much of the tour, he played using only four fingers of his right hand instead of five. The pain he suffered was excruciating. His audiences, wildly enthusiastic about his music, never knew what it cost him.*

Olga Wisinger-Florian, 1844-1926 (82 years), was part of an internationally influential group of Austrian artists who believed women should and could have equal standing with men in the world of the arts, considered heretical in her time. The Chicago World's Fair in 1893 gave Wisinger-Florian and others an unprecedented platform for winning international consideration of both their art and their case for justice in this and in other areas of human endeavor.

Scott Joplin, 1868-1917 (49 years), King of Ragtime, gained national and international acclaim at the Chicago World's Fair in 1893. Ironically, though some were invited to perform, not on the main stage but in other venues, Black people were not permitted even to attend the Fair except at designated times and conditions. Frederick Douglass and Ida B. Wells distributed a pamphlet at the Haitian Exhibit protesting the fair's depiction of Black people and Native Americans as inferior to whites and the exclusion of African Americans from the planning and exhibitions—a sad commentary on prevalent prejudices. How different Scott Joplin's life might have been had he not been subjected to the humiliations of Jim Crow.

Susan B. Anthony, 1820-1906 (86 years), grew up in a Quaker family, and from age 17 dedicated her life at great personal sacrifice to causes of justice, particularly for slaves and for women. Quakers were the first to take a public abolitionist stand as a group, influenced in large measure by John Woolman (1720-1772), who did not live long enough to see his dreams realized, but whose life and writings impacted the generations who followed him. In 1776 the Society of Friends declared no member could own slaves, and fourteen years later they first petitioned Congress to end slavery in the United States. For Anthony, the plight of women, with no rights or politically recognized voice, was equally intolerable. She first became involved with the Temperance movement by watching countless families destroyed through male alcoholism. But she quickly realized this was a symptom of a much more poisonous social reality, the prevailing belief that women existed to serve men and had little value apart from that. Along with Quaker minister Lucretia Mott and other courageous women and men, Anthony suffered social disdain and even physical attacks to a degree we perhaps forget one hundred years after women were finally granted what we now take for granted, the right to have a voice, the right to vote. I don't know whether she and her loyal sister Mary ever played a role in children's lives like the one I imagined for her in Cally and Teddy's lives, but it would have been consistent with their character.

Dr. George A. Tann, 1835-1907 (72 years), the first black physician in the state of Kansas, also served the Cherokee and Osage communities in the Oklahoma Territory a few miles south of his home near Independence, Kansas. "Kansas State Historical Society documents record that the people of Independence held Dr. Tann in such high regard that he was not buried in the traditionally separate black section of the cemetery but was laid to rest in a prominent spot in gratitude for his selfless service to the community. His gravesite can be seen today in the Mt. Hope Cemetery in Independence" (from https://littlehouseontheprairie.com/dr-george-a-tann-pioneer-physician-and-neighbor-to-the-ingalls/). Dr. Tann was born in Pennsylvania and moved to Kansas in 1869 at age 34 to devote the rest of his life (38 more years) to his work in Kansas and the Oklahoma Territory. He and his wife Eliza had two daughters, Stella and Naomi ("Dr. George Tann, Black Frontier Physician," by Susan Thurlow and *A Doctor Fetched by the Family Dog: the story of Dr.*

George A. Tann, pioneer Black physician. Springfield, MO, Independent Publishing Co., 1984).

Professor Michele Esposito, 1855-1929, a prize-winning Italian composer and pianist who spent most of his professional life in Dublin, Ireland, teaching piano at the Royal Irish Academy of Music for more than forty years. He inaugurated chamber-music recitals, established and conducted the Dublin Orchestral Society, and conducted the London Symphony Orchestra for two years. In addition to the pianoforte, he composed orchestral, chamber music, stage music, and numerous songs. He died in Florence at age 74.

Discussion Guide

Chapters 1-13

1. What have you most enjoyed in the story so far?

2. Cally and Charlie are growing up only about sixty miles apart in southern Ireland, but their family contexts are quite different. In what ways are they distinct?

3. Despite the differences, what similarities do you notice between the families?

4. In what ways has Peter grown up to be like his father Joseph, from the glimpse you had of Joseph in the Prologue? How does this affect Peter's son Charlie?

5. In what ways did Peter and Cathleen make counter-cultural decisions for their time in history? In what ways is their family structure consistent with their culture?

6. What primary challenges face the main characters, Cally, Charlie and their families?

7. What do you think about the way Peter handled Charlie's disobedience in the storm?

8. Cally believes her mother and sister's deaths, her father's depression, and Teddy's accident are all her fault. How do you evaluate her feelings of guilt?

9. Cathleen tells Charlie that Cora is rich every way but financially. What types of richness do you see in Cally's family and experiences?

10. Would you prefer to have Frank or Peter as your father?

11. Charlie grows up without much contact with other children. How does this affect him?

12. Cathleen is not as content with her life as we might expect. What does she want to see change? What makes her sad?

13. Louise is known as a *seanachie* (shan-a-kee), a storyteller. What do you think of the story she tells Frank in chapter 13? Do you think it encourages him in his decision to emigrate?

14. In what ways can you see God caring for Cally, Teddy and Charlie?

Chapters 14-23

1. What most caught your interest in this section?

2. Can you think of at least three reasons the author named chapter 14 "The Crossing"?

3. Charlie, Peter, and Cally all believe Frank's death was their fault. What would you like to say to each of them?

4. Peter was profoundly impacted by Frank's and Colin's deaths. Describe how he changed, including examples from later chapters in this section.

5. Describe the ways Cathleen cared for each of the three, Charlie, Peter, and Cally.

6. In what ways can you see God caring for Cally and Teddy before and after they were kidnapped?

7. How did you react to Margaret's perspective both on the ship and when Cally and Peter ran away? How might you have felt in her place?

8. What biblical story does the ending of chapter 20 remind you of?

9. From what you've learned about the treatment of children in the 1890s in the U.S., especially homeless children, do you think our society and legal system handles this better now?

10. What most disappointed you about what happened in these chapters?

11. Cally and Teddy have a serious disagreement at the end of chapter 22. If you could change Cally's conclusion, what would you want her to decide?

12. Do you think Teddy might one day run away from Cally? Why? Do you think he will return to Killeagh?

13. How did you feel about the Malcomsons leaving Albany without locating Cally and Teddy? Which Malcomson would most likely embrace your perspective?

Chapters 24-34

1. What do you think of Paddy and his gang? How does Cally feel about his decision-making, including making her become Calvin?
2. What was the important role Cash played for Cally and Teddy?
3. Were you surprised that Cally returned to the church where she had seen Cousin Roisin?
4. If you were Father Callahan in Albany, how would you care for the children of the gangs? Do you think you could have done better? What do you think of the idea of orphan trains?
5. PTSD wasn't yet understood at the time Charlie suffered from his terror of storms. What good decision did his parents make to help him?
6. Had you already connected the dots between Charlie and Cathleen and wee Cally receiving her treasure in front of the Old Thatch Bar?
7. How do you feel about Cap? Do you agree with Aunt Mary that he's not fit to have Cally and Teddy? How would you define his legacy?
8. What was the emotional impact on Charlie of his accident?
9. Though Scott Joplin played at the Chicago World's Fair, Black people were only allowed into the fair on specified days. And allowing them in at all was considered "progressive." How do you respond to that, in light of what was done for women at the fair?
10. Did you anticipate Teddy joining the Oneida? Why do you think he didn't return to Ireland when he ran away? Cally mourns Teddy's rejection of her. Did she deserve it?
11. What did you think of Charlie trying to be "ordinary"? Did you anticipate what happened to him with Mr. Barrow? How did Mr. Paderewski help him?
12. What touches of grace do you see in the tragedies of Chapter 34?
13. What do you think about Cally "borrowing" Felicity?

Chapters 35-38

1. When did you first suspect Cora would play a critical role in Cally's life?

2. What do you think of Richard's scheme to free Cally from her fate as a horse thief? Do you think Dr. Tann's letter was ethical?

3. What are your thoughts on attributing a questionable action to a historical person?

4. Based on the Epilogue, what do you think might happen next in regard to the horse thief?

5. Dr. Tann's story first came to the attention of twentieth century readers through Laura Ingalls Wilder's book *Little House on the Prairie.* He was so esteemed by his white patients they "honored" him with burial in the white people's cemetery. What do you think about that?

6. Quakers keep showing up in this book. The author did not expect or plan for that to happen. What characteristics of Quakers does this story highlight?

7. How did Charlie change after Mr. Barrow visited him in Dublin? How did Mr. Paderewski help him once again? Have you ever experienced a similar emotional catharsis?

8. The book does not relate what happened to Cally and Felicity Rose in relation to the Malcomsons after their re-crossing. What do you imagine, given the limited information in the Epilogue? Cally was contracted to be a nanny for Cora's children. Did she continue in that role, do you think?

9. In what ways do Cally and Charlie still need emotional healing? What "big picture" problems do they each still face? (Spoiler alert: this will be important in Book Two.)

10. Think about Teddy. What problems or issues might he still face?

11. The author claims Cally and Charlie told her their stories and all she did was write them down. What do you think about that?

12. What is your main takeaway from this book?

Coming next . . .

Trains have largely replaced wagons on the old Oregon Trail. But an enigmatic invitation reaches Thomas from eccentric (and now deceased) Uncle William Malcomson, who tried to rob his nephew Peter during Margaret's wedding. A treasure hunt or a wild goose chase? To escape the ruckus in Kansas City raised by an old gravedigger, Charlie and Cally decide to find out—and discover treasure in Idaho Uncle William never imagined.

Treasure Hunt 1904

Book Two of the Cally and Charlie series